# H. G. WELLS

# A Modern Utopia

*Edited by* GREGORY CLAEYS *and* PATRICK PARRINDER
*With an Introduction by* FRANCIS WHEEN
*and Notes by* GREGORY CLAEYS *and* ANDY SAWYER

PENGUIN BOOKS

PENGUIN BOOKS

Published by the Penguin Group
Penguin Books Ltd, 80 Strand, London WC2R ORL, England
Penguin Group (USA) Inc., 375 Hudson Street, New York, New York 10014, USA
Penguin Group (Canada), 10 Alcorn Avenue, Toronto, Ontario, Canada M4V 3B2
(a division of Pearson Penguin Canada Inc.)
Penguin Ireland, 25 St Stephen's Green, Dublin 2, Ireland
(a division of Penguin Books Ltd)
Penguin Group (Australia), 250 Camberwell Road,
Camberwell, Victoria 3124, Australia (a division of Pearson Australia Group Pty Ltd)
Penguin Books India Pvt Ltd, 11 Community Centre,
Panchsheel Park, New Delhi – 110 017, India
Penguin Group (NZ), cnr Airborne and Rosedale Roads, Albany,
Auckland 1310, New Zealand (a division of Pearson New Zealand Ltd)
Penguin Books (South Africa) (Pty) Ltd, 24 Sturdee Avenue,
Rosebank 2196, South Africa

Penguin Books Ltd, Registered Offices: 80 Strand, London WC2R ORL, England

www.penguin.com

First published 1905
This edition first published in Penguin Classics 2005

3

Text copyright © the Literary Executors of the Estate of H. G. Wells
Biographical Note, Further Reading, Note on the Text
copyright © Patrick Parrinder, 2005
Introduction copyright © Francis Wheen, 2005
Notes copyright © Gregory Claeys and Andy Sawyer, 2005
All rights reserved

Quotation of George Orwell on p. xxiii courtesy of the estate of the
late Sonia Brownell Orwell and Secker & Warburg Ltd

The moral right of the editors has been asserted

Set in 10.25/12.25 pt PostScript Adobe Sabon
Typeset by Rowland Phototypesetting Ltd, Bury St Edmunds, Suffolk
Printed in England by Clays Ltd, St Ives plc

PENGUIN CLASSICS

# A MODERN UTOPIA

H. G. WELLS, the third son of a small shopkeeper, was born in Bromley in 1866. After two years' apprenticeship in a draper's shop, he became a pupil-teacher at Midhurst Grammar School and won a scholarship to study under T. H. Huxley at the Normal School of Science, South Kensington. He taught biology before becoming a professional writer and journalist. He wrote more than a hundred books, including novels, essays, histories and programmes for world regeneration.

Wells, who rose from obscurity to world fame, had an emotionally and intellectually turbulent life. His prophetic imagination was first displayed in pioneering works of science fiction such as *The Time Machine* (1895), *The Island of Doctor Moreau* (1896), *The Invisible Man* (1897) and *The War of the Worlds* (1898). Later he became an apostle of socialism, science and progress, whose anticipations of a future world state include *The Shape of Things to Come* (1933). His controversial views on sexual equality and women's rights were expressed in the novels *Ann Veronica* (1909) and *The New Machiavelli* (1911). He was, in Bertrand Russell's words, 'an important liberator of thought and action'.

Wells drew on his own early struggles in many of his best novels, including *Love and Mr Lewisham* (1900), *Kipps* (1905), *Tono-Bungay* (1909) and *The History of Mr Polly* (1910). His educational works, some written in collaboration, include *The Outline of History* (1920) and *The Science of Life* (1930). His *Experiment in Autobiography* (2 vols., 1934) reviews his world. He died in London in 1946.

GREGORY CLAEYS is Professor of History at Royal Holloway, University of London. He is the author of several books on the history of radicalism and socialism, and has edited sixteen volumes of utopian writings.

PATRICK PARRINDER took his MA and Ph.D at Cambridge University, where he held a Fellowship at King's College and published his first two books on Wells, *H. G. Wells* (1970) and *H. G. Wells: The Critical Heritage* (1972). He has been Chairman of the

H. G. Wells Society and editor of *The Wellsian*, and has also written on James Joyce, science fiction, literary criticism and the history of the English novel. His book *Shadows of the Future* (1995) brings together his interests in Wells, science fiction and literary prophecy. Since 1986 he has been Professor of English at the University of Reading.

FRANCIS WHEEN is a journalist, author and broadcaster. He has written for most British national newspapers, and was named Columnist of the Year in 1997 for his 'Wheen's World' page in the *Guardian*. His biography of Karl Marx, which won the Isaac Deutscher Memorial Prize, has been translated into more than twenty languages. His other books include *Tom Driberg: His Life and Indiscretions, Who Was Dr Charlotte Bach?* and *Hoo-Hahs and Passing Frenzies*, which won the George Orwell Prize in 2003. His latest book is *How Mumbo-Jumbo Conquered the World: A Short History of Modern Delusions*. He is deputy editor of *Private Eye* and a regular panellist on the BBC programme *The News Quiz*.

ANDY SAWYER is the librarian of the Science Fiction Foundation Collection at the University of Liverpool Library, and Course Director of the MA in Science Fiction Studies offered by the School of English. He also teaches a science fiction module for undergraduates. He has published widely on science fiction and related literatures, and co-edited the collection of essays *Speaking Science Fiction* (Liverpool University Press, 2000). He is also Reviews Editor of *Foundation: the International Review of Science Fiction* and Associate Editor of the forthcoming *Encyclopedia of Themes in Science Fiction and Fantasy* (Greenwood Press).

# CONTENTS

Biographical Note                          vii
Introduction                               xiii
Further Reading                            xxvii
Note on the Text                           xxix

A MODERN UTOPIA                            1

Appendix: Scepticism of the
    Instrument                             249
Notes                                      267

# Biographical Note

Herbert George Wells was born on 21 September 1866 at Bromley, Kent, a small market town soon to be swallowed up by the suburban growth of outer London. His father, formerly a professional gardener and a county cricketer renowned for his fast bowling, owned a small business in Bromley High Street selling china goods and cricket bats. The house was grandly known as Atlas House, but the centre of family life was a cramped basement kitchen underneath the shop. Soon Joseph Wells's cricketing days were cut short by a broken leg, and the family fortunes looked bleak.

Young 'Bertie' Wells had already shown great academic promise, but when he was thirteen his family broke up and he was forced to earn his own living. His father was bankrupt, and his mother left home to become resident housekeeper at Uppark, the great Sussex country house where she had worked as a lady's maid before her marriage. Wells was taken out of school to follow his two elder brothers into the drapery trade. After serving briefly as a pupil-teacher and a pharmacist's assistant, in 1881 he was apprenticed to a department store in Southsea, working a thirteen-hour day and sleeping in a dormitory with his fellow-apprentices. This was the unhappiest period of his life, though he would later revisit it in comic romances such as *Kipps* (1905) and *The History of Mr Polly* (1910). Kipps and Polly both manage to escape from their servitude as drapers, and in 1883, helped by his long-suffering mother, Wells cancelled his indentures and obtained a post as teaching assistant at Midhurst Grammar School near Uppark. His intellectual development, long held back, now progressed astonishingly. He passed a series of examinations in science subjects and, in September 1884, entered the Normal School of Science, South Kensington (later to become part of Imperial College of Science and Technology) on a government scholarship.

Wells was a born teacher, as many of his books would show, and at first he was an enthusiastic student. He had the good fortune to be taught biology and zoology by one of the most influential scientific thinkers of the Victorian age, Darwin's friend and supporter T. H. Huxley. Wells never forgot Huxley's teaching, but the other professors were more humdrum, and his interest in their courses rapidly waned. He scraped through second-year physics, but failed his third-year geology exam and left South Kensington in 1887 without taking a degree. He was thrilled by the theoretical framework and imaginative horizons of natural science, but impatient of practical detail and the grinding, routine tasks of laboratory work. He cut his classes and spent his time reading literature and history, satisfying the curiosity he had earlier felt while exploring the long-neglected library at Uppark. He started a college magazine, the *Science Schools Journal*, and argued for socialism in student debates.

In the summer of 1887 Wells became science master at a small private school in North Wales, but a few weeks later he was knocked down and injured by one of his pupils on the football field. Sickly and undernourished as a result of three years of student poverty, he suffered severe kidney and lung damage. After months of convalescence at Uppark he was able to return to science teaching at Henley House School, Kilburn. In 1890 he passed his University of London B.Sc. (Hons.) with a first class in zoology and obtained a post as a biology tutor for the University Correspondence College. In 1891 he married his cousin Isabel Wells, but they had little in common and soon Wells fell in love with one of his students, Amy Catherine Robbins (usually known as 'Jane'). They started living together in 1893, and married two years later when his divorce came through.

During his years as a biology tutor Wells slowly began making his way as a writer and journalist. He wrote for the

*Educational Times*, edited the *University Correspondent*, and in 1891 published a philosophical essay, 'The Rediscovery of the Unique', in the prestigious *Fortnightly Review*. His first book was a *Textbook of Biology* (1893). But no sooner was it published than his health again collapsed, forcing him to give up teaching and rely entirely on his literary earnings. His future seemed highly precarious, yet soon he was in regular demand as a writer of short stories and humorous essays for the burgeoning newspapers and magazines of the period. He became a fiction reviewer and, for a short period in 1895, a theatre critic.

Ever since his student days Wells had worked intermittently on a story about time-travelling and the possible future of the human race. An early version was published in the *Science Schools Journal* as 'The Chronic Argonauts', but now, after numerous redrafts and much encouragement from the poet and editor W. E. Henley, it finally took shape as *The Time Machine* (1895). Its success was instantaneous, and while it was running as a magazine serial Wells was already being spoken of as a 'man of genius'. He was celebrated as the inventor of the 'scientific romance', a combination of adventure novel and philosophical tale in which the hero becomes involved in a life-and-death struggle resulting from some unforeseen scientific development. There was now a ready market for his fiction, and *The Island of Doctor Moreau* (1896), *The Invisible Man* (1897), *The War of the Worlds* (1898), *When the Sleeper Wakes* (1899; later revised as *The Sleeper Awakes*, 1910), *The First Men in the Moon* (1901) and several other volumes followed quickly from his pen.

By the turn of the twentieth century Wells was established as a popular author in England and America, and his books were rapidly being translated into French, German, Spanish, Russian and other European languages. Already his fame had begun to eclipse that of his predecessor in scientific romance, the French author Jules Verne, who had dominated the field since the 1860s. But Wells, an increasingly self-conscious artist, had larger ambitions than to go down in history as a boys' adventure novelist like Jules Verne. *Love and Mr Lewisham* (1900) was his first attempt at realistic fiction, comic in spirit and manifestly reflecting his own experiences as a student and teacher. By the end of the Edwardian decade, when he wrote his 'Condition of England' novels *Tono-Bungay* (1909) and *The New Machiavelli* (1911), Wells had become one of the leading novelists of his day, the friend and rival of such literary figures as Arnold Bennett, Joseph Conrad, Ford Madox Ford and Henry James.

But Wells was never a devotee of art for art's sake; he was a prophetic writer with a social and political message. His first major non-fictional work was *Anticipations* (1902), a book of futurological essays setting out the possible effects of scientific and technological progress in the twentieth century. *Anticipations* brought him into contact with the Fabian Society and launched his career as a political journalist and an influential voice of the British left. During his Fabian period Wells wrote *A Modern Utopia* (1905), but failed in his attempt to challenge the bureaucratic, reformist outlook of the Society's leaders such as Bernard Shaw (a lifelong friend and rival) and Beatrice Webb. Wells's Edwardian scientific romances such as *The Food of the Gods* (1904) and *The War in the Air* (1908), though full of humorous touches, are propagandist in intent. In other 'future war' stories of this period he predicted the tank and the atomic bomb.

Success as an author brought about great changes in his personal life. Ill-health had forced him to leave London for the Kent coast in 1898, but in the long run the only legacy of his footballing injury was the diabetes that affected him in old age. He commissioned a house, Spade House, overlooking the English Channel at Sandgate, from the architect C. F. A. Voysey, and here his and Jane's two sons were born – George Philip or 'Gip', who became a zoology professor and collaborated with his father and Julian Huxley on the biology encyclopedia *The Science of Life* (1930), and Frank, who worked in the film industry. Wells gave generous support to his parents and to his eldest brother, who was a fellow-fugitive from the drapery trade. Increasingly, however, he looked for emotional fulfilment outside the family, and his sexual affairs became notorious. He had a daughter in 1909 with Amber Reeves, a leading young Fabian economist, and in 1914 the novelist and critic Rebecca West gave birth to his son Anthony West, whose troubled childhood would later be reflected in his own novel *Heritage* (1955) and in his biography of his father.

As Wells's personal life became the gossip of literary London, his roles as imaginative writer and political journalist or prophet came increasingly into conflict. *Ann Veronica* (1909) was an example of topical, controversial fiction, dramatizing and commenting on such issues as women's rights, sexual equality and contemporary morals. It was the first of Wells's 'discussion novels' in which his personal relationships were often very thinly disguised. His later fiction takes a great variety of forms, but it all belongs to the broad category of the novel of ideas. At one extreme is the realistic reporting of *Mr Britling Sees It Through* (1916) – still valuable and unique as a portrayal of the English 'home front' in the First World War – while at the other extreme are brief fables such as *The Undying Fire* (1919) and *The Croquet Player* (1936), political allegories about world events each cast in the form of a prophetic dialogue.

Wells was by no means an experimental novelist like his younger contemporaries James Joyce and Virginia Woolf, but he was often technically innovative, and in some of his books the boundaries between fiction and non-fiction begin to break down. Sometimes he would take a classic from an earlier, pre-modern epoch as his literary model: *A Modern Utopia* (1905), for example, refers back to Sir Thomas More's *Utopia* and Plato's *Republic*. His bestselling historical works *The Outline of History* (1920) and *A Short History of the World* (1922) break with historical conventions by looking forward to the next stage in history. These works were written in order to draw the lessons of the First World War and to ensure that, if possible, its carnage would never be repeated; Wells saw history as a 'race between education and catastrophe'. The same concerns led to his future-history novel *The Shape of Things to Come* (1933), later rewritten for the cinema as *Things to Come*, an epic science-fiction film produced in 1936 by Alexander Korda. Both novel and film contain dire warnings about the inevitable outbreak and disastrous consequences of the Second World War.

By the 1920s, Wells was not only a famous author but a public figure whose name was rarely out of the newspapers. He briefly worked for the Ministry of Propaganda in 1918, producing a memorandum on war aims which anticipated the setting-up of the League of Nations. In 1922 and 1923 he stood for Parliament as a Labour candidate. He sought to influence world leaders, including two US Presidents, Theodore Roosevelt and Franklin D. Roosevelt. His meeting with Lenin in the Kremlin in 1920 and his interview in 1934 with Lenin's successor Josef Stalin were publicized all over the world. His high-pitched, piping voice was often heard on BBC radio. In 1933 he was elected president of International PEN, the writers' organization campaigning for intellectual freedom. In the same year his books were publicly burnt by the Nazis in Berlin, and he was banned from visiting Fascist Italy. His ideas strongly influenced the Pan-European Union, the pressure group advocating European unity between the wars.

But Wells became convinced that nothing less than global unity was needed if humanity was not to destroy itself. In *The Open Conspiracy* (1928) and other books he outlined his theories of world citizenship and world government. As the Second World War drew nearer he felt that his mission had been a failure and his warnings had gone unheeded. His last great campaign, for which he tried to obtain international support, was for human rights. The proposal set out in his Penguin Special *The Rights of Man* (1940) helped to bring about the United Nations declaration of 1948. He spent the war years at his house in Hanover Terrace, Regent's Park, and was awarded a D.Litt. by London University in 1943. His last book, *Mind at the End of Its Tether* (1945), was a despairing, pessimistic work, even bleaker in its prospects for mankind than *The Time Machine* fifty years earlier. He died at Hanover Terrace on 13 August 1946. He was restless and tireless to the end, a prophet eternally dissatisfied with himself and with humanity. 'Some day', he had written in a whimsical 'Auto-Obituary' three years earlier, 'I shall write a book, a *real* book.' He had published over fifty works of fiction and, in total, some 150 books and pamphlets.

Patrick Parrinder

# Introduction

'A map of the world that does not include Utopia,' Oscar Wilde wrote, 'is not worth glancing at.'[1] But who would wish to book a holiday in such a place, still less take up permanent residence? A recent Utopian visionary, Francis Fukuyama, acknowledged the problem in his famous announcement that the end of the Cold War marked 'the end of history as such: that is the end point of mankind's ideological evolution'.[2] While celebrating the ultimate triumph of liberal capitalism, and the universal peace and prosperity it would create, he was obliged to concede that since all the really big questions had now been settled 'in the post-historical period there will be neither art nor philosophy, just the perpetual caretaking of the museum of human history'. The only threat to this brave new world, he suggested, might be the sheer boredom of its citizens. As it turned out, however, there was no time for tedium to set in: history soon returned with a vengeance.

Nothing is more transient than eternal bliss. As H. G. Wells's narrator says in Chapter 11 of *A Modern Utopia*, 'I have no thought that my tenure of Utopia becomes every moment more precarious . . . I forget that a Utopia is a thing of the imagination that becomes more fragile with every added circumstance, that, like a soap-bubble, it is most brilliantly and variously coloured at the very instant of its dissolution.' Moments later, the bubble duly bursts.

Why, then, might anyone still read *A Modern Utopia*, or Thomas More's *Utopia*, or Plato's *Republic*? In a radio broadcast towards the end of his life, Wells suggested that Utopias had a continuing resonance which futuristic fictions such as his earlier novels *The Time Machine* and *The War of the Worlds* couldn't achieve.

> There is little prospect of any futuristic writings becoming permanent literature. We prophets write for our own time and pass almost before we are dead, but some of the Utopias are among the most enduring gems in the literary treasure house. They throw down no such self-destructive challenge as the futurist writer does, when he says, 'This is the way things are going – and this is what is coming about'. The Utopian says merely, 'If only', and escapes from time, death and judgment.[3]

Utopias are inverted pictures – photographic negatives – of their own era, and their composition reveals the intellectual and aesthetic impulses of those who imagined them. *A Modern Utopia*, published in 1905, is thus most illuminating not as a manifesto but as a vivid account of late-Victorian and Edwardian preoccupations.

One of Wells's abiding obsessions was the sheer grubbiness of London, a city of smoke and horse-shit. In *The Invisible Man* (1897) the title character complains that, while walking in the capital, 'I gathered dirt about my ankles, floating smuts and dust upon my skin. I did not know how long it would be before I should become visible from that cause also. But I saw clearly it could not be for long. Not in London at any rate.' Wells's 1906 novel *In the Days of the Comet*, in which the swish of a comet's tail 'cools and cleanses the human atmosphere', includes a vile litany of the contents of English houses – 'their dank, dark cupboards, the verminous papers from their scaly walls, their dust and dirt-sodden carpets ... the old dirt-saturated books, their ornaments – their dirty, decayed, and altogether painful ornaments ...' He also describes with 'peculiar horror' what people wore in pre-comet England:

> The men's clothes were worn without any cleansing process at all, except an occasional superficial brushing, for periods of a year or so; they were made of dark obscurely mixed patterns to conceal the stage of defilement they had reached, and they were

of a felted and porous texture admirably calculated to accumulate drifting matter. Many women wore skirts of similar substances, and of so long and inconvenient a form that they inevitably trailed among all the abomination of our horse-frequented roads.

As the heroine of *Ann Veronica* (1909) says: 'You see, dear, one *is* passionately anxious for something – what is it? One wants to be *clean* . . . But I'm always trying to make things happen. And I get myself dirty . . . it's all dirt that washes off, dear, but it's dirt.'

Wells's modern Utopia, by contrast, is spotless. The apartment where the narrator spends his first night is 'very clear and clean and simple', with 'no corners to gather dirt', no 'dust-collecting hangings', no 'dusty carpets', no 'dirty, black-leaded fireplace' (Ch. 3). In Utopia, he is impressed to learn, 'ragged and dirty' citizens are taken into custody by the police, and the State will 'confiscate and clear and clean' houses that seem 'unduly crowded or dirty' (Ch. 5). When the narrator reaches the Utopian version of London, he finds that 'the air is as clear and less dusty than it is among high mountains . . . all heating is done by electricity, and no coal ever enters the town; there are no horses or dogs, and so there is not a suspicion of smoke and scarcely a particle of any sort of dirt' (Ch. 9). It is the reappearance of grime, rather than the altered skyline, that strikes him most forcibly when he returns to the real Edwardian London: within moments he is confronted by a 'shrivelled, dirt-lined old woman', a 'pinched and dirty little girl', a 'ragged and filthy nursing mother' (Ch. 11). 'What a lot of filthy, torn paper is scattered about the world!' he exclaims in Trafalgar Square. 'We walk slowly side by side towards the dirt-littered basin of the fountain, and stand regarding two grimy tramps' (Ch. 11). Nothing futuristic or prophetic here: this is pure social realism.

Prophecy hasn't been entirely forsworn, of course. Wells cannot resist bringing out his crystal ball occasionally, and as we travel through his parallel world we notice many now-familiar features – air-conditioning, central-heating thermostats, electric coffee-makers. When the Wellsian narrator –

rather ponderously identified as the Owner of the Voice –
travels to England, he naturally does so by train via the Channel
Tunnel. The rulers of his Utopia apply a strict no-smoking
policy indistinguishable from that of Mayor Bloomberg in New
York. Most remarkably, Wells appears to have invented a form
of Keynesianism at a time when J. M. Keynes himself was still
a Cambridge undergraduate. 'The State will stand at the back
of the economic struggle as the reserve employer of labour,' he
writes in Chapter 5. 'There are many durable things bound
finally to be useful that could be made and stored whenever the
tide of more highly paid employment ebbed . . . new roads could
be made and public buildings reconstructed, inconveniences of
all sorts removed, until under the stimulus of accumulating
material, accumulating investments or other circumstances, the
tide of private enterprise flowed again.' There are also some
charming whims that could usefully be implemented in our own
century, notably the annual plebiscite to choose 'the ugliest
local building' – which is then demolished.

Even so, Wells's *A Modern Utopia* is recognizably a creature
of its time, and the fact that he wrote such a book at all shows
how well attuned he was to the zeitgeist: almost a hundred
Utopian fantasies were published between 1875 and 1905, an
efflorescence unparalleled before or since. Most are now forgotten, except for William Morris's *News from Nowhere*, but at
the time they had a large audience in Britain and elsewhere.
Edward Bellamy's *Looking Backward* (1888) – in which industry, trade and social welfare are all controlled by a vast, benign
corporate state – has been described as 'probably the most
widely-read American novel since *Uncle Tom's Cabin*'.

Previous Utopias, whether rural idylls or urban polities, had
been pre-technological and therefore (in Wells's word) 'sessile'
(Ch. 5). The kinetic energy of the industrial revolution rendered
them instantly obsolete, since the capitalist dynamic required
ceaseless development of new machinery, new products and new
markets. As Karl Marx wrote in *The Communist Manifesto*:

> Constant revolutionising of production, uninterrupted disturb-
> ance of all social conditions, everlasting uncertainty and agitation

distinguish the bourgeois epoch from all earlier ones. All fixed,
fast-frozen relations, with their train of ancient and venerable
prejudices and opinions, are swept away, all new-formed ones
become antiquated before they can ossify. All that is solid melts
into air . . .[4]

The twentieth-century economist Joseph Schumpeter described
capitalism as a system of 'creative destruction',[5] and by the
1880s its destructive consequences were increasingly apparent
in the industrial cities of Britain – slums, unemployment,
hunger, disease. 'The contrasts of rich and poor are unendur-
able and ought not to be endured by either rich or poor,'
William Morris protested in 1883.[6] 'The system of chattel slavery had to give its place to the feudal system of seigneur and
serf; and this has been swept away in favour of our present
contract system between rich and poor, and this in turn will
give place to socialism.'

Morris was a leading member of the Democratic Foundation
(later renamed the Social Democratic Federation), a socialist
party founded by H. M. Hyndman in June 1881 – the same
month in which Hyndman introduced Marx's economic
theories to the British public for the first time through his
manifesto *England For All*, which advocated universal suffrage,
abolition of the House of Lords and the nationalization of
land. Although its membership was never large, the Federation
undoubtedly articulated a far wider discontent: its pamphlet
*Socialism Made Plain* sold 100,000 copies in 1883.

But what did socialism mean? There was already a bewilder-
ing variety of alternatives – guild socialism, Christian socialism,
scientific socialism, anarchism and so on. Some saw it as the
violent culmination of the class struggle, others merely as the
most efficient and equitable form of economic organization.
For William Morris, as an artist, it was an aesthetic ideal.
'Morris passed from art to socialism, because he saw that under
capitalism there could be no art and no happiness for the great
majority,' G. D. H. Cole observed.[7]

H. G. Wells, by contrast, was a scientist. As an undergraduate
in the 1880s he had been taught by the biologist T. H. Huxley,

Charles Darwin's great friend and ally, and like many of his contemporaries Wells thought Marx's *Capital* a far less revolutionary treatise than Darwin's *Origin of Species* (1859) and his *Descent of Man* (1871). Darwin himself may have been reluctant to discuss the political and religious implications of his work, but his disciples had no such inhibition. 'Just as Darwin discovered the law of evolution in human nature,' Frederick Engels declared in his graveside oration at Karl Marx's funeral, 'so Marx discovered the law of evolution in human history'.[8] This analogy between a biological organism and social life had first been suggested by the philosopher Herbert Spencer, but for very different purposes: it was he who coined the phrase 'survival of the fittest' as a summary of Darwinian theory, which he then applied as a justification for unfettered laissez-faire capitalism. Inspired by Spencer, many business tycoons would cite the ideas of 'social Darwinism' as proof that rich and poor alike deserved their fate, and that any form of state regulation (or even philanthropy) would interfere with the 'natural' laws of survival.

For Utopian writers, however, the most exciting strand of evolutionary theory was that developed by Darwin's cousin Francis Galton, who invented the term 'eugenics' in 1883 to describe 'the study of agencies under social control that may improve or impair the racial qualities of future generations, whether physically or mentally'.[9] Galton himself wrote a short Utopian essay, 'Kantsaywhere',[10] in which only those superior physical specimens of humanity who obtain a 'eugenic certificate' are allowed to have children. Inferior members of the species – whose skull-size or ancestry classifies them as 'undesirable as individuals, and dangerous to the community' – are kept under close surveillance and punished severely if they attempt to breed.

Modern readers for whom eugenics is synonymous with Nazism may be surprised to learn that a century ago the most prominent eugenicists were progressives and socialists, for whom laissez-faire was no more acceptable in the propagation of the species than in economics. Sidney Webb – founder of the Fabian Society, the London School of Economics and the *New*

*Statesman* – wrote in an 1896 Fabian pamphlet that private property promotes 'wrong production, both of commodities and of human beings; the preparation of senseless luxuries whilst there is need for more bread; and the breeding of degenerate hordes of demoralised "residuum" unfit for social life.'[11] Webb's horror at the 'indiscriminate multiplication of the unfit' was shared by fellow-Fabians such as George Bernard Shaw. 'It is one of the troubles of our present civilisation,' Shaw wrote in *The Intelligent Woman's Guide to Socialism*, 'that the inferior stocks are outbreeding the superior ones.'[12]

Bernard Shaw and H. G. Wells attended a lecture given by Francis Galton in May 1904, when Wells was already working on *A Modern Utopia*, and both were invited to comment on Galton's proposal that eugenics

> must be introduced into the national conscience, like a new religion. It has, indeed, strong claims to become an orthodox religious tenet of the future, for eugenics co-operate with the workings of nature by securing that humanity shall be represented by the fittest races. What nature does blindly, slowly, and ruthlessly, man may do providently, quickly, and kindly. As it lies within his power, so it becomes his duty to work in that direction. The improvement of our stock seems to me one of the highest objects that we can reasonably attempt.[13]

Shaw gave his unqualified approval, declaring that 'there is now no reasonable excuse for refusing to face the fact that nothing but a eugenic religion can save our civilisation from the fate that has overtaken all previous civilisations'.[14] Wells's reaction was more cautious. He admitted that 'the way of nature has always been to slay the hindmost, and there is still no other way, unless we can prevent those who would become the hindmost being born. It is in the sterilisation of failures . . . that the possibility of an improvement of the human stock lies'.[15] Nevertheless, most of his speech was clearly intended to distance himself from the eugenicist zealots. 'Dr Galton has resorted in the past to the device of inquiring how many judges and bishops and such-like eminent persons a family can boast,' he said. 'Dr Galton . . . seemed to me to ignore the consideration of social advantage, of what Americans call the "pull" that follows any striking success. The fact that the sons and nephews of a distinguished judge or great scientific man are themselves eminent judges or successful scientific men may, after all, be far more due to a special knowledge of the channels of professional advancement than to any distinctive family gift . . . I think we want a much more elaborate analysis.'

Wells was already retreating from the position set out in his sociological tract *Anticipations of the Reaction of Mechanical Progress upon Human Life and Thought*, published in 1901, which proposed that the poor and ill-educated – 'the People of the Abyss' – should have all their state support withdrawn, and be killed if they tried to reproduce. He had also argued that the social status of the intellectual elite proved their innate superiority, a view he repudiated three years later when challenging Galton's contention that criminals should be prevented from breeding: 'Many eminent criminals appear to me to be persons superior in many respects – in intelligence, initiative, originality – to the average judge.' He had clearly taken to heart the hostile (indeed horrified) criticism of *Anticipations* from reviewers and friends. 'What we miss in Mr Wells's view of humanity,' the *Spectator* had noted, 'is any allowance for humanity itself' – a point echoed in a letter from Joseph Conrad, who urged Wells to cast 'a wide and generous net, where there would be room for everybody' instead of establishing 'a sort of select circle to which you address yourself, leaving the rest of the world outside the pale'.[16] As a writer with a mass readership, Wells took the point. Perhaps recalling the *Daily Telegraph*'s appalled reaction to his advocacy of 'such extreme doctrines as the lethal chamber for the criminal and the lunatic', in *A Modern Utopia* he hastened to assure readers that 'there would be no killing, no lethal chambers . . . I doubt even if there will be jails' (Ch. 5).

He didn't retreat very far, however. In Chapter 5 – 'Failure in a Modern Utopia' – he asks what his parallel world will do with congenital invalids, drunks, madmen and 'lumpish, unteachable and unimaginative people'. His answer: 'These people will have to be in the descendent phase, the species must be engaged in eliminating them; there is no escape from that . . .' The ideal state would seek to 'achieve the maximum elimination of its feeble and spiritless folk in every generation' – the only concession being that it would do so 'with the minimum of suffering'.

So much for the underclass: what of the rulers? While the lumpish and spiritless types are eliminated, 'conversely the people of exceptional quality must be in the ascendant'. After reading *Anticipations*, Winston Churchill had sent a letter to Wells warning that 'nothing would be more fatal than for the government of states to get in the hands of experts. Expert knowledge is limited knowledge, and the unlimited ignorance of the plain man who knows where it hurts is a safer guide than any rigorous direction of a specialised character.'[17] He protested in vain. Like many of his Fabian contemporaries, Wells believed that the modern world required a ruling class of professional technocrats, economists and intellectuals: the old aristocratic amateurs weren't up to the job, but nor was 'the plain man'. In November 1902 he became one of twelve founder-members of the Coefficients' Club, formed by Sidney and Beatrice Webb as 'a kind of non-party Shadow Cabinet of experts, roughly paralleling the general structure of departmental functions'.[18] The Webbs themselves oversaw Local Government and Labour, Bertrand Russell advised on Science, while H. G. Wells acted as 'Cultural Minister without Portfolio'.

This self-appointed administrative elite reappeared three years later in *A Modern Utopia* as The Order of the Samurai, a group of 'voluntary noblemen' who rule the world. 'Voluntary noblemen!' the narrator's sceptical travelling companion splut-ters. 'Voluntary Gods, I fancy they think themselves' (Ch. 4). There is no universal suffrage, since 'the large intricacy of Utopian organization demands a more powerful and efficient method of control than electoral methods can give' (Ch. 9), but membership of the Samurai is open to any intelligent, healthy and efficient adult – 'provided he follows the Rule' (Ch. 9). Or, rather, the Rules. Samurai mustn't drink alcohol, smoke tobacco or eat meat. Acting, singing and reciting are all for-bidden to them, though 'they may lecture authoritatively or debate' (Ch. 9). They cannot work in any kind of service industry – restaurants, hotels, barbershops. Nor can they 'play games in public or ... watch them being played' (Ch. 9). They must take cold baths every day, maintain lifelong fidelity to their spouses and sleep alone at least four nights in five.

One wonders just how seriously Wells (an inveterate womanizer) intended this to be taken; and sometimes one senses that he wondered too. His description of the fictional narrator on the first page is a recognizable self-portrait of the author, a short, tubby, balding man whose speaking voice is 'an unattractive tenor' – not exactly the very model of a modern Übermensch. The implication is that we should keep this figure in mind when reading his paeans to the tall, fit, hearty supermen of Utopia, and realize that his dreamy paradise isn't necessarily the ideal habitat for the person who imagined it. (We might also recall that the only characters in his novels who have real warmth and human appeal – the clerks and servants and draper's assistants, the Kippses and Hoopdrivers and Mr Pollys – are those who would be classified as 'inferior' in this Utopia.) There is a further hint at the very end, when the Utopist bubble bursts and the narrator finds himself dumped in central London. 'But from the front seat on the top of an omnibus on a sunny September afternoon,' he grumbles, 'the Strand and Charing Cross corner and Whitehall and the great multitude of people, the great uproar of vehicles, streaming in all directions, is apt to look a world altogether too formidable. It has a glare, it has a tumult and vigour that shout one down' (Ch. 11). But does he really yearn for the deep contemplative peace of Utopia? Wells himself was practically synonymous with tumult and vigour – a prolific writer, a noisy public figure, a fearless controversialist, as unignorable as a double-decker bus in the Strand. As John Carey conceded in *The Intellectuals and the Masses* (1992), after a long chapter denouncing Wellsian misanthropy, 'Wells's greatness as a writer depends not only on the intensity with which he hates but on the imaginative duplicity that qualifies his hatred. He is nearly always in two minds, and this saves him from mere prescription. The utopias he invents seem to waver and change into dystopias as we watch, robbing us of certainty.'[19]

That is certainly true of *A Modern Utopia* – though its transformation into dystopia owes rather more to events in the real world, and to subsequent counterblasts such as Aldous Huxley's *Brave New World* (a straight parody of Wells) and George Orwell's *Nineteen Eighty-Four*. In a famous essay titled 'Wells, Hitler and the World State', published by *Horizon* in 1941, Orwell noted that much of H. G. Wells's work – novels, Utopias, essays, films, pamphlets – depended on a supposed antithesis between the man of science who is working towards a planned World State and the reactionary who is trying to restore a disorderly past:

On the one side science, order, progress, internationalism, aeroplanes, steel, concrete, hygiene: on the other side war, nationalism, religion, monarchy, peasants, Greek professors, poets, horses. History as he sees it is a series of victories won by the scientific man over the romantic man . . . But unfortunately the equation of science with common sense does not really hold good. The aeroplane, which was looked forward to as a civilising influence but in practice has hardly been used except for dropping bombs, is the symbol of that fact. Modern Germany is far more scientific than England, and far more barbarous. Much of what Wells has imagined and worked for is physically there in Nazi Germany. The order, the planning, the State encouragement of science, the steel, the concrete, the aeroplanes, are all there, but all in the service of ideas appropriate to the Stone Age . . . Obviously it is impossible for Wells to accept this. It would contradict the world-view on which his own works are based.[20]

The essay infuriated Wells, who wrote to Orwell denouncing him as 'a shit',[21] but he had brought it on himself. In his autobiography, published in 1934, Wells maintained that his invention of the Samurai had solved 'a primary problem of government'[22] better than any method previously suggested. 'The experience of the thirty years that have passed since I launched this scheme,' he continued, 'and particularly the appearance of such successful organisations as the Communist Party and the Italian Fascists has greatly strengthened my belief in the essential soundness of this conception of the governing order of the future.' Wells had strong ideological objections to both Marxism and Fascism, but his tribute to some of the organizational methods of the Soviet Communist Party and the Italian Fascist Party – clearly identified here and elsewhere as experiments in Samurai government – explains why his political writings have been out of fashion (and out of print) for so long.

He must not be kept in this self-inflicted exile indefinitely, however – not least because readers deserve a chance to discover what an extraordinary literary artist he was. Here are a couple of paragraphs chosen more or less at random from Chapter 9, where he describes the Samurai's obligation to disappear to a wild and remote place once a year for lone meditation:

> It came to me suddenly as very strange that even as we sat and talked, across deserted seas, on burning sands, through the still aisles of forests, and in all the high and lonely places of the world, beyond the margin where the ways and houses go, solitary men and women sailed alone or marched alone, or clambered – quiet, resolute exiles; they stood alone amidst wildernesses of ice, on the precipitous banks of roaring torrents, in monstrous caverns, or steering a tossing boat in the little circle of the horizon amidst the tumbled, incessant sea, all in their several ways communing with the emptiness, the enigmatic spaces and silences, the winds and torrents and soulless forces that lie about the lit and ordered life of men.
>
> I saw more clearly now something I had seen dimly already in the bearing and the faces of this Utopian chivalry, a faint persistent tinge of detachment from the immediate heats and hurries, the little graces and delights, the tensions and stimulations of the daily world. It pleased me strangely to think of this steadfast yearly pilgrimage of solitude, and how near men might come then to the high distances of God.

Note how in each sentence the swelling waves of subordinate clauses crash on to the shore with a thunderous monosyllable – 'men', 'world', 'God'. (Note, too, the incidental admission that Samurai are immune to graces and delights, another indi-

cation of his imaginative duplicity.) If the poetry of Yeats or
Eliot or Larkin can transcend their political prejudices, so can
Wells's prose.

Yet even his ideas have a surprising resonance. In an era of
globalization and New World Orders, the vision of a World
State no longer seems quite so fanciful. Twenty-first-century
readers may also feel a twinge of recognition when Wells reveals
that every citizen is obliged to carry an unfalsifiable identity
card, whose details are entered on a vast international database
'by which every person in the world can be promptly and
certainly recognized', since the modern Utopia 'must square
itself to the needs of a migratory population, to an endless
coming and going, to a people as fluid and tidal as the sea'
(Ch. 5). And, now that scientists offer the prospect of improving
the human stock and eliminating deformities through gene-
manipulation, Wells's interest in eugenic breeding suddenly
acquires an unnerving topicality. As John Carey says, 'his value
as a writer is that he faces us with facts beyond the normal
scope of fiction'.[23]

A century after its original publication, *A Modern Utopia*
can serve as an inspiration or a warning. H. G. Wells claimed
to be setting out his desires rather than his predictions, but who
would dare to say that those yearnings – so long dismissed as
faded Edwardian nightmares – may not yet be fulfilled?

Francis Wheen

# NOTES

1.   Oscar Wilde, *The Soul of Man Under Socialism and Selected
     Critical Prose* (London: Penguin Classics, 2001).

2.   Francis Fukuyama, 'The End of History?', *The National Interest*,
     No 16, (Summer 1989) pp. 3–18.

3.   H. G. Wells, 'Utopias', broadcast by ABC on 19 January 1939;
     typescript at http://www.depauw.edu/sfs/documents/wells1.htm.

4.   Karl Marx and Friedrich Engels, *The Communist Manifesto*
     (Oxford: Oxford World's Classics, 1992), p. 6.

5.   Joseph A. Schumpeter, *Capitalism, Socialism and Democracy*
     (London: Routledge, 1994).

6.   Norman Kelvin (ed.), *The Collected Letters of William Morris* (Princeton: Princeton University Press, 1984), Vol. 2, p. 202.

7.   G. D. H. Cole, *Self-Government in Industry* (Bell & Sons, 1917).

8.   Francis Wheen, *Karl Marx* (London: Fourth Estate, 1999), p. 364.

9.   Francis Galton, *Inquiries into Human Faculty and Its Development* (Basingstoke: Macmillan, 1883).

10.  Francis Galton, 'Kantsaywhere' in Karl Pearson, *The Life, Letters and Labours of Francis Galton* (Cambridge: Cambridge University Press, 1914–30), pp. 411–25.

11.  Sidney Webb, 'The Difficulties of Individualism' (London: Fabian Society, 1896).

12.  George Bernard Shaw, *The Intelligent Woman's Guide to Socialism* (London, Constable, 1928)

13.  Francis Galton, 'Eugenics: Its Definition, Scope and Aims', paper read before the Sociological Society at the School of Economics (London University) on 16 May 1904, reprinted in *The American Journal of Sociology*, Vol. X, No. 1 (July 1904).

14.  *The American Journal of Sociology*, op. cit.

15.  Ibid.

16.  The quotes from reviews in the *Spectator* and *Daily Telegraph* and from Conrad's letter come from John S. Partington, *Building Cosmopolis: The Political Thought of H. G. Wells* (Aldershot: Ashgate, 2003).

17.  Winston Churchill, 17 November 1902, quoted in Harold Perkin, *The Rise of Professional Society: England since 1880* (London: Routledge, 1989), p. 169.

18.  Description of the Coefficients' Club is in Robert Scally, *The Origins of the Lloyd George Coalition* (Princeton: Princeton University Press, 1975).

19.  John Carey, *The Intellectuals and the Masses* (London: Faber & Faber, 1992).

20.  George Orwell, 'Wells, Hitler and the World State', *Horizon*, August 1941.

21.  Wells's description of Orwell is quoted in D. J. Taylor, *Orwell: The Life* (London: Chatto & Windus, 2003).

22.  H. G. Wells, *Experiment in Autobiography*, Vol. II (London: Gollancz and Cresset Press, 1934), p. 659.

23.  John Carey, *The Intellectuals and the Masses* (London: Faber & Faber, 1992).

# Further Reading

The most vivid and memorable account of Wells's life and times is his own *Experiment in Autobiography* (2 vols., London: Gollancz and Cresset Press, 1934). It has been reprinted several times. A 'postscript' containing the previously suppressed narrative of his sexual liaisons was published as *H. G. Wells in Love*, edited by his son G. P. Wells (London: Faber & Faber, 1984) His more recent biographers draw on this material, as well as on the large body of letters and personal papers archived at the University of Illinois and elsewhere. The fullest and most scholarly biographies are *The Time Traveller* by Norman and Jeanne Mackenzie (2nd edn, London: Hogarth Press, 1987) and *H. G. Wells: Desperately Mortal* by David C. Smith (New Haven and London: Yale University Press, 1986). Smith has also edited a generous selection of Wells's *Correspondence* (4 vols., London: Pickering & Chatto, 1998). Another highly readable, if controversial and idiosyncratic, biography is *H. G. Wells: Aspects of a Life* (London: Hutchinson, 1984) by Wells's son Anthony West. Michael Foot's *H. G.: The History of Mr Wells* (London and New York: Doubleday, 1995) is enlivened by its author's personal knowledge of Wells and his circle.

Two illuminating general interpretations of Wells and his writings are Michael Draper's *H. G. Wells* (Basingstoke: Macmillan, 1987) and Brian Murray's *H. G. Wells* (New York: Continuum, 1990). Both are introductory in scope, but Draper's approach is critical and philosophical, while Murray packs a remarkable amount of biographical and historical detail into a short space. John Hammond's *An H. G. Wells Companion* (London and Basingstoke: Macmillan, 1979) and

*H. G. Wells* (Harlow and London: Longman, 2001) combine criticism with useful contextual material. *H. G. Wells: The Critical Heritage*, edited by Patrick Parrinder (London: Routledge, 1972), is a collection of reviews and essays of Wells published during his lifetime. A number of specialized critical and scholarly studies of Wells concentrate on his scientific romances. These include Bernard Bergonzi's pioneering study of *The Early H. G. Wells* (Manchester: Manchester University Press, 1961); John Huntington, *The Logic of Fantasy: H. G. Wells and Science Fiction* (New York: Columbia University Press, 1982); and Patrick Parrinder, *Shadows of the Future: H. G. Wells, Science Fiction and Prophecy* (Liverpool: Liverpool University Press, 1995). Peter Kemp's *H. G. Wells and the Culminating Ape* (London and Basingstoke: Macmillan, 1982) offers a lively and, at times, lurid tracing of Wells's 'biological themes and imaginative obsessions', while Roslynn D. Haynes's *H. G. Wells: Discoverer of the Future* (London and Basingstoke: Macmillan, 1980) surveys his use of scientific ideas. W. Warren Wagar, *H. G. Wells and the World State* (New Haven: Yale University Press, 1961) and John S. Partington, *Building Cosmopolis* (Aldershot: Ashgate, 2003) are studies of his political thought and his schemes for world government. John S. Partington has also edited *The Wellsian* (The Netherlands: Equilibris, 2003), a selection of essays from the H. G. Wells Society's annual critical journal of the same name. The American branch of the Wells Society maintains a highly informative website at http://hgwellsusa.50megs.com

P. P.

# Note on the Text

In September 1903 H. G. Wells went on a two-week walking tour in the Swiss Alps with Graham Wallas (1858–1932), then a lecturer in Political Science at the London School of Economics. Wells, who found Wallas a somewhat trying companion, wrote to his wife during the holiday that 'I shall use W. freely in the next novel'.[1] This may have been the genesis of *A Modern Utopia*. Wells's paper 'Scepticism of the Instrument' was read to the Oxford Philosophical Society in November, and later incorporated into the book as an appendix. Early in the following year Wells found himself unable to take up an invitation to visit his friend Arnold Bennett in Paris. He wrote to Bennett on 29 March that 'I've got a damned book in hand that necessitates reading all Plato and most other things if it is to be done properly'.[2] He had completed *A Modern Utopia* by the end of August, and a month later he told an American socialist, George Sterling, that 'I think it's the best thing I've done'.[3] It was serialized in six instalments in the *Fortnightly Review* (October 1904–April 1905), and published in book form by Chapman & Hall in April. The first American edition was by Scribner's (New York) at the end of May. Subsequent editions appeared in London (1909, 1917) and in New York (1907, 1909, 1916), with relatively few alterations. In 1925 *A Modern Utopia* appeared in Volume 9 of the Atlantic Edition of the Works of H. G. Wells.[4]

The Atlantic edition was intended to provide definitive versions of all Wells's major works, and it is the basis of the current edition, with the modifications set out below. The principal changes from the first London edition are the removal of the seven illustrations by Edmund J. Sullivan – the most interesting of these illustrations, which Wells termed 'meretricious', is 'the Order of the Samurai' which served as a frontispiece – and the omission of the extended 'Note to the Reader' (see list of variants).

Printed in the United States and published simultaneously in New York and London, the Atlantic edition was meant to follow British spelling conventions but frequently fails to do so. In the present text, housestyling of punctuation and spelling has been implemented to make the text more accessible to the reader: single quotation marks (for doubles) with doubles inside singles as needed; end punctuation placed outside end quotation marks when appropriate; spaced N-dashes (for the heavier, longer M-dash) and M-dashes (for the double-length 2M-dash); 'iz' spellings (e.g. recognize, not recognise), and acknowledgements and judgement, not acknowledgments and judgment; no full stop after personal titles (Dr, Mr, Mrs) or chapter titles, which may not follow the capitalization of the copy-text. Hyphens have been removed from some thirty words in accordance with modern British practice, e.g. banknote not bank-note, goodbye not good-bye, cannonball not cannon-ball, tomorrow not to-morrow, worldwide not world-wide, but frock coat not frock-coat, half a dozen not half-a-dozen, free will not free-will, love story not love-story, etc. Some words have been altered in accordance with modern British conventions, for example, vice versa for *vice versâ* and Hindu for Hindoo. The word 'a' has been added before 'more powerful' at p. 174, line 13, correcting an error in the Atlantic text.

## SELECTED VARIANT READINGS

(i) The 1905 edition adds 'A Note to the Reader' before the Table of Contents. This reads:

This book is in all probability the last of a series of writings, of which – disregarding certain earlier disconnected essays – my *Anticipations* was the beginning. Originally I intended *Anticipa-*

*tions* to be my sole digression from my art or trade (or what you will) of an imaginative writer. I wrote that book in order to clear up the muddle in my own mind about innumerable social and political questions, questions I could not keep out of my work, which it distressed me to touch upon in a stupid haphazard way, and which no one, so far as I knew, had handled in a manner to satisfy my needs. But *Anticipations* did not achieve its end. I have a slow constructive hesitating sort of mind, and when I emerged from that undertaking I found I had still most of my questions to state and solve. In *Mankind in the Making*, therefore, I tried to review the social organisation in a different way, to consider it as an educational process instead of dealing with it as a thing with a future history, and if I made this second book even less satisfactory from a literary standpoint than the former (and this is my opinion), I blundered, I think, more edifyingly – at least from the point of view of my own instruction. I ventured upon several themes with a greater frankness than I had used in *Anticipations*, and came out of that second effort guilty of much rash writing, but with a considerable development of formed opinion. In many matters I had shaped out at last a certain personal certitude, upon which I feel I shall go for the rest of my days. In this present book I have tried to settle accounts with a number of issues left over or opened up by its two predecessors, to correct them in some particulars, and to give the general picture of a *Utopia* that has grown up in my mind during the course of these speculations as a state of affairs at once possible and more desirable than the world in which I live. But this book has brought me back to imaginative writing again. In its two predecessors the treatment of social organisation had been purely objective; here my intention has been a little wider and deeper, in that I have tried to present not simply an ideal, but an ideal in reaction with two personalities. Moreover, since this may be the last book of the kind I shall ever publish, I have written into it as well as I can the heretical metaphysical scepticism upon which all my thinking rests, and I have inserted certain sections reflecting upon the established methods of sociological and economic science . . .

The last four words will not attract the butterfly reader, I know. I have done my best to make the whole of this book as lucid and entertaining as its matter permits, because I want it read by as many people as possible, but I do not promise anything but rage and confusion to him who proposes to glance through my pages just to see if I agree with him, or to begin in the middle, or to read without a constantly alert attention. If you are not already a little interested and open-minded with regard to social and political questions, and a little exercised in self-examination, you will find neither interest nor pleasure here. If your mind is 'made up' upon such issues your time will be wasted on these pages. And even if you are a willing reader you may require a little patience for the peculiar method I have this time adopted.

That method assumes an air of haphazard, but it is not so careless as it seems. I believe it to be – even now that I am through with the book – the best way to a sort of lucid vagueness which has always been my intention in this matter. I tried over several beginnings of a Utopian book before I adopted this. I rejected from the outset the form of the argumentative essay, the form which appeals most readily to what is called the 'serious' reader, the reader who is often no more than the solemnly impatient parasite of great questions. He likes everything in hard, heavy lines, black and white, yes and no, because he does not understand how much there is that cannot be presented at all in that way; wherever there is any effect of obliquity, of incommensurables, wherever there is any levity or humour or difficulty of multiplex presentation, he refuses attention. Mentally he seems to be built up upon an invincible assumption that the Spirit of Creation cannot count beyond two, he deals only in alternatives. Such readers I have resolved not to attempt to please here. Even if I presented all my tri-clinic crystals as systems of cubes! Indeed I felt it would not be worth doing. But having rejected the 'serious' essay as a form, I was still greatly exercised, I spent some vacillating months over the scheme of this book. I tried first a recognised method of viewing questions from divergent points that has always attracted me and which I have never succeeded in using, the discussion novel, after the fashion of Peacock's (and Mr Mallock's) development of the ancient dialogue; but this encumbered me with unnecessary characters and the inevitable complication of intrigue among them, and I abandoned it. After that I tried to cast the thing into a shape resembling a little the double personality of Boswell's Johnson, a sort of interplay between monologue and commentator; but that too, although it got nearer to the quality I sought, finally failed. Then I hesitated over what one might call 'hard narrative.' It will be evident to the experienced reader that by omitting certain speculative and metaphysical elements and by elaborating incident, this book might have been reduced to a straightforward story. But I did not want to omit as much on this occasion. I do not see why I should always pander to the vulgar appetite for stark stories. And in short, I made it this. I explain all this in order to make it clear to the reader that, however queer this book appears at the first examination, it is the outcome of trial and deliberation, it is intended to be as it is. I am aiming throughout at a sort of shot-silk texture between philosophical discussion on the one hand and imaginative narrative on the other.

My friend, Mr E. J. Sullivan, has achieved collaboration in his admirably decorative illustrations, and I have to tender him my very warmest thanks.

H. G. WELLS.

(ii) Variants between Atlantic (1925) and Chapman & Hall (1905) readings:

| page:line | Atlantic | Chapman & Hall |
| --- | --- | --- |
| 15:20 | State | state |
| 15:24 | World State | World-state |
| 19:15 | we | us |
| 20:4 | inflections | inflexions |
| 20:13 | also in that parallel planet beyond Sirius | in that parallel planet beyond Sirius also |
| 23:31 | World State | world-state |
| 25:24 | disorganisation | disorganisation? |
| 25:25 | disarrange | disarrange? |
| 25:25 | population | population? |
| 31:7 | modern-minded | modern minded |

| page:line | Atlantic | Chapman & Hall |
|---|---|---|
| 31:32 | individuality – | individuality, |
| 31:33 | hitherto – | hitherto, |
| 33:18 | oddly | odd |
| 34:5 | publicity on the | publicity in the |
| 34:26 | defensive, the | defensive, that too the |
| 36:3 | World State | world-state |
| 36:12 | modern | Modern |
| 41:4 | St. | San |
| 45:37 | man | MAN |
| 46:3 | modern | Modern |
| 49:7 | modern | Modern |
| 50:25 | fire extinguishing | *fire-extincteurs* |
| 53:23 | disc | disk |
| 57:11 | modern | Modern |
| 57:28–9 | products – . . . like – | products, . . . like, |
| 62:19 | by-product | bye-product |
| 62:38 | Political Economy | 'Political Economy' |
| 65:2 | State | state |
| 66:4 | pour | fall |
| 66:4 | exist | are |
| 67:20 | Utopia. | Utopia? |
| 69:3 | modern | Modern |
| 71:4 | portion | moiety |
| 72:fn | Blithedale | Blythedale |
|  | Note Books | *Notebook* |
| 73:28 | make | makes |
| 73:30 | a competent | a too competent |
| 77:8 | modern | Modern |
| 78:8 | modern | Modern |
| 84:10 | to and fro lecturing | from in the earth lecturing |
| 85:29 | modern | Modern |
| 87:22 | modern | Modern |
| 89:22 | They | (They |
| 89:30 | up." | up.") |
| 90:32 | they were | it was |
| 90:32 | they are | it is |
| 91:9 | church | Church |

| page:line | *Atlantic* | *Chapman & Hall* |
|---|---|---|
| 95:13 | modern | Modern |
| 98:27 | There are many | There is a number of |
| 99:21 | gentlewomen | gentle women |
| 103:11 | burdensome | burthensome |
| 107:33 | Modern | modern |
| 108:22 | Public Office | public office |
| 111:15 | Piz | Passo |
| 111:17 | St. | San |
| 114:9 | modern | Modern |
| 114:28–9 | slave. But | slave. You imagine that father of old Liberalism, Rousseau, slinking off from his offspring at the door of the Foundling Hospital, and you can understand what a crime against Natural virtue this quiet eye of the State would have seemed to him. But |
| 115:2 | particles | parties |
| 115:7 | by-products | bye products |
| 117:7 | St. | Saint |
| 118:5 | Kapellbrücke | Kapellbrucke |
| 122:21 | of trees | of little trees |
| 125:34 | modern | Modern |
| 126:38 | to add | and add |
| 128:9 | modern | Modern |
| 128:34 | illness | illnesses |
| 132:5 | licences | licenses |
| 138:11 | pygmy | pigmy |
| 140:25 | code, is | code, are |
| 141:11 | herd, becomes the | herd, the |
| 142:23 | inquiring | enquiring |
| 142:32 | Republic | republic |
| 143:21 | Modern | modern |
| 143:22 | group | grouped |

| page:line | Atlantic | Chapman & Hall |
|---|---|---|
| 143:fn | Hillquit | Hillqurit |
| 146:15 | self-cleaning bedrooms | self-cleaning little bedrooms |
| 147:13 | grey | gray |
| 148:7 | verandas | verandahs |
| 148:15 | oftener | often |
| 149:3 | rare in | rare indeed in |
| 153:7 | inquiries | enquiries |
| 153:28 | inquiries | enquiries |
| 153:32 | Everyone seems | Everyone one meets seems |
| 155:11 | wear | wore |
| 155:23 | of the old | of old |
| 155:24 | Kapellbrücke | Kapelbrucke |
| 157:34 | inexpressibly | inexpressively |
| 158:10 | gets from | gets for example from |
| 160:1 | of puzzling | of one's puzzling |
| 160:12 | exist | exists |
| 160:30 | burden | burthen |
| 161:10 | a sufficient | a small but sufficient |
| 164:24 | commonalty | commonality |
| 168:7 | imposter | impostor |
| 169:13 | I saw her | it was her |
| 172:9 | burned | burnt |
| 176:30 | enthusiasm | enthusiasms |
| 181:5 | emerging | merging |
| 182:4 | uniqueness | uniquenesses |
| 184:3 | Modern | modern |
| 185:1 | to frame it so | to so frame it |
| 185:9 | Modern | modern |
| 186:3 | Salomon | Saloman |
| 189:18 | debatable | debateable |
| 189:20 | Technic | Technique |
| 190:5 | a quantity of | some very obscure |
| 193:33 | *purchasable* | *purchaseable* |
| 203:24 | Tromsö | Tromso |
| 204:24 | night | nights |
| 208:12 | desirous | desiring |

| page:line | *Atlantic* | *Chapman & Hall* |
|---|---|---|
| 210:8 | Modern | modern |
| 210:17 | faces | face |
| 213:31 | of the aggregations | of aggregations |
| 214:14 | wish | want |
| 216:4 | ideas | idea |
| 217:23 | St. | Saint |
| 218:25 | poetic | poietic |
| 220:13 | Dr. J. Deniker | Doctor J. Deinker |
| 224:13 | at all | of all |
| 225:21 | Pygmies | Pigmies |
| 225:22 | their gifts | their little gifts |
| 225:28 | none has | none have |
| 227:24 | modern | Modern |
| 227:33 | tranquillise | tranquilise |
| 228:4 | a while | a little while |
| 229:27 | however, widely | however, very widely |
| 229:28 | But we have | We have, however, |
| 233:10 | jealously | jealousy |
| 236:26 | explain. My | explain very quickly. My |
| 237:35 | asphalt | asphalte |
| 243:9 | shout | shouts |
| 245:29 | farther | further |
| 247:27 | *between the whole and the individual* | *between great and individual* |
| 247:29 | *that scheme* | *that great scheme* |
| 251:1 | SCEPTICISM … 1903. | APPENDIX/ SCEPTICISM OF THE INSTRUMENT/ A PORTION OF A PAPER READ TO THE OXFORD PHILOSOPHICAL SOCIETY, NOVEMBER 8, 1903, AND REPRINTED, WITH SOME REVISION, FROM THE VERSION GIVEN IN |

| page:line | Atlantic | Chapman & Hall |
|---|---|---|
| 251:1 | SCEPTICISM ... 1903. | Mind, vol. xiii. (N.S.), No. 51. (See also Chapter I., § 6, and Chapter X., § § 1 and 2.) |
| 257:7 | a distance | a little distance |
| 258:36 | even to-day | to-day even |
| 259:14 | try to | try and |
| 263:16 | as being in | as in |
| 263:18 | impossible. They ... plane. This | impossible. This |
| 265:3 | cartography. | cartography. Here followed certain comments upon Personal Idealism, and Mr. F. C. S. Schiller's Humanism, of no particular value. |

The manuscript of A Modern Utopia is in the Wells Collection at the Rare Books and Special Collections Library, University of Illinois at Urbana-Champaign.

Gregory Claeys, Patrick Parrinder

## NOTES

1. The Correspondence of H. G. Wells, ed. David C. Smith (London: Pickering & Chatto, 1998), i, p. 424.
2. Arnold Bennett and H. G. Wells, ed. Harris Wilson (London: Hart-Davis, 1960), p. 106.
3. Correspondence, ii, pp. 42, 48.
4. London: T. Fisher Unwin, and New York: Scribner's.

# A MODERN UTOPIA

# Contents

|  | Preface [1925] | 5 |
|  | The Owner of the Voice | 7 |
| 1 | Topographical | 11 |
| 2 | Concerning Freedoms | 28 |
| 3 | Utopian Economics | 53 |
| 4 | The Voice of Nature | 81 |
| 5 | Failure in a Modern Utopia | 95 |
| 6 | Women in a Modern Utopia | 121 |
| 7 | A Few Utopian Impressions | 146 |
| 8 | My Utopian Self | 167 |
| 9 | The Samurai | 174 |
| 10 | Race in Utopia | 212 |
| 11 | The Bubble Bursts | 234 |

# PREFACE [1925]

*A Modern Utopia* was an experiment in form. It was done while I was completing *Kipps*.[1] The intentions of the experiment I tried to make clear in my preface to the first edition, and from that preface I will repeat here as much as will still interest the patient reader.

The method assumes an air of haphazard, but it is not so careless as it seems. I believe it to be the best way to the sort of lucid vagueness which has been my intention in this matter. I tried over several beginnings of a Utopian book before I adopted this. I rejected from the outset the form of the argumentative essay, the form which appeals most readily to what is called the 'serious' reader, the reader who is often no more than the solemnly impatient parasite of great questions. He likes everything in hard, heavy lines, black and white, yes and no, because he does not understand how much there is that cannot be presented at all in that way; wherever there is any effect of obliquity, of incommensurables, wherever there is any levity or humour or difficulty of multiplex presentation, he refuses attention. Mentally he seems to be built up upon an invincible assumption that the Spirit of Creation cannot count beyond two, he deals only in alternatives. Such readers I have resolved not to attempt to please here. Even if I presented all my triclinic crystals[2] as systems of cubes –! Indeed I felt it would not be worth doing. But having rejected the 'serious' essay as a form, I was still greatly exercised, I spent some vacillating months over the scheme of this book. I first tried a recognized method of viewing questions from divergent points that has always attracted me but which I have never succeeded in using, the discussion novel, after the fashion of Peacock's[3] (and Mr Mallock's[4]) development of the ancient dialogue; but this encumbered me with unnecessary characters and the inevitable complication of intrigue among them, and I abandoned it. After that I tried to cast the thing into a shape resembling a little the double personality of Boswell's Johnson,[5] a sort of interplay between monologue and commentator; but that too, although it got nearer to the quality I sought, finally failed. Then I hesitated over what one might call 'hard narrative'. It will be evident to the experienced reader that by omitting certain speculative and metaphysical elements and by elaborating incident, this book might have been reduced to a straightforward story. But I did not want to omit as much on this occasion. I do not see why I should always pander to the vulgar appetite for stark stories. And in short, I made it this. I explain all this in order to make it clear to the reader that, however queer this book appears at the first examination, it is the outcome of trial and deliberation; it is intended to be as it is. I am aiming throughout at a sort of shot-silk texture between philosophical discussion on the one hand and imaginative narrative on the other.

So much for the intention of the book. It had a certain moderate success in both Europe and America, and later on a cheap edition had a considerable sale in Great Britain.

Bound up with it here is a paper called 'Scepticism of the Instrument', which was read to the Oxford Philosophical Society on November 8th, 1903, and which enlarged upon and cleared up various issues raised in *A Modern Utopia*. Following upon that are several papers of unequal merit and various interest that it seems just worthwhile to reprint in a collected edition of the writer's work.[6]

# THE OWNER OF THE VOICE

*There are works, and this is one of them, that are best begun
with a portrait of the author. And here indeed, because of a
very natural misunderstanding, this is the only course to take.
Throughout these papers sounds a note, a distinctive and personal note, a note that tends at times towards stridency; and all
that is not, as these words are, in Italics, is in one Voice. Now
this Voice, and this is the peculiarity of the matter, is not to be
taken as the Voice of the ostensible author who fathers these
pages. You have to clear your mind of any preconceptions in
that respect. The Owner of the Voice you must figure to yourself
as a whitish plump man,[1] a little under the middle size and age,
with such blue eyes as many Irishmen have, and agile in his
movements and with a slight tonsorial baldness – a penny might
cover it – of the crown. His front is convex. He droops at times
like most of us, but for the greater part he bears himself as
valiantly as a sparrow. Occasionally his hand flies out with a
fluttering gesture of illustration. And his Voice (which is our
medium henceforth) is an unattractive tenor that becomes at
times aggressive. Him you must imagine as sitting at a table
reading a manuscript about Utopias, a manuscript he holds in
two hands that are just a little fat at the wrist. The curtain rises
upon him so. But afterwards, if the devices of this declining art
of literature prevail, you will go with him through curious and
interesting experiences. Yet ever and again you will find him
back at that little table, the manuscript in his hand and the
expansion of his ratiocinations about Utopia conscientiously
resumed. The entertainment before you is neither the set drama
of the work of fiction you are accustomed to read, nor the set*

*lecturing of the essay you are accustomed to evade, but a hybrid of these two. If you figure this owner of the Voice as sitting, a little nervously, a little modestly, on a stage, with table, glass of water and all complete, and myself as the intrusive chairman insisting with a bland ruthlessness upon his 'few words' of introduction before he recedes into the wings, and if further-more you figure a sheet behind our friend on which moving pictures intermittently appear, and if finally you suppose his subject to be the story of the adventure of his soul among Utopian inquiries, you will be prepared for some at least of the difficulties of this unworthy but unusual work.*

*But over against this writer here presented, there is also another earthly person in the book, who gathers himself together into a distinct personality only after a preliminary complication with the reader. This person is spoken of as the botanist, and he is a leaner, rather taller, graver and much less garrulous man. His face is weakly handsome and done in tones of grey, he is fairish and grey-eyed, and you would suspect him of dyspepsia. It is a justifiable suspicion. Men of this type, the chairman remarks with a sudden intrusion of exposition, are romantic with a shadow of meanness, they seek at once to conceal and shape their sensuous cravings beneath egregious sentimentalities, they get into mighty tangles and troubles with women, and he has had his troubles. You will hear of them, for that is the quality of his type. He gets no personal expression in this book, the Voice is always that other's, but you gather much of the matter and something of the manner of his interpolations from the asides and the tenor of the Voice.*

*So much by way of portraiture is necessary to present the explorers of the Modern Utopia, which will unfold itself as a background to these two inquiring figures. The image of a cinematograph[2] entertainment is the one to grasp. There will be an effect of these two people going to and fro in front of the circle of a rather defective lantern, which sometimes jams and sometimes gets out of focus, but which does occasionally succeed in displaying on the screen a momentary moving picture of Utopian conditions. Occasionally the picture goes out altogether, the Voice argues and argues and the foot-*

*lights return, and then you find yourself listening again to the rather too plump little man at his table laboriously enunciating propositions, upon whom the curtain rises now.*

# I

# TOPOGRAPHICAL

§ 1

The Utopia of a modern dreamer must needs differ in one fundamental aspect from the Nowheres and Utopias men planned before Darwin[1] quickened the thought of the world. Those were all perfect and static States, a balance of happiness won for ever against the forces of unrest and disorder that inhere in things. One beheld a healthy and simple generation enjoying the fruits of the earth in an atmosphere of virtue and happiness, to be followed by other virtuous, happy and entirely similar generations until the Gods grew weary. Change and development were dammed back by invincible dams for ever. But the Modern Utopia must be not static but kinetic, must shape not as a permanent state but as a hopeful stage leading to a long ascent of stages. Nowadays we do not resist and overcome the great stream of things, but rather float upon it. We build now not citadels, but ships of state. For one ordered arrangement of citizens rejoicing in an equality of happiness safe and assured to them and their children for ever, we have to plan 'a flexible common compromise, in which a perpetually novel succession of individualities may converge most effectually upon a comprehensive onward development'. That is the first, most generalized difference between a Utopia based upon modern conceptions and all the Utopias that were written in the former time.

Our business here is to be Utopian, to make vivid and credible, if we can, first this facet and then that, of an imaginary whole and happy world. Our deliberate intention is to be not, indeed, impossible, but most distinctly impracticable by every scale that reaches only between today and tomorrow. We are to turn our backs for a space upon the insistent examination of the thing that is, and face towards the freer air, the ampler spaces of the thing that perhaps might be, to the projection of a State or city 'worthwhile', to designing upon the sheet of our imaginations the picture of a life conceivably possible, and yet better worth living than our own. That is our present enterprise. We are going to lay down certain necessary starting propositions, and then we shall proceed to explore the sort of world these propositions give us. . . .

It is no doubt an optimistic enterprise. But it is good for a while to be free from the carping note that must needs be audible when we discuss our present imperfections, to release ourselves from practical difficulties and the tangle of ways and means. It is good to stop by the track for a space, put aside the knapsack, wipe the brows, and talk a little of the upper slopes of the mountain we think we are climbing, would but the trees let us see it.

There is to be no inquiry here of policy and method. This is to be a holiday from politics and movements and methods. But, for all that, we must needs define certain limitations. Were we free to have our untrammelled desire, I suppose we should follow Morris to his Nowhere,[2] we should change the nature of man and the nature of things together; we should make the whole race wise, tolerant, noble, perfect – wave our hands to a splendid anarchy, every man doing as it pleases him, and none pleased to do evil, in a world as good in its essential nature, as ripe and sunny, as the world before the Fall. But that golden age, that perfect world, comes out into the possibilities of space and time. In space and time the pervading Will to Live sustains for evermore a perpetuity of aggressions. Our proposal here is upon a more practical plane at least than that. We are to restrict ourselves first to the limitations of human possibility as we know them in the men and women of this world today, and then to all the inhumanity, all the insubordination of nature. We are to shape our state in a world of uncertain seasons, sudden catastrophes, antagonistic diseases, and inimical beasts and vermin, out of men and women with like passions, like uncertainties of mood and desire to our own. And, moreover, we are going to accept this world of conflict, to adopt no attitude of renunciation towards it, to face it in no ascetic spirit, but in the mood of the Western peoples, whose purpose is to survive and overcome. So much we adopt in common with those who deal not in Utopias, but in the world of Here and Now.

Certain liberties, however, following the best Utopian precedents, we may take with existing fact. We assume that the tone of public thought may be entirely different from what it is in the present world. We permit ourselves a free hand with the mental conflict of life, within the possibilities of the human mind as we know it. We permit ourselves also a free hand with all the apparatus of existence that man has, so to speak, made for himself, with houses, roads, clothing, canals, machinery, with laws, boundaries, conventions and traditions, with schools, with literature and religious organization, with creeds and customs, with everything, in fact, that it lies within man's power to alter. That, indeed, is the cardinal assumption of all Utopian speculations old and new; the Republic and Laws of Plato, and More's Utopia, Howells' implicit Altruria, and Bellamy's future Boston, Comte's great Western Republic, Hertzka's Freeland, Cabet's Icaria, and Campanella's City of the Sun are built, just as we shall build, upon that, upon the hypothesis of the complete emancipation of a community of men from tradition, from habits, from legal bonds, and that subtler servitude possessions entail. And much of the essential value of all such speculations lies in this assumption of emancipation, lies in that regard towards human freedom, in the undying interest of the human power of self-escape, the power to resist the causation of the past, and to evade, initiate, endeavour and overcome.

§ 2

There are very definite artistic limitations also. There must always be a certain effect of hardness and thinness about Utopian speculations. Their common fault is to be comprehensively jejune. That which is the blood and warmth and reality of life is largely absent; there are no individualities, but only generalized people. In almost every Utopia – except, perhaps, Morris's *News from Nowhere* – one sees handsome but characterless buildings, symmetrical and perfect cultivations, and a multitude of people, healthy, happy, beautifully dressed, but without any personal distinction whatever. Too often the prospect resembles the key to one of those large pictures of coronations, royal weddings, parliaments, conferences and gatherings so popular in Victorian times, in which, instead of a face, each figure bears a neat oval with its index number legibly inscribed. This burthens us with an incurable effect of unreality, and I do not see how it is altogether to be escaped. It is a disadvantage that has to be accepted. Whatever institution has existed or exists, however irrational, however preposterous, has by virtue of its contact with individualities an effect of realness and rightness no untried thing may share. It has ripened, it has been christened with blood, it has been stained and mellowed by handling, it has been rounded and dented to the softened contours that we associate with life; it has been salted, maybe, in a brine of tears. But the thing that is merely proposed, the thing that is merely suggested, however rational, however necessary, seems strange and inhuman in its clear, hard, uncompromising lines, its unqualified angles and surfaces.

There is no help for it, there it is! The Master suffers with the last and least of his successors. For all the humanity he wins to, through his dramatic device of dialogue, I doubt if anyone has ever been warmed to desire himself a citizen in the Republic of Plato; I doubt if anyone could stand a month of the relentless publicity of virtue planned by More. . . . No one wants to live in any community of intercourse really, save for the sake of the individualities he would meet there. The fertilizing conflict of individualities is the ultimate meaning of the personal life, and all our Utopias no more than schemes for bettering that interplay. At least, that is how life shapes itself more and more to modern perceptions. Until you bring in individualities, nothing comes into being, and a Universe ceases when you shiver the mirror of the least of individual minds.

## § 3

No less than a planet will serve the purpose of a modern Utopia. Time was when a mountain valley or an island seemed to promise sufficient isolation for a polity to maintain itself intact from outward force; the Republic of Plato stood armed ready for defensive war, and the New Atlantis and the Utopia of More in theory, like China and Japan through many centuries of effectual practice, held themselves isolated from intruders. Such late instances as Butler's satirical *Erewhon*, and Mr Stead's queendom of inverted sexual conditions in Central Africa, found the Tibetan method of slaughtering the inquiring visitor a simple, sufficient rule. But the whole trend of modern thought is against the permanence of any such enclosures. We are acutely aware nowadays that, however subtly contrived a State may be, outside your boundary lines the epidemic, the breeding barbarian or the economic power will gather its strength to overcome you. The swift march of invention is all for the invader. Now perhaps you might still guard a rocky coast or a narrow pass; but what of that near tomorrow when the flying machine[3] soars overhead, free to descend at this point or that? A State powerful enough to keep isolated under modern conditions would be powerful enough to rule the world, would be, indeed, if not actively ruling yet passively acquiescent in all other human organizations, and so responsible for them altogether. World State, therefore, it must be.

That leaves no room for a modern Utopia in Central Africa or in South America or round about the pole, those last refuges of ideality. The floating isle of *La Cité Morellyste* no longer avails. We need a planet. Lord Erskine, the author of a Utopia ('Armata') that might have been inspired by Mr Hewins,[4] was the first of all Utopists to perceive this – he joined his twin planets pole to pole by a sort of umbilical cord. But the modern imagination, obsessed by physics, must travel further than that.

Out beyond Sirius,[5] far in the deeps of space, beyond the flight of a cannonball flying for a billion years, beyond the range of unaided vision, blazes the star that is *our* Utopia's sun. To those who know where to look, with a good opera-glass aiding good eyes, it and three fellows that seem in a cluster with it – though they are incredible billions of miles nearer – make just the faintest speck of light. About it go planets, even as our planets, but weaving a different fate, and in its place among them is Utopia, with its sister mate, the Moon. It is a planet like our planet, the same continents, the same islands, the same oceans and seas, another Fujiyama[6] is beautiful there dominating another Yokohama – and another Matterhorn[7] overlooks the icy disorder of another Theodule. It is so like our planet that a terrestrial botanist might find his every species there, even to the meanest pondweed or the remotest Alpine blossom. . . .

Only when he had gathered that last and turned about to find his inn again, perhaps he would not find his inn!

Suppose now that two of us were actually to turn about in just that fashion. Two, I think, for to face a strange planet, even though it be a wholly civilized one, without some other familiar backing, dashes the courage overmuch. Suppose that we were indeed so translated even as we stood. You figure us upon some high pass in the Alps, and though I – being one easily made giddy by stooping – am no botanist myself, if my companion were to have a specimen tin under his arm – so long as it is not painted that abominable popular Swiss apple green – I would make it no occasion for quarrel! We have tramped and botanized and come to a rest, and, sitting among rocks, we have eaten our lunch and finished our bottle of Yvorne, and fallen into a talk of Utopias, and said such things as I have been saying. I could figure it myself upon that little neck of the Lucendro Pass,[8] upon the shoulder of the Piz Lucendro, for there once I lunched and talked very pleasantly, and we are looking down upon the Val Bedretto, and Villa and Fontana and Airolo try to hide from us under the mountain side – three-quarters of a mile they are vertically below. (*Lantern*.)[9] With that absurd nearness of effect one gets in the Alps, we see the little train a dozen miles away, running down the Biaschina to Italy, and the Lukmanier Pass beyond Piora left of us, and the San Giacomo right, mere footpaths under our feet. . . .

And behold! in the twinkling of an eye we are in that other world!

We should scarcely note the change. Not a cloud would have gone from the sky. It might be the remote town below would take a different air, and my companion the botanist, with his educated observation, might almost see as much, and the train, perhaps, would be gone out of the picture, and the embanked straightness of the Ticino in the Ambri-Piotta meadows – that might be altered, but that would be all the visible change. Yet I have an idea that in some obscure manner we should come to feel at once a difference in things.

The botanist's glance would, under a subtle attraction, float back to Airolo. 'It's queer,' he would say quite idly, 'but I never noticed that building there to the right before.'

'Which building?'

'That to the right – with a queer sort of thing—'

'I see now. Yes. Yes, it's certainly an odd-looking affair. . . . And big, you know! Handsome! I wonder—'

That would interrupt our Utopian speculations. We should both discover that the little towns below had changed – but how, we should not have marked them well enough to know. It would be indefinable, a change in the quality of their grouping, a change in the quality of their remote, small shapes.

I should flick a few crumbs from my knee, perhaps. 'It's odd,' I should say, for the tenth or eleventh time, with a motion to rise, and we should get up and stretch ourselves, and, still a little puzzled, turn our faces towards the path that clambers down over the tumbled rocks and runs round by the still clear lake and down towards the Hospice of St Gotthard – if perchance we could still find that path.

Long before we got to that, before even we got to the great high road, we should have hints from the stone cabin in the nape of the pass – it would be gone or wonderfully changed – from the very goats upon the rocks, from the little hut by the rough bridge of stone, that a mighty difference had come to the world of men.

And presently, amazed and amazing, we should happen on a man – no Swiss – dressed in unfamiliar clothing and speaking an unfamiliar speech. . . .

## § 4

Before nightfall we should be drenched in wonders, but still we should have wonder left for the thing my companion, with his scientific training, would no doubt be the first to see. He would glance up, with that proprietary eye of the man who knows his constellations down to the little Greek letters. I imagine his exclamation. He would at first doubt his eyes. I should inquire the cause of his consternation, and it would be hard to explain. He would ask me with a certain singularity of manner for 'Orion',[10] and I should not find him; for the Great Bear, and it would have vanished. 'Where?' I should ask, and 'where?' seeking among that scattered starriness, and slowly I should acquire the wonder that possessed him.

Then, for the first time perhaps, we should realize from this unfamiliar heaven that not the world had changed, but ourselves – that we had come into the uttermost deeps of space.

## § 5

We need suppose no linguistic impediments to intercourse. The whole world will surely have a common language, that is quite elementarily Utopian; and since we are free of the trammels of convincing storytelling, we may suppose that language to be sufficiently our own to understand. Indeed, should we be in Utopia at all if we could not talk to everyone? That accursed bar of language, that hostile inscription in the foreigner's eyes, 'deaf and dumb to you, sir, and so – your enemy', is the very first of the defects and complications one has fled the earth to escape.

But what sort of language would we have the world speak, if we were told the miracle of Babel was presently to be reversed?

If I may take a daring image, a medieval liberty, I would suppose that in this lonely place the Spirit of Creation spoke to us on this matter. 'You are wise men,' that Spirit might say – and I, being a suspicious, touchy, over-earnest man for all my predisposition to plumpness, would instantly scent the irony (while my companion, I fancy, might even plume himself), 'and to beget your wisdom is chiefly why the world was made. You are so good as to propose an acceleration of that tedious multitudinous evolution upon which I am engaged. I gather, a universal tongue would serve you there. While I sit here among these mountains – I have been filing away at them for this last aeon or so, just to attract your hotels, you know – will you be so kind—? A few hints—?'

Then the Spirit of Creation might transiently smile, a smile that would be like the passing of a cloud. All the mountain wilderness about us would be radiantly lit. (You know those swift moments, when warmth and brightness drift by, in lonely and desolate places.)

Yet, after all, why should two men be smiled into apathy by the Infinite? Here we are, with our knobby little heads, our eyes and hands and feet and stout hearts, and if not we or ours, still the endless multitudes about us and in our loins are to come at last to the World State and a greater fellowship and the universal tongue. Let us to the extent of our ability, if not answer that question, at any rate try to think ourselves within sight of the best thing possible. That after all is our purpose, to imagine our best and strive for it; and it is a worse folly and a worse sin than presumption to abandon striving because the best of all our bests looks mean amidst the suns.

Now you as a botanist would, I suppose, incline to something, as they say, 'scientific'. You wince under that most offensive epithet – and I am able to give you my intelligent sympathy – though 'pseudo-scientific' and 'quasi-scientific' are worse by far for the skin. You would begin to talk of scientific languages,[11] of Esperanto, La Langue Bleue, New Latin, Volapuk, and Lord Lytton,[12] of the philosophical language of Archbishop Whateley,[13] Lady Welby's work upon Significs[14] and the like. You would tell me of the remarkable precisions, the encyclopaedic quality of chemical terminology, and at the word terminology I should insinuate a comment on that eminent American biologist, Professor Mark Baldwin,[15] who has carried the language biological to such heights of expressive clearness as to be triumphantly and invincibly unreadable. (Which foreshadows the line of my defence.)

You make your ideal clear; a scientific language you demand, without ambiguity, as precise as mathematical formulae, and with every term in relations of exact logical consistency with every other. It will be a language with all the inflections of verbs and nouns regular and all its constructions inevitable, each word clearly distinguishable from every other word in sound as well as spelling.

That, at any rate, is the sort of thing one hears demanded; and if only because the demand rests upon implications that reach far beyond the region of language, it is worth considering here. It implies, indeed, almost everything that we are endeavouring to repudiate in this particular work. It implies that the whole intellectual basis of mankind is established, that the rules of logic, the systems of counting and measurement, the general categories and schemes of resemblance and difference, are established for the human mind for ever – blank Comte-ism, in fact, of the blankest description. But indeed the science of logic and the whole framework of philosophical thought men have kept since the days of Plato and Aristotle,[16] has no more essential permanence as a final expression of the human mind than the Scottish Longer Catechism. Amidst the welter of modern thought, a philosophy long lost to men rises again into being, like some blind and almost formless embryo that must presently develop sight and form and power, a philosophy in which this assumption is denied.*

All through this Utopian excursion, I must warn you, you shall feel the thrust and disturbance of that insurgent movement. In the reiterated use of 'Unique', you will, as it were, get the gleam of its integument; in the insistence upon individuality and the individual difference as the significance of life, you will feel the texture of its shaping body. Nothing endures, nothing is precise and certain (except the mind of a pedant), perfection is

---

* The serious reader may refer at leisure to Sidgwick's *Use of Words in Reasoning*[17] (particularly), and to Bosanquet's *Essentials of Logic*,[18] Bradley's *Principles of Logic*,[19] and Sigwart's *Logik*;[20] the lighter-minded may read and mark the temper of Professor Case in the British Encyclopaedia, article 'Logic' (vol. XXX). I have appended to this book a rude sketch of a philosophy upon the new lines, originally read by me to the Oxford Phil. Soc. in 1903.

the mere repudiation of that ineluctable marginal inexactitude which is the mysterious inmost quality of Being. Being, indeed! – there is no being, but a universal becoming of individualities, and Plato turned his back on truth when he turned towards his museum of specific ideals. Heraclitus, that lost and misinterpreted giant, may perhaps be coming to his own. . . .

There is no abiding thing in what we know. We change from weaker to stronger lights, and each more powerful light pierces our hitherto opaque foundations and reveals fresh and different opacities below. We can never foretell which of our seemingly assured fundamentals the next change will not affect. What folly, then, to dream of mapping out our minds in however general terms, of providing for the endless mysteries of the future a terminology and an idiom! We follow the vein, we mine and accumulate our treasure, but who can tell which way the vein may trend? Language is the nourishment of the thought of man, that serves only as it undergoes metabolism, and becomes thought and lives, and in its very living passes away. You scientific people, with your fancy of a terrible exactitude in language, of indestructible foundations built, as that Wordsworthian[21] doggerel on the title page of Nature[22] says, 'for aye,' are marvellously without imagination!

The language of Utopia will no doubt be one and indivisible; all mankind will, in the measure of their individual differences in quality, be brought into the same phase, into a common resonance of thought, but the language they will speak will still be a living tongue, an animated system of imperfections, which every individual man will infinitesimally modify. Through the universal freedom of exchange and movement, the developing change in its general spirit will be a worldwide change; that is the quality of its universality. I fancy it will be a coalesced language, a synthesis of many. Such a language as English is a coalesced language; it is a coalescence of Anglo-Saxon and Norman French and Scholar's Latin, welded into one speech more ample and more powerful and beautiful than either. The Utopian tongue might well present a more spacious coalescence, and hold in the frame of such an uninflected or slightly inflected idiom as English already presents, a profuse vocabulary into which have been cast a dozen once separate tongues, super-posed and then welded together through bilingual and trilingual compromises.* In the past ingenious men have speculated on the inquiry, 'Which language will survive?' The question was badly put. I think now that this wedding and survival of several in a common offspring is a far more probable thing.

§ 6

This talk of languages, however, is a digression. We were on our way along the faint path that runs round the rim of the Lake of Lucendro, and we were just upon the point of coming upon our first Utopian man. He was, I said, no Swiss. Yet he would have been a Swiss on mother Earth, and here he would have the same face, with some difference, maybe, in the expression; the same physique, though a little better developed perhaps – the same complexion. He would have different habits, different traditions, different knowledge, different ideas, differ-ent clothing and different appliances, but, except for all that, he would be the same man. We very distinctly provided at the outset that the modern Utopia must have people inherently the same as those in the world.

There is more, perhaps, in that than appears at the first suggestion.

That proposition gives one characteristic difference between a modern Utopia and almost all its predecessors. It is to be a world Utopia, we have agreed, no less; and so we must needs face the fact that we are to have differences of race. Even the lower class of Plato's Republic was not specifically of different race. But this is a Utopia as wide as Christian charity, and white and black, brown, red and yellow, all tints of skin, all types of body and character, will be there. How we are to adjust their differences is a master question, and the matter is not even to be opened in this chapter. It will need a whole chapter even to glance at its issues. But here we underline that stipulation; every race of

* *Vide* an excellent article, *La Langue Française en l'an 2003*, par Léon Bollack, in *La Revue*, 15 juillet, 1903.

this planet Earth is to be found in the strictest parallelism there, in numbers the same – only, as I say, with an entirely different set of traditions, ideals, ideas and purposes, and so moving under those different skies to an altogether different destiny.

There follows a curious development of this to anyone clearly impressed by the uniqueness and the unique significance of individualities. Races are no hard and fast things, no crowd of identically similar persons, but massed sub-races and tribes and families each after its kind unique, and these again are clusterings of still smaller uniques and so down to each several person. So that our first convention works out to this, that not only is every earthly mountain, river, plant and beast, also in that parallel planet beyond Sirius, but every man, woman and child alive has a Utopian parallel. From now onward, of course, the fates of these two planets will diverge, men will die here whom wisdom will save there, and perhaps conversely here we shall save men; children will be born to them and not to us, to us and not to them; but this, this moment of reading, is the starting moment, and for the first and last occasion the populations of our planets are abreast.

We must in these days make some such supposition. The alternative is a Utopia of dolls in the likeness of angels – imaginary laws to fit incredible people, an unattractive undertaking.

For example, we must assume there is a man such as I might have been, better informed, better disciplined, better employed, thinner and more active – and I wonder what he is doing! – and you, Sir or Madam, are in duplicate also, and all the men and women that you know and I. I doubt if we shall meet our doubles, or if it would be pleasant for us to do so; but as we come down from these lonely mountains to the roads and houses and living places of the Utopian World State, we shall certainly find, here and there, faces that will remind us singularly of those who have lived under our eyes.

There are some you never wish to meet again, you say, and some, I gather, you do. 'And One—!'

It is strange, but this figure of the botanist will not keep in place. It sprang up between us, dear reader, as a passing illustrative invention. I do not know what put him into my head, and for the moment it fell in with my humour for a space to foist the man's personality upon you as yours and call you scientific – that most abusive word. But here he is, indisputably, with me in Utopia, and lapsing from our high speculative theme into halting but intimate confidences. He declares he has not come to Utopia to meet again with his sorrows.

What sorrows?

I protest, even warmly, that neither he nor his sorrows were in my intention.

He is a man, I should think, of thirty-nine, a man whose life has been neither tragedy nor a joyous adventure, a man with one of those faces that have gained interest rather than force or nobility from their commerce with life. He is something refined, with some knowledge, perhaps, of the minor pains and all the civil self-controls; he has read more than he has suffered, and suffered rather than done. He regards me with his blue-grey eye, from which all interest in this Utopia has faded.

'It is a trouble,' he says, 'that has come into my life only for a month or so – at least acutely again. I thought it was all over. There was someone—'

It is an amazing story to hear upon a mountain crest in Utopia, this Hampstead affair, this story of a Frognal[23] heart. 'Frognal,' he says, is the place where they met, and it summons to my memory the word on a board at the corner of a flint-dressed new road, an estate development road, with a vista of villas up a hill. He had known her before he got his professorship, and neither her 'people' nor his – he speaks that detestable middle-class dialect in which aunts and things with money and the right of intervention are called 'people'! – approved of the affair. 'She was, I think, rather easily swayed,' he says. 'But that's not fair to her, perhaps. She thought too much of others. If they seemed distressed, or if they seemed to think a course right—' ...

Have I come to Utopia to hear this sort of thing?

## § 7

It is necessary to turn the botanist's thoughts into a worthier channel. It is necessary to override these modest regrets, this intrusive, petty love story. Does he realize this is indeed Utopia? Turn your mind, I insist, to this Utopia of mine and leave these earthly troubles to their proper planet. Do you realize just where the propositions necessary to a modern Utopia are taking us? Everyone on earth will have to be here; – themselves, but with a difference. Somewhere here in this world is, for example, Mr Chamberlain,[24] and the King[25] is here (no doubt *incognito*), and all the Royal Academy, and Sandow,[26] and Mr Arnold White.[27]

But these famous names do not appeal to him.

My mind goes from this prominent and typical personage to that, and for a time I forget my companion. I am distracted by the curious side issues this general proposition trails after it. There will be so-and-so, and so-and-so. The name and figure of Mr Roosevelt[28] jerks into focus, and obliterates an attempt to acclimatize the Emperor of the Germans. What, for instance, will Utopia do with Mr Roosevelt? There drifts across my inner vision the image of a strenuous struggle with Utopian constables, the voice that has thrilled terrestrial millions in eloquent protest. The writ of arrest, drifting loose in the conflict, comes to my feet; I impale the scrap of paper, and read – but can it be? – 'attempted disorganization . . . incitements to disarrange . . . the balance of population'.

The trend of my logic for once has led us into a facetious alley. One might indeed keep in this key and write an agreeable little Utopia, that like the holy families of the medieval artists (or Michelangelo's 'Last Judgement')[29] should compliment one's friends in various degrees. Or one might embark upon a speculative treatment of the entire Almanach de Gotha, something on the lines of Epistemon's vision[30] of the damned great, when

'Xerxes was a crier of mustard.
Romulus was a salter and a patcher of pattens. . . .'

That incomparable catalogue! That incomparable catalogue! Inspired by the Muse of Parody we might go on to the pages of *Who's Who*, and even, with an eye to the obdurate republic, to *Who's Who in America*, and make the most delightful and extensive arrangements. Now where shall we put this most excellent man? And this? . . .

But, indeed, it is doubtful if we shall meet any of these doubles during our Utopian journey, or know them when we meet them. I doubt if anyone will be making the best of both these worlds. The great men in this still unexplored Utopia may be but village Hampdens[31] in our own, and earthly goatherds and obscure illiterates sit here in the seats of the mighty.

That again opens agreeable vistas left of us and right.

But my botanist obtrudes his personality again. His thoughts have travelled by a different route.

'I know,' he says, 'that she will be happier here, and that they will value her better than she has been valued upon earth.'

His interruption serves to turn me back from my momentary contemplation of those popular effigies inflated by old newspapers and windy report, the earthly great. He sets me thinking of more personal and intimate applications, of the human beings one knows with a certain approximation to real knowledge, of the actual common substance of life. He turns me to the thought of rivalries and tendernesses, of differences and disappointments. I am suddenly brought painfully against the things that might have been. What if instead of that Utopia of vacant ovals we meet relinquished loves here, and opportunities lost and faces as they might have looked to us?

I turn to my botanist almost reprovingly. 'You know, she won't be quite the same lady here that you knew in Frognal,' I say, and wrest myself from a subject that is no longer agreeable by rising to my feet.

'And besides,' I say, standing above him, 'the chances against our meeting her are a million to one. . . . And we loiter! This is not the business we have come upon, but a mere incidental kink in our larger plan. The fact remains, these people we have come to see are people with like infirmities to our own – and only the conditions are changed. Let us pursue the tenor of our inquiry.'

With that I lead the way round the edge of the Lake of Lucendro towards our Utopian world. (*You figure him doing it.*)[32] Down the mountain we shall go and down the passes, and as the valleys open the world will open, – Utopia, where men and women are happy and laws are wise, and where all that is tangled and confused in human affairs has been unravelled and made right.

# 2

# CONCERNING FREEDOMS

Now what sort of question would first occur to two men descending upon the planet of a Modern Utopia? Probably grave solicitude about their personal freedom. Towards the Stranger, as I have already remarked, the Utopias of the past displayed their least amiable aspect. Would this new sort of Utopian State, spread to the dimensions of a world, be any less forbidding?

We should take comfort in the thought that universal Toleration is certainly a modern idea, and it is upon modern ideas that this World State rests. But even suppose we are tolerated and admitted to this unavoidable citizenship, there will still remain a wide range of possibility. . . . I think we should try to work the problem out from an inquiry into first principles, and that we should follow the trend of our time and kind by taking up the question as one of 'Man *versus* the State',[1] and discussing the compromise of Liberty.

The idea of individual liberty is one that has grown in importance and grows with every development of modern thought. To the classical Utopists freedom was relatively trivial. Clearly they considered virtue and happiness as entirely separable from liberty, and as being altogether more important things. But the modern view, with its deepening insistence upon individuality and upon the significance of its uniqueness, steadily intensifies the value of freedom, until at last we begin to see liberty as the very substance of life, that indeed it is life, and that only the dead things, the choiceless things, live in absolute obedience to law. To have free play for one's individuality is, in the modern view, the subjective triumph of existence, as survival in creative work and offspring is its objective triumph. But for all men, since man is a social creature, the play of will must fall short of absolute freedom. Perfect human liberty is possible only to a despot who is absolutely and universally obeyed. Then to will would be to command and achieve, and within the limits of natural law we could at any moment do exactly as it pleased us to do. All other liberty is a compromise between our own freedom of will and the wills of those with whom we come in contact. In an organized state each one of us has a more or less elaborate code of what he may do to others and to himself, and what others may do to him. He limits others by his rights, and is limited by the rights of others, and by considerations affecting the welfare of the community as a whole.

Individual liberty in a community is not, as mathematicians would say, always of the same sign. To ignore this is the essential fallacy of the cult called Individualism. But in truth, a general prohibition in a state may increase the sum of liberty, and a general permission may diminish it. It does not follow, as these people would have us believe, that a man is more free where there is least law and more restricted where there is most law. A socialism or a communism is not necessarily a slavery, and there is no freedom under Anarchy. Consider how much liberty we gain by the loss of the common liberty to kill. Thereby one may go to and fro in all the ordered parts of the earth, unencumbered by arms or armour, free of the fear of playful poison, whimsical barbers or hotel trapdoors. Indeed, it means freedom from a thousand fears and precautions. Suppose there existed even the limited freedom to kill in vendetta, and think what would happen in our suburbs. Consider the inconvenience of two households in a modern suburb estranged and provided with modern weapons of precision, the inconvenience not only to each other, but to the neutral pedestrian, the practical loss of freedoms all about them. The butcher, if he came at all, would have to come round in an armoured cart. . . .

It follows, therefore, in a modern Utopia, which finds the final hope of the world in the evolving interplay of unique individualities, that the State will have effectually chipped away just all those spendthrift liberties that waste liberty, and not one liberty more, and so have attained the maximum general freedom.

There are two distinct and contrasting methods of limiting liberty; the first is Prohibition, 'thou shalt not', and the second Command, 'thou shalt'. There is, however, a sort of prohibition that takes the form of a conditional command, and this one needs to bear in mind. It says if you do so-and-so, you must also do so-and-so; if, for example, you go to sea with men you employ, you must go in a seaworthy vessel. But the pure command is unconditional; it says, whatever you have done or are doing or want to do, you are to do this, as when the social system, working through the base necessities of base parents and bad laws, sends a child of thirteen into a factory. Prohib-ition takes one definite thing from the indefinite liberty of a man, but it still leaves him an unbounded choice of actions. He remains free, and you have merely taken a bucketful from the sea of his freedom. But compulsion destroys freedom altogether. In this Utopia of ours there may be many prohib-itions, but no indirect compulsions – if one may so contrive it – and few or no commands. As far as I see it now, in this present discussion, I think indeed there should be no positive compulsions at all in Utopia, at any rate for the adult Utopian – unless they fall upon him as penalties incurred.

## § 2

What prohibitions should we be under, we two Uitlanders in this Utopian world? We should certainly not be free to kill, assault or threaten anyone we met, and in that we earth-trained men would not be likely to offend. And until we knew more exactly the Utopian idea of property we should be very chary of touching anything that might conceivably be appropriated. If it was not the property of individuals it might be the property of the State. But beyond that we might have our doubts. Are we right in wearing the strange costumes we do, in choosing the path that pleases us athwart this rock and turf, in coming striding with unfumigated rucksacks and snow-wet hobnails into what is conceivably an extremely neat and orderly world? We have passed our first Utopian now with an answered vague gesture, and have noted, with secret satisfaction, there is no access of dismay; we have rounded a bend, and down the valley in the distance we get a glimpse of what appears to be a singularly well-kept road. . . .

I submit that to the modern-minded man it can be no sort of Utopia worth desiring that does not give the utmost freedom of going to and fro. Free movement is to many people one of the greatest of life's privileges – to go wherever the spirit moves them, to wander and see – and though they have every comfort, every security, every virtuous discipline, they will still be unhappy if that is denied them. Short of damage to things cherished and made, the Utopians will surely have this right, so we may expect no unclimbable walls and fences, nor the discovery of any laws we may transgress in coming down these mountain places.

And yet, just as civil liberty itself is a compromise defended by prohibitions, so this particular sort of liberty must also have its qualifications. Carried to the absolute pitch, the right of free movement ceases to be distinguishable from the right of free intrusion. We have already, in a comment on More's Utopia, hinted at an agreement with Aristotle's argument against communism, that it flings people into an intolerable continuity of contact. Schopenhauer[2] carried out Aristotle in the vein of his own bitterness and with the truest of images when he likened human society to hedgehogs clustering for warmth, and unhappy when either too closely packed or too widely separated. Empedocles[3] found no significance in life whatever except as an unsteady play of love and hate, of attraction and repulsion, of assimilation and the assertion of difference. So long as we ignore difference, so long as we ignore individuality – and that I hold has been the common sin of all Utopias hitherto – we can make absolute statements, prescribe communisms or individualisms, and all sorts of hard theoretic arrangements. But in the world of reality, which – to modernize Heraclitus[4] and Empedocles – is nothing more nor less than the world of individuality, there are no absolute rights and wrongs, there are no qualitative questions at all, but only quantitative adjustments. Equally strong in the normal civilized man is the desire for freedom of movement and the desire for a certain privacy, for a corner definitely his, and we have to consider where the line of reconciliation comes.

The desire for absolute personal privacy is perhaps never a very strong or persistent craving. In the great majority of human beings, the gregarious instinct is sufficiently powerful to render any but the most temporary isolations not simply disagreeable, but painful. The savage has all the privacy he needs within the compass of his skull; like dogs and timid women, he prefers ill-treatment to desertion; and it is only a scarce and complex modern type that finds comfort and refreshment in lonely places and solitary occupations. Yet such there are, men who can neither sleep well nor think well, nor attain to a full perception of beautiful objects, who do not savour the best of existence until they are securely alone, and for the sake of these even it would be reasonable to draw some limits to the general right of free movement. But their particular need is only a special and exceptional aspect of an almost universal claim to privacy among modern people, not so much for the sake of isolation as for congenial companionship. We want to go apart from the great crowd, not so much to be alone as to be with those who appeal to us particularly and to whom we particularly appeal; we want to form households and societies with them, to give our individualities play in intercourse with them, and in the appointments and furnishings of that intercourse. We want gardens and enclosures and exclusive freedoms for our like and our choice, just as spacious as we can get them – and it is only the multitudinous uncongenial, anxious also for similar developments in some opposite direction, that checks this expansive movement of personal selection and necessitates a compromise on privacy.

Glancing back from our Utopian mountainside down which this discourse marches, to the confusions of old earth, we may remark that the need and desire for privacies there is exceptionally great at the present time, that it was less in the past, that in the future it may be less again, and that under the Utopian conditions to which we shall come when presently we strike yonder road, it may be reduced to quite manageable dimensions. But this is to be effected not by the suppression of individualities to some common pattern,* but by the broadening of public charity and the general amelioration of mind and manners. It is not by assimilation, that is to say, but by understanding that the modern Utopia achieves itself. The ideal community of man's past was one with a common belief, with common customs and common ceremonies, common manners and common formulae; men of the same society dressed in the same fashion, each according to his defined and understood grade, behaved in the same fashion, loved, worshipped and died in the same fashion. They did or felt little that did not find a sympathetic publicity. The natural disposition of all peoples, white, black or brown, a natural disposition that education seeks to destroy, is to insist upon uniformity, to make publicity extremely unsympathetic to even the most harmless departures from the code. To be dressed 'oddly', to behave 'oddly', to eat in a different manner or of different food, to commit, indeed, any breach of the established convention is to give offence and to incur hostility among unsophisticated men. But the disposition of the more original and enterprising minds at all times has been to make such innovations.

This is particularly in evidence in this present age. The almost cataclysmal development of new machinery, the discovery of new materials and the appearance of new social possibilities through the organized pursuit of material science, has given enormous and unprecedented facilities to the spirit of innovation. The old local order has been broken up or is now being broken up all over the earth, and everywhere societies deliquesce, everywhere men are afloat amidst the wreckage of their flooded conventions, and still tremendously unaware of the thing that has happened. The old local orthodoxies of behaviour, of precedence, the old accepted amusements and employments, the old ritual of conduct in the important small things of the

* More's *Utopia*. 'Whoso will may go in, for there is nothing within the houses that is private or anie man's owne.'

daily life and the old ritual of thought in the things that make discussion, are smashed up and scattered and mixed discordantly together, one use with another, and no worldwide culture of toleration, no courteous admission of differences, no wider understanding has yet replaced them. And so publicity on the modern earth has become confusedly unsympathetic for everyone. Classes are intolerable to classes and sets to sets, contact provokes aggressions, comparisons, persecutions and discomforts, and the subtler people are excessively tormented by a sense of observation, unsympathetic always and often hostile. To live without some sort of segregation from the general mass is impossible in exact proportion to one's individual distinction.

Of course things will be very different in Utopia. Utopia will be saturated with consideration. To us, clad as we are in mountain-soiled tweeds and with no money but British banknotes negotiable only at a practically infinite distance, this must needs be a reassuring induction. And Utopian manners will not only be tolerant, but almost universally tolerable. Endless things will be understood perfectly and universally that on earth are understood only by a scattered few; baseness of bearing, grossness of manner, will be the distinctive mark of no section of the community whatever. The coarser reasons for privacy, therefore, will not exist here. And that savage sort of shyness, too, that makes so many half-educated people on earth recluse and defensive the Utopians will have escaped by their more liberal breeding. In the cultivated State we are assuming it will be ever so much easier for people to eat in public, rest and amuse themselves in public, and even work in public. Our present need for privacy in many things marks, indeed, a phase of transition from an ease in public in the past due to homogeneity, to an ease in public in the future due to intelligence and good breeding, and in Utopia that transition will be complete. We must bear that in mind throughout the consideration of this question.

Yet, after this allowance has been made, there still remains a considerable claim for privacy in Utopia. The room or apartments or home or mansion, whatever it may be a man or woman maintains, must be private and under his or her complete dominion; it seems harsh and intrusive to forbid a central garden plot or peristyle, such as one sees in Pompeii, within the house walls, and it is almost as difficult to deny a little private territory beyond the house. Yet if we concede that, it is clear that without some further provision we concede the possibility that the poorer townsman (if there are to be rich and poor in the world) will be forced to walk through endless miles of high fenced villa gardens before he may expand in his little scrap of reserved open country. Such is already the poor Londoner's miserable fate. . . . Our Utopia will have, of course, faultless roads and beautifully arranged interurban communications, swift trains or motor services or what not, to diffuse its population, and without some anticipatory provisions, the prospect of the residential areas becoming a vast area of defensively walled villa Edens is all too possible.

This is a quantitative question, be it remembered, and not to be dismissed by any statement of principle. Our Utopians will meet it, I presume, by detailed regulations, very probably varying locally with local conditions. Privacy beyond the house might be made a privilege to be paid for in proportion to the area occupied, and the tax on these licences of privacy might increase as the square of the area affected. A maximum fraction of private enclosure for each urban and suburban square mile could be fixed. A distinction could be drawn between an absolutely private garden and a garden private and closed only for a day or a couple of days a week, and at other times open to the well-behaved public. Who, in a really civilized community, would grudge that measure of invasion? Walls could be taxed by height and length, and the enclosure of really natural beauties, of rapids, cascades, gorges, viewpoints and so forth made impossible. So a reasonable compromise between the vital and conflicting claims of the freedom of movement and the freedom of seclusion might be attained. . . .

And as we argue thus we draw nearer and nearer to the road that goes up and over the Gotthard crest and down the Val Tremola towards Italy.

What sort of road would that be?

## § 3

Freedom of movement in a Utopia planned under modern conditions must involve something more than unrestricted pedestrian wanderings, and the very proposition of a World State speaking one common tongue carries with it the idea of a world population travelled and travelling to an extent quite beyond anything our native earth has seen. It is now our terrestrial experience that whenever economic and political developments set a class free to travel, that class at once begins to travel; in England, for example, above the five or six hundred pounds a year level, it is hard to find anyone who is not habitually migratory, who has not been frequently, as people say, 'abroad'. In the modern Utopia travel must be in the common texture of life. To go into fresh climates and fresh scenery, to meet a different complexion of humanity and a different type of home and food and apparatus, to mark unfamiliar trees and plants and flowers and beasts, to climb mountains, to see the snowy night of the North and the blaze of the tropical midday, to follow great rivers, to taste loneliness in desert places, to traverse the gloom of tropical forests and to cross the high seas, will be an essential part of the reward and adventure of life, even for the commonest people. . . . This is a bright and pleasant particular in which a modern Utopia must differ again, and differ diametrically, from its predecessors.

We may conclude from what has been done in places upon our earth that the whole Utopian world will be open and accessible and as safe for the wayfarer as France or England is today. The peace of the world will be established for ever, and everywhere, except in remote and desolate places, there will be convenient inns, at least as convenient and trustworthy as those of Switzerland today; the touring clubs and hotel associations that have tariffed that country and France so effectually will have had their fine Utopian equivalents, and the whole world will be habituated to the coming and going of strangers. The greater part of the world will be as secure and cheaply and easily accessible to everyone as is Zermatt or Lucerne to a Western European of the middle-class at the present time.

On this account alone no places will be so congested as these two are now on earth. With freedom to go everywhere, with easy access everywhere, with no dread of difficulties about language, coinage, custom or law, why should everyone continue to go to just a few special places? Such congestions are merely the measure of the general inaccessibility and insecurity and costliness of contemporary life, an awkward transitory phase in the first beginnings of the travel age of mankind.

No doubt the Utopian will travel in many ways. It is unlikely there will be any smoke-disgorging steam-railway trains in Utopia, they are already doomed on earth, already threatened with that obsolescence that will endear them to the Ruskins[5] of tomorrow, but a thin spider's web of inconspicuous special routes will cover the land of the world, pierce the mountain masses and tunnel under the seas. These may be double railways or monorails or what not – we are no engineers to judge between such devices – but by means of them the Utopian will travel about the earth from one chief point to another at a speed of two or three hundred miles or more an hour. That will abolish the greater distances. . . . One figures these main communications as something after the manner of corridor trains, smooth-running and roomy, open from end to end, with cars in which one may sit and read, cars in which one may take refreshment, cars into which the news of the day comes printing itself from the wires beside the track; cars in which one may have privacy and sleep if one is so disposed, bathroom cars, library cars; a train as comfortable as a good club. There will be no distinctions of class in such a train, because in a civilized world there would be no offence between one kind of man and another, and for the good of the whole world such travelling will be as cheap as it can be, and well within the reach of any but the almost criminally poor.

Such great tramways as this will be used when the Utopians wish to travel fast and far; thereby you will glide all over the land surface of the planet; and feeding them and distributing from them, innumerable minor systems, clean little electric tramways I picture them, will spread out over the land in finer reticulations, growing close and dense in the urban regions and thinning as the population thins. And running beside these lighter railways, and spreading beyond their range, will be the smooth minor high roads such as this one we now approach, upon which independent vehicles, motor-cars, cycles and what not, will go. I doubt if we shall see any horses upon this fine, smooth, clean road; I doubt if there will be many horses on the high roads of Utopia, and, indeed, if they will use draught horses at all upon that planet. Why should they? Where the world gives turf or sand, or along special tracts, the horse will perhaps be ridden for exercise and pleasure, but that will be all the use for him; and as for the other beasts of burden, on the remoter mountain tracks the mule will no doubt still be a picturesque survival, in the desert men will still find a use for the camel, and the elephant may linger to play a part in the pageant of the East. But the burden of the minor traffic, if not the whole of it, will certainly be mechanical. This is what we shall see even while the road is still remote, swift and shapely motor-cars going past, cyclists, and in these agreeable mountain regions there will also be pedestrians upon their way. Cycle tracks will abound in Utopia, sometimes following beside the great high roads, but oftener taking their own more agreeable line amidst woods and crops and pastures; and there will be a rich variety of footpaths and minor ways. There will be many footpaths in Utopia. There will be pleasant ways over the scented needles of the mountain pinewoods, primrose-strewn tracks amidst the budding thickets of the lower country, paths running beside rushing streams, paths across the wide spaces of the corn land, and, above all, paths through the flowery garden spaces amidst which the houses in the towns will stand. And everywhere about the world, on road and path, by sea and land, the happy holiday Utopians will go.

The population of Utopia will be a migratory population beyond any earthly precedent, not simply a travelling population, but migratory. The old Utopias were all localized, as localized as a parish councillor; but it is manifest that nowadays even quite ordinary people live over areas that would have made a kingdom in those former days, would have filled the Athenian of the 'Laws' with incredulous astonishment. Except for the habits of the very rich during the Roman Empire, there was never the slightest precedent for this modern detachment from place. It is nothing to us that we go eighty or ninety miles from home to place of business, or take an hour's spin of fifty miles to our weekend golf; every summer it has become a fixed custom to travel wide and far. Only the clumsiness of communications limits us now, and every facilitation of loco-motion widens not only our potential, but our habitual range. Not only this, but we change our habitations with a growing frequency and facility; to Sir Thomas More we should seem a breed of nomads. That old fixity was of necessity and not of choice, it was a mere phase in the development of civilization, a trick of rooting man learnt for a time from his new-found friends, the corn and the vine and the hearth; the untamed spirit of the young has turned for ever to wandering and the sea. The soul of man has never yet in any land been willingly adscript to the glebe. Even Mr Belloc,[6] who preaches the happiness of a peasant proprietor, is so much wiser than his thoughts that he sails about the seas in a little yacht or goes afoot from Belgium to Rome. We are winning our freedom again once more, a freedom renewed and enlarged, and there is now neither neces-sity nor advantage in a permanent life servitude to this place or that. Men may settle down in our modern Utopia for love and the family at last, but first and most abundantly they will see the world.

And with this loosening of the fetters of locality from the feet of men, necessarily there will be all sorts of fresh distributions of the factors of life. On our own poor haphazard earth, wher-ever men work, wherever there are things to be grown, minerals to be won, power to be used, there, regardless of all the joys and decencies of life, the households needs must cluster. But in Utopia there will be wide stretches of cheerless or unhealthy or toilsome or dangerous land with never a household; there will be regions of mining and smelting, black with the smoke of furnaces and gashed and desolated by mines, with a sort of weird inhospitable grandeur of industrial desolation, and the men will come thither and work for a spell and return to civilization again, washing and changing their attire in the swift

gliding train. And by way of compensation there will be beautiful regions of the earth specially set apart and favoured for
children; in them the presence of children will remit taxation,
while in other less wholesome places the presence of children
will be taxed; the lower passes and fore hills of these very Alps,
for example, will be populous with homes, serving the vast
arable levels of Upper Italy.

So we shall see, as we come down by our little lake in the lap
of Lucendro, and even before we reach the road, the first scattered chalets and households in which these migrant people
live, the upper summer homes. With the coming of summer, as
the snows on the high Alps recede, a tide of households and
schools, teachers and doctors, and all such attendant services
will flow up the mountain masses, and ebb again when the
September snows return. It is essential to the modern ideal of life
that the period of education and growth should be prolonged
to as late a period as possible and puberty correspondingly
retarded, and by wise regulation the statesmen of Utopia will
constantly adjust and readjust regulations and taxation to diminish the proportion of children reared in hot and stimulating
conditions. These high mountains will, in the bright sweet summer, be populous with youth. Even up towards this high place
where the snow is scarce gone until July, these households will
extend, and below, the whole long valley of Urseren will be a
scattered summer town.

One figures one of the more urban highways, one of those
along which the light railways of the second order run, such as
that in the valley of Urseren, into which we should presently
come. I figure it as one would see it at night, a band a hundred
yards perhaps in width, the footpath on either side shaded with
high trees and lit softly with orange glowlights; while down the
centre the tramway of the road will go, with sometimes a
nocturnal tram-car gliding, lit and gay but almost noiselessly,
past. Lantern-lit cyclists will flit along the track like fireflies,
and ever and again some humming motor-car will hurry by, to
or from the Rhoneland or the Rhineland or Switzerland or
Italy. Away on either side the lights of the little country homes
up the mountain slopes will glow.

I figure it at night, because so it is we should see it first.

We should come out from our mountain valley into the minor road that runs down the lonely rock wilderness of the St Gotthard Pass, we should descend that nine miles of winding route, and so arrive towards twilight among the clustering homes and upland unenclosed gardens of Realp and Hospenthal and Andermatt. Between Realp and Andermatt, and down the Schoellenen gorge, the greater road would run. By the time we reached it, we should be in the way of understanding our adventure a little better. We should know already, when we saw those two familiar clusters of chalets and hotels replaced by a great dispersed multitude of houses – we should see their window lights, but little else – that we were the victims of some strange transition in space or time, and we should come down by dimly seen buildings into the part that would answer to Hospenthal, wondering and perhaps a little afraid. We should come out into this great main roadway – this roadway like an urban avenue – and look up it and down, hesitating whether to go along the valley Furka-ward, or down by Andermatt through the gorge that leads to Göschenen. . . .

People would pass us in the twilight, and then more people; we should see they walked well and wore a graceful, unfamiliar dress, but more we should not distinguish.

'Goodnight!' they would say to us in clear, fine voices. Their dim faces would turn with a passing scrutiny towards us.

We should answer out of our perplexity: 'Goodnight!' – for by the conventions established in the beginning of this book, we are given the freedom of their tongue.

## § 4

Were this a story, I should tell at length how much we were helped by the good fortune of picking up a Utopian coin of gold, how at last we adventured into the Utopian inn and found it all marvellously easy. You see us the shyest and most watchful of guests; but of the food they put before us and the furnishings of the house, and all our entertainment, it will be better to speak later. We are in a migratory world, we know, one greatly accustomed to foreigners; our mountain clothes are not strange enough to attract acute attention, though ill-made and shabby, no doubt, by Utopian standards; we are dealt with as we might best wish to be dealt with, that is to say as rather untidy, inconspicuous men. We look about us and watch for hints and examples, and, indeed, get through with the thing. And after our queer yet not unpleasant dinner, in which we remark no meat figures, we go out of the house for a breath of air and for quiet counsel one with another, and there it is we discover those strange constellations overhead. It comes to us then, clear and full, that our imagination has realized itself; we dismiss quite finally a Rip-Van-Winkle[7] fancy we have entertained, all the unfamiliarities of our descent from the mountain pass gather together into one fulness of conviction, and we know, we know, we are in Utopia.

We wander under the trees by the main road, watching the dim passers-by as though they were the phantoms of a dream. We say little to one another. We turn aside into a little pathway and come to a bridge over the turbulent Reuss, hurrying down towards the Devil's Bridge[8] in the gorge below. Far away over the Furka ridge a pallid glow preludes the rising of the moon.

Two lovers pass us whispering, and we follow them with our eyes. This Utopia has certainly preserved the fundamental freedom, to love. And then a sweet-voiced bell from somewhere high up towards Oberalp chimes two-and-twenty times.

I break the silence. 'That might mean ten o'clock,' I say.

My companion leans upon the bridge and looks down into the dim river below. I become aware of the keen edge of the moon like a needle of incandescent silver creeping over the crest, and suddenly the river is alive with flashes.

He speaks, and astonishes me with the hidden course his thoughts have taken.

'We two were boy and girl lovers like that,' he says, and jerks a head at the receding Utopians. 'I loved her first, and I do not think I have ever thought of loving anyone but her.'

It is a curiously human thing, and, upon my honour, not one I had designed, that when at last I stand in the twilight in the midst of a Utopian township, when my whole being should be taken up with speculative wonder, this man should be standing by my side, and lugging my attention persistently towards himself, towards his limited futile self. This thing perpetually happens to me, this intrusion of something small and irrelevant and alive upon my great impressions. The time I first saw the Matterhorn, that Queen among the Alpine summits, I was distracted beyond appreciation by the tale of a man who could not eat sardines – always sardines did this with him and that; and my first wanderings along the brown streets of Pompeii,[9] an experience I had anticipated with a strange intensity, was shot with the most stupidly intelligent discourse on vehicular tariffs in the chief capitals of Europe that it is possible to imagine. And now this man, on my first night in Utopia, talks and talks and talks of his poor little love affair.

It shapes itself as the most trite and feeble of tragedies, one of those stories of effortless submission to chance and custom in which Mr Hardy[10] or George Gissing[11] might have found a theme. I do but half listen at first – watching the black figures in the moonlit roadway pacing to and fro. Yet – I cannot trace how he conveys the subtle conviction to my mind – the woman he loves is beautiful.

They were boy and girl together, and afterwards they met again as fellow students in a world of comfortable discretions. He seems to have taken the decorums of life with a confiding good faith, to have been shy and innocent in a suppressed sort of way, and of a mental type not made for worldly successes; but he must have dreamt about her and loved her well enough. How she felt for him I could never gather; it seemed to be all of that fleshless friendliness into which we train our girls. Then abruptly happened stresses. The man who became her husband appeared, with a very evident passion. He was a year or so older than either of them, and he had the habit and quality of achieving his ends; he was already successful and with the promise of wealth, and I, at least, perceived from my botanist's phrasing that his desire was for her beauty.

As my botanist talked I seemed to see the whole little drama, rather clearer than his words gave it me, the actors all absurdly in Hampstead middle-class raiment, meetings of a Sunday after church (the men in silk hats, frock coats, and tightly rolled umbrellas), rare excursions into evening dress, the decorously vulgar fiction read in their homes, its ambling sentimentalities of thought, the amiably worldly mothers, the respectable fathers, the aunts, the 'people' – his 'people' and her 'people' – the piano music and the song, and in this setting our friend, 'quite clever' at botany and 'going in' for it 'as a profession', and the girl, gratuitously beautiful; so I figured the arranged and orderly environment into which this claw of an elemental force had thrust itself to grip.

The stranger who had come in got what he wanted; the girl considered that she thought she had never loved the botanist, had had only friendship for him – though little she knew of the meaning of those fine words – they parted a little incoherently and in tears, and it had not occurred to the young man to imagine she was not going off to conventional life in some other of the endless Frognals he imagined as the cellular tissue of the world.

But she wasn't.

He had kept her photograph and her memory sweet, and if ever he had strayed from the severest constancy, it seemed only in the end to strengthen with the stuff of experience, to enhance by comparative disappointment his imagination of what she might have meant to him. . . . Then eight years afterwards they met again.

By the time he gets to this part of his story we have, at my initiative, left the bridge and are walking towards the Utopian guest house. The Utopian guest house! His voice rises and falls, and sometimes he holds my arm. My attention comes and goes. 'Goodnight,' two sweet-voiced Utopians cry to us in their universal tongue, and I answer them 'Goodnight.'

'You see,' he persists, 'I saw her only a week ago. It was in Lucerne, while I was waiting for you to come on from England. I talked to her three or four times altogether. And her face – the change in her! I can't get it out of my head – night or day. The miserable waste of her. . . .'

Before us, through the tall pine stems, shine the lights of our Utopian inn.

He talks vaguely of ill-usage. 'The husband is vain, boastful, dishonest to the very confines of the law, and a drunkard. There are scenes and insults—'

'She told you?'

'Not much, but someone else did. He brings other women almost into her presence to spite her.'

'And it's going on?' I interrupt.

'Yes. *Now.*'

'Need it go on?'

'What do you mean?'

'Lady in trouble,' I say. 'Knight at hand. Why not stop this dismal grizzling and carry her off?' (*You figure the heroic sweep of the arm that belongs to the Voice.*)[12] I positively forget for the moment that we are in Utopia at all.

'You mean?'

'Take her away from him! What's all this emotion of yours worth if it isn't equal to that!'

Positively he seems aghast at me.

'Do you mean elope with her?'

'It seems a most suitable case.'

For a space he is silent, and we go on through the trees. A Utopian tram-car passes and I see his face, poor, bitted[13] wretch! looking pinched and scared in its trailing glow of light.

'That's all very well in a novel,' he says. 'But how could I go back to my laboratory, mixed classes with young ladies, you know, after a thing like that? How could we live and where could we live? We might have a house in London, but who would call upon us? ... Besides, you don't know her. She is not the sort of woman.... Don't think I'm timid or conventional. Don't think I don't feel.... Feel! *You* don't know what it is to feel in a case of this sort....'

He halts and then flies out viciously: 'Ugh! There are times when I could strangle him with my hands.'

Which is nonsense.

He flings out his lean botanizing hands in an impotent gesture.

'My dear man!' I say, and say no more.

For a moment I forget we are in Utopia altogether.

## § 5

Let us come back to Utopia. We were speaking of travel.

Besides roadways and railways and tramways, for those who go to and fro in the earth the modern Utopians will have very many other ways of travelling. There will be rivers, for example, with a vast variety of boats; canals with diverse sorts of haulage; there will be lakes and lagoons; and when one comes at last to the borders of the land, the pleasure craft will be there, coming and going, and the swift great passenger vessels, very big and steady, doing thirty knots an hour or more, will trace long wakes as they go dwindling out athwart the restless vastness of the sea.

They will be just beginning to fly in Utopia. We owe much to M. Santos Dumont;[14] the world is immeasurably more disposed to believe this wonder is coming, and coming nearly, than it was five years ago. But unless we are to suppose Utopian scientific knowledge far in advance of ours – and though that supposition was not proscribed in our initial undertaking, it would be inconvenient for us and not quite in the vein of the rest of our premises – they, too, will only be in the same experimental stage as ourselves. In Utopia, however, they will conduct research by the army corps while we conduct it – we don't conduct it! We let it happen. Fools make researches and wise men exploit them – that is our earthly way of dealing with the question, and we thank Heaven for an assumed abundance of financially impotent and sufficiently ingenious fools.

In Utopia, a great multitude of selected men, chosen volunteers, will be collaborating upon this new step in man's struggle with the elements. Bacon's visionary House of Salomon* will be a thing realized, and it will be humming with this business. Every university in the world will be urgently working for priority in this aspect of the problem or that. Reports of experiments, as full and as prompt as the telegraphic reports of cricket in our more sportive atmosphere, will go about the world. All this will be passing, as it were, behind the act drop of our first

* In the *New Atlantis*.

experience, behind this first picture of the urbanized Urseren valley. The literature of the subject will be growing and developing with the easy swiftness of an eagle's swoop as we come down the hillside; unseen in that twilight, unthought of by us until this moment, a thousand men at a thousand glowing desks, a busy specialist press, will be perpetually sifting, criticizing, condensing, and clearing the ground for further speculation. Those who are concerned with the problems of public locomotion will be following these aeronautic investigations with a keen and enterprising interest, and so will the physiologist and the sociologist. That Utopian research will, I say, go like an eagle's swoop in comparison with the blind-man's fumbling of our terrestrial way. Even before our own brief Utopian journey is out, we may get a glimpse of the swift ripening of all this activity that will be in progress at our coming. Tomorrow, perhaps, or in a day or so, some silent, distant thing will come gliding into view over the mountains, will turn and soar and pass again beyond our astonished sight. . . .

§ 6

But my friend and his great trouble turn my mind from these questions of locomotion and the freedoms that cluster about them. In spite of myself I find myself framing his case. He is a lover, the most conventional of Anglican lovers, with a heart that has had its training, I should think, in the clean but limited schoolroom of Mrs Henry Wood. . . .[15]

In Utopia I think they will fly with stronger pinions, it will not be in the superficialities of life merely that movement will be wide and free, they will mount higher and swoop more steeply than he in his cage can believe. What will their range be, their prohibitions? what jars to our preconceptions will he and I receive here?

My mind flows with the free, thin flow that it has at the end of an eventful day, and as we walk along in silence towards our inn I rove from issue to issue, I find myself ranging amidst the fundamental things of the individual life and all the perplexity

of desires and passions. I turn my questionings to the most
difficult of all sets of compromises, those mitigations of spon-
taneous freedom that constitute the marriage laws, the mystery
of balancing justice against the good of the future, amidst
these violent and elusive passions. Where falls the balance of
freedoms here? I pass for a time from Utopianizing altogether,
to ask the question that, after all, Schopenhauer failed completely to answer, why sometimes in the case of hurtful, point-
less, and destructive things we want so vehemently. . . .

I come back from this unavailing glance into the deeps to the
general question of freedoms in this new relation. I find myself
far adrift from the case of the Frognal botanist, and asking how
far a modern Utopia will deal with personal morals.

As Plato demonstrated long ago, the principles of the relation
of State control to personal morals may be best discussed in the
case of intoxication, the most isolated and least complicated of
all this group of problems. But Plato's treatment of this issue
as a question of who may or may not have the use of wine,
though suitable enough in considering a small State in which
everybody was the effectual inspector of everybody, is entirely
beside the mark under modern conditions, in which we are to
have an extraordinarily higher standard of individual privacy
and an amplitude and quantity of migration inconceivable to
the Academic imagination. We may accept his principle and
put this particular freedom (of the use of wine) among the
distinctive privileges of maturity, and still find all that a modern
would think of as the Drink Question untouched.

That question in Utopia will differ perhaps in the proportion
of its factors, but in no other respect, from what it is upon
earth. The same desirable ends will be sought, the maintenance
of public order and decency, the reduction of inducements
to form this bad and wasteful habit to their lowest possible
minimum, and the complete protection of the immature. But
the modern Utopians, having systematized their sociology, will
have given some attention to the psychology of minor officials,
a matter altogether too much neglected by the social reformer
on earth. They will not put into the hands of a common policeman powers direct and indirect that would be dangerous to the

public in the hands of a judge. And they will have avoided the immeasurable error of making their control of the drink traffic a source of public revenue. Privacies they will not invade, but they will certainly restrict the public consumption of intoxicants to specified licensed places and the sale of them to unmistakable adults, and they will make the temptation of the young a grave offence. In so migratory a population as the modern Utopian, the licensing of inns and bars would be under the same control as the railways and high roads. Inns exist for the stranger and not for the locality, and we shall meet with nothing there to correspond with our terrestrial absurdity of Local Option.

The Utopians will certainly control this trade, and as certainly punish personal excesses. Public drunkenness (as distinguished from the mere elation that follows a generous but controlled use of wine) will be an offence against public decency, and will be dealt with in some very drastic manner. It will, of course, be an aggravation of, and not an excuse for, crime.

But I doubt whether the State will go beyond that. Whether an adult shall use wine or beer or spirits or not, seems to me entirely a matter for his doctor and his own private conscience. I doubt if we explorers shall meet any drunken men, and I doubt not we shall meet many who have never availed themselves of their adult freedom in this respect. The conditions of physical happiness will be better understood in Utopia, it will be worthwhile to be well there, and the intelligent citizen will watch himself closely. Half and more of the drunkenness of earth is an attempt to lighten dull days and hopelessly sordid and disagreeable lives, and in Utopia they do not suffer these things. Assuredly Utopia will be temperate, not only drinking, but eating with the soundest discretion. Yet I do not think wine and good ale will be altogether wanting there, nor good mellow whisky, nor, upon occasion, the engaging various liqueur. I do not think so. My botanist, who abstains altogether, is of another opinion. We differ here and leave the question to the earnest reader. I have the utmost respect for all Teetotallers, Prohibitionists, and Haters and Persecutors of Innkeepers, their energy of reform awakens responsive notes in me, and to their species I look for a large part of the urgent repair of our earth; yet for all that—

There is Burgundy, for example, a bottle of soft and kindly
Burgundy, taken to make a sunshine on one's lunch when four
strenuous hours of toil have left one on the further side of
appetite. Or ale, a foaming tankard of ale, ten miles of sturdy
tramping in the sleet and slush as a prelude, and then good
bread and good butter and a ripe hollow Stilton and celery and
ale – ale with a certain quantitative freedom. Or again, where
is the sin in a glass of tawny port three or four times, or it may
be five, a year, when the walnuts come round in their season?
If you drink no port, then what are walnuts for? Such things I
hold for the reward of vast intervals of abstinence; they justify
your wide, immaculate margin, which is else a mere unmeaning
blankness on the page of palate God has given you! I write of
these things as a fleshly man, confessedly and knowingly fleshly,
and more than usually aware of my liability to err; I know
myself for a gross creature more given to sedentary world-
mending than to brisk activities, and not one-tenth as active as
the dullest newspaper boy in London. Yet still I have my uses,
uses that vanish in monotony, and still I must ask why should
we bury the talent of these bright sensations altogether? Under
no circumstances can I think of my Utopians maintaining their
fine order of life on ginger ale and lemonade and the ale that is
Kops'.[16] Those terrible Temperance Drinks, solutions of qualified sugar mixed with vast volumes of gas, as, for example,
soda, seltzer, lemonade and fire-extinguishing hand grenades –
*minerals*, they call such stuff in England – fill a man with wind
and self-righteousness. Indeed they do! Coffee destroys brain
and kidney, a fact now universally recognized and advertised
throughout America; and tea, except for a kind of green tea
best used with discretion in punch, tans the entrails and turns
honest stomachs into leather bags. Rather would I be Metchni-
koffed* at once and have a clean, good stomach of German
silver. No! If we are to have no ale in Utopia, give me the one
clean temperance drink that is worthy to set beside wine, and
that is simple water. Best it is when not quite pure and with a
trace of organic matter, for then it tastes and sparkles. . . .

* See *The Nature of Man*, by Professor Elie Metchnikoff.[17]

My botanist would still argue.

Thank Heaven this is my book, and that the ultimate decision rests with me. It is open to him to write his own Utopia and arrange that everybody shall do nothing except by the consent of the savants of the Republic, either in his eating, drinking, dressing or lodging even as Cabet proposed. It is open to him to try a *News from Nowhere* Utopia with the wine left out. I have my short way with him here quite effectually. I turn in the entrance of our inn to the civil but by no means obsequious landlord, and with a careful ambiguity of manner – for the thing may be considered an outrage, and I try to make it possible the idea is a jest – put my test demand. . . .

'You see, my dear Teetotaler? – he sets before me tray and glass and . . .' Here follows the necessary experiment and a deep sigh. . . . 'Yes, a bottle of quite *excellent* light beer! So there are also cakes and ale in Utopia! Let us in this saner and more beautiful world drink perdition to all earthly excesses. Let us drink more particularly to the coming of the day when men beyond there will learn to distinguish between qualitative and quantitative questions, to temper good intentions with good intelligence, and righteousness with wisdom. One of the darkest evils of our world is surely the unteachable wildness of the Good.'

§ 7

So presently to bed and to sleep, but not at once to sleep. At first my brain, like a dog in unfamiliar quarters, must turn itself round for a time or so before it lies down. This strange mystery of a world of which I have seen so little as yet – a mountain slope, a twilit road, a traffic of ambiguous vehicles and dim shapes, the window lights of many homes – fills me with curiosities. Figures and incidents come and go, the people we have passed, our landlord, quietly attentive and yet, I feel, with the keenest curiosity peeping from his eyes, the unfamiliar forms of the house parts and furnishings, the unfamiliar courses of the meal. Outside this little bedroom is a world, a whole unimagined world. A thousand million things lie outside in the darkness beyond this lit inn of ours, unthought-of possibilities, overlooked considerations, surprises, riddles, incommensurables, a whole monstrous intricate universe of consequences that I have to do my best to unravel. I attempt impossible recapitulations and mingle the weird quality of dream stuff with my thoughts.

Athwart all this tumult of my memory goes this queer figure of my unanticipated companion, so obsessed by himself and his own egotistical love that this sudden change to another world seems only a change of scene for his gnawing, uninvigorating passion. It occurs to me that she also must have an equivalent in Utopia, and then that idea and all ideas grow thin and vague, and are dissolved at last in the rising tide of sleep. . . .

# 3

# UTOPIAN ECONOMICS

## § 1

These modern Utopians with the universally diffused good manners, the universal education, the fine freedoms we shall ascribe to them, their world unity, world language, worldwide travellings, worldwide freedom of sale and purchase, will remain mere dream stuff, incredible even by twilight, until we have shown that at that level the community will still sustain itself. At any rate, the common liberty of the Utopians will not embrace the common liberty to be unserviceable, the most perfect economy of organization still leaves the fact untouched that all order and security in a State rests on the certainty of getting work done. How will the work of this planet be done? What will be the economics of a modern Utopia?

Now in the first place, a state so vast and complex as this world Utopia, and with so migratory a people, will need some handy symbol to check the distribution of services and commodities. Almost certainly they will need to have money. They will have money, and it is not inconceivable that, for all his sorrowful thoughts, our botanist with his trained observation, his habit of looking at little things upon the ground, would be the one to see and pick up the coin that has fallen from some wayfarer's pocket. (This, in our first hour or so before we reach the inn in the Urserenthal.) You figure us upon the high Gotthard road, heads together over the little disc that contrives to tell us so much of this strange world.

It is, I imagine, of gold, and it will be a convenient accident if it is sufficient to make us solvent for a day or so, until we are a little more informed of the economic system into which we have come. It is, moreover, of a fair round size, and the inscription declares it one Lion, equal to 'twaindy'[1] bronze Crosses. Unless the ratio of metals is very different here, this latter must be a token coin, and therefore legal tender for but a small amount. (That would be pain and pleasure to Mr Wordsworth Donisthorpe[2] if he were to chance to join us, for once he planned a Utopian coinage,* and the words Lion and Cross are his. But a token coinage and 'legal tender' he cannot abide. They make him argue.) And being in Utopia, that unfamiliar 'twaindy' suggests at once we have come upon that most Utopian of all things, a duodecimal system of counting.

My author's privilege of details serves me here. This Lion is distinctly a beautiful coin, admirably made, with its value in fine, clear letters circling the obverse side, and a head thereon – of Newton,[3] as I live! One detects American influence here. Each year, as we shall find, each denomination of coins celebrates a centenary. The reverse shows the universal goddess of the Utopian coinage – Peace, as a beautiful woman, reading with a child out of a great book, and behind them are stars, and an hour-glass, halfway run. Very human these Utopians, after all, and not by any means above the obvious in their symbolism!

So for the first time we learn definitely of the World State, and we get our first clear hint, too, that there is an end to Kings. But our coin raises other issues also. It would seem that this Utopia has no simple community of goods, that there is, at any rate, a restriction upon what one may take, a need for evidences of equivalent value, a limitation to human credit.

It dates – so much of this present Utopia of ours dates. Those former Utopists were bitterly against gold. You will recall the undignified use[4] Sir Thomas More would have us put it to, and how there was no money at all in the Republic of Plato, and in that later community for which he wrote his 'Laws' an iron coinage of austere appearance and doubtful efficacy. . . . It may be these great gentlemen were a little hasty with a complicated difficulty, and not a little unjust to a highly respectable element.

---

* *A System of Measures*, by Wordsworth Donisthorpe.

Gold is abused and made into vessels of dishonour, and abolished from ideal society as though it were the cause instead of the instrument of human baseness; but, indeed, there is nothing bad in gold. Making gold into vessels of dishonour and banishing it from the State is punishing the hatchet for the murderer's crime. Money, did you but use it right, is a good thing in life, a necessary thing in civilized human life; as complicated indeed for its purposes, but as natural a growth as the bones in a man's wrist, and I do not see how one can imagine anything at all worthy of being called a civilization without it. It is the water of the body social, it distributes and receives, and renders growth and assimilation and movement and recovery possible. It is the reconciliation of human interdependence with liberty. What other device will give a man so great a freedom with so strong an inducement to effort? The economic history of the world, where it is not the history of the theory of property, is very largely the record of the abuse, not so much of money as of credit devices to supplement money, to amplify the scope of this most precious invention; and no device of labour credits* or free demand of commodities from a central store† or the like has ever been suggested that does not give ten thousand times more scope for that inherent moral dross in man that must be reckoned with in any sane Utopia we may design and plan. . . . Heaven knows where progress may not end, but at any rate this developing State, into which we two men have fallen, this twentieth-century Utopia, has still not passed beyond money and the use of coins.

§ 2

Now if this Utopian world is to be in some degree parallel to contemporary thought, it must have been concerned, it may be still concerned, with many unsettled problems of currency, and with the problems that centre about a standard of value. Gold is perhaps of all material substances the best adapted to the

---

* Edward Bellamy's *Looking Backward*, chap. IX.
† More's *Utopia* and Cabet's *Icaria*.

monetary purpose, but even at that best it falls far short of an imaginable ideal. It undergoes spasmodic and irregular cheapening through new discoveries of gold, and at any time it may undergo very extensive and sudden and disastrous depreciation through the discovery of some way of transmuting less valuable elements. The liability to such depreciations introduces an undesirable speculative element into the relations of debtor and creditor. When, on the one hand, there is for a time a check in the increase of the available stores of gold, or an increase in the energy applied to social purposes, or a checking of the public security that would impede the free exchange of credit and necessitate a more frequent production of gold in evidence, then there comes an undue appreciation of money as against the general commodities of life, and an automatic impoverishment of the citizens in general as against the creditor class. The common people are mortgaged into the bondage of debt. And on the other hand an unexpected spate of gold production, the discovery of a single nugget as big as St Paul's, let us say – a quite possible thing – would result in a sort of jail delivery of debtors and a financial earthquake.

It has been suggested by an ingenious thinker that it is possible to use as a standard of monetary value no substance whatever, but instead, force, and that value might be measured in units of energy. An excellent development this, in theory at any rate, of the general idea of the modern State as kinetic and not static; it throws the old idea of the social order and the new into the sharpest antithesis. The old order is presented as a system of institutions and classes ruled by men of substance; the new, of enterprises and interests led by men of power.

Now I glance at this matter in the most incidental manner, as a man may skim through a specialist's exposition in a popular magazine. You must figure me, therefore, finding from a casual periodical paper in our inn, with a certain surprise at not having anticipated as much, the Utopian self of that same ingenious person quite conspicuously a leader of thought, and engaged in organizing the discussion of the currency changes Utopia has under consideration. The article, as it presents itself to me, contains a complete and lucid, though occasionally rather technical, explanation of his newest proposals. They have been published, it seems, for general criticism; and one gathers that in the modern Utopia the administration presents the most elaborately detailed schemes of any proposed alteration in law or custom, some time before any measure is taken to carry it into effect, and the possibilities of every detail are acutely criticized, flaws anticipated, side issues raised, and the whole minutely tested and fined down by a planetful of critics, before the actual process of legislation begins.

The explanation of these proposals involves an anticipatory glance at the local administration of a modern Utopia. To anyone who has watched the development of technical science during the last decade or so, there will be no shock in the idea that a general consolidation of a great number of common public services over areas of considerable size is now not only practicable, but very desirable. In a little while heating and lighting and the supply of power for domestic and industrial purposes and for urban and interurban communications will all be managed electrically from common generating stations. And the trend of political and social speculation points decidedly to the conclusion that so soon as it passes out of the experimental stage, the supply of electrical energy, just like drainage and the supply of water, will fall to the local authority. Moreover, the local authority will be the universal landowner. Upon that point so extreme an individualist as Herbert Spencer was in agreement with the Socialist. In Utopia we conclude that, whatever other types of property may exist, all natural sources of force, and indeed all strictly natural products – coal, water-power and the like – are inalienably vested in the local authorities (which, in order to secure the maximum of convenience and administrative efficiency, will probably control areas as large sometimes as half England); they will generate electricity by water-power, by combustion, by wind or tide or whatever other natural force is available, and this electricity will be devoted, some of it to the authority's lighting and other public works, some of it, as a subsidy, to the World-State authority which controls the high roads, the great railways, the inns and other apparatus of world communication, and the rest will pass on to private individuals or to distributing companies at a uniform fixed rate for private lighting and heating, for machinery and industrial applications of all sorts. Such an arrangement of affairs will necessarily involve a vast amount of bookkeeping between the various authorities, the World-State government and the customers, and this bookkeeping will naturally be done most conveniently in units of physical energy.

It is not incredible that the assessment of the various local administrations for the central world government would be already calculated upon the estimated total of energy periodically available in each locality, and booked and spoken of in these physical units. Accounts between central and local governments could be kept in these terms. Moreover, one may imagine Utopian local authorities making contracts in which payment would be no longer in coinage upon the gold basis, but in notes good for so many thousands or millions of units of energy at one or other of the generating stations.

Now the problems of economic theory will have undergone an enormous clarification if, instead of measuring in fluctuating money values, the same scale of energy units can be extended to their discussion; if, in fact, the idea of trading could be entirely eliminated. In my Utopia, at any rate, this has been done; the production and distribution of common commodities have been expressed as a problem in the conversion of energy, and the scheme that Utopia was now discussing was the application of this idea of energy as the standard of value to the entire Utopian coinage. Every one of those giant local authorities was to be free to issue energy notes against the security of its surplus of saleable available energy, and to make all its contracts for payment in those notes up to a certain maximum defined by the amount of energy produced and disposed of in that locality in the previous year. This power of issue was to be renewed just as rapidly as the notes came in for redemption. In a world without boundaries, with a population largely migratory and emancipated from locality, the price of the energy notes of these various local bodies would constantly tend to be uniform, because employment would constantly shift into the areas where energy was cheap. Accordingly, the price of so many millions of units of energy at any particular moment in coins of the gold currency would be approximately the same throughout the world. It was proposed to select some particular day when the economic atmosphere was distinctly equable, and to declare a fixed ratio between the gold coinage and the energy notes; each gold Lion and each Lion of credit representing exactly the number of energy units it could buy on that day. The old gold coinage was at once to cease to be legal tender beyond certain defined limits, except to the central government, which would not reissue it as it came in. It was, in fact, to become a temporary token coinage, a token coinage of full value for the day of conversion at any rate, if not afterwards, under the new standard of energy, and to be replaceable by an ordinary token coinage as time went on. The old computation by Lions and the values of the small change of daily life were therefore to suffer no disturbance whatever.

The economists of Utopia, as I apprehended them, had a different method and a very different system of theories from those I have read on earth, and this makes my exposition considerably more difficult. This article upon which I base my account floated before me in an unfamiliar, perplexing and dreamlike phraseology. Yet I brought away an impression that here was a rightness that earthly economists have failed to grasp. Few earthly economists have been able to disentangle themselves from patriotisms and politics, and their obsession has always been international trade. Here in Utopia the World State cuts that away from beneath their feet; there are no imports but meteorites, and no exports at all. Trading is the earthly economists' initial notion, and they start from perplexing and insoluble riddles about exchange value, insoluble because all trading finally involves individual preferences which are incalculable and unique. Nowhere do they seem to be handling really defined standards, every economic dissertation and discussion reminds one more strongly than the last of the game of croquet Alice played in Wonderland,[5] when the mallets were flamingoes and the balls were hedgehogs and crawled away, and the hoops were soldiers and kept getting up and walking about. But economics in Utopia must be, it seems to me, not a theory of trading based on bad psychology, but physics applied to problems in the theory of sociology. The general problem of Utopian economics is to state the conditions of the most efficient application of the steadily increasing quantities of material energy the progress of science makes available for human service, to the general needs of mankind. Human labour and existing material are dealt with in relation to that. Trading and relative wealth are merely episodical in such a scheme. The trend of the article I read, as I understood it, was that a monetary system based upon a relatively small amount of gold, upon which the business of the whole world had hitherto been done, fluctuated unreasonably and supplied no real criterion of wellbeing, that the nominal values of things and enterprises had no clear and simple relation to the real physical prosperity of the community, that the nominal wealth of a community in millions of pounds or dollars or Lions, measured nothing but the quantity of hope in the air, and an increase of confidence meant an inflation of credit and a pessimistic phase a collapse of this hallucination of possessions. The new standards, this advocate reasoned, were to alter all that, and it seemed to me they would.

I have tried to indicate the drift of these remarkable proposals, but about them clustered an elaborate mass of keen and temperate discussion. Into the details of that discussion I will not enter now, nor am I sure I am qualified to render the multitudinous aspect of this complicated question at all precisely. I read the whole thing in the course of an hour or two of rest after lunch – it was either the second or third day of my stay in Utopia – and we were sitting in a little inn at the end of the Lake of Uri. We had loitered there, and I had fallen reading because of a shower of rain.... But certainly as I read it the proposition struck me as a singularly simple and attractive one, and its exposition opened out to me for the first time clearly, in a comprehensive outline, the general conception of the economic nature of the Utopian State.

§ 3

The difference between the social and economic sciences as they exist in our world* and in this Utopia deserves perhaps a word or so more. I write with the utmost diffidence, because upon earth economic science has been raised to a very high level of tortuous abstraction by the industry of its professors, and I can claim neither a patient student's intimacy with their productions nor – what is more serious – anything but the most generalized knowledge of what their Utopian equivalents have achieved. The vital nature of economic issues to a Utopia necessitates, however, some attempt at interpretation between the two.

In Utopia there is no distinct and separate science of economics. Many problems that we should regard as economic come within the scope of Utopian psychology. My Utopians make two divisions of the science of psychology, first the general psychology of individuals, a sort of mental physiology separated by no definite line from physiology proper, and secondly the psychology of relationship between individuals. This second is an exhaustive study of the reaction of people upon each other and of all possible relationships. It is a science of human aggregations, of all possible family groupings, of neighbours and neighbourhood, of companies, associations, unions, secret and public societies, religious groupings, of common ends and intercourse, and of the methods of intercourse and collective decision that hold human groups together, and finally of government and the State. The elucidation of economic relationships, depending as it does on the nature of the hypothesis of human aggregation actually in operation at any time, is considered to be subordinate and subsequent to this general science of Sociology. Political economy and economics, in our world now, consist of a hopeless muddle of social assumptions and preposterous psychology, and a few geographical and physical generalizations. Its ingredients will be classified out and widely

* But see Giddings' *Principles of Sociology*,[6] a modern and richly suggestive American work, imperfectly appreciated by the British student. See also Walter Bagehot's *Economic Studies*.[7]

separated in Utopian thought. On the one hand there will
be the study of physical economies, ending in the descriptive
treatment of society as an organization for the conversion of all
the available energy in nature to the material ends of mankind –
a physical sociology which will be already at such a stage of
practical development as to be giving the world this token
coinage representing energy – and on the other there will be the
study of economic problems as problems in the division of
labour, having regard to a social organization whose main ends
are reproduction and education in an atmosphere of personal
freedom. Each of these inquiries, working unencumbered by
the other, will be continually contributing fresh valid conclusions for the use of the practical administrator.

In no region of intellectual activity will our hypothesis of
freedom from tradition be of more value in devising a Utopia
than here. From its beginning the earthly study of economics
has been infertile and unhelpful, because of the mass of unana-
lysed and scarcely suspected assumptions upon which it rested.
The facts were ignored that trade is a by-product and not an
essential factor in social life, that property is a plastic and
fluctuating convention, that value is capable of impersonal
treatment only in the case of the most generalized requirements.
Wealth was measured by the standards of exchange. Society
was regarded as a practically unlimited number of avaricious
adult units incapable of any other subordinate groupings than
business partnerships, and the sources of competition were
assumed to be inexhaustible. Upon such quicksands rose an
edifice that aped the securities of material science, developed a
technical jargon and professed the discovery of 'laws'. Our
liberation from these false presumptions through the rhetoric
of Carlyle[8] and Ruskin, and the activities of the Socialists, is
more apparent than real. The old edifice oppresses us still,
repaired and altered by indifferent builders, underpinned in
places, and with a slight change of name. 'Political Economy'
has been painted out, and instead we read 'Economics – under
entirely new management'. Modern Economics differs mainly
from old Political Economy in having produced no Adam
Smith. The old Political Economy made certain generalizations,

and they were mostly wrong; the new Economics evades generalizations, and seems to lack the intellectual power to make them. The science hangs like a gathering fog in a valley, a fog which begins nowhere and goes nowhere, an incidental, unmeaning inconvenience to passers-by. Its most typical exponents display a disposition to disavow generalizations altogether, to claim consideration as 'experts', and to make immediate political application of that conceded claim. Now Newton, Darwin, Dalton,[9] Davy,[10] Joule[11] and Adam Smith[12] did not affect this 'expert' hankey-pankey, becoming enough in a hairdresser or a fashionable physician but indecent in a philosopher or a man of science. In this state of impotent expertness, however, or in some equally unsound state, economics must struggle on – a science that is no science, a floundering lore wallowing in a mud of statistics – until either the study of the material organization of production on the one hand as a development of physics and geography, or the study of social aggregation on the other, renders enduring foundations possible.

§ 4

The older Utopias were all relatively small states; Plato's Republic, for example, was to be smaller than the average English borough, and no distinction was made between the Family, the Local Government and the State. Plato and Campanella – for all that the latter was a Christian priest – carried communism to its final point and prescribed even a community of husbands and wives, an idea that was brought at last to the test of effectual experiment in the Oneida Community[13] of New York State (1848–1879). This latter body did not long survive its founder, at least as a veritable communism, by reason of the insurgent individualism of its vigorous sons. More, too, denied privacy and ruled an absolute community of goods at any rate, and so, coming to the Victorian Utopias, did Cabet. But Cabet's communism was one of the 'free store' type, and the goods were yours only after you had requisitioned them. That seems the case in the *Nowhere* of Morris also. Compared with the older writers Bellamy and Morris have a vivid sense of individual separation, and their departure from the old homogeneity is sufficiently marked to justify a doubt whether there will be any more thoroughly communistic Utopias for ever.

A Utopia such as this present one, written in the opening of the twentieth century and after the most exhaustive discussion – nearly a century long – between Communistic and Socialistic ideas on the one hand, and Individualism on the other, emerges upon a sort of effectual conclusion to those controversies. The two parties have so chipped and amended each other's initial propositions that, indeed, except for the labels still flutteringly adhesive to the implicated men, it is hard to choose between them. Each side established a good many propositions, and we profit by them all. We of the succeeding generation can see quite clearly that for the most part the heat and zeal of these discussions arose in the confusion of a quantitative for a qualitative question. To the onlooker, both Individualism and Socialism are, in the absolute, absurdities; the one would make men the slaves of the violent or rich, the other the slaves of the State official, and the way of sanity runs, perhaps even sinuously, down the intervening valley. Happily the dead past buries its dead, and it is not our function now to adjudicate the preponderance of victory. In the very days when our political and economic order is becoming steadily more Socialistic, our ideals of intercourse turn more and more to a fuller recognition of the claims of individuality. The State is to be progressive, it is no longer to be static, and this alters the general condition of the Utopian problem profoundly; we have to provide not only for food and clothing, for order and health, but for initiative. The factor that leads the World State on from one phase of development to the next is the interplay of individualities; to speak teleologically, the world exists for the sake of and through initiative, and individuality is the method of initiative. Each man and woman, to the extent that his or her individuality is marked, breaks the law of precedent, transgresses the general formula, and makes a new experiment for the direction of the life force. It is impossible, therefore, for the State, which represents all and is preoccupied by the average, to make effectual experiments and intelligent innovations, and so supply the essential substance of life. As against the individual the State represents the species; in the case of the Utopian World State it absolutely represents the species. The individual emerges from the species, makes his experiment, and either fails, dies and comes to an end, or succeeds and impresses himself in offspring, in consequences and results, intellectual, material and moral, upon the world.

Biologically the species is the accumulation of the experiments of all its successful individuals since the beginning, and the World State of the Modern Utopist will, in its economic aspect, be a compendium of established economic experience, about which individual enterprise will be continually experimenting, either to fail and pass, or to succeed and at last become incorporated with the undying organism of the World State. This organism is the universal rule, the common restriction, the rising level platform on which individualities stand.

The World State in this ideal presents itself as the sole land-owner of the earth, with the great local governments I have adumbrated, the local municipalities, holding, as it were, feudally under it as landlords. The State or these subordinates holds all the sources of energy, and either directly or through its tenants, farmers and agents, develops these sources, and renders the energy available for the work of life. It or its tenants will produce food, and so human energy; and the exploitation of coal and electric power, and the powers of wind and wave and water will be within its right. It will pour out this energy by assignment and lease and acquiescence and what not upon its individual citizens. It will maintain order, maintain roads, maintain a cheap and efficient administration of justice, maintain cheap and rapid locomotion and be the common carrier of the planet, convey and distribute labour, control, let or administer all natural productions, pay for and secure healthy births and a healthy and vigorous new generation, maintain the public health, coin money and sustain standards of measurement, subsidize research, and reward such commercially unprofitable undertakings as benefit the community as a whole; subsidize when needful chairs of criticism and authors and publications, and collect and distribute information. The energy developed and the employment afforded by the State will descend like water that the sun has sucked out of the sea to pour upon a mountain range; and back to the sea again it will come at last, debouching in ground rent and royalty and licence fees, in the fees of travellers and profits upon carrying and coinage and the like, in death duty, transfer tax, legacy and forfeiture, returning to the sea. Between the clouds and the sea it will run, as a river system runs, down through a great region of individual enterprise and interplay, whose freedom it will sustain. In that intermediate region between the kindred heights and deeps those beginnings and promises will arise that are the essential significance, the essential substance, of life. From our human point of view the mountains and sea exist for the habitable lands that lie between. So likewise the State is for Individualities. The State is for Individuals, the law is for freedoms, the world is for experiment, experience and change: these are the fundamental beliefs upon which a modern Utopia must go.

## § 5

Within this scheme, which makes the State the source of all energy and the final legatee, what will be the nature of the property a man may own? Under modern conditions – indeed, under any conditions – a man without some negotiable property is a man without freedom, and the extent of his property is very largely the measure of his freedom. Without any property, without even shelter or food, a man has no choice but to set about getting these things; he is in servitude to his needs until he has secured property to satisfy them. But with a certain small property a man is free to do many things, to take a fortnight's holiday when he chooses, for example, and to try this new departure from his work or that; with so much more, he may take a year of freedom and go to the ends of the earth; with so much more, he may obtain elaborate apparatus and try curious novelties, build himself houses and make gardens, establish businesses and make experiments at large. Very speedily, under terrestrial conditions, the property of a man may reach such proportions that his freedom oppresses the freedom of others. Here, again, is a quantitative question, an adjustment of conflicting freedoms, a quantitative question that too many people insist on making a qualitative one.

The object sought in the code of property laws that one would find in operation in Utopia would be the same object that pervades the whole Utopian organization, namely, a universal maximum of individual freedom. Whatever far-reaching movements the State or great rich men or private corporations may make, the starvation by any complication of employment, the unwilling deportation, the destruction of alternatives to servile submissions, must not ensue. Beyond such qualifications, the object of Modern Utopian statesmanship will be to secure to a man the freedom given by all his legitimate property, that is to say, by all the values his toil or skill or foresight and courage have brought into being. Whatever he has justly made he has a right to keep, that is obvious enough; but he will also have a right to sell and exchange, and so this question of what may be property takes really the form of what a man may buy in Utopia.

A modern Utopian most assuredly must have a practically unqualified property in all those things that become, as it were, by possession, extensions and expressions of his personality; his clothing, his jewels, the tools of his employment, his books, the objects of art he may have bought or made, his personal weapons (if Utopia have need of such things), insignia and so forth. All such things that he has bought with his money or acquired – provided he is not a professional or habitual dealer in such property – will be inalienably his, his to give or lend or keep, free even from taxation. So intimate is this sort of property that I have no doubt Utopia will give a man posthumous rights over it – will permit him to assign it to a successor with at the utmost the payment of a small redemption. A horse, perhaps, in certain districts, or a bicycle, or any such mechanical conveyance personally used, the Utopians might find it well to rank with these possessions. No doubt, too, a house and privacy owned and occupied by a man, and even a man's own household furniture, might be held to stand as high or almost as high in the property scale, might be taxed as lightly and transferred under only a slightly heavier redemption, provided he had not let these things on hire, or otherwise alienated them from his intimate self. A thoroughgoing, Democratic Socialist will no doubt be inclined at first to object that if the Utopians make these things a specially free sort of property in this way, men would spend much more upon them than they would otherwise do, but indeed that will be an excellent thing. We are too much affected by the needy atmosphere of our own mismanaged world. In Utopia no one will have to hunger because some love to make and have made and own and cherish beautiful things. To give this much of property to individuals will tend to make clothing, ornamentation, implements, books and all the arts finer and more beautiful, because by buying such things a man will secure something inalienable – save in the case of bankruptcy – for himself and for those who belong to him. Moreover, a man may in his lifetime set aside sums to ensure special advantages of education and care for the immature children of himself and others, and in this manner also exercise a posthumous right.*

For all other property, the Utopians will have a scantier respect; even money unspent by a man, and debts to him that bear no interest, will at his death stand upon a lower level than these things. What he did not choose to gather and assimilate to himself, or assign for the special education of his children, the State will share in the lion's proportion with heir and legatee.

This applies, for example, to the property that a man creates and acquires in business enterprises, which are presumably undertaken for gain and as a means of living rather than for themselves. All new machinery, all new methods, all uncertain and variable and non-universal undertakings, are no business for the State; they commence always as experiments of unascertained value, and next after the invention of money, there is no invention has so facilitated freedom and progress as the invention of the limited liability company to do this work of trial

---

* But a Statute of Mortmain[14] will set a distinct time limit to the continuance of such benefactions. A periodic revision of endowments is a necessary feature in any modern Utopia.

and adventure. The abuses, the necessary reforms of company law on earth, are no concern of ours here and now, suffice it that in a modern Utopia such laws must be supposed to be as perfect as mortal laws can possibly be made. *Caveat vendor*[15] will be a sound qualification of *Caveat emptor* in the beautifully codified Utopian law. Whether the Utopian company will be allowed to prefer this class of share to that or to issue debentures, whether indeed usury, that is to say lending money at fixed rates of interest, will be permitted at all in Utopia, one may venture to doubt. But whatever the nature of the shares a man may hold, they will all be sold at his death, and whatever he has not clearly assigned for special educational purposes will – with possibly some fractional concession to near survivors – lapse to the State. The 'safe investment', that permanent, undying claim upon the community, is just one of those things Utopia will discourage; which indeed the developing security of civilization quite automatically discourages through the fall in the rate of interest. As we shall see at a later stage, the State will insure the children of every citizen, and those legitimately dependent upon him, against the inconvenience of his death; it will carry out all reasonable additional dispositions he may have made for them in the same event; and it will insure him against old age and infirmity; and the object of Utopian economics will be to give a man every inducement to spend his surplus money in intensifying the quality of his surroundings, either by economic adventures and experiments, which may yield either losses or large profits, or in increasing the beauty, the pleasure, the abundance and promise of life.

Besides strictly personal possessions and shares in business adventures, Utopia will no doubt permit associations of its citizens to have a property in various sorts of contracts and concessions, in leases of agricultural and other land, for example; in houses they may have built, factories and machinery they may have made, and the like. And if a citizen prefer to adventure into business single-handed, he will have all the freedoms of enterprise enjoyed by a company; in business affairs he will be a company of one, and his single share will be dealt with at his death like any other shares. . . . So much for the second kind of property. And these two kinds of property will probably exhaust the sorts of property a Utopian may possess.

The trend of modern thought is entirely against private property in land or natural objects or products, and in Utopia these things will be the inalienable property of the World State. Subject to the rights of free locomotion, land will be leased out to companies or individuals, but – in view of the unknown necessities of the future – never for a longer period than, let us say, fifty years.

The property of a parent in his children, and of a husband in his wife, seems to be undergoing a steadily increasing qualification in the world of today, but the discussion of the Utopian state of affairs in regard to such property may be better reserved until marriage becomes our topic. Suffice it here to remark, that the increasing control of a child's welfare and upbringing by the community, and the growing disposition to limit and tax inheritance are complementary aspects of the general tendency to regard the welfare and free interplay of future generations no longer as the concern of parents and altruistic individuals, but as the predominant issue of statesmanship, and the duty and moral meaning of the world community as a whole.

§ 6

From the conception of mechanical force as coming in from Nature to the service of man, a conception the Utopian proposal of a coinage based on energy units would emphasize, arise profound contrasts between the modern and the classical Utopias. Except for a meagre use of water-power for milling, and the wind for sailing – so meagre in the latter case that the classical world never contrived to do without the galley slave – and a certain restricted help from oxen in ploughing and from horses in locomotion, all the energy that sustained the old-fashioned State was derived from the muscular exertion of toiling men. They ran their world by hand. Continual bodily labour was a condition of social existence. It is only with the coming of coal burning, of abundant iron and steel, and of scientific knowledge that this condition has been changed. Today, I suppose, if it were possible to indicate in units of energy the grand total of work upon which the social fabric of the United States or England rests, it would be found that a vastly preponderating portion is derived from non-human sources, from coal and liquid fuel, and explosives and wind and water. There is every indication of a steady increase in this proportion of mechanical energy, in this emancipation of men from the necessity of physical labour. There appears no limit to the invasion of life by the machine.

Now it is only in the last three hundred years that any human being seems to have anticipated this. It stimulates the imagination to remark how entirely it was overlooked as a modifying cause in human development.* Plato clearly had no ideas about machines at all as a force affecting social organization. There was nothing in his world to suggest them to him. I suppose there arose no invention, no new mechanical appliance or method of the slightest social importance through all his length of years. He never thought of a State that did not rely for its force upon human muscle, just as he never thought of a State that was not primarily organized for warfare hand to hand. Political and moral inventions he saw enough of and to spare, and in that direction he still stimulates the imagination. But in regard to all material possibilities he deadens rather than stimulates.† An infinitude of nonsense about the Greek mind would never have been written if the distinctive intellectual and artistic quality of Plato's time, its extraordinarily clear definition of certain material conditions as absolutely permanent, coupled with its politico-social instability, had been borne in mind. The food of the Greek imagination was the very antithesis of our own nourishment. We are educated by our circumstances to think no revolution in appliances and economic organization incredible, our minds play freely about possibilities that would have struck the men of the Academy as outrageous extravagance, and it is

* It is interesting to note how little even Bacon seems to see of this in his *New Atlantis*.
† The lost *Utopia* of Hippodamus[16] provided rewards for inventors, but unless Aristotle misunderstood him, and it is certainly the fate of all Utopias to be more or less misread, the inventions contemplated were political devices.

in regard to politico-social expedients that our imaginations fail. Sparta, for all the evidence of history, is scarcely more credible to us than a motor-car throbbing in the agora[17] would have been to Socrates.

By sheer inadvertence, therefore, Plato commenced the tradition of Utopias without machinery, a tradition we find Morris still loyally following, except for certain mechanical barges and such-like toys, in his *News from Nowhere*. There are some foreshadowings of mechanical possibilities in the *New Atlantis*, but it is only in the nineteenth century that Utopias appeared in which the fact is clearly recognized that the social fabric rests no longer upon human labour. It was, I believe, Cabet* who first in a Utopian work insisted upon the escape of man from irksome labours through the use of machinery. He is the great primitive of modern Utopias, and Bellamy is his American equivalent. Hitherto, either slave labour (Phaleas),† or at least class distinctions involving unavoidable labour in the lower class, have been assumed – as Plato does, and as Bacon in the *New Atlantis* probably intended to do (More gave his Utopians bondsmen *sans phrase* for their most disagreeable toil); or there is – as in Morris and the outright Return-to-Nature Utopians – a bold make-believe that all toil may be made a joy, and with that a levelling down of all society to an equal participation in labour. But indeed this is against all the observed behaviour of mankind. It needed the Olympian unworldliness of an irresponsible rich man of the shareholding type, a Ruskin or a Morris playing at life, to imagine as much. Road-making under Mr Ruskin's auspices[18] was a joy at Oxford no doubt, and a distinction, and it still remains a distinction; it proved the least contagious of practices. And Hawthorne[19] did not find bodily toil anything more than the curse the Bible says it is, at Brook Farm.‡

If toil is a blessing, never was blessing so effectually disguised, and the very people who tell us that, hesitate to suggest more than a beautiful ease in the endless day of Heaven. A certain

---

* Cabet, *Voyage en Icarie*, 1848.
† Aristotle's *Politics*, bk. II, chap. VIII.
‡ *The Blithedale Romance*, and see also his *Note Books*.

amount of bodily or mental exercise, a considerable amount of doing things under the direction of one's free imagination is quite another matter. Artistic production, for example, when it is at its best, when a man is freely obeying himself and not troubling to please others, is really not toil at all. It is quite a different thing digging potatoes, as boys say, 'for a lark', and digging them because otherwise you will starve, digging them day after day as a dull, unavoidable imperative. The essence of toil is that imperative, and the fact that the attention *must* cramp itself to the work in hand – that it excludes freedom, and not that it involves fatigue. So long as anything but a quasi-savage life depended upon toil, so long was it hopeless to expect mankind to do anything but struggle to confer just as much of this blessing as possible upon one another. But now that the new conditions physical science is bringing about, not only dispense with man as a source of energy but supply the hope that all routine work may be made automatic, it is becoming conceivable that presently there may be no need for anyone to toil habitually at all; that a labouring class – that is to say a class of workers without personal initiative – will become unnecessary to the world of men.

The plain message physical science has for the world at large is this, that were our political and social and moral devices only as well contrived to their ends as a linotype machine,[20] an antiseptic operating plant, or an electric tram-car, there need now at the present moment be no appreciable toil in the world, and only the smallest fraction of the pain, the fear and the anxiety that now make human life so doubtful in its value. There is more than enough for everyone alive. Science stands, a competent servant, behind her wrangling underbred masters, holding out resources, devices and remedies they are too stupid to use.* And on its material side a modern Utopia must needs present these gifts as taken, and show a world that is really abolishing the need of labour, abolishing the last base reason for anyone's servitude or inferiority.

* See that most suggestive little book, *Twentieth Century Inventions*, by Mr George Sutherland.[21]

# § 7

The effectual abolition of a labouring and servile class will make itself felt in every detail of the inn that will shelter us, of the bedrooms we shall occupy. You conceive my awakening to all these things on the morning after our arrival. I shall lie for a minute or so with my nose peeping over the coverlet, agreeably and gently coming awake, and with some vague nightmare of sitting at a common table with an unavoidable dustman in green and gold called Boffin,* fading out of my mind. Then I should start up. You figure my apprehensive, startled inspection of my chamber. 'Where am I?' that classic phrase, recurs. Then I perceive quite clearly that I am in bed in Utopia.

Utopia! The word is enough to bring anyone out of bed to the nearest window; but thence I see no more than the great mountain mass behind the inn, a very terrestrial-looking mountain mass. I return to the contrivances about me, and make my examination as I dress, pausing garment in hand to hover over first this thing of interest and then that.

The room is, of course, very clear and clean and simple; not by any means cheaply equipped, but designed to economize the labour of redding and repair just as much as is possible. It is beautifully proportioned, and rather lower than most rooms I know on earth. There is no fireplace, and I am perplexed by that until I find a thermometer beside six switches on the wall. Above this switchboard is a brief instruction: one switch warms the floor, which is not carpeted, but covered by a substance like soft oilcloth; one warms the mattress (which is of metal with resistance coils threaded to and fro in it); and the others warm the wall in various degrees, each directing current through a separate system of resistances. The casement does not open, but above, flush with the ceiling, a noiseless rapid fan pumps air out of the room. The air enters by a Tobin shaft.[22] There is a recess dressing-room, equipped with a bath and all that is necessary to one's toilette, and the water, one remarks, is warmed, if one desires it warm, by passing it through an electrically heated

* *Vide* William Morris's *News from Nowhere.*

spiral of tubing. A cake of soap drops out of a store machine on the turn of a handle, and when you have done with it, you drop that and your soiled towels and so forth, which also are given you by machines, into a little box, through the bottom of which they fall at once and sail down a smooth shaft. A little notice tells you the price of your room, and you gather the price is doubled if you do not leave the toilette as you found it. Beside the bed, and to be lit at night by a handy switch over the pillow, is a little clock, its face flush with the wall. The room has no corners to gather dirt, wall meets floor with a gentle curve, and the apartment could be swept out effectually by a few strokes of a mechanical sweeper. The door frames and window frames are of metal, rounded and impervious to draught. You are politely requested to turn a handle at the foot of your bed before leaving the room, and forthwith the frame turns up into a vertical position, and the bedclothes hang airing. You stand at the doorway and realize that there remains not a minute's work for anyone to do. Memories of the foetid disorder of many an earthly bedroom after a night's use float across your mind.

And you must not imagine this dustless, spotless, sweet apartment as anything but beautiful. Its appearance is a little unfamiliar of course, but all the muddle of dust-collecting hangings and witless ornament that cover the earthly bedroom, the valances, the curtains to check the draught from the ill-fitting wood windows, the worthless irrelevant pictures, usually a little askew, the dusty carpets and all the paraphernalia about the dirty, black-leaded fireplace are gone. But the faintly tinted walls are framed with just one clear-coloured line, as finely placed as the member of a Greek capital;[23] the door handles and the lines of the panels of the door, the two chairs, the framework of the bed, the writing-table, have all that final simplicity, that exquisite finish of contour that is begotten of sustained artistic effort. The graciously shaped windows each frame a picture – since they are draughtless the window seats are no mere mockeries as are the window seats of earth – and on the sill, the sole thing to need attention in the room, is one little bowl of blue Alpine flowers.

The same exquisite simplicity meets one downstairs.

Our landlord sits down at table with us for a moment, and seeing we do not understand the electrically heated coffee-pot before us, shows us what to do. Coffee and milk we have, in the Continental fashion, and some excellent rolls and butter.

He is a swarthy little man, our landlord, and overnight we saw him preoccupied with other guests. But we have risen either late or early by Utopian standards, we know not which, and this morning he has us to himself. His bearing is kindly and inoffensive, but he cannot conceal the curiosity that possesses him. His eye meets ours with a mute inquiry, and then as we fall to, we catch him scrutinizing our cuffs, our garments, our boots, our faces, our table manners. He asks nothing at first, but says a word or so about our night's comfort and the day's weather, phrases that have an air of being customary. Then comes a silence that is interrogative.

'Excellent coffee,' I say to fill the gap.

'And excellent rolls,' says my botanist.

Our landlord indicates his sense of our approval.

A momentary diversion is caused by the entry of an elfin-tressed little girl, who stares at us half impudently, half shyly, with bright black eyes, hesitates at the botanist's clumsy smile and nod, and then goes and stands by her father and surveys us steadfastly.

'You have come far?' ventures our landlord, patting his daughter's shoulder.

I glance at the botanist. 'Yes,' I say, 'we have.'

I expand. 'We have come so far that this country of yours seems very strange indeed to us.'

'The mountains?'

'Not only the mountains.'

'You came up out of the Ticino valley?'

'No – not that way.'

'By the Oberalp?'

'No.'

'The Furka?'

'No.'

'Not up from the lake?'

'No.'

He looks puzzled.

'We came,' I say, 'from another world.'

He seems trying to understand. Then a thought strikes him, and he sends away his little girl with a needless message to her mother.

'Ah!' he says. 'Another world – eh? Meaning—?'

'Another world – far in the deeps of space.'

Then at the expression of his face one realizes that a modern Utopia will probably keep its more intelligent citizens for better work than inn-tending. He is evidently inaccessible to the idea we think of putting before him. He stares at us a moment and then remarks, 'There's the book to sign.'

We find ourselves confronted with a book, a little after the fashion of the familiar hotel visitors' book of earth. He places this before us, and beside it puts pen and ink and a slab, upon which ink has been freshly smeared.

'Thumbmarks,' says my scientific friend hastily in English.

'You show me how to do it,' I say as quickly.

He signs first, and I look over his shoulder.

He is displaying more readiness than I should have expected. The book is ruled in broad transverse lines, and has a space for a name, for a number and a thumbmark. He puts his thumb upon the slab and makes the thumbmark first with the utmost deliberation. Meanwhile he studies the other two entries. The 'numbers' of the previous guests above are complex muddles of letters and figures. He writes his name, then with a calm assurance writes down his number, A.M.a.1607.2.$\alpha\beta\oplus$. I am wrung with momentary admiration. I follow his example, and fabricate an equally imposing signature. We think ourselves very clever. The landlord proffers finger bowls for our thumbs, and his eye goes, just a little curiously, to our entries.

I decide it is advisable to pay and go before any conversation about our formulae arises.

As we emerge into the corridor, and the morning sunlight of the Utopian world, I see the landlord bending over the book.

'Come on,' I say. 'The most tiresome thing in the world is explanations, and I perceive that if we do not get along, they will fall upon us now.'

I glance back to discover the landlord and a gracefully robed woman standing outside the pretty simplicity of the Utopian inn, watching us doubtfully as we recede.

'Come on,' I insist.

§ 8

We should go towards the Schoellenen gorge, and as we went, our fresh morning senses would gather together a thousand factors for our impression of this more civilized world. A modern Utopia will have done with yapping about nationality, and so the ugly fortifications, the barracks and military defilements of the earthly vale of Urseren will be wanting. Instead there will be a great multitude of gracious little houses, clustering in college-like groups, no doubt about their common kitchens and halls, down and about the valley slopes. And there will be many more trees, and a great variety of trees – all the world will have been ransacked for winter conifers. Despite the height of the valley there will be a double avenue along the road. This high road with its tramway would turn with us to descend the gorge, and we should hesitate upon the adventure of boarding the train. But now we should have the memory of our landlord's curious eye upon us, and we should decide at last to defer the risk of explanations such an enterprise might precipitate.

We should go by the great road for a time, and note something of the difference between Utopian and terrestrial engineering.

The tramway, the train road, the culverts and bridges, the Urnerloch tunnel, into which the road plunges, will all be beautiful things.

There is nothing in machinery, there is nothing in embankments and railways and iron bridges and engineering devices to oblige them to be ugly. Ugliness is the measure of imperfection; a thing of human making is for the most part ugly in proportion to the poverty of its constructive thought, to the failure of its producer fully to grasp the purpose of its being. Everything to which men continue to give thought and attention, which they make and remake in the same direction, and with a continuing desire to do as well as they can, grows beautiful inevitably. Things made by mankind under modern conditions are ugly, primarily because our social organization is ugly, because we live in an atmosphere of snatch and uncertainty, and do everything in an underbred strenuous manner. This is the misfortune of machinery, and not its fault. Art, like some beautiful plant, lives on its atmosphere, and when the atmosphere is good it will grow everywhere, and when it is bad nowhere. If we smashed and buried every machine, every furnace, every factory in the world, and without any further change set ourselves to home industries, hand labour, spade husbandry, sheepfolding and pig minding, we should still do things in the same haste, and achieve nothing but dirtiness, inconvenience, bad air and another gaunt and gawky reflection of our intellectual and moral disorder. We should mend nothing.

But in Utopia a man who designs a tram road will be a cultivated man, an artist craftsman; he will strive, as a good writer or a painter strives, to achieve the simplicity of perfection. He will make his girders and rails and parts as gracious as that first engineer, Nature, has made the stems of her plants and the joints and gestures of her animals. To esteem him a sort of anti-artist, to count every man who makes things with his unaided thumbs an artist and every man who uses machinery as a brute, is merely a passing phase of human stupidity. This tram road beside us will be a triumph of design. The idea will be so unfamiliar to us that for a time it will not occur to us that it is a system of beautiful objects at all. We shall admire its ingenious adaptation to the need of a district that is buried half the year in snow, the hard bed below, curved and guttered to do its own clearing, the great arched sleeper masses, raising the rails a good two yards above the ground, the easy, simple standards and insulators. Then it will creep in upon our minds, 'But, by Jove! *This is designed!*'

Indeed the whole thing will be designed.

Later on, perhaps, we may find students in an art school working in competition to design an electric tram, students who know something of modern metallurgy and something of

electrical engineering, and we shall find people as keenly critical
of a signal box or an iron bridge as they are on earth of—!
Heavens! what *are* they critical about on earth?

The quality and condition of a dress tie!

We should make some unpatriotic comparisons with our
own planet, no doubt.

# 4

# THE VOICE OF NATURE

## § 1

Presently we recognize the fellow of the earthly Devil's Bridge, still intact as a footway, spanning the gorge; and old memories turn us off the road down the steep ruin of an ancient mule track towards it. It is our first reminder that Utopia too must have a history. We cross it and find the Reuss, for all that it has already lit and warmed and ventilated and cleaned several thousands of houses in the dale above, and for all that it drives those easy trams in the gallery overhead, is yet capable of as fine a cascade as ever it flung on earth. So we come to a rocky path, wild as one could wish, and descend, discoursing how good and fair an ordered world may be, but with a certain unformulated qualification in our minds about those thumbmarks we have left behind.

'Do you recall the Zermatt valley?' says my friend, 'and how on earth it reeks and stinks with smoke?'

'People make that an argument for obstructing change, instead of helping it forward!'

And here perforce an episode intrudes. We are invaded by a talkative person.

He overtakes us and begins talking forthwith in a fluty, but not unamiable, tenor. He is a great talker, this man, and a fairly respectable gesticulator, and to him it is we make our first ineffectual tentatives at explaining who indeed we are; but his flow of talk washes that all away again. He has a face of that rubicund, knobby type I have heard an indignant mineralogist speak of as botryoidal,[1] and about it waves a quantity of disorderly blond hair. He is dressed in leather doublet and knee breeches, and he wears over these a streaming woollen cloak of faded crimson that gives him a fine dramatic outline as he comes down towards us over the rocks. His feet, which are large and handsome but bright pink with the keen morning air, are bare except for sandals of leather. (It was the only time that we saw anyone in Utopia with bare feet.) He salutes us with a scroll-like waving of his stick, and falls in with our slower paces.

'Climbers, I presume?' he says, 'and you scorn these trams of theirs? I like you. So do I! Why a man should consent to be dealt with as a bale of goods holding an indistinctive ticket – when God gave him legs and a face – passes my understanding.'

As he speaks, his staff indicates the great mechanical road that runs across the gorge and high overhead through a gallery in the rock, follows it along until it turns the corner, picks it up as a viaduct far below, traces it until it plunges into an arcade through a jutting crag, and there dismisses it with a spiral whirl. '*No!*' he says.

He seems sent by Providence, for just now we had been discussing how we should broach our remarkable situation to these Utopians before our money is spent.

Our eyes meet, and I gather from the botanist that I am to open our case.

I do my best.

'You came from the other side of space!' says the man in the crimson cloak, interrupting me. 'Precisely! I like that – it's exactly my note! So do I! And you find this world strange! Exactly my case! We are brothers! We shall be in sympathy. I am amazed, I have been amazed as long as I can remember, and I shall die, most certainly, in a state of incredulous amazement at this remarkable world. Eh? . . . You found yourselves suddenly upon a mountain top! Fortunate men!' He chuckled. 'For my part I found myself in the still stranger position of infant to two parents of the most intractable dispositions!'

'The fact remains,' I protest.

'A position, I can assure you, demanding Tact of an altogether superhuman quality!'

We desist for a space from the attempt to explain our re-markable selves, and for the rest of the time this picturesque

and exceptional Utopian takes the talk entirely under his
control. . . .

§ 2

An agreeable person, though a little distracting, he was; and
he talked, we recall, of many things. He impressed us, we found
afterwards, as a poseur[2] beyond question, a conscious Ishmaelite[3]
in the world of wit, and in some subtly inexplicable way as a
most consummate ass. He talked first of the excellent and
commodious trams that came from over the passes, and ran
down the long valley towards middle Switzerland, and of all
the growth of pleasant homes and chalets amidst the heights
that made the opening gorge so different from its earthly
parallel, with a fine disrespect. 'But they are beautiful,' I protested. 'They are graciously proportioned, they are placed in
well-chosen positions; they give no offence to the eye.'

'What do we know of the beauty they replace? They are a
mere rash. Why should we men play the part of bacteria upon
the face of our Mother?'

'All life is that!'

'No! not natural life, not the plants and the gentle creatures
that live their wild shy lives in forest and jungle. That is a part
of her. That is the natural bloom of her complexion. But these
houses and tramways and things, all made from ore and stuff
torn from her veins—! You can't better my image of the rash.
It's a morbid breaking out! I'd give it all for one – what is it? –
free and natural chamois.'

'You live at times in a house?' I asked.

He ignored my question. For him, untroubled Nature was
the best, he said, and, with a glance at his feet, the most beautiful. He professed himself a Nazarite,[4] and shook back his Teutonic poet's shock of hair. So he came to himself; and for the
rest of our walk he kept to himself as the thread of his discourse,
and went over himself from top to toe, and strung thereon all
topics under the sun by way of illustrating his splendours. But
especially his foil was the relative folly, the unnaturalness and
want of logic in his fellow men. He held strong views about

the extreme simplicity of everything, only that men, in their muddle-headedness, had confounded it all. 'Hence, for example, these trams! They are always running up and down as though they were looking for the lost simplicity of nature. "We dropped it here!"' He earned a living, we gathered, 'some considerable way above the minimum wage', which threw a chance light on the labour problem – by perforating records for automatic musical machines – no doubt of the Pianotist and Pianola[5] kind – and he spent all the leisure he could gain in going to and fro lecturing on 'The Need of a Return to Nature', and on 'Simple Foods and Simple Ways'. He did it for the love of it. It was very clear to us he had an inordinate impulse to lecture, and esteemed us fair game. He had been lecturing on these topics in Italy, and he was now going back through the mountains to lecture in Saxony, lecturing on the way, to perforate a lot more records, lecturing the while, and so start out lecturing again. He was undisguisedly glad to have us to lecture to by the way.

He called our attention to his costume at an early stage. It was the embodiment of his ideal of Nature-clothing, and it had been made especially for him at very great cost. 'Simply because naturalness has fled the earth, and has to be sought now, and washed out from your crushed complexities like gold.'

'I should have thought,' said I, 'that any clothing whatever was something of a slight upon the natural man.'

'Not at all,' said he, 'not at all! You forget his natural vanity!'

He was particularly severe on our artificial hoofs, as he called our boots, and our hats or hair destructors. 'Man is the real King of Beasts and should wear a mane. The lion only wears it by consent and in captivity.' He tossed his head.

Subsequently while we lunched and he waited for the specific natural dishes he ordered – they taxed the culinary resources of the inn to the utmost – he broached a comprehensive generalization. 'The animal kingdom and the vegetable kingdom are easily distinguished, and for the life of me I see no reason for confusing them. It is, I hold, a sin against Nature. I keep them distinct in my mind and I keep them distinct in my person. No animal substance inside, no vegetable without; – what could be simpler or more logical? Nothing upon me but leather and all-wool garments; within, cereals, fruit, nuts, herbs and the like. Classification – order – man's function. He is here to observe and accentuate Nature's simplicity. These people' – he swept an arm that tried not too personally to include us – 'are filled and covered with confusion.'

He ate great quantities of grapes and finished with a cigarette. He demanded and drank a great horn of unfermented grape juice, and it seemed to suit him well.

We three sat about the board – it was in an agreeable little arbour on a hill hard by the place where Wassen stands on earth, and it looked down the valley to the Uri Rothstock, and ever and again we sought to turn his undeniable gift of exposition to the elucidation of our own difficulties.

But we seemed to get little, his style was so elusive. Afterwards, indeed, we found much information and many persuasions had soaked into us, but at the time it seemed to us he told us nothing. He indicated things by dots and dashes, instead of by good hard assertive lines. He would not pause to see how little we knew. Sometimes his wit rose so high that he would lose sight of it himself, and then he would pause, purse his lips as if he whistled, and then till the bird came back to the lure, fill his void mouth with grapes. He talked of the relations of the sexes, and love – a passion he held in great contempt as being in its essence complex and disingenuous – and afterwards we found we had learned much of what the marriage laws of Utopia allow and forbid.

'A simple natural freedom,' he said, waving a grape in an illustrative manner, and so we gathered the modern Utopia did not at any rate go to that. He spoke, too, of the regulation of unions, of people who were not allowed to have children, of complicated rules and interventions. 'Man,' he said, 'had ceased to be a natural product!'

We tried to check him with questions at this most illuminating point, but he drove on like a torrent, and carried his topic out of sight. The world, he held, was overmanaged, and that was the root of all evil. He talked of the overmanagement of the world, and among other things of the laws that would not let a poor simple idiot, a 'natural', go at large. And so we had our first glimpse of what Utopia did with the feeble and insane. 'We make all these distinctions between man and man, we exalt this and favour that, and degrade and seclude that; we make birth artificial, life artificial, death artificial.'

'You say *We*,' said I, with the first glimmering of a new idea, 'but *you* don't participate?'

'Not I! I'm not one of your samurai,[6] your voluntary noblemen who have taken the world in hand. I might be, of course, but I'm not.'

'Samurai!' I repeated, 'voluntary noblemen!' and for the moment could not frame a question.

He whirled on to an attack on science, that stirred the botanist to controversy. He denounced with great bitterness all specialists whatever, and particularly doctors and engineers.

'Voluntary noblemen!' he said, 'voluntary Gods I fancy they think themselves,' and I was left behind for a space in the perplexed examination of this parenthesis, while he and the botanist – who is sedulous to keep his digestion up to date with all the newest devices – argued about the good of medicine men.

'The natural human constitution,' said the blond-haired man, 'is perfectly simple, with one simple condition – you must leave it to Nature. But if you mix up things so distinctly and essentially separated as the animal and vegetable kingdoms for example, and ram *that* in for it to digest, what can you expect?

'Ill health! There isn't such a thing – in the course of Nature. But you shelter from Nature in houses, you protect yourselves by clothes that are useful instead of being ornamental, you wash – with such abstersive chemicals as soap for example – and above all you consult doctors.' He approved himself with a chuckle. 'Have you ever found anyone seriously ill without doctors and medicine about? Never! You say a lot of people would die without shelter and medical attendance! No doubt – but a natural death. A natural death is better than an artificial life, surely? That's – to be frank with you – the very citadel of my position.'

That led him, and rather promptly, before the botanist could rally to reply, to a great tirade against the laws that forbade 'sleeping out'. He denounced them with great vigour; and alleged that for his own part he broke that law whenever he could, found some corner of moss, shaded from an excess of dew, and there sat up to sleep. He slept, he said, always in a sitting position, with his head on his wrists and his wrists on his knees – the simple natural position for sleep in man. . . . He said it would be far better if all the world slept out, and all the houses were pulled down.

You will understand, perhaps, the subdued irritation I felt as I sat and listened to the botanist entangling himself in the logical net of this wild nonsense. It impressed me as being irrelevant. When one comes to a Utopia one expects a Cicerone,[7] one expects a person as precise and insistent and instructive as an American advertisement – the advertisement of one of those land agents, for example, who print their own engaging photographs to instil confidence and begin, 'You want to buy real estate.' One expects to find all Utopians absolutely convinced of the perfection of their Utopia, and incapable of receiving a hint against its order. And here was this purveyor of absurdities!

And yet now that I come to think it over, is not this too one of the necessary differences between a modern Utopia and those finite compact settlements of the older school of dreamers? It is not to be a unanimous world any more, it is to have all and more of the mental contrariety we find in the world of the real; it is no longer to be perfectly explicable, it is just our own vast mysterious welter, with some of the blackest shadows gone, with a clearer illumination, and a more conscious and intelligent will. Irrelevance is not irrelevant to such a scheme, and our blond-haired friend is exactly just where he ought to be here.

Still—

§ 3

I ceased to listen to the argumentation of my botanist with this apostle of Nature. The botanist, in his scientific way, was, I believe, defending the learned professions. (He thinks and argues like drawing on squared paper.) It struck me as transiently remarkable that a man who could not be induced to forget himself and his personal troubles on coming into a whole new world, who could waste our first evening in Utopia upon a paltry egotistical love story, should presently become quite heated and impersonal in the discussion of scientific professionalism. He was – absorbed. I can't attempt to explain these vivid spots and blind spots in the imaginations of sane men; there they are!

'You say,' said the botanist, with a prevalent index finger, and the resolute deliberation of a big siege gun being lugged into action over rough ground by a number of inexperienced men, 'you prefer a natural death to an artificial life. But what is your *definition* (stress) of artificial? . . .'

And after lunch too! I ceased to listen, flicked the end of my cigarette ash over the green trellis of the arbour, stretched my legs with a fine restfulness, leant back, and gave my mind to the fields and houses that lay adown the valley.

What I saw interwove with fragmentary things our garrulous friend had said, and with the trend of my own speculations. . . .

The high road, with its tramways and its avenues on either side, ran in a bold curve, and with one great loop of descent, down the opposite side of the valley, and below crossed again on a beautiful viaduct and dipped into an arcade in the side of the Bristenstock. Our inn stood out boldly, high above the level this took. The houses clustered in their collegiate groups over by the high road, and near the subordinate way that ran almost vertically below us and past us and up towards the valley of the Meien Reuss. There were one or two Utopians cutting and packing the flowery mountain grass in the carefully levelled and irrigated meadows by means of swift, light machines that ran on things like feet and seemed to devour the herbage, and there were many children and a woman or so, going to and fro among the houses near at hand. I guessed a central building towards the high road must be the school from which these children were coming. I noted the health and cleanliness of these young heirs of Utopia as they passed below.

The pervading quality of the whole scene was a sane order, the deliberate solution of problems, a progressive intention steadily achieving itself; and the aspect that particularly occupied me was the incongruity of this with our blond-haired friend.

On the one hand here was a state of affairs that implied a power of will, an organizing and controlling force, the co-operation of a great number of vigorous people to establish and sustain its progress; and on the other this creature of pose and vanity, with his restless wit, his perpetual giggle at his own cleverness, his manifest incapacity for comprehensive co-operation.

Now, had I come upon a hopeless incompatibility? Was this the *reductio ad absurdum*[8] of my vision, and must it even as I sat there fade, dissolve and vanish before my eyes?

There was no denying our blond friend. If this Utopia is indeed to parallel our earth, man for man – and I see no other reasonable choice to that – there must be this sort of person and kindred sorts of persons in great abundance. The desire and gift to see life whole is not the lot of the great majority of men, the service of truth is the privilege of the elect, and these clever fools who choke the avenues of the world of thought, who stick at no inconsistency, who oppose, obstruct, confuse, will find only the freer scope amidst Utopian freedoms.

They argued on, these two, as I worried my brains with riddles. It was like a fight between a cock sparrow and a tortoise; they both went on in their own way, regardless of each other's proceedings. The encounter had an air of being extremely lively, and the moments of contact were few. 'But you mistake my point,' the blond man was saying, disordering his hair – which had become unruffled in the preoccupation of dispute – with a hasty movement of his hand, 'you don't appreciate the position I take up.'

'Ugh!' said I privately, and lighted another cigarette and went away into my own thoughts with that.

The position he takes up! That's the way of your intellectual fool, the Universe over. He takes up a position, and he's going to be the most brilliant, delightful, engaging and invincible of gay delicious creatures defending that position you can possibly imagine. And even when the case is not so bad as that, there still remains the quality. We 'take up our positions', silly little

contentious creatures that we are, we will not see the right in
one another, we will not patiently state and restate, and honestly accommodate and plan, and so we remain at sixes and
sevens. We've all a touch of Gladstone[9] in us, and try to the
last moment to deny we have made a turn. And so our poor
broken-springed world jolts athwart its trackless destiny. Try to
win into line with some fellow weakling, and see the little host of
suspicions, aggressions, misrepresentations, your approach will
stir – like summer flies on a high road – the way he will try to
score a point and claim you as a convert to what he has always
said, his fear lest the point should be scored to you.

It is not only such gross and palpable cases as our blond and
tenoring friend. I could find the thing negligible were it only
that. But when one sees the same thread woven into men who
are leaders, men who sway vast multitudes, who are indeed
great and powerful men; when one sees how unfair they can
be, how unteachable, the great blind areas in their eyes also,
their want of generosity, then one's doubts gather like mists
across this Utopian valley, its vistas pale, its people become
unsubstantial phantoms, all its order and its happiness dim and
recede. . . .

If we are to have any Utopia at all, we must have a clear
common purpose, and a great and steadfast movement of will to
override all these incurably egotistical dissentients. Something is
needed wide and deep enough to float the worst of egotisms
away. The world is not to be made right by acclamation and in
a day, and then for ever more trusted to run alone. It is manifest
this Utopia could not come about by chance and anarchy, but
by co-ordinated effort and a community of design, and to
tell of just land laws and wise government, a wisely balanced
economic system, and wise social arrangements without telling
how they were brought about, and how they are sustained
against the vanity and self-indulgence, the moody fluctuations
and uncertain imaginations, the heat and aptitude for partisan-
ship that lurk, even when they do not flourish, in the texture of
every man alive, is to build a palace without either door or
staircase.

I had not this in mind when I began.

Somewhere in the Modern Utopia there must be adequate men, men the very antithesis of our friend, capable of self-devotion, of intentional courage, of honest thought and steady endeavour. There must be a literature to embody their common idea, of which this Modern Utopia is merely the material form; there must be some organization, however slight, to keep them in touch one with the other.

Who will these men be? Will they be a caste? a race? an organization in the nature of a church? . . . And there came into my mind the words of our acquaintance, that he was not one of these 'voluntary noblemen'.

At first that phrase struck me as being merely queer, and then I began to realize certain possibilities that were wrapped up in it.

The animus of our chance friend, at any rate, went to suggest that here was his antithesis. Evidently what he is not, will be the class to contain what is needed here. Evidently.

## § 4

I was recalled from my meditations by the hand of the blond-haired man upon my arm.

I looked up to discover the botanist had gone into the inn.

The blond-haired man was for a moment almost stripped of pose.

'I say,' he said. 'Weren't you listening to me?'

'No,' I said bluntly.

His surprise was manifest. But by an effort he recalled what he had meant to say.

'Your friend,' he said, 'has been telling me, in spite of my sustained interruptions, a most incredible story.'

I wondered how the botanist managed to get it in. 'About that woman?' I said.

'About a man and a woman who hate each other and can't get away from each other.'

'I know,' I said.

'It sounds absurd.'

'It is.'

'Why can't they get away? What is there to keep them together? It's ridiculous. I—'

'Quite.'

'He *would* tell it to me.'

'It's his way.'

'He interrupted me. And there's no point in it. Is he—' he hesitated, 'mad?'

'There's a whole world of people mad with him,' I answered after a pause.

The perplexed expression of the blond-haired man intensified. It is vain to deny that he enlarged the scope of his inquiry, visibly if not verbally. 'Dear me!' he said, and took up something he had nearly forgotten. 'And you found yourselves suddenly on a mountainside? . . . I thought you were joking.'

I turned round upon him with a sudden access of earnestness. At least I meant my manner to be earnest, but to him it may have seemed wild.

'You,' I said, 'are an original sort of man. Do not be alarmed. Perhaps you will understand. . . . We were not joking.'

'But, my dear fellow!'

'I mean it! We come from an inferior world! Like this, but out of order.'

'No world could be more out of order—'

'You play at that and have your fun. But there's no limit to the extent to which a world of men may get out of gear. In our world—'

He nodded, but his eye had ceased to be friendly.

'Men die of starvation; people die by the hundred thousand needlessly and painfully; men and women are lashed together to make hell for each other; children are born – abominably, and reared in cruelty and folly; there is a thing called war, a horror of blood and vileness. The whole thing seems to me at times a cruel and wasteful wilderness of muddle. You in this decent world have no means of understanding—'

'No?' he said, and would have begun, but I went on too quickly.

'No! When I see you dandering through this excellent and hopeful world, objecting, obstructing and breaking the law, displaying your wit on science and order, on the men who toil so ingloriously to swell and use the knowledge that is salvation, this salvation for which *our* poor world cries to heaven—'

'You don't mean to say,' he said, 'that you really come from some other world where things are different and worse?'

'I do.'

'And you want to talk to me about it instead of listening to me?'

'Yes.'

'Oh, nonsense!' he said abruptly. 'You can't do it – really. I can assure you this present world touches the nadir of imbecility. You and your friend, with his love for the lady who's so mysteriously tied – you're romancing! People could not possibly do such things. It's – if you'll excuse me – ridiculous. *He* began – he would begin. A most tiresome story – simply bore me down. We'd been talking very agreeably before that, or rather *I* had, about the absurdity of marriage laws, the interference with a free and natural life, and so on, and suddenly he burst like a dam. No!' He paused. 'It's really impossible. You behave perfectly well for a time, and then you begin to interrupt. . . . And such a childish story, too!'

He spun round upon his chair, got up, glanced at me over his shoulder, and walked out of the arbour. He stepped aside hastily to avoid too close an approach to the returning botanist. 'Impossible,' I heard him say. He was evidently deeply aggrieved by us. I saw him presently a little way off in the garden, talking to the landlord of our inn, and looking towards us as he talked – they both looked towards us – and after that, without the ceremony of a farewell, he disappeared, and we saw him no more. We waited for him a little while, and then I expounded the situation to the botanist. . . .

'We are going to have a very considerable amount of trouble explaining ourselves,' I said in conclusion. 'We are here by an act of the imagination, and that is just one of those metaphysical operations that are so difficult to make credible. We are, by the standard of bearing and clothing I remark about us, unattractive in dress and deportment. We have nothing to produce to explain our presence here, no bit of a flying-machine or a space-travelling sphere or any of the apparatus customary on these occasions. We have no means beyond a dwindling amount of small change out of a gold coin, upon which I suppose in ethics and the law some native Utopian had a better claim. We may already have got ourselves into trouble with the authorities with that confounded number of yours!'

'You did one too!'

'All the more bother, perhaps, when the thing is brought home to us. There's no need for recriminations. The thing of moment is that we find ourselves in the position – not to put too fine a point upon it – of tramps in this admirable world. The question of all others of importance to us at present is what do they do with their tramps? Because sooner or later, and the balance of probability seems to incline to sooner, whatever they do with their tramps that they will do with us.'

'Unless we can get some work.'

'Exactly – unless we can get some work.'

'Get work!'

The botanist leant forward on his arms and looked out of the arbour with an expression of despondent discovery. 'I say,' he remarked; 'this is a strange world – quite strange and new. I'm only beginning to realize just what it means for us. The mountains there are the same, the old Bristenstock and all the rest of it; but these houses, you know, and that roadway, and the costumes, and that machine that is licking up the grass there – only. . . .'

He sought expression. 'Who knows what will come in sight round the bend of the valley there? Who knows what may happen to us anywhere? We don't know who rules over us even . . . we don't know that!'

'No,' I echoed, 'we don't know *that*.'

# 5
# FAILURE IN A MODERN UTOPIA

The old Utopias – save for the breeding schemes of Plato and Campanella – ignored that reproductive competition among individualities which is the substance of life, and dealt essentially with its incidentals. The endless variety of men, their endless gradation of quality, over which the hand of selection plays, and to which we owe the unmanageable complication of real life, is tacitly set aside. The real world is a vast disorder of accidents and incalculable forces in which men survive or fail. A modern Utopia, unlike its predecessors, dare not pretend to change the last condition; it may order and humanize the conflict, but men must still survive or fail.

Most Utopias present themselves as going concerns, as happiness in being; they make it an essential condition that a happy land can have no history, and all the citizens one is permitted to see are well looking and upright and mentally and morally in tune. But we are under the dominion of a logic that obliges us to take over the actual population of the world with only such moral and mental and physical improvements as lie within their inherent possibilities, and it is our business to ask what Utopia will do with its congenital invalids, its idiots and madmen, its drunkards and men of vicious mind, its cruel and furtive souls, its stupid people, too stupid to be of use to the community, its lumpish, unteachable and unimaginative people? And what will it do with the man who is 'poor' all round, the rather spiritless, rather incompetent low-grade man who on earth sits in the den of the sweater,[1] tramps the streets under the banner of the unemployed, or trembles – in another

man's cast-off clothing, and with an infinity of hat-touching –
on the verge of rural employment?

These people will have to be in the descendent phase, the
species must be engaged in eliminating them; there is no escape
from that, and conversely the people of exceptional quality
must be ascendant. The better sort of people, so far as they can
be distinguished, must have the fullest freedom of public service,
and the fullest opportunity of parentage. And it must be open
to every man to approve himself worthy of ascendency.

The way of Nature in this process is to kill the weaker and
the sillier, to crush them, to starve them, to overwhelm them,
using the stronger and more cunning as her weapon. But man
is the unnatural animal, the rebel child of Nature, and more
and more does he turn himself against the harsh and fitful
hand that reared him. He sees with a growing resentment the
multitude of suffering ineffectual lives over which his species
tramples in its ascent. In the Modern Utopia he will have set
himself to change the ancient law. No longer will it be that
failures must suffer and perish lest their breed increase, but the
breed of failure must not increase, lest they suffer and perish,
and the race with them.

Now we need not argue here to prove that the resources of
the world and the energy of mankind, were they organized
sanely, are amply sufficient to supply every material need of
every living human being. And if it can be so contrived that
every human being shall live in a state of reasonable physical
and mental comfort, without the reproduction of inferior types,
there is no reason whatever why that should not be secured.
But there must be a competition in life of some sort to determine
who are to be pushed to the edge, and who are to prevail
and multiply. Whatever we do, man will remain a competitive
creature, and though moral and intellectual training may vary
and enlarge his conception of success and fortify him with
refinements and consolations, no Utopia will ever save him
completely from the emotional drama of struggle, from exul-
tations and humiliations, from pride and prostration and
shame. He lives in success and failure just as inevitably as he
lives in space and time.

But we may do much to make the margin of failure endurable. On earth, for all the extravagance of charity, the struggle for the mass of men at the bottom resolves itself into a struggle, and often a very foul and ugly struggle, for food, shelter and clothing. Deaths outright from exposure and starvation are now perhaps uncommon, but for the multitude there are only miserable houses, uncomfortable clothes, and bad and insufficient food; fractional starvation and exposure, that is to say. A Utopia planned upon modern lines will certainly have put an end to that. It will insist upon every citizen being properly housed, well nourished, and in good health, reasonably clean and clothed healthily, and upon that insistence its labour laws will be founded. In a phrasing that will be familiar to everyone interested in social reform, it will maintain a standard of life. Any house, unless it be a public monument, that does not come up to its rising standard of healthiness and convenience, the Utopian State will incontinently pull down, and pile the material and charge the owner for the labour; any house unduly crowded or dirty, it must in some effectual manner, directly or indirectly, confiscate and clear and clean. And any citizen indecently dressed, or ragged and dirty, or publicly unhealthy, or sleeping abroad homeless, or in any way neglected or derelict, must come under its care. It will find him work if he can and will work, it will take him to it, it will register him and lend him the money wherewith to lead a comely life until work can be found or made for him, and it will give him credit and shelter him and strengthen him if he is ill. In default of private enterprises it will provide inns for him and food, and it will – by itself acting as the reserve employer – maintain a minimum wage which will cover the cost of a decent life. The State will stand at the back of the economic struggle as the reserve employer of labour. This most excellent idea does, as a matter of fact, underlie the British institution of the workhouse, but it is jumbled up with the relief of old age and infirmity, it is administered parochially and on the supposition that all population is static and localized whereas every year it becomes more migratory; it is administered without any regard to the rising standards of comfort and self-respect in a progressive civilization, and it is administered grudgingly. The thing that is done is done as unwilling charity by administrators who are often, in the rural districts at least, competing for low-priced labour, and who regard want of employment as a crime. But if it were possible for any citizen in need of money to resort to a place of public employment as a right, and there work for a week or month without degradation upon certain minimum terms, it seems fairly certain that no one would work, except as the victim of some quite exceptional and temporary accident, for less.

The work publicly provided would have to be toilsome, but not cruel nor incapacitating. A choice of occupations would need to be afforded, occupations adapted to different types of training and capacity, with some residual employment of a purely laborious and mechanical sort for those who were incapable of doing the things that required intelligence. Necessarily this employment by the State would be a relief of economic pressure, but it would not be considered a charity done to the individual, but a public service. It need not pay, any more than the police need pay, but it could probably be done at a small margin of loss. There are many durable things bound finally to be useful that could be made and stored whenever the tide of more highly paid employment ebbed and labour sank to its minimum: bricks, iron from inferior ores, shaped and preserved timber, pins, nails, plain fabrics of cotton and linen, paper, sheet glass, artificial fuel and so on; new roads could be made and public buildings reconstructed, inconveniences of all sorts removed, until under the stimulus of accumulating material, accumulating investments or other circumstances, the tide of private enterprise flowed again.

The State would provide these things for its citizen as though it was his right to require them; he would receive as a shareholder in the common enterprise and not with any insult of charity. But on the other hand it will require that the citizen who renders the minimum of service for these concessions shall not become a parent until he is established in work at a rate above the minimum, and free of any debt he may have incurred. The State will never press for its debt, nor put a limit to its accumulation so long as a man or woman remains childless; it will not even grudge them temporary spells of good fortune when they may lift their earnings above the minimum wage. It will pension the age of everyone who cares to take a pension, and it will maintain special guest homes for the very old to which they may come as paying guests, spending their pensions there. By such obvious devices it will achieve the maximum elimination of its feeble and spiritless folk in every generation with the minimum of suffering and public disorder.

§ 2

But the mildly incompetent, the spiritless and dull, the poorer sort who are ill, do not exhaust our Utopian problem. There remain idiots and lunatics, there remain perverse and incompetent persons, there are people of weak character who become drunkards, drug takers, and the like. Then there are persons tainted with certain foul and transmissible diseases. All these people spoil the world for others. They may become parents, and with most of them there is manifestly nothing to be done but to seclude them from the great body of the population. You must resort to a kind of social surgery. You cannot have social freedom in your public ways, your children cannot speak to whom they will, your girls and gentlewomen cannot go abroad while some sorts of people go free. And there are violent people, and those who will not respect the property of others, thieves and cheats; they, too, so soon as their nature is confirmed, must pass out of the free life of our ordered world. So soon as there can be no doubt of the disease or baseness of the individual, so soon as the insanity or other disease is assured, or the crime repeated a third time, or the drunkenness or misdemeanour past its seventh occasion (let us say), so soon must he or she pass out of the common ways of men.

The dreadfulness of all such proposals as this lies in the possibility of their execution falling into the hands of hard, dull and cruel administrators. But in the case of a Utopia one assumes the best possible government, a government as merciful and deliberate as it is powerful and decisive. You must not too hastily imagine these things being done – as they would be done on earth at present – by a number of zealous half-educated people in a state of panic at a quite imaginary 'Rapid Multiplication of the Unfit'.

No doubt for first offenders, and for all offenders under five-and-twenty, the Modern Utopia will attempt cautionary and remedial treatment. There will be disciplinary schools and colleges for the young, fair and happy places, but with less confidence and more restraint than the schools and colleges of the ordinary world. In remote and solitary regions these enclosures will lie, they will be fenced in and forbidden to the common run of men, and there, remote from all temptation, the defective citizen will be schooled. There will be no masking of the lesson; 'which do you value most, the wide world of humanity, or this evil trend in you?' From that discipline at last the prisoners will return.

But the others; what would a saner world do with them?

Our world is still vindictive, but the all-reaching State of Utopia will have the strength that begets mercy. Quietly the outcast will go from among his fellow men. There will be no drumming of him out of the ranks, no tearing off of epaulettes, no smiting in the face. The thing must be just public enough to obviate secret tyrannies, and that is all.

There would be no killing, no lethal chambers. No doubt Utopia will kill all deformed and monstrous and evilly diseased births, but for the rest, the State will hold itself accountable for their being. There is no justice in Nature perhaps, but the idea of justice must be sacred in any good society. Lives that statesmanship has permitted, errors it has not foreseen and educated against, must not be punished by death. If the State does not keep faith, no one will keep faith. Crime and bad lives are the measure of a State's failure, all crime in the end is the crime of the community. Even for murder Utopia will not, I think, kill.

I doubt even if there will be jails. No men are quite wise enough, good enough and cheap enough to staff jails as a jail ought to be staffed. Perhaps islands will be chosen, islands lying apart from the highways of the sea, and to these the State will send its exiles, most of them thanking Heaven, no doubt, to be quit of a world of prigs. The State will, of course, secure itself against any children from these people, that is the primary object in their seclusion, and perhaps it may even be necessary to make these island prisons a system of island monasteries and island nunneries. Upon that I am not competent to speak, but if I may believe the literature of the subject – unhappily a not very well criticized literature – it is not necessary to enforce this separation.*

About such islands patrol boats will go, there will be no freedoms of boat building, and it may be necessary to have armed guards at the creeks and quays. Beyond that the State will give these segregated failures just as full a liberty as they can have. If it interferes any further it will be simply to police the islands against the organization of serious cruelty, to maintain the freedom of any of the detained who wish it to transfer themselves to other islands, and so to keep a check upon tyranny. The insane, of course, will demand care and control, but there is no reason why the islands of the hopeless drunkard, for example, should not each have a virtual autonomy, have at the most a Resident and a guard. I believe that a community of drunkards might be capable of organizing even its own bad habit to the pitch of tolerable existence. I do not see why such an island should not build and order for itself and manufacture and trade. 'Your ways are not our ways,' the World State will say; 'but here is freedom and a company of kindred souls. Elect your jolly rulers, brew if you will and distil; here are vine cuttings and barley fields; do as it pleases you to do. We will take care of the knives, but for the rest – deal yourselves with God!'

And you see the big convict steamship standing in to the Island of Incurable Cheats. The crew are respectfully at their quarters, ready to lend a hand overboard, but wide awake, and the captain is hospitably on the bridge to bid his guests goodbye and keep an eye on the movables. The new citizens for this particular Alsatia,[2] each no doubt with his personal belongings

* See, for example, Dr W. A. Chapple's *The Fertility of the Unfit*.[3]

securely packed and at hand, crowd the deck and study the nearing coast. Bright, keen faces would be there, and we, were we by any chance to find ourselves beside the captain, might recognize the double of this great earthly magnate or that, Petticoat Lane and Park Lane[4] cheek by jowl. The landing part of the jetty is clear of people, only a government man or so stands there to receive the boat and prevent a rush, but beyond the gates a number of engagingly smart-looking individuals loiter speculatively. One figures a remarkable building labelled Custom House, an interesting fiscal revival this population has made, and beyond, crowding up the hill, the painted walls of a number of comfortable inns clamour loudly. One or two inhabitants in reduced circumstances would act as hotel touts, there are several hotel omnibuses and a Bureau de Change, certainly a Bureau de Change. And a small house with a large board, aimed point-blank seaward, declares itself a Gratis Information Office, and next to it rises the graceful dome of a small Casino. Beyond, great hoardings proclaim the advantages of many island specialties, a hustling commerce, and the opening of a Public Lottery. There is a large cheap-looking barrack, the school of Commercial Science for gentlemen of inadequate training. . . .

Altogether a very go-ahead looking little port it would be, and though this disembarkation would have none of the flow of hilarious good fellowship that would throw a halo of genial noise about the Islands of Drink, it is doubtful if the new arrivals would feel anything very tragic in the moment. Here at last was scope for adventure after their hearts.

This sounds more fantastic than it is. But what else is there to do, unless you kill? You must seclude, but why should you torment? All modern prisons are places of torture by restraint, and the habitual criminal plays the part of a damaged mouse at the mercy of the cat of our law. He has his little painful run and back he comes again to a state more horrible even than destitution. There are no Alsatias left in the world. For my own part I can think of no crime, unless it is reckless begetting or the wilful transmission of contagious disease, for which the bleak terrors, the solitudes and ignominies of the modern prison do not seem outrageously cruel. If you want to go so far as that, then kill. Why, once you are rid of them, should you pester criminals to respect an uncongenial standard of conduct? Into such islands of exile as this a modern Utopia will have to purge itself. There is no alternative that I can contrive.

§ 3

Will a Utopian be free to be idle?

Work has to be done, every day humanity is sustained by its collective effort, and without a constant recurrence of effort in the single man as in the race as a whole, there is neither health nor happiness. The permanent idleness of a human being is not only burdensome to the world, but his own secure misery. But unprofitable occupation is also intended by idleness, and it may be considered whether that freedom also will be open to the Utopian. Conceivably it will, like privacy, locomotion, and almost all the freedoms of life, and on the same terms – if he possess the money to pay for it.

That last condition may produce a shock in minds accustomed to the proposition that money is the root of all evil, and to the idea that Utopia necessarily implies something rather oaken and hand-made and primitive in all these relations. Of course, money is not the root of any evil in the world; the root of all evil in the world, and the root of all good too, is the Will to Live, and money becomes harmful only when by bad laws and bad economic organization it is more easily attained by bad men than good. It is as reasonable to say food is the root of all disease, because so many people suffer from excessive and unwise eating. The sane economic ideal is to make the possession of money the clear indication of public service-ableness, and the more nearly that ideal is attained, the smaller is the justification of poverty and the less the hardship of being poor. In barbaric and disorderly countries it is almost honourable to be indigent and unquestionably virtuous to give to a beggar; and even in the more or less civilized societies of earth, so many children come into life hopelessly handicapped that austerity to the poor is regarded as the meanest of mean virtues.

But in Utopia everyone will have had an education and a certain minimum of nutrition and training; everyone will be insured against ill health and accidents; there will be the most efficient organization for balancing the pressure of employment and the presence of disengaged labour, and so to be moneyless will be clear evidence of unworthiness. In Utopia no one will dream of giving to a casual beggar, and no one will dream of begging.

There will need to be, in the place of the British casual wards, simple but comfortable inns with a low tariff – controlled to a certain extent no doubt, and even in some cases maintained, by the State. This tariff will have such a definite relation to the minimum permissible wage, that a man who has incurred no liabilities through marriage or the like relationship, will be able to live in comfort and decency upon that minimum wage, pay his small insurance premium against disease, death, disablement or ripening years, and have a margin for clothing and other personal expenses. But he will get neither shelter nor food, except at the price of his freedom, unless he can produce money.

But suppose a man without money in a district where employment is not to be found for him; suppose the amount of employment to have diminished in the district with such suddenness as to have stranded him there. Or suppose he has quarrelled with the only possible employer, or that he does not like his particular work. Then no doubt the Utopian State, which wants everyone to be just as happy as the future welfare of the race permits, will come to his assistance. One imagines him resorting to a neat and business-like post office, and stating his case to a civil and intelligent official. In any sane State the economic conditions of every quarter of the earth will be watched as constantly as its meteorological phases, and a daily map of the country within a radius of three or four hundred miles showing all the places where labour is needed will hang upon the post-office wall. To this his attention will be directed. The man out of work will decide to try his luck in this place or that; and the public servant, the official, will make a note of his name, verify his identity – the freedom of Utopia will not be incompatible with the universal registration of thumbmarks – and issue passes for travel and coupons for any necessary inn accommodation on his way to the chosen destination. There he will seek a new employer.

Such a free change of locality once or twice a year from a region of restricted employment to a region of labour shortage will be among the general privileges of the Utopian citizen.

But suppose that in no district in the world is there work within the capacity of this particular man?

Before we suppose that, we must take into consideration the general assumption one is permitted to make in all Utopian speculations. All Utopians will be reasonably well educated upon Utopian lines; there will be no illiterates unless they are unteachable imbeciles, no rule-of-thumb toilers as inadaptable as trained beasts. The Utopian worker will be as versatile as any well-educated man is on earth today, and no Trade Union will impose a limit to his activities. The world will be his Union. If the work he does best and likes best is not to be found, there is still the work he likes second best. Lacking his proper employment, he will turn to some kindred trade.

But even with that adaptability, it may be that sometimes he will not find work. Such a disproportion between the work to be done and the people to do it may arise as to present a surplus of labour everywhere. This disproportion may be due to two causes: to an increase of population without a corresponding increase of enterprises, or to a diminution of employment throughout the world due to the completion of great enterprises, to economies achieved, or to the operation of new and more efficient labour-saving appliances. Through either cause, a World State may find itself doing well except for an excess of citizens of mediocre and lower quality.

But the first cause may be anticipated by wise marriage laws. . . . The full discussion of these laws will come later, but here one may insist that Utopia will control the increase of its population. Without the determination and ability to limit that increase as well as to stimulate it whenever it is necessary, no Utopia is possible. That was clearly demonstrated by Malthus[5] for all time.

The second cause is not so easily anticipated, but then, though its immediate result in glutting the labour market is similar, its final consequences are entirely different from those of the first. The whole trend of a scientific mechanical civilization is continually to replace labour by machinery and to increase it in its effectiveness by organization; and so, quite independently of any increase in population, labour must either fall in value until it can compete against and check the cheapening process, or, if that is prevented as it will be in Utopia by a minimum wage, come out of employment. There is no apparent limit to this process. But a surplus of efficient labour at the minimum wage is exactly the condition that should stimulate new enterprises, and that in a State saturated with science and prolific in invention will stimulate new enterprises. An increasing surplus of available labour without an absolute increase of population, an increasing surplus of labour due to increasing economy and not to proliferation, and which, therefore, does not press on and disarrange the food supply, is surely the ideal condition for a progressive civilization. I am inclined to think that, since labour will be regarded as a delocalized and fluid force, it will be the World State and not the big municipalities ruling the force areas that will be the reserve employer of labour. Very probably it will be convenient for the State to hand over the surplus labour for municipal purposes, but that is another question. All over the world the labour exchanges will be reporting the fluctuating pressure of economic demand and transferring workers from this region of excess to that of scarcity; and whenever the excess is universal, the World State – failing an adequate development of private enterprise – will either reduce the working day and so absorb the excess, or set on foot some permanent special works of its own, paying the minimum wage and allowing them to progress just as slowly or just as rapidly as the ebb and flow of labour dictated. But with sane marriage and birth laws there is no reason to suppose such calls upon the resources and initiative of the world more than temporary and exceptional occasions.

# § 4

The existence of our blond bare-footed friend was evidence enough that in a modern Utopia a man will be free to be just as idle or uselessly busy as it pleases him, after he has earned the minimum wage. He must do that, of course, to pay for his keep, to pay his assurance tax against ill-health or old age, and any charge or debt paternity may have brought upon him. The World State of the modern Utopist is no state of moral compulsions. If, for example, under the restricted Utopian scheme of inheritance, a man inherited sufficient money to release him from the need to toil, he would be free to go where he pleased and do what he liked. A certain proportion of men at ease is good for the world; work as a moral obligation is the morality of slaves, and so long as no one is overworked there is no need to worry because some few are underworked. Utopia does not exist as a solace for envy. From leisure, in a good moral and intellectual atmosphere, come experiments, come philosophy and the new departures.

In any modern Utopia there must be many leisurely people. We are all too obsessed in the real world by the strenuous ideal, by the idea that the vehement incessant fool is the only righteous man. Nothing done in a hurry, nothing done under strain, is really well done. A State where all are working hard, where none go to and fro, easily and freely, loses touch with the purpose of freedom.

But inherited independence will be the rarest and least permanent of Utopian facts, for the most part that wider freedom will have to be earned, and the inducements to men and women to raise their personal value far above the minimum wage will be very great indeed. Thereby will come privacies, more space in which to live, liberty to go everywhere and do no end of things, the power and freedom to initiate interesting enterprises and assist and co-operate with interesting people, and indeed all the best things of life. The Modern Utopia will give a universal security indeed, and exercise the minimum of compulsions to toil, but it will offer some acutely desirable prizes. The aim of all these devices, the minimum wage, the standard of

life, provision for all the feeble and unemployed and so
forth, is not to rob life of incentives but to change their nature,
to make life not less energetic, but less panic-stricken and
violent and base, to shift the incidence of the struggle for existence from our lower to our higher emotions, so to anticipate
and neutralize the motives of the cowardly and bestial, that
the ambitious and energetic imagination which is man's finest
quality may become the incentive and determining factor in
survival.

§ 5

After we have paid for our lunch in the little inn that corres-
ponds to Wassen, the botanist and I would no doubt spend the
rest of the forenoon in the discussion of various aspects and
possibilities of Utopian labour laws. We should examine our
remaining change, copper coins of an appearance ornamental
rather than reassuring, and we should decide that after what
we had gathered from the man with the blond hair, it would,
on the whole, be advisable to come to the point with the labour
question forthwith. At last we should draw the deep breath of
resolution and arise and ask for the Public Office. We should
know by this time that the labour bureau sheltered with the
post office and other public services in one building.

The Public Office of Utopia would of course contain a few
surprises for two men from terrestrial England. You imagine us
entering, the botanist lagging a little behind me, and my first
attempts to be offhand and commonplace in a demand for
work.

The office is in charge of a quick-eyed little woman of six
and thirty perhaps, and she regards us with a certain keenness
of scrutiny.

'Where are your papers?' she asks.

I think for a moment of the documents in my pocket, my
passport chequered with visas and addressed in my commen-
dation and in the name of her late Majesty by *We, Robert
Arthur Talbot Gascoigne Cecil, Marquess of Salisbury, Earl of
Salisbury, Viscount Cranborne, Baron Cecil*[6] and so forth, to

all whom it may concern, my *Carte d'Identité* (useful on minor occasions) of the Touring Club de France, my green ticket to the Reading Room of the British Museum and my Lettre d'Indication from the London and County Bank. A foolish humour prompts me to unfold all these, hand them to her and take the consequences, but I resist.

'Lost,' I say, briefly.

'Both lost?' she asks, looking at my friend.

'Both,' I answer.

'How?'

I astonish myself by the readiness of my answer.

'I fell down a snow slope and they came out of my pocket.'

'And exactly the same thing happened to both of you?'

'No. He'd given me his to put with my own.' She raised her eyebrows. 'His pocket is defective,' I add, a little hastily.

Her manners are too Utopian for her to follow that up. She seems to reflect on procedure.

'What are your numbers?' she asks, abruptly.

A vision of that confounded visitors' book at the inn above comes into my mind. 'Let me *see*,' I say, and pat my forehead and reflect, refraining from the official eye before me. 'Let me *see*.'

'What is yours?' she asks the botanist.

'A. B.,' he says, slowly, 'little *a*, nine four seven, I *think* —'

'Don't you know?'

'Not exactly,' says the botanist, very agreeably. 'No.'

'Do you mean to say neither of you know your own numbers?' says the little post-mistress, with a rising note.

'Yes,' I say with an engaging smile and trying to keep up a good social tone. 'It's queer, isn't it? We've both forgotten.'

'You're joking,' she suggests.

'Well,' I temporize.

'I suppose you've got your thumbs?'

'The fact is —' I say and hesitate. 'We've got our thumbs, of course.'

'Then I shall have to send a thumbprint down to the office and get your number from that. But are you sure you haven't your papers or numbers? It's very queer.'

We admit rather sheepishly that it's queer, and question one another silently.

She turns thoughtfully for the thumbmarking slab, and as she does so, a man enters the office. At the sight of him she asks with a note of relief, 'What am I to do, sir, here?'

He looks from her to us gravely, and his eye lights to curiosity at our dress. 'What is the matter, madam?' he asks, in a courteous voice.

She explains.

So far the impression we have had of our Utopia is one of a quite unearthly sanity, of good management and comprehensive design in every material thing, and it has seemed to us a little incongruous that all the Utopians we have talked to, our host of last night, the post-mistress and our garrulous tramp, have been of the most commonplace type. But suddenly there looks out from this man's pose and regard a different quality, a quality altogether nearer that of the beautiful tramway and of the gracious order of the mountain houses. He is a well-built man of perhaps five and thirty, with the easy movement that comes with perfect physical condition, his face is clean shaven and shows the firm mouth of a disciplined man, and his grey eyes are clear and steady. His legs are clad in some woven stuff deep-red in colour, and over this he wears a white shirt fitting pretty closely, and with a woven purple hem. His general effect reminds me somehow of the Knights Templars.[7] On his head is a cap of thin leather and still thinner steel, and with the vestiges of ear-guards – rather like an attenuated version of the caps that were worn by Cromwell's Ironsides.[8]

He looks at us and we interpolate a word or so as she explains, and feel a good deal of embarrassment at the foolish position we have made for ourselves. I determine to cut my way out of this entanglement before it complicates itself further.

'The fact is—' I say.

'Yes?' he says, with a faint smile.

'We've perhaps been disingenuous. Our position is so entirely exceptional, so difficult to explain—'

'What have you been doing?'

'No,' I say with decision; 'it can't be explained like that.'

He looks down at his feet. 'Go on,' he says.

I try to give the thing a quiet, matter-of-fact air. 'You see,' I say, in the tone one adopts for really lucid explanations, 'we come from another world. Consequently, whatever thumbmark registration or numbering you have in this planet doesn't apply to us, and we don't know our numbers because we haven't got any. We are really, you know, explorers, strangers—'

'But what world do you mean?'

'It's a different planet – a long way away. Practically at an infinite distance.'

He looks up in my face with the patient expression of a man who listens to nonsense.

'I know it sounds impossible,' I say, 'but here is the simple fact – we *appear* in your world. We appeared suddenly upon the neck of Lucendro – the Piz Lucendro – yesterday afternoon, and I defy you to discover the faintest trace of us before that time. Down we marched into the St Gotthard road and here we are! That's our fact. And as for papers—! Where in your world have you seen papers like this?'

I produce my pocketbook, extract my passport and present it to him.

His expression has changed. He takes the document and examines it, turns it over, looks at me, and smiles that faint smile of his again.

'Have some more,' I say, and proffer the card of the T.C.F.

I follow up that blow with my green British Museum ticket, as tattered as a flag in a knight's chapel.

'You'll get found out,' he says, with my documents in his hand. 'You've got your thumbs. You'll be measured. They'll refer to the central registers, and there you'll be!'

'That's just it,' I say, 'we shan't be.'

He reflects. 'It's a queer sort of joke for you two men to play,' he decides, handing me back my documents.

'It's no joke at all,' I say, replacing them in my pocketbook.

The post-mistress intervenes. 'What would you advise me to do?'

'No money?' he asks.

'No.'

He makes some suggestions. 'Frankly,' he says, 'I think you
have escaped from some island. How you got so far as here
I can't imagine, or what you think you'll do. . . . But anyhow,
there's the stuff for your thumbs.'

He points to the thumbmarking apparatus and turns to
attend to his own business.

Presently we emerge from the office in a state between dis-
comfiture and amusement, each with a tramway ticket for
Lucerne in his hand and with sufficient money to pay our
expenses until the morrow. We are to go to Lucerne because
there there is a demand for comparatively unskilled labour in
carving wood, which seems to us a sort of work within our
range and a sort that will not compel our separation.

§ 6

The old Utopias are sessile organizations; the new must square
itself to the needs of a migratory population, to an endless
coming and going, to a people as fluid and tidal as the sea. It
does not enter into the scheme of earthly statesmanship, but
indeed all local establishments, all definitions of place, are even
now melting under our eyes. Presently all the world will be
awash with anonymous stranger men.

Now the simple laws of custom, the homely methods of
identification that served in the little communities of the past
when everyone knew everyone, fail in the face of this liquefac-
tion. If the modern Utopia is indeed to be a world of responsible
citizens, it must have devised some scheme by which every
person in the world can be promptly and certainly recognized,
and by which anyone missing can be traced and found.

This is by no means an impossible demand. The total population of the world is, on the most generous estimate, not more
than 1,500,000,000, and the effectual indexing of this number
of people, the record of their movement hither and thither, the
entry of various material facts such as marriage, parentage,
criminal convictions and the like, the entry of the newborn and
the elimination of the dead, colossal task though it would be,
is still not so great as to be immeasurably beyond comparison

with the work of the post offices in the world of today, or the cataloguing of such libraries as that of the British Museum, or such collections as that of the insects in Cromwell Road.[9] Such an index could be housed quite comfortably on one side of Northumberland Avenue,[10] for example. It is only a reasonable tribute to the distinctive lucidity of the French mind to suppose the central index housed in a vast series of buildings at or near Paris. The index would be classified primarily by some unchanging physical characteristic, such as we are told the thumbmark and fingermark afford, and to these would be added any other physical traits that were of material value. The classification of thumbmarks and of inalterable physical characteristics goes on steadily, and there is every reason for assuming it possible that each human being could be given a distinct formula, a number or 'scientific name', under which he or she could be docketed.* About the buildings in which this great main index would be gathered, would be a system of other indices with cross references to the main one, arranged under names, under professional qualifications, under diseases, crimes and the like.

These index cards might conceivably be transparent and so contrived as to give a photographic copy promptly whenever it was needed, and they could have an attachment into which would slip a ticket bearing the name of the locality in which the indidivual was last reported. A little army of attendants would be at work upon this index day and night. From sub-stations constantly engaged in checking back thumbmarks and numbers, an incessant stream of information would come, of births, of deaths, of arrivals at inns, of applications to post offices for letters, of tickets taken for long journeys, of criminal convictions, marriages, applications for public doles and the like. A filter of offices would sort the stream, and all day and all night for ever a swarm of clerks would go to and fro correcting this central register, and photographing copies of its entries for transmission to the subordinate local stations, in

* It is quite possible that the actual thumbmark may play only a small part in the work of identification, but it is an obvious convenience to our thread of story to assume that it is the one sufficient feature.

response to their inquiries. So the inventory of the State would watch its every man and the wide world write its history as the fabric of its destiny flowed on. At last, when the citizen died, would come the last entry of all, his age and the cause of his death and the date and place of his cremation, and his card would be taken out and passed on to the universal pedigree, to a place of greater quiet, to the ever-growing galleries of the records of the dead.

Such a record is inevitable if a modern Utopia is to be achieved.

Yet at this, too, our blond-haired friend would no doubt rebel. One of the many things to which some will make claim as a right, is that of going unrecognized and secret whither one will. But that, so far as one's fellow wayfarers were concerned, would still be possible. Only the State would share the secret of one's little concealment. To the eighteenth-century Liberal, to the old-fashioned nineteenth-century Liberal, that is to say to all professed Liberals, brought up to be against the Government on principle, this organized clairvoyance will be the most hateful of dreams. Perhaps, too, the Individualist would see it in that light. But these are only the mental habits acquired in an evil time. The old Liberalism assumed bad government, the more powerful the government the worse it was, just as it assumed the natural righteousness of the free individual. Darkness and secrecy were, indeed, the natural refuges of liberty when every government had in it the near possibility of tyranny, and the Englishman or American looked at the papers of a Russian or a German as one might look at the chains of a slave. But suppose we do not assume that government is necessarily bad, and the individual necessarily good – and the hypothesis upon which we are working practically abolishes either alternative – then we alter the case altogether. The government of a modern Utopia will be no perfection of intentions ignorantly ruling the world. . . .*

---

* In the typical modern State of our own world, with its population of many millions, and its extreme facility of movement, undistinguished men who adopt an alias can make themselves untraceable with the utmost ease. The temptation of the opportunities thus offered has developed a new type of criminality, the

Such is the eye of the State that is now slowly beginning to apprehend our existence as two queer and inexplicable particles disturbing the fine order of its field of vision, the eye that will presently be focusing itself upon us with a growing astonishment and interrogation. 'Who in the name of Galton[11] and Bertillon,'[12] one fancies Utopia exclaiming, 'are *you*?'

I perceive I shall cut a queer figure in that focus. I shall affect a certain spurious ease of carriage no doubt. 'The fact is,' I shall begin. . . .

§ 7

And now see how an initial hypothesis may pursue and overtake its maker. Our thumbmarks have been taken, they have travelled by pneumatic tube to the central office of the municipality hard by Lucerne, and have gone on thence to the headquarters of the index at Paris. There, after a rough preliminary classification, I imagine them photographed on glass, and flung by means of a lantern in colossal images upon a screen, all finely squared, and the careful experts marking and measuring their several convolutions. And then off goes a brisk clerk to the long galleries of the index building.

I have told them they will find no sign of us, but you see him going from gallery to gallery, from bay to bay, from drawer to drawer, and from card to card. 'Here he is!' he mutters to himself, and he whips out a card and reads. 'But that is impossible!' he says. . . .

You figure us returning after a day or so of such Utopian experiences as I must presently describe, to the central office in Lucerne, even as we have been told to do.

---

Deeming or Crossman[13] type, base men who subsist and feed their heavy imaginations in the wooing, betrayal, ill-treatment and sometimes even the murder of undistinguished women. This is a large, a growing, and, what is gravest, a prolific class, fostered by the practical anonymity of the common man. It is only the murderers who attract much public attention, but the supply of low-class prostitutes is also largely due to these free adventures of the base. It is one of the by-products of State Liberalism, and at present it is very probably drawing ahead in the race against the development of police organization.

I make my way to the desk of the man who has dealt with us before. 'Well?' I say, cheerfully, 'have you heard?'

His expression dashes me a little. 'We've heard,' he says, and adds, 'it's very peculiar.'

'I told you you wouldn't find out about us,' I say, triumphantly.

'But we have,' he says; 'but that makes your freak none the less remarkable.'

'You've heard! You know who we are! Well – tell us! We had an idea, but we're beginning to doubt.'

'You,' says the official, addressing the botanist, 'are—!'

And he breathes his name. Then he turns to me and gives me mine.

For a moment I am dumbfounded. Then I think of the entries we made at the inn in the Urserenthal, and then in a flash I have the truth. I rap the desk smartly with my fingertips and shake my index finger in my friend's face.

'By Jove!' I say in English. 'They've got our doubles!'

The botanist snaps his fingers. 'Of course! I didn't think of that.'

'Do you mind,' I say to this official, 'telling us some more about ourselves?'

'I can't think why you keep it up,' he remarks, and then almost wearily tells me the facts about my Utopian self. They are a little difficult to understand. He says I am one of the samurai, which sounds Japanese, 'but you will be degraded,' he says, with a gesture almost of despair. He describes my position in this world in phrases that convey very little.

'The queer thing,' he remarks, 'is that you were in Norway only three days ago.'

'I am there still. At least – I'm sorry to be so much trouble to you, but do you mind following up that last clue and inquiring if the person to whom the thumbmark really belongs isn't in Norway still?'

The idea needs explanation. He says something incomprehensible about a pilgrimage. 'Sooner or later,' I say, 'you will have to believe there are two of us with the same thumbmark. I won't trouble you with any apparent nonsense about other planets and so forth again. Here I am. If I was in Norway a few days ago, you ought to be able to trace my journey hither. And my friend?'

'He was in India.' The official is beginning to look perplexed.

'It seems to me,' I say, 'that the difficulties in this case are only just beginning. How did I get from Norway hither? Does my friend look like hopping from India to the St Gotthard at one hop? The situation is a little more difficult than that—'

'But here!' says the official, and waves what are no doubt photographic copies of the index cards.

'But we are not those individuals!'

'You *are* those individuals.'

'You will see,' I say.

He dabs his finger argumentatively upon the thumbmarks. 'I see now,' he says.

'There is a mistake,' I maintain, 'an unprecedented mistake. There's the difficulty. If you inquire you will find it begin to unravel. What reason is there for us to remain casual work-men here, when you allege we are men of position in the world, if there isn't something wrong? We shall stick to this wood-carving work you have found us here, and meanwhile I think you ought to inquire again. That's how the thing shapes to me.'

'Your case will certainly have to be considered further,' he says, with the faintest of threatening notes in his tone. 'But at the same time' – hand out to those copies from the index again – 'there you are, you know!'

§ 8

When my botanist and I have talked over and exhausted every possibility of our immediate position, we should turn, I think, to more general questions.

I should tell him the thing that was becoming more and more apparent in my own mind. Here, I should say, is a world, obviously on the face of it well organized. Compared with our world, it is like a well-oiled engine beside a scrap heap. It has even got this confounded visual organ swivelling about in the most alert and lively fashion. But that's by the way. . . . You have only to look at all these houses below. (We should be sitting on a seat on the Gütsch and looking down on the Lucerne of Utopia, a Lucerne that would, I insist quite arbitrarily, still keep the Wasserthurm and the Kapellbrücke.) You have only to mark the beauty, the simple cleanliness and balance of this world, you have only to see the free carriage, the unaffected graciousness of even the common people, to understand how fine and complete the arrangements of this world must be. How are they made so? We of the twentieth century are not going to accept the sweetish, faintly nasty slops of Rousseauism[14] that so gratified our great-great-grandparents in the eighteenth. We know that order and justice do not come by Nature – 'if only the policeman would go away'. These things mean intention, will, carried to a scale that our poor vacillating, hot and cold earth has never known. What I am really seeing more and more clearly is the will beneath this visible Utopia. Convenient houses, admirable engineering that is no offence amidst natural beauties, beautiful bodies and a universally gracious carriage, these are only the outward and visible signs of an inward and spiritual grace. Such an order means discipline. It means triumph over the petty egotisms and vanities that keep men on our earth apart; it means devotion and a nobler hope; it cannot exist without a gigantic process of inquiry, trial, forethought and patience in an atmosphere of mutual trust and concession. Such a world as this Utopia is not made by the chance occasional co-operations of self-indulgent men, by autocratic rulers or by the bawling wisdom of the democratic leader. And an unrestricted competition for gain, an enlightened selfishness, that too fails us. . . .

I have compared the system of indexing humanity we have come upon to an eye, an eye so sensitive and alert that two strangers cannot appear anywhere upon the planet without discovery. Now an eye does not see without a brain, an eye does not turn round and look without a will and purpose. A Utopia that deals only with appliances and arrangements is a dream of superficialities; the essential problem here, the body within these garments, is a moral and an intellectual problem.

Behind all this material order, these perfected communications, perfected public services and economic organizations, there must be men and women willing these things. There must be a considerable number and a succession of these men and women of will. No single person, no transitory group of people, could order and sustain this vast complexity. They must have a collective if not a common width of aim, and that involves a spoken or written literature, a living literature to sustain the harmony of their general activity. In some way they must have put the more immediate objects of desire into a secondary place, and that means renunciation. They must be effectual in action and persistent in will, and that means discipline. But in the modern world in which progress advances without limits, it will be evident that whatever common creed or formula they have must be of the simplest sort; that whatever organization they have must be as mobile and flexible as a thing alive. All this follows inevitably from the general propositions of our Utopian dream. When we made those, we bound ourselves helplessly to come to this. . . .

The botanist would nod an abstracted assent.

I should cease to talk. I should direct my mind to the confused mass of memories three days in Utopia will have given us. Besides the personalities with whom we have come into actual contact, our various hosts, our foreman and work-fellows, the blond man, the public officials and so on, there will be a great multitude of other impressions. There will be many bright snapshots of little children, for example, of girls and women and men, seen in shops and offices and streets, on quays, at windows and by the wayside, people riding hither and thither and walking to and fro. A very human crowd it has seemed to me. But among them were there any who might be thought of as having a wider interest than the others, who seemed in any way detached from the rest by a purpose that passed beyond the seen?

Then suddenly I recall that clean-shaven man who talked with us for a little while in the public office at Wassen, the man who reminded me of my boyish conception of a Knight Templar, and with him come momentary impressions of other lithe and serious-looking people dressed after the same manner, words and phrases we have read in such scraps of Utopian reading as have come our way, and expressions that fell from the loose mouth of the man with the blond hair. . . .

# 6

# WOMEN IN A MODERN UTOPIA

But though I have come to a point where the problem of a Utopia has resolved itself very simply into the problem of government and direction, I find I have not brought the botanist with me. Frankly he cannot think so steadily onward as I can. I feel to think, he thinks to feel. It is I and my kind that have the wider range, because we can be impersonal as well as personal. We can escape ourselves. In general terms, at least, I understand him, but he does not understand me in any way at all. He thinks me an incomprehensible brute because his obsession is merely one of my incidental interests, and wherever my reasoning ceases to be explicit and full, the slightest ellipsis, the most transitory digression, he evades me and is back at himself again. He may have a personal liking for me, though I doubt it, but also he hates me pretty distinctly, because of this bias he cannot understand. My philosophical insistence that things shall be reasonable and hang together, that what can be explained shall be explained, and that what can be done by calculation and certain methods shall not be left to chance, he loathes. He just wants adventurously to feel. He wants to feel the sunset, and he thinks that on the whole he would feel it better if he had not been taught the sun was about ninety-two million miles away. He wants to feel free and strong, and he would rather feel so than be so. He does not want to accomplish great things, but to have dazzling things occur to him. He does not know that there are feelings also up in the clear air of the philosophic mountains, in the long ascents of effort and design. He does not know that thought itself is only a finer sort of feeling than his – good hock to the mixed gin, porter and treacle of his emotions, a perception of similitudes and oppositions that carries even thrills. And naturally he broods on the source of all his most copious feelings and emotions, women, and particularly upon the woman who has most made him feel. He forces me also to that.

Our position is unfortunate for me. Our return to the Utopian equivalent of Lucerne revives in him all the melancholy distresses that so preoccupied him when first we were transferred to this better planet. One day, while we are still waiting there for the public office to decide about us, he broaches the matter. It is early evening, and we are walking beside the lake after our simple dinner. 'About here,' he says, 'the quays would run and all those big hotels would be along here, looking out on the lake. It's so strange to have seen them so recently, and now not to see them at all. . . . Where have they gone?'

'Vanished by hypothesis.'

'What?'

'Oh! They're there still. It's we that have come hither.'

'Of course. I forgot. But still— You know, there was an avenue of trees along this quay with seats, and she was sitting looking out upon the lake. . . . I hadn't seen her for ten years.'

He looks about him still a little perplexed. 'Now we are here,' he says, 'it seems as though that meeting and the talk we had must have been a dream.'

He falls musing.

Presently he says: 'I knew her at once. I saw her in profile. But, you know, I didn't speak to her directly. I walked past her seat and on for a little way; trying to control myself. . . . Then I turned back and sat down beside her, very quietly. She looked up at me. Everything came back – everything. For a moment or so I felt I was going to cry. . . .'

That seems to give him a sort of satisfaction even in the reminiscence.

'We talked for a time just like casual acquaintances – about the view and the weather, and things like that.'

He muses again.

'In Utopia everything would have been different,' I say.

'I suppose it would.'

He goes on before I can say anything more.

'Then, you know, there was a pause. I had a sort of intuition that the moment was coming. So I think had she. You may scoff, of course, at these intuitions—'

I don't, as a matter of fact. Instead, I swear secretly. Always this sort of man keeps up the pretence of highly distinguished and remarkable mental processes, whereas – have not I, in my own composition, the whole diapason of emotional fool? Is not the suppression of these notes my perpetual effort, my undying despair? And then am I to be accused of poverty?

But to his story.

'She said, quite abruptly, "I am not happy," and I told her, "I knew that the instant I saw you." Then, you know, she began to talk to me very quietly, very frankly, about everything. It was only afterwards I began to feel just what it meant, her talking to me like that.'

I cannot listen to this!

'Don't you understand,' I cry, 'that we are in Utopia? She may be bound unhappily upon earth and you may be bound, but not here. Here I think it will be different. Here the laws that control all these things will be humane and just. So that all you said and did, over there, does not signify here – does not signify here!'

He looks up for a moment at my face, and then carelessly at my wonderful new world.

'Yes,' he says, without interest, with something of the tone of an abstracted elder speaking to a child, 'I dare say it will be all very fine here.' And he lapses, thwarted from his confidences, into musing.

There is something almost dignified in this withdrawal into himself. For a moment I entertain an illusion that really I am unworthy to hear the impalpable inconclusiveness of what he said to her and of what she said to him.

I am snubbed. I am also amazed to find myself snubbed. I become breathless with indignation. We walk along side by side, but now profoundly estranged.

I regard the façade of the Utopian public offices of Lucerne – I had meant to call his attention to some of the architectural features of these – with a changed eye, with all the spirit gone out of my vision. I wish I had never brought this introspective carcass, this mental ingrate, with me.

I incline to fatalistic submission. I suppose I had no power to leave him behind. . . . I wonder and I wonder. The old Utopists never had to encumber themselves with this sort of man.

§ 2

How would things be 'different' in the Modern Utopia? After all it is time we faced the riddle of the problems of marriage and motherhood. . . .

The Modern Utopia is not only to be a sound and happy World State, but it is to be one progressing from good to better. But as Malthus* demonstrated for all time, a State whose population continues to increase in obedience to unchecked instinct, can progress only from bad to worse. From the view of human comfort and happiness, the increase of population that occurs at each advance in human security is the greatest evil of life. The way of Nature is for every species to increase nearly to its possible maximum of numbers, and then to improve through the pressure of that maximum against its limiting conditions by the crushing and killing of all the feebler individuals. The way of Nature has also been the way of human-ity so far, and except when a temporary alleviation is obtained through an expansion of the general stock of sustenance by invention or discovery, the amount of starvation and of the physical misery of privation in the world must vary almost exactly with the excess of the actual birth rate over that required to sustain population at a number compatible with a universal contentment. Neither has Nature evolved, nor has man so far put into operation, any device by which paying this price of progress, this misery of a multitude of starved and unsuccessful lives, can be evaded. A mere indiscriminating restriction of the birth rate – an end practically attained in the homely, old-fashioned civilization of China by female infanticide –

* 'Essay on the Principles of Population'.[1]

involves not only the cessation of distresses but stagnation, and the minor good of a sort of comfort and social stability is won at too great a sacrifice. Progress depends essentially on competitive selection, and that we may not escape.

But it is a conceivable and possible thing that this margin of futile struggling, pain and discomfort and death might be reduced to nearly nothing without checking physical and mental evolution, with indeed an acceleration of physical and mental evolution, by preventing the birth of those who would in the unrestricted interplay of natural forces be born to suffer and fail. The method of Nature 'red in tooth and claw'[2] is to degrade, thwart, torture and kill the weakest and least adapted members of every species in existence in each generation, and so keep the specific average rising; the ideal of a scientific civilization is to prevent those weaklings being born. There is no other way of evading Nature's punishment of sorrow. The struggle for life among the beasts and uncivilized men means misery and death for the inferior individuals, misery and death in order that they may not increase and multiply; in the civilized State it is now clearly possible to make the conditions of life tolerable for every living creature, provided the inferiors can be prevented from increasing and multiplying. But this latter condition must be respected. Instead of competing to escape death and wretchedness, we may compete to give birth and we may heap every sort of consolation prize upon the losers in that competition. The modern State tends to qualify inheritance, to insist upon education and nurture for children, to come in more and more in the interests of the future between father and child. It is taking over the responsibility of the general welfare of the children more and more; and as it does so, its right to decide which children it will shelter becomes more and more reasonable.

How far will such conditions be prescribed? How far can they be prescribed in a modern Utopia?

Let us set aside at once all nonsense of the sort one hears in certain quarters about the human stud farm.* State breeding of

* See *Mankind in the Making*, chap. II.[3]

the population was a reasonable proposal for Plato to make, in view of the biological knowledge of his time and the purely tentative nature of his metaphysics; but from anyone in the days after Darwin, it is preposterous. Yet we have it given to us as the most brilliant of modern discoveries by a certain school of sociological writers, who seem totally unable to grasp the modification of meaning 'species' and 'individual' have undergone in the last fifty years. They do not seem capable of the suspicion that the boundaries of species have vanished, and that individuality now carries with it the quality of the unique! To them individuals are still defective copies of a Platonic ideal of the species, and the purpose of breeding no more than an approximation to that perfection. Individuality is indeed a negligible difference to them, an impertinence, and the whole flow of modern biological ideas has washed over them in vain.

But to the modern thinker individuality is the significant fact of life, and the idea of the State, which is necessarily concerned with the average and general, selecting individualities in order to pair them and improve the race, an absurdity. It is like fixing a crane on the plain in order to raise the hill tops. In the initiative of the individual above the average lies the reality of the future, which the State, presenting the average, may subserve but cannot control. And the natural centre of the emotional life, the cardinal will, the supreme and significant expression of individuality, should lie in the selection of a partner for procreation.

But compulsory pairing is one thing, and the maintenance of general limiting conditions is another, and one well within the scope of State activity. The State is justified in saying, before you may add children to the community for the community to educate and in part to support, you must be above a certain minimum of personal efficiency, and this you must show by holding a position of solvency and independence in the world; you must be above a certain age, and a certain minimum of physical development, and free of any transmissible disease. You must not be a criminal unless you have expiated your offence. Failing these simple qualifications, if you and some person conspire to add to the population of the State, we will, for the sake of humanity, take over the innocent victim of your passions, but we shall insist that you are under a debt to the State of a peculiarly urgent sort, and one you will certainly pay, even if it is necessary to use restraint to get the payment out of you: it is a debt that has in the last resort your liberty as a security, and, moreover, if this thing happens a second time, or if it is disease or imbecility you have multiplied, we will take an absolutely effectual guarantee that neither you nor your partner offend again in this matter.

'Harsh!' you say, and 'Poor Humanity!'

You have the gentler alternative to study in your terrestrial slums and asylums.

It may be urged that to permit conspicuously inferior people to have one or two children in this way would be to fail to attain the desired end, but indeed this is not so. A suitably qualified permission, as every statesman knows, may produce the social effects without producing the irksome pressure of an absolute prohibition. Amidst bright and comfortable circumstances, and with an easy and practicable alternative, people will exercise foresight and self-restraint to escape even the possibilities of hardship and discomfort; and free life in Utopia is to be well worth this trouble even for inferior people. The growing comfort, self-respect and intelligence of the English is shown, for example, in the fall in the proportion of illegitimate births from 2.2 per 1,000 in 1846–50 to 1.2 per 1,000 in 1890–1900, and this without any positive preventive laws whatever. This most desirable result is pretty certainly not the consequence of any great exaltation of our moral tone, but simply of a rising standard of comfort and a livelier sense of consequences and responsibilities. If so marked a change is possible in response to such progress as England has achieved in the past fifty years, if discreet restraint can be so effectual as this, it seems reasonable to suppose that in the ampler knowledge and the cleaner, franker atmosphere of our Utopian planet the birth of a child to diseased or inferior parents, and contrary to the sanctions of the State, will be the rarest of disasters.

And the death of a child, too, that most tragic event, Utopia will rarely know. Children are not born to die in childhood.

But in our world, at present, through the defects of our medical science and nursing methods, through defects in our organization, through poverty and carelessness, and through the birth of children that never ought to have been born, one out of every five children born dies within five years. It may be the reader has witnessed this most distressful of all human tragedies. It is sheer waste of suffering. There is no reason why ninety-nine out of every hundred children born should not live to a ripe age. Accordingly, in any modern Utopia, it must be insisted they will.

## § 3

All former Utopias have, by modern standards, erred on the side of over-regulation in these matters. The amount of State interference with the marriage and birth of the citizens of a modern Utopia will be much less than in any terrestrial State. Here, just as in relation to property and enterprise, the law will regulate only in order to secure the utmost freedom and initiative.

Up to the beginning of this chapter, our Utopian speculations, like many Acts of Parliament, have ignored the difference of sex. 'He' indeed is to be read as 'He and She' in all that goes before. But we may now come to the sexual aspects of the modern ideal of a constitution of society in which, for all purposes of the individual, women are to be as free as men. This will certainly be realized in the Modern Utopia if it can be realized at all – not only for woman's sake, but for man's.

But women may be free in theory and not in practice, and as long as they suffer from their economic inferiority, from the inability to produce as much value as a man for the same amount of work – and there can be no doubt of this inferiority – so long will their legal and technical equality be a mockery. It is a fact that almost every point in which a woman differs from a man is an economic disadvantage to her, her incapacity for great stresses of exertion, her frequent liability to slight illness, her weaker initiative, her inferior invention and resourcefulness, her relative incapacity for organization and combination, and the possibilities of emotional complications whenever she is in economic dependence on men. So long as women are compared economically with men and boys they will be inferior in precisely the measure in which they differ from men. All that constitutes this difference they are supposed not to trade upon except in one way, and that is by winning or luring a man to marry, selling themselves in an almost irrevocable bargain, and then following and sharing his fortunes for 'better or worse'.

But – do not let the proposition in its first crudity alarm you – suppose the Modern Utopia equalizes things between the sexes in the only possible way, by insisting that motherhood is a service to the State and a legitimate claim to a living; and that, since the State is to exercise the right of forbidding or sanctioning motherhood, a woman who is, or is becoming, a mother is as much entitled to wages above the minimum wage, to support, to freedom, and to respect and dignity, as a policeman, a solicitor-general, a king, a bishop in the State Church, a Government professor, or anyone else the State sustains. Suppose the State secures to every woman who is, under legitimate sanctions, becoming or likely to become a mother, that is to say who is duly married, a certain wage from her husband to secure her against the need of toil and anxiety, suppose it pays her a certain gratuity upon the birth of a child, and continues to pay at regular intervals sums sufficient to keep her and her child in independent freedom, so long as the child keeps up to the minimum standard of health and physical and mental development. Suppose it pays more upon the child when it rises markedly above certain minimum qualifications, physical or mental, and, in fact, does its best to make thoroughly efficient motherhood a profession worth following. And suppose in correlation with this it forbids the industrial employment of married women and of mothers who have children needing care, unless they are in a position to employ qualified efficient substitutes to take care of their offspring. What differences from terrestrial conditions will ensue?

This extent of intervention will at least abolish two or three salient hardships and evils of the civilized life. It will abolish the hardship of the majority of widows, who on earth are poor and encumbered exactly in proportion as they have discharged the chief distinctive duty of a woman, and miserable just in proportion as their standard of life and of education is high. It will abolish the hardship of those who do not now marry on account of poverty, or who do not dare to have children. The fear that often turns a woman from a beautiful to a mercenary marriage will vanish from life. In Utopia a career of wholesome motherhood would be, under such conditions as I have suggested, the normal and remunerative calling for a woman; and a capable woman who has borne, bred and begun the education of eight or nine well-built, intelligent and successful sons and daughters would be an extremely prosperous woman, quite irrespective of the economic fortunes of the man she has married. She would need to be an exceptional woman, and she would need to have chosen a man at least a little above the average as her partner in life. But his death or misbehaviour or misfortunes would not ruin her.

Now such an arrangement is merely the completed induction from the starting propositions that make some measure of education free and compulsory for every child in the State. If you prevent people making profit out of their children – and every civilized State, even that compendium of old-fashioned Individualism, the United States of America, is now disposed to admit the necessity of that prohibition – and if you provide for the aged instead of leaving them to their children's sense of duty, the practical inducements to parentage, except among very wealthy people, are greatly reduced. The sentimental factor in the case rarely leads to more than a solitary child or at most two to a marriage, and with a high and rising standard of comfort and circumspection it is unlikely that the birth rate will ever rise very greatly again. The Utopians will hold that if you keep the children from profitable employment for the sake of the future, then if you want any but the exceptionally rich, secure, pious, unselfish or reckless to bear children freely, you must be prepared to throw the cost of their maintenance upon the general community.

In short, Utopia will hold that sound childbearing and rearing is a service done not to a particular man but to the whole community, and all its legal arrangements for motherhood will be based on that conception.

## § 4

And after these preliminaries we must proceed to ask, first, what will be the Utopian marriage law, and then what sort of customs and opinions are likely to be superadded to that law?

The trend of our reasoning has brought us to the conclusion that the Utopian State will feel justified in intervening between men and women on two accounts, first on account of paternity, and secondly on account of the clash of freedoms that may otherwise arise. The Utopian State will effectually interfere with and prescribe conditions for all sorts of contract, and for this sort of contract in particular it will be in agreement with almost every earthly State, in defining in the completest fashion what things a man or woman may be bound to do, and what they cannot be bound to do. From the point of view of a statesman, marriage is the union of a man and woman in a manner so intimate as to involve the probability of offspring, and it is of primary importance to the State, first in order to secure good births, and secondly good home conditions, that these unions should not be free nor promiscuous nor practically universal throughout the adult population.

Prolific marriage must be a profitable privilege. It must occur only under certain obvious conditions: the contracting parties must be in health and condition, free from specific transmissible taints, above a certain minimum age, and sufficiently intelligent and energetic to have acquired a minimum education. The man at least must be in receipt of a net income above the minimum wage, after any outstanding charges against him have been paid. All this much it is surely reasonable to insist upon before the State becomes responsible for the prospective children. The age at which men and women may contract to marry is difficult to determine. But if we are, as far as possible, to put women on an equality with men, if we are to insist upon a universally educated population, and if we are seeking to reduce the infantile death rate to zero, it must be much higher than it is in any terrestrial State. The woman should be at least one and twenty; the man twenty-six or twenty-seven.

One imagines the parties to a projected marriage first obtaining licences which will testify that these conditions are satisfied. From the point of view of the theoretical Utopian State, these licences are the feature of primary importance. Then, no doubt, that universal register at Paris would come into play. As a matter of justice, there must be no deception between the two people, and the State will insure that in certain broad essentials this is so. They would have to communicate their joint intention to a public office after their personal licences were granted, and each would be supplied with a copy of the index card of the projected mate, on which would be recorded his or her age, previous marriages, legally important diseases, offspring, domiciles, public appointments, criminal convictions, registered assignments of property and so forth. Possibly it might be advisable to have a little ceremony for each party, for each in the absence of the other, in which this record could be read over in the presence of witnesses, together with some prescribed form of address of counsel in the matter. There would then be a reasonable interval for consideration and withdrawal on the part of either spouse. In the event of the two people persisting in their resolution, they would after this minimum interval signify as much to the local official and the necessary entry would be made in the registers. These formalities would be quite independent of any religious ceremonial the contracting parties might choose, for with religious belief and procedure the modern State has no concern.

So much for the preliminary conditions of matrimony. For those men and women who chose to ignore these conditions and to achieve any sort of union they liked the State would have no concern, unless offspring were born illegitimately. In that case, as we have already suggested, it would be only reasonable to make the parents chargeable with every duty, with maintenance, education and so forth, that in the normal course of things would fall to the State. It would be necessary to impose a life-assurance payment upon these parents, and to exact effectual guarantees against every possible evasion of the responsibility they had incurred. But the further control of private morality, beyond the protection of the immature from corruption and evil example, will be no concern of the State's. When a child comes in, the future of the species comes in; and the State comes in as the guardian of interests wider than the individual's; but the adult's private life is the entirely private life into which the State may not intrude.

Now what will be the nature of the Utopian contract of matrimony?

From the first of the two points of view named above, that of parentage, it is obvious that one unavoidable condition will be the chastity of the wife. Her infidelity being demonstrated, must at once terminate the marriage and release both her husband and the State from any liability for the support of her illegitimate offspring. That, at any rate, is beyond controversy; a marriage contract that does not involve that, is a triumph of metaphysics over common sense. It will be obvious that under Utopian conditions it is the State that will suffer injury by a wife's misconduct, and that a husband who condones anything of the sort will participate in her offence. A woman, therefore, who is divorced on this account will be divorced as a public offender, and not in the key of a personal quarrel; not as one who has inflicted a private and personal wrong. This, too, lies within the primary implications of marriage.

Beyond that, what conditions should a marriage contract in Utopia involve?

A reciprocal restraint on the part of the husband is clearly of no importance whatever, so far as the first end of matrimony goes, the protection of the community from inferior births. It is no wrong to the State. But it does carry with it a variable amount of emotional offence to the wife; it may wound her pride and cause her violent perturbations of jealousy; it may lead to her neglect, her solitude and unhappiness, and it may even work to her physical injury. There should be an implication that it is not to occur. She has bound herself to the man for the good of the State, and clearly it is reasonable that she should look to the State for relief if it does occur. The extent of the offence given her is the exact measure of her injury; if she does not mind nobody minds, and if her self-respect does not suffer nothing whatever is lost to the world; and so it should rest with her to establish his misconduct, and, if she thinks fit, to terminate the marriage.

A failure on either side to perform the elementary duties of companionship, desertion, for example, should obviously give the other mate the right to relief, and clearly the development of any disqualifying habit, drunkenness, or drug-taking, or the like, or any serious crime or acts of violence, should give grounds for a final release. Moreover, the modern Utopian State intervenes between the sexes only because of the coming generation, and for it to sustain restrictions upon conduct in a continually fruitless marriage is obviously to lapse into purely moral intervention. It seems reasonable, therefore, to set a term to a marriage that remains childless, to let it expire at the end of three or four or five unfruitful years, but with no restriction upon the right of the husband and wife to marry each other again.

These are the fairly easy primaries of this question. We now come to the more difficult issues of the matter. The first of these is the question of the economic relationships of husband and wife, having regard to the fact that even in Utopia women, at least until they become mothers, are likely to be on the average poorer than men. The second is the question of the duration of a marriage. But the two interlock, and are, perhaps, best treated together in one common section. And they both ramify in the most complicated manner into the consideration of the general morale of the community.

§ 5

This question of marriage is the most complicated and difficult in the whole range of Utopian problems. But it is happily not the most urgent necessity that it should be absolutely solved. The urgent and necessary problem is the ruler. With rulers rightly contrived and a provisional defective marriage law, a Utopia may be conceived as existing and studying to perfect itself, but without rulers a Utopia is impossible though the theory of its matrimony be complete. And the difficulty in this question is not simply the difficulty of a complicated chess problem, for example, in which the whole tangle of considerations does at least lie in one plane, but a series of problems upon different levels and containing incommensurable factors.

It is very easy to repeat our initial propositions, to recall that we are on another planet, and that all the customs and traditions of the earth are set aside, but the faintest realization of that demands a feat of psychological insight. We have all grown up into an invincible mould of suggestion about sexual things; we regard this with approval, that with horror and this again with contempt, very largely because the thing has always been put to us in this light or that. The more emancipated we think ourselves the more subtle are our bonds. The disentanglement of what is inherent in these feelings from what is acquired is an extraordinarily complex undertaking. Probably all men and women have a more or less powerful disposition to jealousy, but what exactly they will be jealous about and what exactly they will suffer seems part of the superposed factor. Probably all men and women are capable of ideal emotions and wishes beyond merely physical desires, but the shape these take are almost entirely a reaction to external images. And you really cannot strip the external off; you cannot get your stark natural man, jealous, but not jealous about anything in particular, imaginative without any imaginings, proud at large. Emotional dispositions can no more exist without form than a man without air. Only a very observant man who had lived all over the planet Earth, in all sorts of social strata, and with every race and tongue, and who was endowed with great imaginative insight, could hope to understand the possibilities and the limitations of human plasticity in this matter; and say what any men and any women could be induced to do willingly, and just exactly what no man and no woman would stand, provided one had the training of them. Though very young men will tell you readily enough. The proceedings of other races and other ages do not seem to carry conviction; what our ancestors did, or what the Greeks or Egyptians did, though it is the direct physical cause of the modern young man or the modern young lady, is apt to impress these remarkable consequences merely as an arrangement of quaint, comical or repulsive proceedings.

But there emerges to the modern inquirer certain ideals and desiderata that at least go some way towards completing and expanding the crude primaries of a Utopian marriage law set out in § 4.

The sound birth being assured, does there exist any valid reason for the persistence of the Utopian marriage union?

There are two lines of reasoning that go to establish a longer duration for marriage. The first of these rests upon the general necessity for a home and for individual attention in the case of children. Children are the results of a choice between individuals; they grow well, as a rule, only in relation to sympathetic and kindred individualities, and no wholesale character-ignoring method of dealing with them has ever had a shadow of the success of the individualized home. Neither Plato nor Socrates,[4] who repudiated the home, seems ever to have had to do with anything younger than a young man. Procreation is only the beginning of parentage, and even where the mother is not the direct nurse and teacher of her child, even where she delegates these duties, her supervision is, in the common case, essential to its welfare. Moreover, though the Utopian State will pay the mother, and the mother only, for the being and welfare of her legitimate children, there will be a clear advantage in fostering the natural disposition of the father to associate his child's welfare with his individual egotism, and to dispense some of his energies and earnings in supplementing the common provision of the State. It is an absurd disregard of a natural economy to leave the innate philoprogenitiveness of either sex uncultivated. Unless the parents continue in close relationship, if each is passing through a series of marriages, the dangers of a conflict of rights, and of the frittering away of emotions, become very grave. The family will lose homogeneity, and its individuals will have for the mother varied and perhaps incompatible emotional associations. The balance of social advantage is certainly on the side of much more permanent unions, on the side of an arrangement that, subject to ample provisions for a formal divorce without disgrace in cases of incompatibility, would bind, or at least enforce ideals that would tend to bind, a man and woman together for the whole term of her maternal activity, until, that is, the last born of her children was no longer in need of her help.

The second system of considerations arises out of the artificiality of woman's position. It is a less conclusive series than the first, and it opens a number of interesting side vistas.

A great deal of nonsense is talked about the natural equality or inferiority of women to men. But it is only the same quality that can be measured by degrees and ranged in ascending and descending series, and the things that are essentially feminine are different qualitatively from and incommensurable with the distinctly masculine things. The relationship is in the region of ideals and conventions, and a State is perfectly free to determine that men and women shall come to intercourse on a footing of conventional equality or with either the man or woman treated as the predominating individual. Aristotle's criticism of Plato in this matter, his insistence upon the natural inferiority of slaves and women, is just the sort of confusion between inherent and imposed qualities that was his most characteristic weakness. The spirit of the European people, of almost all the peoples now in the ascendant, is towards a convention of equality; the spirit of the Mahometan world is towards the intensification of a convention that the man alone is a citizen and that the woman is very largely his property. There can be no doubt that the latter of these two convenient fictions is the more primitive way of regarding this relationship. It is quite unfruitful to argue between these ideals as if there were a demonstrable conclusion, the adoption of either is an arbitrary act, and we shall simply follow our age and time if we display a certain bias for the former.

If one looks closely into the various practical expansions of these ideas, we find their inherent falsity works itself out in a very natural way so soon as reality is touched. Those who insist upon equality work in effect for assimilation, for a similar treatment of the sexes. Plato's women of the governing class, for example, were to strip for gymnastics like men, to bear arms and go to war, and follow most of the masculine occupations of their class. They were to have the same education and to be assimilated to men at every doubtful point. The Aristotelian attitude, on the other hand, insists upon specialization. The men are to rule and fight and toil; the women are to support motherhood in a state of natural inferiority. The trend of evolutionary forces through long centuries of human development has been on the whole in this second direction, has been towards differentiation.* An adult white woman differs far more from a white man than a negress or pygmy woman from her equivalent male. The education, the mental disposition, of a white or Asiatic woman, reeks of sex; her modesty, her decorum is not to ignore sex but to refine and put a point to it; her costume is clamorous with the distinctive elements of her form. The white woman in the materially prosperous nations is more of a sexual specialist than her sister of the poor and austere peoples, of the prosperous classes more so than the peasant woman. The contemporary woman of fashion who sets the tone of occidental intercourse is a stimulant rather than a companion for a man. Too commonly she is an unwholesome stimulant turning a man from wisdom to appearance, from beauty to beautiful pleasures, from form to colour, from persistent aims to brief and stirring triumphs. Arrayed in what she calls distinctively 'dress', scented, adorned, displayed, she achieves by artifice a sexual differentiation profounder than that of any other vertebrated animal. She outshines the peacock's excess above his mate; one must probe among the domestic secrets of the insects and crustacea to find her living parallel. And it is a question by no means easy and yet of the utmost importance, to determine how far the wide and widening differences between the human sexes is inherent and inevitable, and how far it is an accident of social development that may be converted and reduced under a different social regimen. Are we going to recognize and accentuate this difference and to arrange our Utopian organization to play upon it, are we to have two primary classes of human

* See Havelock Ellis's *Man and Woman*.[5]

being, harmonizing indeed and reacting, but following essentially different lives, or are we going to minimize this difference in every possible way?

The former alternative leads either to a romantic organization of society in which men will live and fight and die for wonderful, beautiful, exaggerated creatures, or it leads to the harem. It would probably lead through one phase to the other. Women would be enigmas and mysteries and maternal dignitaries that one would approach in a state of emotional excitement and seclude piously when serious work was in hand. A girl would blossom from the totally negligible to the mystically desirable at adolescence, and boys would be removed from their mother's educational influence at as early an age as possible. Whenever men and women met together, the men would be in a state of inflamed competition towards one another, and the women likewise, and the intercourse of ideas would be in suspense. Under the latter alternative the sexual relation would be subordinated to friendship and companionship; boys and girls would be co-educated – very largely under maternal direction, and women, disarmed of their distinctive barbaric adornments, the feathers, beads, lace and trimmings that enhance their clamorous claim to a directly personal attention, would mingle according to their quality in the counsels and intellectual development of men. Such women would be fit to educate boys even up to adolescence. It is obvious that a marriage law embodying a decision between these two sets of ideas would be very different according to the alternative adopted. In the former case a man would be expected to earn and maintain in an adequate manner the dear delight that had favoured him. He would tell her beautiful lies about her wonderful moral effect upon him, and keep her sedulously from all responsibility and knowledge. And since there is an undeniably greater imaginative appeal to men in the first bloom of a woman's youth, she would have a distinct claim upon his energies for the rest of her life. In the latter case a man would no more pay for and support his wife than she would do so for him. They would be two friends, differing in kind no doubt but differing reciprocally, who had linked themselves in a matrimonial relationship. Our Utopian marriage so far as we have discussed it, is indeterminate between these alternatives.

We have laid it down as a general principle that the private morals of an adult citizen are no concern for the State. But that involves a decision to disregard certain types of bargain. A sanely contrived State will refuse to sustain bargains wherein there is no plausibly fair exchange, and if private morality is really to be outside the scope of the State then the affections and endearments most certainly must not be regarded as negotiable commodities. The State, therefore, will absolutely ignore the distribution of these favours unless children, or at least the possibility of children, is involved. It follows that it will refuse to recognize any debts or transfers of property that are based on such considerations. It will be only consistent, therefore, to refuse recognition in the marriage contract to any financial obligation between husband and wife, or any settlements qualifying that contract, except when they are in the nature of accessory provision for the prospective children.* So far the Utopian State will throw its weight upon the side of those who advocate the independence of women and their conventional equality with men.

But to any further definition of the marriage relation the World State of Utopia will not commit itself. The wide range of relationships that are left possible within and without the marriage code, is entirely a matter for the individual choice and imagination. Whether a man treat his wife in private as a goddess to be propitiated, as a 'mystery' to be adored, as an agreeable auxiliary, as a particularly intimate friend, or as the wholesome mother of his children, is entirely a matter for their private intercourse: whether he keep her in Oriental idleness or active co-operation, or leave her to live her independent life, rests with the couple alone; and all the possible friendships and intimacies outside marriage also lie quite beyond the organization of the modern State. Religious teaching and literature

---

* Unqualified gifts for love by solvent people will, of course, be quite possible and permissible, unsalaried services and the like, provided the standard of life is maintained and the joint income of the couple between whom the services hold does not sink below twice the minimum wage.

may affect these; customs may arise; certain types of relationship may involve social isolation; the justice of the statesman is
blind to such things. It may be urged that according to Atkinson's illuminating analysis* the control of love-making was the
very origin of the human community. In Utopia, nevertheless,
love-making is no concern of the State's beyond the province
that the protection of children covers.† Change of function is
one of the ruling facts in life; the sac that was in our remotest
ancestors a swimming bladder is now a lung; and the State
which was once, perhaps, no more than the jealous and tyran-
nous will of the strongest male in the herd, becomes the instrument of justice and equality. The State intervenes now only
where there is want of harmony between individuals – individuals who exist or who may presently come into existence.

§ 6

It must be reiterated that our reasoning still leaves Utopian
marriage an institution with wide possibilities of variation. We
have tried to give effect to the ideal of a virtual equality, an
equality of spirit between men and women, and in doing so we
have overridden the accepted opinion of the great majority of
mankind. Probably the first writer to do as much was Plato.
His argument in support of this innovation upon natural human
feeling was thin enough – a mere analogy to illustrate the spirit
of his propositions; it was his creative instinct that determined
him. In the atmosphere of such speculations as this, Plato looms
very large indeed, and in view of what we owe to him, it seems
reasonable that we should hesitate before dismissing, as a thing

---

* See Lang and Atkinson's *Social Origins* and *Primal Law*.[6]
† It cannot be made too clear that though the control of morality is outside the
law the State must maintain a general decorum, a systematic suppression of
powerful and moving examples, and of incitations and temptations of the
young and inexperienced; and to that extent it will, of course, in a sense
exercise a control over morals. But this will be only part of a wider law to
safeguard the tender mind. For example, lying advertisements and the like,
when they lean towards adolescent interests, will encounter a specially disagreeable disposition in the law, over and above the treatment of their general
dishonesty.

prohibited and evil, a type of marriage that he made almost the central feature in the organization of the ruling class, at least, of his ideal State. He was persuaded that the narrow monogamic family is apt to become illiberal and antisocial, to withdraw the imagination and energies of the citizen from the services of the community as a whole, and the Roman Catholic Church has so far endorsed and substantiated his opinion as to forbid family relations to its priests and significant servants. He conceived of a poetic devotion to the public idea, a devotion of which the mind of Aristotle, as his criticisms of Plato show, was incapable, as a substitute for the warm and tender but illiberal emotions of the home. But while the Church made the alternative to family ties celibacy* and participation in an organization, Plato was far more in accordance with modern ideas in perceiving the disadvantage that would result from precluding the nobler types of character from offspring. He sought a way to achieve progeny, therefore, without the narrow concentration of the sympathies about the home, and he found it in a multiple marriage in which every member of the governing class was considered to be married to all the others. But the detailed operation of this system he put tentatively and very obscurely. His suggestions have the experimental inconsistency of an inquiring man. He left many things altogether open, and it is unfair to him to adopt Aristotle's forensic method and deal with his discussion as though it was a fully worked-out project. It is clear that Plato intended every member of his governing class to be so 'changed at birth' as to leave paternity untraceable; mothers were not to know their children, nor children their parents, but there is nothing to forbid the supposition that he intended these people to select and adhere to congenial mates within the great family. Aristotle's assertion that the Platonic Republic left no scope for the virtue of continence shows that he had jumped to just the same conclusions a contemporary London errand boy, hovering a little shamefacedly over Jowett[7] in a public library, might be expected to reach.

* The warm imagination of Campanella, that quaint Calabrian monastic, fired by Plato, reversed this aspect of the Church.

Aristotle obscures Plato's intention, it may be accidentally, by speaking of his marriage institution as a community of wives. When reading Plato he could not or would not escape reading in his own conception of the natural ascendency of men, his idea of property in women and children. But as Plato intended women to be conventionally equal to men, this phrase belies him altogether; community of husbands and wives would be truer to his proposal. Aristotle condemns Plato as roundly as any commercial room would condemn him today, and in much the same spirit; he asserts rather than proves that such a grouping is against the nature of man. He wanted to have women property just as he wanted to have slaves property, he did not care to ask why, and it distressed his conception of convenience extremely to imagine any other arrangement. It is no doubt true that the natural instinct of either sex is exclusive of participators in intimacy during a period of intimacy, but it was probably Aristotle who gave Plato an offensive interpretation in this matter. No one would freely submit to such a condition of affairs as multiple marriage carried out, in the spirit of the Aristotelian interpretation, to an obscene completeness, but that is all the more reason why the Modern Utopia should not refuse a group marriage to three or more freely consenting persons. There is no sense in prohibiting institutions which no sane people could ever want to abuse. It is claimed – though the full facts are difficult to ascertain – that a group marriage of over two hundred persons was successfully organized by John Humphrey Noyes at Oneida Creek.* It is fairly certain in the latter case that there was no 'promiscuity', and that the members mated for variable periods, and often for life, within the group. The documents are reasonably clear upon that point. This Oneida community was, in fact, a league of two hundred persons to regard their children as 'common'. Choice and preference were not abolished in the community, though in some cases they were set aside – just as they are by many parents

* See John H. Noyes's *History of American Socialisms*[8] and his writings generally. The bare facts of this and the other American experiments are given, together with more recent matter, by Morris Hillquit, in *The History of Socialism in the United States*.[9]

under our present conditions. There seems to have been a premature attempt at 'stirpiculture', at what Mr Francis Galton now calls 'Eugenics', in the mating of the members, and there was also a limitation of offspring. Beyond these points the inner secrets of the community do not appear to be very profound; its atmosphere was almost commonplace, it was made up of very ordinary people. There is no doubt that it had a career of exceptional success throughout the whole lifetime of its founder, and it broke down with the advent of a new generation, with the onset of theological differences, and the loss of its guiding intelligence. The Anglo-Saxon spirit, it has been said by one of the ablest children of the experiment, is too individualistic for communism. It is possible to regard the temporary success of this complex family as a strange accident, as the wonderful exploit of what was certainly a very exceptional man. Its final disintegration into frankly monogamic couples – it is still a prosperous business association – may be taken as an experimental verification of Aristotle's common-sense psychology, and was probably merely the public acknowledgement of conditions already practically established.

Out of respect for Plato we cannot ignore this possibility of multiple marriage altogether in our Utopian theorizing, but even if we leave this possibility open we are still bound to regard it as a thing so likely to be rare as not to come at all under our direct observation during our Utopian journeyings. But in one sense, of course, in the sense that the State guarantees care and support for all properly born children, our entire Utopia is to be regarded as a comprehensive marriage group.*

It must be remembered that a modern Utopia must differ from the Utopias of any preceding age in being worldwide; it is not, therefore, to be the development of any special race or type of culture, as Plato's developed an Athenian-Spartan blend, or More, Tudor England. The modern Utopia is to be, before all things, synthetic. Politically and socially, as linguistically, we must suppose it a synthesis; politically it will be a synthesis

---

* The Thelema of Rabelais,[10] with its principle of 'Fay ce que vouldras' within the limits of the order, is probably intended to suggest a Platonic complex marriage after the fashion of our interpretation.

of once widely different forms of government; socially and morally, a synthesis of a great variety of domestic traditions and ethical habits. Into the modern Utopia there must have entered the mental tendencies and origins that give our own world the polygamy of the Zulus and of Utah, the polyandry of Tibet, the latitudes of experiment permitted in the United States, and the divorceless wedlock of Comte. The tendency of all synthetic processes in matters of law and custom is to reduce and simplify the compulsory canon, to admit alternatives and freedoms; what were laws before become traditions of feeling and style, and in no matter will this be more apparent than in questions affecting the relations of the sexes.

# 7

# A FEW UTOPIAN
# IMPRESSIONS

§ 1

But now we are in a better position to describe the houses and
ways of the Utopian townships about the Lake of Lucerne, and
to glance a little more nearly at the people who pass. You figure
us as curiously settled down in Utopia, as working for a low
wage at wood-carving until the authorities at the central registry
in Paris can solve the perplexing problem we have set them. We
stay in an inn looking out upon the lake, and go to and fro for
our five hours' work a day with a curious effect of having been
born Utopians. The rest of our time is our own.

Our inn is one of those inns and lodging-houses which have
a minimum tariff, inns which are partly regulated and, in the
default of private enterprise, maintained and controlled by the
World State throughout the entire world. It is one of several
such establishments in Lucerne. It possesses many hundreds of
practically self-cleaning bedrooms, equipped very much after
the fashion of the rooms we occupied in the similar but much
smaller inn at Hospenthal, differing only a little in the decoration. There is the same dressing-room recess with its bath,
the same graceful proportion in the succinct simplicity of its
furniture. This particular inn is a quadrangle after the fashion
of an Oxford college; it is perhaps forty feet high, and with
about five storeys of bedrooms above its lower apartments;
the windows of the rooms look either outward or inward to
the quadrangle, and the doors give upon artificially lit passages
with staircases passing up and down. These passages are
carpeted with a sort of cork carpet, but are otherwise bare.
The lower storey is occupied by the equivalent of a London

club, kitchens and other offices, dining-room, writing-room, smoking and assembly rooms, a barber's shop and a library. A colonnade with seats runs about the quadrangle, and in the middle is a grass-plot. In the centre of this a bronze figure, a sleeping child, reposes above a little basin and fountain, in which water lilies are growing. The place has been designed by an architect happily free from the hampering traditions of Greek temple building, and of Roman and Italian palaces; it is simple, unaffected, gracious. The material is some artificial stone with the dull surface and something of the tint of yellow ivory; the colour is a little irregular, and a partial confession of girders and pillars breaks this front of tender colour with lines and mouldings of greenish grey that blend with the tones of the leaden gutters and rain pipes from the light red roof. At one point only does any explicit effort towards artistic effect appear, and that is in the great arched gateway opposite my window. Two or three abundant yellow roses climb over the face of the building, and when I look out of my window in the early morning – for the usual Utopian working day commences within an hour of sunrise – I see Pilatus[1] above this outlook, rosy in the morning sky.

This quadrangle type of building is the prevalent element in Utopian Lucerne, and one may go from end to end of the town along corridors and covered colonnades without emerging by a gateway into the open roads at all. Small shops are found in these colonnades, but the larger stores are usually housed in buildings specially adapted to their needs. The majority of the residential edifices are far finer and more substantial than our own modest shelter, though we gather from such chance glimpses as we get of their arrangements that the labour-saving ideal runs through every grade of this servantless world; and what we should consider a complete house in earthly England is hardly known here.

The autonomy of the household has been reduced far below terrestrial conditions by hotels and clubs, and all sorts of co-operative expedients. People who do not live in hotels seem usually to live in clubs. The fairly prosperous Utopian belongs, in most cases, to one or two residential clubs of congenial men and women. These clubs usually possess in addition to furnished bedrooms more or less elaborate suites of apartments, and if a man prefers it one of these latter can be taken and furnished according to his personal taste. A pleasant boudoir, a private library and study, a private garden plot, are among the commonest of such luxuries. Devices to secure roof gardens, loggias, verandas, and such-like open-air privacies to the more sumptuous of these apartments, give interest and variety to Utopian architecture. There are sometimes little cooking corners in these flats – as one would call them on earth – but the ordinary Utopian would no more think of a special private kitchen for his dinners than he would think of a private flour mill or dairy farm. Business, private work and professional practice go on sometimes in the house apartments, but oftener in special offices in the great warren of the business quarter. A common garden, an infant school, play rooms and a playing garden for children, are universal features of the club quadrangles.

Two or three main roads with their tramways, their cyclists' paths and swift traffic paths, will converge on the urban centre, where the public offices will stand in a group close to the two or three theatres and the larger shops; and hither, too, in the case of Lucerne, the head of the swift railway to Paris and England and Scotland, and to the Rhineland and Germany will run. And as one walks out from the town centre one will come to that mingling of homesteads and open country which will be the common condition of all the more habitable parts of the globe.

Here and there, no doubt, will stand quite solitary homesteads, homesteads that will nevertheless be lit and warmed by cables from the central force station, that will share the common water supply, will have their perfected telephonic connection with the rest of the world, with doctor, shop and so forth, and may even have a pneumatic tube for books and small parcels to the nearest post office. But the solitary homestead, as a permanent residence, will be something of a luxury – the resort of rather wealthy garden lovers; and most people with a bias for retirement will probably get as much residential solitude as they care for in the hire of a holiday chalet in a forest, by remote lagoons or high up the mountainside.

The solitary house may indeed prove to be very rare in Utopia. The same forces, the same facilitation of communications that will diffuse the towns will tend to little concentrations of the agricultural population over the countryside. The field workers will probably take their food with them to their work during the day, and for the convenience of an interesting dinner and of civilized intercourse after the working day is over, they will most probably live in a college quadrangle with a common room and club. I doubt if there will be any agricultural labourers drawing wages in Utopia. I am inclined to imagine farming done by tenant associations, by little democratic unlimited-liability companies working under elected managers, and paying not a fixed rent but a share of the produce to the State. Such companies could reconstruct annually to weed out indolent members.* A minimum standard of efficiency in farming would be ensured by fixing a minimum beneath which the rent must not fall, and perhaps by inspection. The general laws respecting the standard of life would, of course, apply to such associations. This type of co-operation presents itself to me as socially the best arrangement for productive agriculture and horticulture, but such enterprises as stock breeding, seed farming and the stocking and loan of agricultural implements are probably, and agricultural research and experiment certainly, best handled directly by large companies or the municipality or the State.

But I should do little to investigate this question; these are presented as quite incidental impressions. You must suppose that for the most part our walks and observations keep us within the more urban quarters of Lucerne. From a number of beautifully printed placards at the street corners, adorned with caricatures of considerable pungency, we discover an odd little election is in progress. This is the selection, upon strictly democratic lines, with a suffrage that includes every permanent

---

* Schemes for the co-operative association of producers will be found in Dr Hertzka's *Freeland*.

resident in the Lucerne ward over the age of fifteen, of the ugliest local building. The old little urban and local governing bodies, we find, have long since been superseded by great provincial municipalities for all the more serious administrative purposes, but they still survive to discharge a number of curious minor functions, and not the least among these is this sort of aesthetic ostracism. Every year every minor local governing body pulls down a building selected by local plebiscite, and the greater Government pays a slight compensation to the owner, and resumes possession of the land it occupies. The idea would strike us at first as simply whimsical, but in practice it appears to work as a cheap and practical device for the aesthetic education of builders, engineers, businessmen, opulent persons and the general body of the public. But when we come to consider its application to our own world we should perceive it was the most Utopian thing we had so far encountered.

§ 2

The factory that employs us is something very different from the ordinary earthly model. Our business is to finish making little wooden toys – bears, cattle men and the like – for children. The things are made in the rough by machinery, and then finished by hand, because the work of unskilful but interested men – and it really is an extremely amusing employment – is found to give a personality and interest to these objects no machine can ever attain.

We carvers – who are the riffraff of Utopia – work in a long shed together, nominally by time; we must keep at the job for the length of the spell, but we are expected to finish a certain number of toys for each spell of work. The rules of the game as between employer and employed in this particular industry hang on the wall behind us; they are drawn up by a conference of the Common Council of Wages Workers with the employers, a common council which has resulted in Utopia from a synthesis of the old Trades Unions, and which has become a constitutional power; but any man who has skill or humour is presently making his own bargain with our employer more or less above that datum line.

Our employer is a quiet blue-eyed man with a humorous smile. He dresses wholly in an indigo blue, that later we come to consider a sort of voluntary uniform for Utopian artists. As he walks about the workshop, stopping to laugh at this production or praise that, one is reminded inevitably of an art school. Every now and then he carves a little himself or makes a sketch or departs to the machinery to order some change in the rough shapes it is turning out. Our work is by no means confined to animals. After a time I am told to specialize in a comical little Roman-nosed pony; but several of the better-paid carvers work up caricature images of eminent Utopians. Over these our employer is most disposed to meditate, and from them he darts off most frequently to improve the type.

It is high summer, and our shed lies open at either end. On one hand is a steep mountainside down which there comes, now bridging a chasm, now a mere straight groove across a meadow, now hidden among green branches, the water-slide that brings our trees from the purple forest overhead. Above us, but nearly hidden, hums the machine shed, but we see a corner of the tank into which, with a mighty splash, the pine trees are delivered. Every now and then, bringing with him a gust of resinous smell, a white-clad machinist will come in with a basketful of crude, unwrought little images, and will turn them out upon the table from which we carvers select them.

(Whenever I think of Utopia that faint and fluctuating smell of resin returns to me, and whenever I smell resin, comes the memory of the open end of the shed looking out upon the lake, the blue-green lake, the boats mirrored in the water, and far and high beyond floats the atmospheric fairyland of the mountains of Glarus, twenty miles away.)

The cessation of the second and last spell of work comes about midday, and then we walk home through this beautiful intricacy of a town to our cheap hotel beside the lake.

We should go our way with a curious contentment, for all that we were earning scarcely more than the minimum wage. We should have, of course, our uneasiness about the final decisions of that universal eye which has turned upon us, we should have those ridiculous sham numbers on our consciences; but that general restlessness, that brooding stress that pursues the weekly worker on earth, that aching anxiety that drives him so often to stupid betting, stupid drinking, and violent and mean offences will have vanished out of mortal experience.

## § 3

I should find myself contrasting my position with my preconceptions about a Utopian visit. I had always imagined myself as standing outside the general machinery of the State – in the distinguished visitors' gallery, as it were – and getting the new world in a series of comprehensive perspective views. But this Utopia, for all the sweeping floats of generalization I do my best to maintain, is swallowing me up. I find myself going between my work and the room in which I sleep and the place in which I dine, very much as I went to and fro in that real world into which I fell five-and-forty years ago. I find about me mountains and horizons that limit my view, institutions that vanish also without an explanation beyond the limit of sight, and a great complexity of things I do not understand and about which, to tell the truth, I do not formulate acute curiosities. People, very unrepresentative people, people just as casual as people in the real world, come into personal relations with us, and little threads of private and immediate interest spin themselves rapidly into a thickening grey veil across the general view. I lose the comprehensive interrogation of my first arrival; I find myself interested in the grain of the wood I work, in birds among the tree branches, in little irrelevant things; and it is only now and then that I get fairly back to the mood that takes all Utopia for its picture.

We spend our first surplus of Utopian money in the reorganization of our wardrobes upon more Utopian lines; we develop acquaintance with several of our fellow workers, and of those who share our table at the inn. We pass insensibly into acquaintanceships and the beginnings of friendships. The World Utopia, I say, seems for a time to be swallowing me up. At the thought of detail it looms too big for me. The question of government, of its sustaining ideas, of race and the wider future, hang like the arch of the sky over these daily incidents, very great indeed, but very remote. These people about me are everyday people, people not so very far from the minimum wage, accustomed much as the everyday people of earth are accustomed to take their world as they find it. Such inquiries as I attempt are pretty obviously a bore to them, pass outside their range as completely as Utopian speculation on earth outranges a stevedore or a member of Parliament or a working plumber. Even the little things of daily life interest them in a different way. So I get on with my facts and reasoning rather slowly; I find myself looking among the pleasant multitudes of the streets for types that promise congenial conversation.

My sense of loneliness is increased during this interlude by the better social success of the botanist. I find him presently falling into conversation with two women who are accustomed to sit at a table near our own. They wear the loose, coloured robes of soft material that are the usual wear of common adult Utopian women; they are both dark and sallow, and they affect amber and crimson in their garments. Their faces strike me as a little unintelligent, and there is a faint touch of middle-aged coquetry in their bearing that I do not like. Yet on earth we should consider them women of exceptional refinement. But the botanist evidently sees in this direction scope for the feelings that have wilted a little under my inattention, and he begins that petty intercourse of a word, of a slight civility, of vague inquiries and comparisons that leads at last to associations and confidences. Such superficial confidences, that is to say, as he finds satisfactory.

This throws me back upon my private observations.

The general effect of a Utopian population is vigour. Everyone seems to be not only in good health but in training; one rarely meets fat people, bald people, or bent or grey. People who would be obese or bent and obviously aged on earth are here in good repair, and as a consequence the whole effect of a crowd is livelier and more invigorating than on earth. The dress is varied and graceful; that of the women reminds one most of

the Italian fifteenth century; they have an abundance of soft
and beautifully coloured stuffs, and the clothes, even of the
poorest, fit admirably. Their hair is very simply but very carefully and beautifully dressed, and except in very sunny weather
they do not wear hats or bonnets. There is little difference in
deportment between one class and another; they all are graceful
and bear themselves with quiet dignity, and among a group of
them a European woman of fashion in her lace and feathers,
her hat and metal ornaments, her mixed accumulations of
'trimmings', would look like a barbarian tricked out with the
miscellaneous plunder of a museum. Boys and girls wear much
the same sort of costume – brown leather shoes, then a sort of
combination of hose and close-fitting trousers that reaches from
toe to waist, and over this a beltless jacket fitting very well, or
a belted tunic. Many slender women wear the same sort of
costume. We should see them in it very often in such a place as
Lucerne, as they returned from expeditions in the mountains.
The older men would wear long robes very frequently, but the
greater proportion of the men would go in variations of much
the same costume as the children. There would certainly be
hooded cloaks and umbrellas for rainy weather, high boots for
mud and snow, and cloaks and coats and furry robes for the
winter. There would be no doubt a freer use of colour than
terrestrial Europe sees in these days, but the costume of the
women at least would be soberer and more practical, and (in
harmony with our discussion in the previous chapter) less differentiated from the men's.

But these, of course, are generalizations. These are the mere
translation of the social facts we have hypotheticated into the
language of costume. There will be a great variety of costume
and no compulsions. The doubles of people who are naturally
foppish on earth will be foppish in Utopia, and people who
have no natural taste on earth will have inartistic equivalents.
Everyone will not be quiet in tone, or harmonious, or beautiful.
Occasionally as I go through the streets to my work, I shall
turn round to glance again at some robe shot with gold
embroidery, some slashing of the sleeves, some eccentricity of
cut, or some discord or untidiness. But these will be but transi-

ent flashes in a general flow of harmonious graciousness; dress will have scarcely any of that effect of disorderly conflict, of self-assertion qualified by the fear of ridicule, that it has in the crudely competitive civilizations of earth.

I shall have the seeker's attitude of mind during those few days at Lucerne. I shall become a student of faces. I shall be, as it were, looking for someone. I shall see heavy faces, dull faces, faces with an uncongenial animation, alien faces, and among these some with an immediate quality of appeal. I should see desirable men approaching me, and I should think: 'Now, if I were to speak to *you*?' Many of these latter I should note wear the same clothing as the man who spoke to us at Wassen; I should begin to think of it as a sort of uniform. . . .

Then I should see grave-faced girls, girls of that budding age when their bearing becomes delusively wise, and the old deception of my youth will recur to me; 'Could you and I but talk together?' I should think. Women will pass me lightly, women with open and inviting faces, but they will not attract me; and there will come beautiful women, women with that touch of claustral preoccupation which forbids the thought of any near approach. They are private and secret, and I may not enter, I know, into their thoughts. . . .

I go as often as I can to the seat by the end of the old Kapellbrücke, and watch the people passing over.

I shall find a quality of dissatisfaction throughout all these days. I shall come to see this period more and more distinctly as a pause, as a waiting interlude; and the idea of an encounter with my double, which came at first as if it were a witticism, as something verbal and surprising, begins to take substance. The idea grows in my mind that after all this is the 'someone' I am seeking, this Utopian self of mine. I had at first an idea of a grotesque encounter, as of something happening in a looking-glass; but presently it dawns on me that my Utopian self must be a very different person from me. His training will be different, his mental content different. But between us there will be a strange link of essential identity, a sympathy, an understanding. I find the thing rising suddenly to a preponderance in my mind. I find the interest of details dwindling to the vanishing-point. That I have come to Utopia is the lesser thing now; the greater is that I have come to meet myself.

I spend hours trying to imagine the encounter, inventing little dialogues. I go alone to the Bureau to find if any news has come to hand from the Great Index in Paris, but I am told to wait another twenty-four hours. I cease absolutely to be interested in anything else, except so far as it leads towards intercourse with this being who is to be at once so strangely alien and so totally mine.

§ 4

Wrapped up in these preoccupations as I am, it will certainly be the botanist who will notice the comparative absence of animals about us.

He will put it in the form of a temperate objection to the Utopian planet.

He is a professed lover of dogs and there are none. We have seen no horses and only one or two mules on the day of our arrival, and there seems not a cat in the world. I bring my mind round to his suggestion. 'This follows,' I say.

It is only reluctantly that I allow myself to be drawn from my secret musings into a discussion of Utopian pets.

I try to explain that a phase in the world's development is inevitable when a systematic worldwide attempt will be made to destroy for ever a great number of contagious and infectious diseases, and that this will involve, for a time at any rate, a stringent suppression of the free movement of familiar animals. Utopian houses, streets and drains will be planned and built to make rats, mice and suchlike house parasites impossible; the race of cats and dogs – providing, as it does, living fastnesses to which such diseases as plague, influenza, catarrhs and the like, can retreat to sally forth again – must pass for a time out of freedom, and the filth made by horses and the other brutes of the highway vanish from the face of the earth. These things make an old story to me, and perhaps explicitness suffers through my brevity.

My botanist fails altogether to grasp what the disappearance of diseases means. His mind has no imaginative organ of that compass. As I talk his mind rests on one fixed image. This presents what the botanist would probably call a 'dear old doggie' – which the botanist would make believe did not possess any sensible odour – and it has faithful brown eyes and understands everything you say. The botanist would make believe it understood him mystically, and I figure his long white hand – which seems to me, in my more jaundiced moments, to exist entirely for picking things and holding a lens – patting its head, while the brute looked things unspeakable. . . .

The botanist shakes his head after my explanation and says quietly, 'I do not like your Utopia, if there are to be no dogs.'

Perhaps that makes me a little malicious. Indeed I do not hate dogs, but I care ten thousand times more for a man than for all the brutes on the earth, and I can see, what the botanist I think cannot, that a life spent in the delightful atmosphere of many pet animals may have too dear a price. . . .

I find myself back again at the comparison of the botanist and myself. There is a profound difference in our imaginations, and I wonder whether it is the consequence of innate character or of training and whether he is really the human type or I. I am not altogether without imagination, but what imagination I have has the most insistent disposition to square itself with every fact in the universe. It hypothesizes very boldly, but on the other hand it will not gravely make believe. Now the botanist's imagination is always busy with the most impossible make-believe. That is the way with all children I know. But it seems to me one ought to pass out of it. It isn't as though the world was an untidy nursery; it is a place of splendours indescribable for all who will lift its veils. It may be he is essentially different from me, but I am much more inclined to think he is simply more childish. Always it is make-believe. He believes that horses are beautiful creatures, for example, dogs are beautiful creatures, that some women are inexpressibly lovely, and he makes believe that this is always so. Never a word of criticism of horse or dog or woman! Never a word of criticism of his impeccable friends! Then there is his botany. He makes believe that all the vegetable kingdom is mystically perfect and exemplary, that all flowers smell deliciously and are exquisitely beautiful, that *Drosera* does not hurt flies very much, and that onions do not smell. Most of the universe does not interest this nature lover at all. But I know, and I am querulously incapable of understanding why everyone else does not know, that a horse is beautiful in one way and quite ugly in another, that everything has this shot-silk quality, and is all the finer for that. When people talk of a horse as an ugly animal I think of its beautiful moments, but when I hear a flow of indiscriminate praise of its beauty I think of such an aspect as one gets from a dog-cart, the fiddle-shaped back and that distressing blade of the neck, the narrow clumsy place between the ears, and the ugly glimpse of cheek. There is, indeed, no beauty whatever save that transitory thing that comes and comes again; all beauty is really the beauty of expression, is really kinetic and momentary. That is true even of those triumphs of static endeavour achieved by Greece. The Greek temple, for example, is a barn with a face that at a certain angle of vision and in a certain light has a great calm beauty.

But where are we drifting? All such things, I hold, are cases of more and less, and of the right moment and the right aspect, even the things I most esteem. There is no perfection, there is no enduring treasure. This pet dog's beautiful affection, I say, or this other sensuous or imaginative delight, is no doubt good, but it can be put aside if it is incompatible with some other and wider good. You cannot focus all good things together.

All right action and all wise action is surely sound judgement and courageous abandonment in the matter of such incompatibilities. If I cannot imagine thoughts and feelings in a dog's brain that cannot possibly be there, at least I can imagine things in the future of men that might be there had we the will to demand them. . . .

'I don't like this Utopia,' the botanist repeats. 'You don't understand about dogs. To me they're human beings – and more! There used to be such a jolly old dog at my aunt's at Frognal when I was a boy—'

But I do not heed his anecdote. Something – something of the nature of conscience – has suddenly jerked back the memory of that beer I drank at Hospenthal, and puts an accusing finger on the memory.

I never have had a pet animal, I confess, though I have been fairly popular with kittens. But with regard to a certain petting of myself—?

Perhaps I was premature about that beer. I have had no pet animals, but I perceive if the Modern Utopia is going to demand the sacrifice of the love of animals, which is, in its way, a very fine thing indeed, so much the more readily may it demand the sacrifice of many other indulgences, some of which are not even fine in the lowest degree.

It is curious this haunting insistence upon sacrifice and discipline!

It is slowly becoming my dominant thought that the sort of people whose will this Utopia embodies must be people a little heedless of small pleasures. You cannot focus all good things at the same time. That is my chief discovery in these meditations at Lucerne. Much of the rest of this Utopia I had in a sort of way anticipated, but not this. I wonder if I shall see my Utopian self for long and be able to talk to him freely. . . .

We lie in the petal-strewn grass under some Judas trees beside the lake shore, as I meander among these thoughts, and each of us, disregardful of his companion, follows his own associations.

'Very remarkable,' I say, discovering that the botanist has come to an end with his story of that Frognal dog.

'You'd wonder how he knew,' he says.

'You would.'

I nibble a green blade.

'Do you realize quite,' I ask, 'that within a week we shall face our Utopian selves and measure something of what we might have been?'

The botanist's face clouds. He rolls over, sits up abruptly and puts his lean hands about his knees.

'I don't like to think about it,' he says. 'What is the good of reckoning . . . might-have-beens?'

## § 5

It is pleasant to think of puzzling the organized wisdom of so superior a planet as this Utopia, this moral monster State my Frankenstein[2] of reasoning has made, and to that pitch we have come. When we are next in the presence of our Lucerne official, he has the bearing of a man who faces a mystification beyond his powers, an incredible disarrangement of the order of Nature. Here, for the first time in the records of Utopian science, are two cases – not simply one but two, and these in each other's company! – of duplicated thumbmarks. This, coupled with a cock-and-bull story of an instantaneous transfer from some planet unknown to Utopian astronomy. That he and all his world exist only upon a hypothesis that would explain every one of these difficulties absolutely, is scarcely likely to occur to his obviously unphilosophic mind.

The official eye is more eloquent than the official lips and asks almost urgently, 'What in this immeasurable universe have you managed to do to your thumbs? And why?' But he is only a very inferior sort of official indeed, a mere clerk of the post, and he has all the guarded reserve of your thoroughly unoriginal man. 'You are not the two persons I ascertained you were,' he says, with the note of one resigned to communion with un-reason; 'because you' – he indicates me – 'are evidently at your residence in London.' I smile. 'That gentleman' – he points a pen at the botanist in a manner that is intended to dismiss my smile once for all – 'will be in London next week. He will be returning next Friday from a special mission to investigate the fungoid parasites that have been attacking the cinchona trees in Ceylon.'

The botanist blesses his heart.

'Consequently' – the official sighs at the burden of such nonsense, 'you will have to go and consult with – the people you ought to be.'

I betray a faint amusement.

'You will have to end by believing in our planet,' I say.

He waggles a negation with his head. He would intimate his position is too responsible a one for jesting, and both of us in our several ways enjoy the pleasure we poor humans have in meeting with intellectual inferiority. 'The Standing Committee of Identification,' he says, with an eye on a memorandum, 'has remitted your case to the Research Professor of Anthropology in the University of London, and they want you to go there, if you will, and talk to him.'

'What else can we do?' says the botanist.

'There's no positive compulsion,' he remarks, 'but your work here will probably cease. Here –' he pushed the neat slips of paper towards us – 'are your tickets for London, and a sufficient supply of money,' – he indicates two piles of coins and paper on either hand of him – 'for a day or so there.' He proceeds in the same dry manner to inform us we are invited to call at our earliest convenience upon our doubles, and upon the Professor who is to investigate our case.

'And then?'

He pulls down the corners of his mouth in a wry deprecatory smile, eyes us obliquely under a crumpled brow, shrugs his shoulders and shows us the palms of his hands.

On earth, where there is nationality, this would have been a Frenchman – the inferior sort of Frenchman – the sort whose only happiness is in the routine security of Government employment.

§ 6

London will be the first Utopian city centre we shall see.

We shall find ourselves there with not a little amazement. It will be our first experience of the swift long-distance travel of Utopia, and I have an idea – I know not why – that we should make the journey by night. Perhaps I think so because the ideal of long-distance travel is surely a restful translation less suitable for the active hours.

We shall dine and gossip and drink coffee at the pretty little tables under the lantern-lit trees, we shall visit the theatre, and decide to sup in the train, and so come at last to the station. There we shall find pleasant rooms with seats and books – luggage all neatly elsewhere – and doors that we shall imagine give upon a platform. Our cloaks and hats and such like out-door impedimenta will be taken in the hall and neatly labelled for London, we shall exchange our shoes for slippers there, and we shall sit down like men in a club. An officious little bell will presently call our attention to a label 'London' on the doorway, and an excellent phonograph will enforce that notice with infinite civility. The doors will open, and we shall walk through into an equally comfortable gallery.

'Where is the train for London?' we shall ask a uniformed fellow Utopian.

'This is the train for London,' he will say.

There will be a shutting of doors, and the botanist and I, trying not to feel too childish, will walk exploring through the capacious train.

The resemblance to a club will strike us both. 'A *good* club,' the botanist will correct me.

When one travels beyond a certain speed, there is nothing but fatigue in looking out of a window, and this corridor train, twice the width of its poor terrestrial brother, will have no need of that distraction. The simple device of abandoning any but a few windows, and those set high, gives the wall space of the long corridors to books; the middle part of the train is indeed a comfortable library with abundant armchairs and couches, each with its green-shaded light, and soft carpets upon the soundproof floor. Further on will be a newsroom, with a noiseless but busy tape at one corner, printing off messages from the wires by the wayside, and further still, rooms for gossip and smoking, a billiard-room, and the dining car. Behind we shall come to bedrooms, bathrooms, the hairdresser and so forth.

'When shall we start?' I ask presently as we return, rather like bashful yokels, to the library, and the old gentleman reading the *Arabian Nights* in the armchair in the corner glances up at me with a sudden curiosity.

The botanist touches my arm and nods towards a pretty little lead-paned window, through which we see a village sleeping under cloudy moonlight go flashing by. Then a skylit lake, and then a string of swaying lights, gone with the leap of a camera shutter.

Two hundred miles an hour!

We resort to a dignified Chinese steward and secure our berths. It is perhaps terrestrial of us that we do not think of reading the Utopian literature that lines the middle part of the train. I find a bed of the simple Utopian pattern, and lie for a time thinking – quite tranquilly – of this marvellous adventure.

I wonder why it is that to lie securely in bed, with the light out, seems ever the same place, wherever in space one may chance to be? And asleep, there is no space for us at all. I become drowsy and incoherent and metaphysical. . . .

The faint and fluctuating drone of the wheels below the car, re-echoed by the flying track, is more perceptible now, but it is not unpleasantly loud, merely a faint tinting of the quiet. . . .

No sea crossing breaks our journey; there is nothing to prevent a Channel tunnel[3] in that other planet; and I wake in London.

The train has been in London some time when I awake, for these marvellous Utopians have discovered that it is not necessary to bundle out passengers from a train in the small hours, simply because they have arrived. A Utopian train is just a peculiar kind of hotel corridor that flies about the earth while one sleeps.

§ 7

How will a great city of Utopia strike us?

To answer that question well one must needs be artist and engineer, and I am neither. Moreover, one must employ words and phrases that do not exist, for this world still does not dream of the things that may be done with thought and steel, when the engineer is sufficiently educated to be an artist, and the artistic intelligence has been quickened to the accomplishment of an engineer. How can one write of these things for a generation which rather admires that inconvenient and gawky muddle of ironwork and Flemish architecture, the London Tower Bridge? When before this, temerarious anticipators have written of the mighty buildings that might someday be, the illustrator has blended with the poor ineffectual splutter of the author's words, his powerful suggestion that it amounted simply to something bulbous, florid and fluent in the vein of the onion and L'Art Nouveau.[4] But here, it may be, the illustrator will not intervene.

Art has scarcely begun in the world.

There have been a few forerunners and that is all. Leonardo,[5] Michelangelo; how they would have exulted in the liberties of steel! There are no more pathetic documents in the archives of art than Leonardo's memoranda. In these one sees him again and again reaching out as it were, with empty desirous hands, towards the unborn possibilities of the engineer. And Dürer,[6] too, was a Modern, with the same turn towards creative invention. In our times these men would have wanted to make viaducts, to bridge wild and inaccessible places, to cut and straddle great railways athwart the mountain masses of the world. You can see, time after time, in Dürer's work, as you can see in the imaginary architectural landscape of the Pompeian walls, the dream of structures lighter and bolder than stone or brick can yield. . . . These Utopian town buildings will be the realization of such dreams.

Here will be one of the great meeting places of mankind. Here – I speak of Utopian London – will be the traditional centre of one of the great races in the commonalty of the World State – and here will be its social and intellectual exchange. There will be a mighty University here, with thousands of professors and tens of thousands of advanced students, and here great journals of thought and speculation, mature and splendid books of philosophy and science, and a glorious fabric of literature will be woven and shaped, and with a teeming leisureliness, put forth. Here will be stupendous libraries, and a mighty organization of museums. About these centres will cluster a great swarm of people, and close at hand will be another centre, for I who am an Englishman must needs stipulate that Westminster shall still be a seat of world Empire, one of several seats, if you will – where the ruling council of the world assembles. Then the arts will cluster round this city, as gold gathers about wisdom, and here Englishmen will weave into wonderful prose and beautiful rhythms and subtly atmospheric forms, the intricate, austere and courageous imagination of our race.

One will come into this place as one comes into a noble mansion. They will have flung great arches and domes of glass above the wider spaces of the town, the slender beauty of the perfect metalwork far overhead will be softened to a fairy-like unsubstantiality by the mild London air. It will be the London air we know, clear of filth and all impurity, the same air that gives our October days their unspeakable clarity and makes every London twilight mysteriously beautiful. We shall go along avenues of architecture that will be emancipated from the last memories of the squat temple boxes of the Greek, the buxom curvatures of Rome; the Goth in us will have taken to steel and countless new materials as kindly as once he took to stone. The gay and swiftly moving platforms of the public ways will go past on either hand, carrying sporadic groups of people, and very speedily we shall find ourselves in a sort of central space, rich with palms and flowering bushes and statuary. We shall look along an avenue of trees, down a wide gorge between the cliffs of crowded hotels, the hotels that are still glowing with internal lights, to where the shining morning river streams dawnlit out to sea.

Great multitudes of people will pass softly to and fro in this central space, beautiful girls and youths going to the University classes that are held in the stately palaces about us, grave and capable men and women going to their businesses, children meandering along to their schools, holidaymakers, lovers, setting out upon a hundred quests; and here we shall ask for the two we more particularly seek. A graceful little telephone kiosk will put us within reach of them, and with a queer sense of unreality I shall find myself talking to my Utopian twin. He has heard of me, he wants to see me and he gives me clear directions how to come to him.

I wonder if my own voice sounds like that.

'Yes,' I say, 'then I will come as soon as we have been to our hotel.'

We indulge in no eloquence upon this remarkable occasion.

Yet I feel an unusual emotional stir. I tremble greatly, and the telephonic mouthpiece rattles as I replace it.

And thence the botanist and I walk on to the apartments that have been set aside for us, and into which the poor little rolls of the property that has accumulated about us in Utopia, our earthly raiment, and a change of linen and the like, have already been delivered. As we go I find I have little to say to my companion, until presently I am struck by a transitory wonder that he should have so little to say to me.

'I can still hardly realize,' I say, 'that I am going to see myself – as I might have been.'

'No,' he says, and relapses at once into his own preoccupation.

For a moment my wonder as to what he should be thinking about brings me near to a double self-forgetfulness.

I realize we are at the entrance of our hotel before I can formulate any further remark.

'This is the place,' I say.

# 8

# MY UTOPIAN SELF

## § 1

It falls to few of us to interview our better selves. My Utopian self is, of course, my better self – according to my best endeavours – and I must confess myself fully alive to the difficulties of the situation. When I came to this Utopia I had no thought of any such intimate self-examination.

The whole fabric of that other universe sways for a moment as I come into his room, into his clear and ordered workroom. I am trembling. A figure rather taller than myself stands against the light.

He comes towards me, and I, as I advance to meet him, stumble against a chair. Then, still without a word, we are clasping hands.

I stand now so that the light falls upon him, and I can see his face better. He is a little taller than I, younger looking and sounder looking; he has missed an illness or so, and there is no scar over his eye. His training has been subtly finer than mine; he has made himself a better face than mine. . . . These things I might have counted upon. I can fancy he winces with a twinge of sympathetic understanding at my manifest inferiority. Indeed I come, trailing clouds of earthly confusion and weakness; I bear upon me all the defects of my world. He wears, I see, that white tunic with the purple band that I have already begun to consider the proper Utopian clothing for grave men, and his face is clean shaven. We forget to speak at first in the intensity of our mutual inspection. When at last I do gain my voice it is to say something quite different from the fine, significant openings of my premeditated dialogues.

'You have a pleasant room,' I remark, and look about a little disconcerted because there is no fireplace for me to put my back against, or hearthrug to stand upon. He pushes me a chair, into which I plump, and we hang over an immensity of conversational possibilities.

'I say,' I plunge, 'what do you think of me? You don't think I'm an impostor?'

'Not now that I have seen you. No.'

'Am I so like you?'

'Like me and your story – exactly.'

'You haven't any doubt left?' I ask.

'Not in the least, since I saw you enter. You come from the world beyond Sirius, twin to this. Eh?'

'And you don't want to know how I got here?'

'I've ceased even to wonder how *I* got here,' he says, with a laugh that echoes mine.

He leans back in his chair, and I in mine, and the absurd parody of our attitude strikes us both.

'Well?' we say, simultaneously, and laugh together.

I will confess this meeting is more difficult even than I anticipated.

## § 2

Our conversation at that first encounter would do very little to develop the Modern Utopia in my mind. Inevitably, it would be personal and emotional. He would tell me how he stood in his world, and I how I stood in mine. I should have to tell him things, I should have to explain things—

No, the conversation would contribute nothing to a modern Utopia.

And so I leave it out.

## § 3

But I should go back to my botanist in a state of emotional relaxation. At first I should not heed the fact that he, too, had been in some manner stirred. 'I have seen him,' I should say needlessly, and seem to be on the verge of telling the untellable. Then I should fade off into: 'It's the strangest thing.'

He would interrupt me with his own preoccupation. 'You know,' he would say, 'I've seen someone.'

I should pause and look at him.

'She is in this world,' he says.

'Who is in this world?'

'Mary!'

I have not heard her name before, but I understand, of course, at once.

'I saw her,' he explains.

'Saw her?'

'I'm certain I saw her. Certain. She was far away across those gardens near here – and before I had recovered from my amazement she had gone! But it was Mary.'

He takes my arm. 'You know I did not understand this,' he says. 'I did not really understand that when you said Utopia, you meant I was to meet her – in happiness.'

'I didn't.'

'It works out at that.'

'You haven't met her yet.'

'I shall. It makes everything different. To tell you the truth I've rather hated this Utopia of yours at times. You mustn't mind my saying it, but there's something of the Gradgrind[1] —'

Probably I should swear at that.

'What?' he says.

'Nothing.'

'But you spoke?'

'I was purring. I'm a Gradgrind – it's quite right – anything you can say about Herbert Spencer, vivisectors, materialistic Science or Atheists, applies without correction to me. Begbie away![2] But now you think better of a modern Utopia? Was the lady looking well?'

'It was her real self. Yes. Not the broken woman I met – in the real world.'

'And as though she was pining for you.'

He looks puzzled.

'Look there!' I say.

He looks.

We are standing high above the ground in the loggia into which our apartments open, and I point across the soft haze of the public gardens to a tall white mass of University buildings that rises with a free and fearless gesture, to lift saluting pinnacles against the clear evening sky. 'Don't you think that rather more beautiful than – say – our National Gallery?'

He looks at it critically. 'There's a lot of metal in it,' he objects. 'What?'

'I purred. But anyhow, whatever you can't see in that, you can, I suppose, see that it is different from anything in your world – it lacks the kindly humanity of a red-brick Queen Anne villa[3] residence, with its gables and bulges and bow windows, and its stained-glass fanlight and so forth. It lacks the self-complacent unreasonableness of Board of Works classicism. There's something in its proportions – as though someone with brains had taken a lot of care to get it quite right, someone who not only knew what metal can do, but what a University ought to be, somebody who had found the Gothic spirit enchanted, petrified, in a cathedral, and had set it free.'

'But what has this,' he asks, 'to do with her?'

'Very much,' I say. 'This is not the same world. If she is here, she will be younger in spirit and wiser. She will be in many ways more refined—'

'No one—' he begins, with a note of indignation.

'No, no! She couldn't be. I was wrong there. But she will be different. Grant that at any rate. When you go forward to speak to her, she may not remember – very many things *you* may remember. Things that happened at Frognal – dear romantic walks through the Sunday summer evenings, practically you two alone, you in your adolescent silk hat and your nice gentlemanly gloves. . . . Perhaps that did not happen here! And she may have other memories – of things – that down there haven't happened. You noted her costume. She wasn't by any chance one of the samurai?'

He answers, with a note of satisfaction, 'No! She wore a womanly dress of greyish green.'

'Probably under the Lesser Rule.'

'I don't know what you mean by the Lesser Rule. She wasn't one of the samurai.'

'And, after all, you know – I keep on reminding you, and you keep on losing touch with the fact that this world contains your double.'

He pales, and his countenance is disturbed. Thank Heaven, I've touched him at last!

'This world contains your double. But, conceivably, everything may be different here. The whole romantic story may have run a different course. It was as it was in our world by the accidents of custom and proximity. Adolescence is a defenceless plastic period. You are a man to form great affections – noble, great affections. You might have met anyone almost at that season and formed the same attachment.'

For a time he is perplexed and troubled by this suggestion.

'No,' he says, a little doubtfully. 'No. It was herself.' ... Then, emphatically, '*No!*'

## § 4

For a time we say no more, and I fall musing about my strange encounter with my Utopian double. I think of the confessions I have just made to him, the strange admissions both to him and myself. I have stirred up the stagnations of my own emotional life, the pride that has slumbered, the hopes and disappointments that have not troubled me for years. There are things that happened to me in my adolescence that no discipline of reason will ever bring to a just proportion for me, the first humiliations I was made to suffer, the waste of all the fine irrecoverable loyalties and passions of my youth. The dull base caste of my little personal tragi-comedy I have ostensibly forgiven, I have for the most part forgotten – and yet when I recall them I hate each actor still. Whenever it comes into my mind – I do my best to prevent it – there it is, and these detestable people blot out the stars for me.

I have told all that story to my double, and he has listened with understanding eyes. But for a little while those squalid memories will not sink back into the deeps.

We lean, side by side, over our balcony, lost in such egotistical absorptions, quite heedless of the great palace of noble dreams to which our first enterprise has brought us.

## § 5

I can understand the botanist this afternoon; for once we are in the same key. My own mental temper has gone for the day, and I know what it means to be untempered. Here is a world and a glorious world, and it is for me to take hold of it, to have to do with it, here and now, and behold! I can only think that I am burnt and scarred, and there rankles that wretched piece of business, the mean unimaginative triumph of my antagonist—

I wonder how many men have any real freedom of mind, are in truth unhampered by such associations, to whom all that is great and noble in life does not, at times at least if not always, seem secondary to obscure rivalries and considerations, to the petty hates that are like germs in the blood, to the lust for self-assertion, to dwarfish pride, to affections they gave in pledge even before they were men.

The botanist beside me dreams, I know, of vindications for that woman.

All this world before us, and its order and liberty, are no more than a painted scene before which he is to meet Her at last, freed from 'that scoundrel'.

He expects 'that scoundrel' really to be present and, as it were, writhing under their feet. . . .

I wonder if that man *was* a scoundrel. He has gone wrong on earth, no doubt, has failed and degenerated, but what was it sent him wrong? Was his failure inherent, or did some net of cross purposes tangle about his feet? Suppose he is not a failure in Utopia! . . .

I wonder that this has never entered the botanist's head.

He, with his vaguer mind, can overlook – spite of my ruthless reminders – all that would mar his vague anticipations. That, too, if I suggested it, he would overcome and disregard. He has the most amazing power of resistance to uncongenial ideas; amazing, that is, to me. He hates the idea of meeting his double, and consequently so soon as I cease to speak of that, with scarcely an effort of his will, it fades again from his mind.

Down below in the gardens two children pursue one another, and one, near caught, screams aloud and rouses me from my reverie.

I follow their little butterfly antics until they vanish beyond a thicket of flowering rhododendra, and then my eyes go back to the great façade of the University buildings.

But I am in no mood to criticize architecture.

Why should a modern Utopia insist upon slipping out of the hands of its creator and becoming the background of a personal drama – of such a silly little drama?

The botanist will not see Utopia in any other way. He tests it entirely by its reaction upon the individual persons and things he knows; he dislikes it because he suspects it of wanting to lethal-chamber his aunt's 'dear old doggie', and now he is reconciled to it because a certain 'Mary' looks much younger and better here than she did on earth. And here am I, near fallen into the same way of dealing!

We agreed to purge this State and all the people in it of traditions, associations, bias, laws and artificial entanglements, and begin anew; but we have no power to liberate ourselves. Our past, even its accidents, its accidents above all, and ourselves, are one.

# 9

# THE SAMURAI

Neither my Utopian double nor I love emotion sufficiently to cultivate it, and my feelings are in a state of seemly subordination when we meet again. He is now in possession of some clear general ideas about my own world, and I can broach almost at once the thoughts that have been growing and accumulating since my arrival in this planet of my dreams. We find our interest in a humanized state-craft makes us, in spite of our vast difference in training and habits, curiously akin.

I put it to him that I came to Utopia with but very vague ideas of the method of government, biassed, perhaps, a little in favour of certain electoral devices but for the rest indeterminate, and that I have come to perceive more and more clearly that the large intricacy of Utopian organization demands a more powerful and efficient method of control than electoral methods can give. I have come to distinguish among the varied costumes and the innumerable types of personality Utopia presents, certain men and women of a distinctive costume and bearing, and I know now that these people constitute an order, the samurai, the 'voluntary nobility', which is essential in the scheme of the Utopian State. I know that this order is open to every physically and mentally healthy adult in the Utopian State who will observe its prescribed austere rule of living, that much of the responsible work of the State is reserved for it, and I am inclined now at the first onset of realization to regard it as far more significant than it really is in the Utopian scheme, as being, indeed, in itself and completely the Utopian scheme. My predominant curiosity concerns the organization of this order. As it has developed in my mind, it has reminded me more and more closely of that strange class of guardians which constitutes the essential substance of Plato's Republic, and it is with an implicit reference to Plato's profound intuitions that I and my double discuss this question.

To clarify our comparison he tells me something of the history of Utopia, and incidentally it becomes necessary to make a correction in the assumptions upon which I have based my enterprise. We are assuming a world identical in every respect with the real planet Earth, except for the profoundest differences in the mental content of life. This implies a different literature, a different philosophy and a different history, and so soon as I come to talk to him I find that though it remains unavoidable that we should assume the correspondence of the two populations, man for man – unless we would face unthinkable complications – we must assume also that a great succession of persons of extraordinary character and mental gifts who on earth died in childhood or at birth, or who never learnt to read, or who lived and died amidst savage or brutalizing surroundings that gave their gifts no scope, did in Utopia encounter happier chances, and take up the development and application of social theory – from the time of the first Utopists in a steady onward progress down to the present hour.* The differences of condition, therefore, had widened with each successive year. Jesus Christ had been born into a liberal and progressive Roman Empire that spread from the Arctic Ocean to the Bight of Benin,[1] and was to know no Decline and Fall, and Mahomet,[2] instead of embodying the dense prejudices of Arab ignorance, opened his eyes upon an intellectual horizon already nearly as wide as the world.

And through this empire the flow of thought, the flow of intention, poured always more abundantly. There were wars, but they were conclusive wars that established new and more permanent relations, that swept aside obstructions, and abolished

---

* One might assume as an alternative to this that amidst the four-fifths of the Greek literature now lost to the world, there perished, neglected, some book of elementary significance, some earlier 'Novum Organum', that in Utopia survived to achieve the profoundest consequences.

centres of decay; there were prejudices tempered to an ordered criticism, and hatreds that merged at last in tolerant reactions. It was several hundred years ago that the great organization of the samurai came into its present form. And it was this organization's widely sustained activities that had shaped and established the World State in Utopia.

This organization of the samurai was a quite deliberate invention. It arose in the course of social and political troubles and complications, analogous to those of our own time on earth, and was, indeed, the last of a number of political and religious experiments dating back to the first dawn of philosophical statecraft in Greece. That hasty despair of specialization for government that gave our poor world individualism, democratic liberalism and anarchism, and that curious disregard of the fund of enthusiasm and self-sacrifice in men which is the fundamental weakness of worldly economics, do not appear in the history of Utopian thought. All that history is pervaded with the recognition of the fact that self-seeking is no more the whole of human life than the satisfaction of hunger; that it is an essential of a man's existence no doubt, and that under stress of evil circumstances it may as entirely obsess him as would the food hunt during famine, but that life may pass beyond to an illimitable world of emotions and effort. Every sane person consists of possibilities beyond the unavoidable needs, is capable of disinterested feeling even if it amounts only to enthusiasm for a sport or an industrial employment well done, for an art, or for a locality or class. In our world now, as in the Utopian past, this impersonal energy of a man goes out into religious emotion and work, into patriotic effort, into artistic enthusiasm, into games and amateur employments; and an enormous proportion of the whole world's fund of effort wastes itself in religious and political misunderstandings and conflicts, and in unsatisfying amusements and unproductive occupations. In a modern Utopia there will, indeed, be no perfection; in Utopia there must also be friction, conflicts and waste, but the waste will be enormously less than in our world. And the co-ordination of activities this relatively smaller waste will measure, will be the achieved end for which the order of the samurai was first devised.

Inevitably such an order must have first arisen among a clash of social forces and political systems as a revolutionary organization. It must have set before itself the attainment of some such Utopian ideal as this modern Utopia does, in the key of mortal imperfection, realize. At first it may have directed itself to research and discussion, to the elaboration of its ideal, to the discussion of a plan of campaign, but at some stage it must have assumed a more militant organization, and have prevailed against and assimilated the pre-existing political organizations, and to all intents and purposes have become this present synthesized World State. Traces of that militancy would, therefore, pervade it still, and a campaigning quality – no longer against specific disorders, but against universal human weaknesses and the inanimate forces that trouble man – still remain as its essential quality.

'Something of this kind,' I should tell my double, 'had arisen in our thought' – I jerk my head back to indicate an infinitely distant planet – 'just before I came upon these explorations. The idea had reached me, for example, of something to be called a New Republic, which was to be in fact an organization for revolution something after the fashion of your samurai, as I understand them – only most of the organization and the rule of life still remained to be invented. All sorts of people were thinking of something in that way about the time of my coming. The idea, as it reached me, was pretty crude in several respects. It ignored the high possibility of a synthesis of languages in the future; it came from a literary man who wrote only English, and, as I read him – he was a little vague in his proposals – it was to be a purely English-speaking movement. And his ideas were coloured too much by the peculiar opportunism of his time; he seemed to have more than half an eye for a prince or a millionaire of genius; he seemed looking here and there for support and the structural elements of a party. Still, the idea of a comprehensive movement of disillusioned and illuminated men behind the shams and patriotisms, the spites and personalities of the ostensible world was there.'

I added some particulars.

'Our movement had something of that spirit in the beginning,' said my Utopian double. 'But while your men seem to be thinking disconnectedly, and upon a very narrow and fragmentary basis of accumulated conclusions, ours had a fairly comprehensive science of human association, and a very careful analysis of the failures of preceding beginnings to draw upon. After all, your world must be as full as ours was of the wreckage and decay of previous attempts; churches, aristocracies, orders, cults. . . .'

'Only at present we seem to have lost heart altogether, and now there are no new religions, no new orders, no new cults – no beginnings any more.'

'But that's only a resting phase, perhaps. You were saying—'

'Oh! – let that distressful planet alone for a time! Tell me how you manage in Utopia.'

§ 2

The social theorists of Utopia, my double explained, did not base their schemes upon the classification of men into labour and capital, the landed interest, the liquor trade and the like. They esteemed these as accidental categories, indefinitely amenable to statesmanship, and they looked for some practical and real classification upon which to base organization.* But, on the other hand, the assumption that men are unclassifiable, because practically homogeneous, which underlies modern democratic methods and all the fallacies of our equal justice, is even more alien to the Utopian mind. Throughout Utopia there is, of course, no other than provisional classifications, since every being is regarded as finally unique, but for political and social purposes things have long rested upon a classification of

---

* In that they seem to have profited by a more searching criticism of early social and political speculations than our earth has yet undertaken. The social speculations of the Greeks, for example, had just the same primary defect as the economic speculations of the eighteenth century – they began with the assumption that the general conditions of the prevalent state of affairs were permanent.

temperaments, which attends mainly to differences in the range and quality and character of the individual imagination.

This Utopian classification was a rough one, but it served its purpose to determine the broad lines of political organization; it was so far unscientific that many individuals fall between or within two or even three of its classes. But that was met by giving the correlated organization a compensatory looseness of play. Four main classes of mind were distinguished, called, respectively, the Poietic, the Kinetic, the Dull and the Base. The former two are supposed to constitute the living tissue of the State; the latter are the fulcra and resistances, the bone and cover of its body. They are not hereditary classes, nor is there any attempt to develop any class by special breeding, simply because the intricate interplay of heredity is untraceable and incalculable. They are classes to which people drift of their own accord. Education is uniform until differentiation becomes unmistakable, and each man (and woman) must establish his position with regard to the lines of this abstract classification by his own quality, choice and development. . . .

The Poietic or creative class of mental individuality embraces a wide range of types, but they agree in possessing imaginations that range beyond the known and accepted, and that involve the desire to bring the discoveries made in such excursions, into knowledge and recognition. The scope and direction of the imaginative excursion may vary very greatly. It may be the invention of something new or the discovery of something hitherto unperceived. When the invention or discovery is primarily beauty then we have the artistic type of Poietic mind; when it is not so, we have the true scientific man. The range of discovery may be narrowed as it is in the art of Whistler[3] or the science of a cytologist, or it may embrace a wide extent of relevance until at last both artist or scientific inquirer merge in the universal reference of the true philosopher. To the accumulated activities of the Poietic type reacted upon by circumstances, are due almost all the forms assumed by human thought and feeling. All religious ideas, all ideas of what is good or beautiful, entered life through the poietic inspirations of man. Except for processes of decay, the forms of the human future

must come also through men of this same type, and it is a
primary essential to our modern idea of an abundant secular
progress that these activities should be unhampered and
stimulated.

The Kinetic class consists of types, various, of course, and
merging insensibly along the boundary into the less representa-
tive constituents of the Poietic group, but distinguished by a
more restricted range of imagination. Their imaginations do
not range beyond the known, experienced and accepted, though
within these limits they may imagine as vividly or more vividly
than members of the former group. They are often very clever
and capable people, but they do not do, and they do not desire
to do, new things. The more vigorous individuals of this class
are the most teachable people in the world, and they are generally more moral and more trustworthy than the Poietic types.
They live – while the Poietics are always something of experi-
mentalists with life. The characteristics of either of these two
classes may be associated with a good or bad physique, with
excessive or defective energy, with exceptional keenness of the
senses in some determinate direction or suchlike 'bent', and the
Kinetic type, just as the Poietic type, may display an imagination
of restricted or of the most universal range. But a fairly energetic
Kinetic is probably the nearest thing to that ideal our earthly
anthropologists have in mind when they speak of the 'Normal'
human being. The very definition of the Poietic class involves a
certain abnormality.

The Utopians distinguished two extremes of this Kinetic class
according to the quality of their imaginative preferences, the
Dan and Beersheba,[4] as it were, of this division. At one end is
the mainly intellectual, unoriginal type, which, with energy of
personality, makes an admirable judge or administrator and
without it an uninventive, laborious, common mathematician,
or common scholar, or common scientific man; while at the
other end is the mainly emotional, unoriginal man, the type to
which – at a low level of personal energy – my botanist inclines.
The second type includes, amidst its energetic forms, great
actors, and popular politicians and preachers. Between these
extremes is a long and wide region of varieties, into which one

would put most of the people who form the reputable workmen, the men of substance, the trustworthy men and women, the pillars of society on earth.

Below these two classes in the Utopian scheme of things, and emerging insensibly into them, come the Dull. The Dull are persons of altogether inadequate imagination, the people who never seem to learn thoroughly, or hear distinctly, or think clearly. (I believe if everyone is to be carefully educated they would be considerably in the minority in the world, but it is quite possible that will not be the reader's opinion. It is clearly a matter of an arbitrary line.) They are the stupid people, the incompetent people, the formal, imitative people, the people who, in any properly organized State, should, as a class, gravitate towards and below the minimum wage that qualifies for marriage. The laws of heredity are far too mysterious for such offspring as they do produce to be excluded from a fair chance in the world; but for themselves, they count neither for work nor direction in the State.

Finally, with a bold disregard of the logician's classificatory rules, these Utopian statesmen who devised the World State hewed out in theory a class of the Base. The Base may, indeed, be either poietic, kinetic or dull, though most commonly they are the last, and their definition concerns not so much the quality of their imagination as a certain bias in it, that to a statesman makes it a matter for special attention. The Base have a narrower and more persistent egoistic reference than the common run of humanity; they may boast, but they have no frankness; they have relatively great powers of concealment, and they are capable of, and sometimes have an aptitude and inclination towards, cruelty. In the queer phrasing of earthly psychology with its clumsy avoidance of analysis, they have no 'moral sense'. They count as an antagonism to the State organization.

Obviously this is the rudest of classifications, and no Utopian has ever supposed it to be a classification for individual application, a classification so precise that one can say, this man is 'poietic', and that man is 'base'. In actual experience these qualities mingle and vary in every possible way. It is not a classification for Truth, but a classification to an end. Taking humanity as a multitude of unique individuals in mass, one may, for practical purposes, deal with it far more conveniently by disregarding its uniqueness and its mixed cases altogether and supposing it to be an assembly of poietic, kinetic, dull and base people. In many respects it behaves as if it were that. The State, dealing as it does only with non-individualized affairs, is not only justified in disregarding, but is bound to disregard, a man's special distinction, and to provide for him on the strength of his prevalent aspect as being on the whole poietic, kinetic or what not. In a world of hasty judgements and carping criticism, it cannot be repeated too often that the fundamental ideas of a modern Utopia imply, everywhere and in everything, margins and elasticities, a certain universal compensatory looseness of play.

§ 3

Now these Utopian statesmen who founded the World State put the problem of social organization in the following fashion: To contrive a revolutionary movement that shall absorb all existing governments and fuse them with itself, and that must be rapidly progressive and adaptable, and yet coherent, persistent, powerful and efficient.

The problem of combining progress with political stability had never been accomplished in Utopia before that time, any more than it has been accomplished on earth. Just as on earth, Utopian history was a succession of powers rising and falling in an alternation of efficient conservative with unstable liberal States. Just as on earth, so in Utopia, the kinetic type of men had displayed a more or less unintentional antagonism to the poietic. The general life-history of a State had been the same on either planet. First, through poietic activities, the idea of a community has developed, and the State has shaped itself; poietic men have arisen first in this department of national life and then that, and have given place to kinetic men of a high type – for it seems to be in their nature that poietic men should be mutually repulsive, and not succeed and develop one another consecutively – and a period of expansion and vigour has set in. The general poietic activity has declined with the development of an efficient and settled social and political organization; the statesman has given way to the politician who has incorporated the wisdom of the statesman with his own energy, the original genius in arts, letters, science and every department of activity to the cultivated and scholarly man. The kinetic man of wide range, who has assimilated his poietic predecessor, succeeds with far more readiness than his poietic contemporary in almost every human activity. The latter is by his very nature undisciplined and experimental, and is positively hampered by precedents and good order. With this substitution of the efficient for the creative type, the State ceases to grow, first in this department of activity and then in that, and so long as its conditions remain the same it remains orderly and efficient. But it has lost its power of initiative and change, its power of adaptation is gone; and with that secular change of conditions which is the law of life, stresses must arise within and without, and bring at last either through revolution or through defeat the release of fresh poietic power. The process, of course, is not in its entirety simple; it may be masked by the fact that one department of activity may be in its poietic stage, while another is in a phase of realization. In the United States of America, for example, during the nineteenth century, there was great poietic activity in industrial organization, and none whatever in political philosophy; but a careful analysis of the history of any period will show the rhythm almost invariably present, and the initial problem before the Utopian philosopher, therefore, was whether this was an inevitable alternation, whether human progress was necessarily a series of developments, collapses and fresh beginnings, after an interval of disorder, unrest and often great unhappiness, or whether it was possible to maintain a secure, happy and progressive State beside an unbroken flow of poietic activity.

Clearly they decided upon the second alternative. If, indeed, I am listening to my Utopian self, then they not only decided the problem could be solved, but they solved it.

He tells me how they solved it.

A modern Utopia differs from all the older Utopias in its recognition of the need of poietic activities – one sees this new consideration creeping into thought for the first time in the phrasing of Comte's insistence that 'spiritual' must precede political reconstruction, and in his admission of the necessity of recurrent books and poems about Utopias – and at first this recognition appears to admit only an added complication to a problem already unmanageably complex. Comte's separation of the activities of a State into the spiritual and material does, to a certain extent, anticipate this opposition of poietic and kinetic; but the intimate texture of his mind was dull and hard, the conception slipped from him again, and his suppression of literary activities, and his imposition of a rule of life upon the poietic types, who are least able to sustain it, mark how deeply he went under. To a large extent he followed the older Utopists in assuming that the philosophical and constructive problem could be done once for all; and he worked the results out simply under an organized kinetic government. But what seems to be merely an addition to the difficulty may in the end turn out to be a simplification, just as the introduction of a fresh term to an intricate irreducible mathematical expression will at times bring it to unity.

Now philosophers after my Utopian pattern, who find the ultimate significance in life in individuality, novelty and the undefined, would not only regard the poietic element as the most important in human society, but would perceive quite clearly the impossibility of its organization. This, indeed, is simply the application to the moral and intellectual fabric of the principles already applied in discussing the State control of reproduction (in Chapter 6, § 2). But just as in the case of births it was possible for the State to frame limiting conditions within which individuality plays more freely than in the void, so the founders of this Modern Utopia believed it possible to define conditions under which every individual born with poietic gifts should be enabled and encouraged to give them a full development, in art, philosophy, invention or discovery. Certain general conditions presented themselves as obviously reasonable: to give every citizen as good an education as he or she could acquire, for example; to frame it so that the directed educational process would never at any period occupy the whole available time of the learner, but would provide throughout a marginal free leisure with opportunities for developing idiosyncrasies, and to ensure by the expedient of a minimum wage for a specified amount of work, that leisure and opportunity did not cease throughout life.

But in addition to thus making poietic activities universally possible, the founders of this Modern Utopia sought to supply incentives, which was an altogether more difficult research, a problem in its nature irresolvably complex and admitting of no systematic solution. But my double told me of a great variety of devices by which poietic men and women were given honour and enlarged freedoms, so soon as they produced an earnest of their quality; and he explained to me how great an ambition they might entertain.

There were great systems of laboratories attached to every municipal force station at which research could be conducted under the most favourable conditions; and every mine, and indeed almost every great industrial establishment, was saddled under its lease with similar obligations. So much for poietic ability and research in physical science. The World State tried the claims of every living contributor to any materially valuable invention, and paid or charged a royalty on its use that went partly to him personally and partly to the research institution that had produced him. In the matter of literature and the philosophical and sociological sciences, every higher educational establishment carried its studentships, its fellowships, its occasional lectureships; and to produce a poem, a novel, a speculative work of force or merit, was to become the object of a generous competition between rival Universities. In Utopia, any author has the option either of publishing his works through the public bookseller as a private speculation, or, if he is of sufficient merit, of accepting a University endowment and conceding his copyright to the University press. All sorts of grants in the hands of committees of the most varied constitution, supplemented these academic resources, and ensured that no possible contributor to the wide flow of the Utopian

mind slipped into neglect. Apart from those who engaged
mainly in teaching and administration, my double told me that
the worldwide House of Salomon*[5] thus created sustained over
a million men. For all the rarity of large fortunes, therefore, no
original man with the desire and capacity for material or mental
experiments went long without resources and the stimulus of
attention, criticism and rivalry.

'And finally,' said my double, 'our Rules ensure a considerable understanding of the importance of poietic activities in the
majority of the samurai in whose hands as a class all the real
power of the world resides.'

'Ah!' said I, 'and now we come to the thing that interests me
most. For it is quite clear, in my mind, that these samurai form
the real body of the State. All this time that I have spent going
to and fro in this planet, it has been growing upon me that this
order of men and women, wearing such a uniform as you wear,
and with faces strengthened by discipline and touched with
devotion, is the Utopian reality; but that for them, the whole
fabric of these fair appearances would crumble and tarnish,
shrink and shrivel, until at last, back I should be amidst the
grime and disorders of the life of earth. Tell me about these
samurai, who remind me of Plato's guardians, who look like
Knights Templars, who bear a name that recalls the swordsmen
of Japan ... and whose uniform you yourself are wearing.
What are they? Are they an hereditary caste, a specially educated order, an elected class? For certainly this world turns
upon them as a door upon its hinges.'

§ 4

'I follow the Common Rule, as many men do,' said my double,
answering my allusion to his uniform almost apologetically.
'But my own work is, in its nature, poietic; there is much
dissatisfaction with our isolation of criminals upon islands, and
I am analysing the psychology of prison officials and criminals
in general with a view to some better scheme. I am supposed to

* The *New Atlantis*.

be ingenious with expedients in this direction. Typically, the samurai are engaged in administrative work. Practically the whole of the responsible rule of the world is in their hands; all our head teachers and disciplinary heads of colleges, our judges, barristers, employers of labour beyond a certain limit, practising medical men, legislators, must be samurai, and all the executive committees, and so forth, that play so large a part in our affairs are drawn by lot exclusively from them. The order is not hereditary – we know just enough of biology and the uncertainties of inheritance to know how silly that would be – and it does not require an early consecration or novitiate or ceremonies and initiations of that sort. The samurai are, in fact, volunteers. Any intelligent adult in a reasonably healthy and efficient state may, at any age after five-and-twenty, become one of the samurai, and take a hand in the universal control.'

'Provided he follows the Rule.'

'Precisely – provided he follows the Rule.'

'I have heard the phrase, "voluntary nobility".'

'That was the idea of our Founders. They made a noble and privileged order – open to the whole world. No one could complain of an unjust exclusion, for the only thing that could exclude from the order was unwillingness or inability to follow the Rule.'

'But the Rule might easily have been made exclusive of special lineages and races.'

'That wasn't their intention. The Rule was planned to exclude the dull, to be unattractive to the base, and to direct and co-ordinate all sound citizens of good intent.'

'And it has succeeded?'

'As well as anything finite can. Life is still imperfect, still a thick felt of dissatisfactions and perplexing problems, but most certainly the quality of all its problems has been raised, and there has been no war, no grinding poverty, not half the disease, and an enormous increase of the order, beauty and resources of life since the samurai, who began as a private aggressive cult, won their way to the rule of the world.'

'I would like to have that history,' I said. 'I expect there was fighting?' He nodded. 'But first – tell me about the Rule.'

'The Rule aims to exclude the dull and base altogether, to discipline the impulses and emotions, to develop a moral habit and sustain a man in periods of stress, fatigue and temptation, to produce the maximum co-operation of all men of good intent, and, in fact, to keep all the samurai in a state of moral and bodily health and efficiency. It does as much of this as well as it can, but, of course, like all general propositions, it does not do it in any case with absolute precision. On the whole, it is so good that most men who, like myself, are doing poietic work, and who would be just as well off without obedience, find a satisfaction in adhesion. At first, in the militant days, it was a trifle hard and uncompromising; it had rather too strong an appeal to the moral prig and harshly righteous man; but it has undergone, and still undergoes, revision and expansion, and every year it becomes a little better adapted to the need of a general rule of life that all men may try to follow. We have now a whole literature, with many very fine things in it, written about the Rule.'

He glanced at a little book on his desk, took it up as if to show it me, then put it down again.

'The Rule consists of three parts: there is the list of things that qualify, the list of things that must not be done and the list of things that must be done. Qualification exacts a little exertion, as evidence of good faith; and it is designed to weed out the duller dull and many of the base. Our schooling period ends now about fourteen, and a small number of boys and girls – about three per cent – are set aside then as unteachable, as, in fact, nearly idiotic; the rest go on to a college or upper school.'

'All your population?'

'With that exception.'

'Free?'

'Of course. And they pass out of college at eighteen. There are several different college courses, but one or other must be followed and a satisfactory examination passed at the end – perhaps ten per cent fail – and the Rule requires that the candidate for the samurai must have passed.'

'But a very good man is sometimes an idle schoolboy.'

'We admit that. And so anyone who has failed to pass the

college-leaving examination may at any time in later life sit for it again – and again and again. Certain carefully specified things excuse it altogether.'

'That makes it fair. But aren't there people who cannot pass examinations?'

'People of nervous instability—'

'But they may be people of great though irregular poietic gifts.'

'Exactly. That is quite possible. But we don't want that sort of people among our samurai. Passing an examination is a proof of a certain steadiness of purpose, a certain self-control and submission—'

'Of a certain "ordinariness".'

'Exactly what is wanted.'

'Of course, those others can follow other careers.'

'Yes. That's what we want them to do. And besides these two educational qualifications, there are two others of a similar kind of more debatable value. One is practically not in operation now. Our Founders put it that a candidate for the samurai must possess what they called a Technic and, as it operated in the beginning, he had to hold the qualification for a doctor, for a lawyer, for a military officer, or an engineer, or teacher, or have painted acceptable pictures, or written a book, or something of the sort. He had in fact, as people say, to "be something", or to have "done something". It was a regulation of vague intention even in the beginning, and it became catholic to the pitch of absurdity. To play a violin skilfully has been accepted as sufficient for this qualification. There may have been a reason in the past for this provision; in those days there were many daughters of prosperous parents – and even some sons – who did nothing whatever but idle uninterestingly in the world, and the organization might have suffered by their invasion; but that reason has gone now, and the requirement remains a merely ceremonial requirement. But, on the other hand, another has developed. Our Founders made a collection of several volumes which they called, collectively, the Book of the Samurai, a compilation of articles and extracts, poems and prose pieces, which were supposed to embody the idea of the order. It was to play the part for the samurai that the Bible did for the ancient Hebrews. To tell you the truth, the stuff was of very unequal merit; there was a lot of very second-rate rhetoric, and some nearly namby-pamby verse. There was also included a quantity of verse and prose that had the trick of seeming wise. But for all such defects, much of the Book from the very beginning was splendid and inspiring matter. From that time to this, the Book of the Samurai has been under revision; much has been added, much rejected, and some deliberately rewritten. Now there is hardly anything in it that is not beautiful and perfect in form. The whole range of noble emotions finds expression there, and all the guiding ideas of our Modern State. We have recently admitted some terse criticism of its contents by a man named Henley.'[6]

'Old Henley!'

'A man who died a little time ago.'

'I knew that man on earth. And he was in Utopia too! He was a great red-faced man, with fiery hair, a noisy, intolerant maker of enemies, with a tender heart – and he was one of the samurai?'

'He defied the Rules.'

'He was a great man with wine. He wrote like wine; in our world he wrote wine; red wine with the light shining through.'

'He was on the Committee that revised our Canon. For the revising and bracing of our Canon is work for poietic as well as kinetic men. You knew him in your world?'

'I wish I had. But I have seen him. On earth he wrote a thing . . . it would run—

> "Out of the night that covers me,
>   Black as the pit from pole to pole,
> I thank whatever Gods may be,
>   For my unconquerable soul. . . ."

'We have that here. All good earthly things are in Utopia also. We put that in the Canon almost as soon as he died,' said my double.

§ 5

'We have now a double Canon, a very fine First Canon, and a Second Canon of work by living men and work of inferior quality, and a satisfactory knowledge of both of these is the fourth intellectual qualification for the samurai.'

'It must keep a sort of uniformity in your tone of thought.'

'The Canon pervades our whole world. As a matter of fact, very much of it is read and learnt in the schools. . . . Next to the intellectual qualification comes the physical, the man must be in sound health, free from certain foul, avoidable and demoralizing diseases, and in good training. We reject men who are fat, or thin and flabby, or whose nerves are shaky – we refer them back to training. And finally the man or woman must be fully adult.'

'Twenty-one? But you said twenty-five!'

'The age has varied. At first it was twenty-five or over; then the minimum became twenty-five for men and twenty-one for women. Now there is a feeling that it ought to be raised. We don't want to take advantage of mere boy and girl emotions – men of my way of thinking, at any rate, don't – we want to get our samurai with experiences, with a settled mature conviction. Our hygiene and regimen are rapidly pushing back old age and death, and keeping men hale and hearty to eighty and more. There's no need to hurry the young. Let them have a chance of wine, love and song; let them feel the bite of full-bodied desire, and know what devils they have to reckon with.'

'But there is a certain fine sort of youth that knows the desirability of the better things at nineteen.'

'They may keep the Rule at any time – without its privileges. But a man who breaks the Rule after his adult adhesion at five and twenty is no more in the samurai for ever. Before that age he is free to break it and repent.'

'And now, what is forbidden?'

'We forbid a good deal. Many small pleasures do no great harm, but we think it well to forbid them, none the less, so that we can weed out the self-indulgent. We think that a constant resistance to little seductions is good for a man's quality. At

any rate, it shows that a man is prepared to pay something for
his honour and privileges. We prescribe a regimen of food,
forbid tobacco, wine or any alcoholic drink, all narcotic
drugs—'

'Meat?'

'In all the round world of Utopia there is no meat. There
used to be. But now we cannot stand the thought of slaughter-
houses. And in a population that is all educated, and at about
the same level of physical refinement, it is practically impossible
to find anyone who will hew a dead ox or pig. We never settled
the hygienic question of meat-eating at all. This other aspect
decided us. I can still remember, as a boy, the rejoicings over
the closing of the last slaughterhouse.'

'You eat fish.'

'It isn't a matter of logic. In our barbaric past horrible flayed
carcasses of brutes dripping blood, were hung for sale in the
public streets.' He shrugged his shoulders.

'They do that still in London – in *my* world,' I said.

He looked again at my laxer, coarser face, and did not say
whatever thought had passed across his mind.

'Originally the samurai were forbidden usury, that is to say
the lending of money at fixed rates of interest. They are still
under that interdiction, but since our commercial code practically prevents usury altogether, and our law will not recognize
contracts for interest upon private accommodation loans to
unprosperous borrowers, it is now scarcely necessary. The idea
of a man growing richer by mere inaction and at the expense
of an impoverishing debtor, is profoundly distasteful to Utopian
ideas, and our State insists pretty effectually now upon the
participation of the lender in the borrower's risks. This, however, is only one part of a series of limitations of the same
character. It is felt that to buy simply in order to sell again
brings out many unsocial human qualities; it makes a man seek
to enhance profits and falsify values, and so the samurai are
forbidden to buy to sell on their own account or for any
employer save the State, unless some process of manufacture
changes the nature of the commodity (a mere change in bulk
or packing does not suffice), and they are forbidden salesman-

ship and all its arts. Consequently they cannot be hotel-keepers, or hotel proprietors, or hotel shareholders, and a doctor – all practising doctors must be samurai – cannot sell drugs except as a public servant of the municipality or the State.'

'That, of course, runs counter to all our current terrestrial ideas,' I said. 'We are obsessed by the power of money. These rules will work out as a vow of moderate poverty, and if your samurai are an order of poor men—'

'They need not be. Samurai who have invented, organized and developed new industries have become rich men, and many men who have grown rich by brilliant and original trading have subsequently become samurai.'

'But these are exceptional cases. The bulk of your money-making business must be confined to men who are not samurai. You must have a class of rich, powerful outsiders—'

'*Have* we?'

'I don't see the evidences of them.'

'As a matter of fact, we have such people! There are rich traders, men who have made discoveries in the economy of distribution, or who have called attention by intelligent, truthful advertisement to the possibilities of neglected commodities, for example.'

'But aren't they a power?'

'Why should they be?'

'Wealth *is* power.'

I had to explain that phrase.

He protested. 'Wealth,' he said, 'is no sort of power at all unless you make it one. If it is so in your world it is so by inadvertency. Wealth is a State-made thing, a convention, the most artificial of powers. You can, by subtle statesmanship, contrive what it shall buy and what it shall not. In your world it would seem you have made leisure, movement, any sort of freedom, life itself, *purchasable*. The more fools you! A poor working man with you is a man in discomfort and fear. No wonder your rich have power. But here a reasonable leisure, a decent life, is to be had by every man on easier terms than by selling himself to the rich. And rich as men are here, there is no private fortune in the whole world that is more than a little thing beside the wealth of the State. The samurai control the State and the wealth of the State, and by their vows they may not avail themselves of any of the coarser pleasures wealth can still buy. Where, then, is the power of your wealthy man?'

'But, then – where is the incentive—?'

'Oh! a man gets things for himself with wealth – no end of things. But little or no power over his fellows – unless they are exceptionally weak or self-indulgent persons.'

I reflected. 'What else may not the samurai do?'

'Acting, singing or reciting are forbidden them, though they may lecture authoritatively or debate. But professional mimicry is not only held to be undignified in a man or woman, but to weaken and corrupt the soul; the mind becomes foolishly dependent on applause, overskilful in producing tawdry and momentary illusions of excellence; it is our experience that actors and actresses as a class are loud, ignoble and insincere. If they have not such flamboyant qualities then they are tepid and ineffectual players. Nor may the samurai do personal services, except in the matter of medicine or surgery; they may not be barbers, for example, nor inn waiters, nor boot cleaners. But nowadays we have scarcely any barbers or boot cleaners; men do these things for themselves. Nor may a man under the Rule be any man's servant, pledged to do whatever he is told. He may neither be a servant nor keep one; he must shave and dress and serve himself, carry his own food from the helper's place to the table, redd his sleeping room and leave it clean. . . .'

'That is all easy enough in a world as ordered as yours. I suppose no samurai may bet?'

'Absolutely not. He may insure his life and his old age for the better equipment of his children, or for certain other specified ends, but that is all his dealings with chance. And he is also forbidden to play games in public or to watch them being played. Certain dangerous and hardy sports and exercises are prescribed for him, but not competitive sports between man and man or side and side. That lesson was learnt long ago before the coming of the samurai. Gentlemen of honour, according to the old standards, rode horses, raced chariots, fought and played competitive games of skill; and the dull, cowardly and base came in thousands to admire, and howl, and bet. The gentlemen of honour degenerated fast enough into a sort of athletic prostitute, with all the defects, all the vanity, trickery and self-assertion of the common actor, and with even less intelligence. Our Founders made no peace with this organization of public sports. They did not spend their lives to secure for all men and women on the earth freedom, health and leisure, in order that they might waste lives in such folly.'

'We have those abuses,' I said, 'but some of our earthly games have a fine side. There is a game called cricket. It is a fine, generous game.'

'Our boys play that, and men too. But it is thought rather puerile to give very much time to it; men should have graver interests. It was undignified and unpleasant for the samurai to play conspicuously ill, and impossible for them to play so constantly as to keep hand and eye in training against the man who was fool enough and cheap enough to become an expert. Cricket, tennis, fives, billiards – you will find clubs and a class of men to play all these things in Utopia, but not the samurai. And they must play their games as games, not as displays; the price of a privacy for playing cricket, so that they could charge for admission, would be overwhelmingly high. . . . Negroes are often very clever at cricket. For a time, most of the samurai had their swordplay, but few do those exercises now; and until about fifty years ago they went out for military training, a fortnight in every year, marching long distances, sleeping in the open, carrying provisions and sham-fighting over unfamiliar ground dotted with disappearing targets. There was a curious inability in our world to realize that war was really over for good and all.'

'And now,' I said, 'haven't we got very nearly to the end of your prohibitions? You have forbidden alcohol, drugs, smoking, betting, and usury, games, trade, servants. But isn't there a vow of Chastity?'

'That is the Rule for your earthly orders?'

'Yes – except, if I remember rightly, for Plato's Guardians.'

'There is a Rule of Chastity here – but not of Celibacy. We

know quite clearly that civilization is an artificial arrangement, and that all the physical and emotional instincts of man are too strong, and his natural instinct of restraint too weak, for him to live easily in the civilized State. Civilization has developed far more rapidly than man has modified. Under the unnatural perfection of security, liberty and abundance our civilization has attained, the normal untrained human being is disposed to excess in almost every direction; he tends to eat too much and too elaborately, to drink too much, to become lazy faster than his work can be reduced, to waste his interest upon displays, and to make love too much and too elaborately. He gets out of training, and concentrates upon egoistic or erotic broodings. The past history of our race is very largely a history of social collapses due to demoralization by indulgences following security and abundance. In the time of our Founders the signs of a worldwide epoch of prosperity and relaxation were plentiful. Both sexes drifted towards sexual excesses, the men towards sentimental extravagances, imbecile devotions, and the complication and refinement of physical indulgences; the women towards those expansions and differentiations of feeling that find expression in music and costly and distinguished dress. Both sexes became unstable and promiscuous. The whole world seemed disposed to do exactly the same thing with its sexual interest as it had done with its appetite for food and drink – make the most of it.'

He paused.

'Satiety came to help you,' I said.

'Destruction may come before satiety. Our Founders organized motives from all sorts of sources, but I think the chief force to give men self-control is Pride. Pride may not be the noblest thing in the soul, but it is the best King there, for all that. They looked to it to keep a man clean and sound and sane. In this matter, as in all matters of natural desire, they held no appetite must be glutted, no appetite must have artificial whets, and also and equally that no appetite should be starved. A man must come from the table satisfied, but not replete. And in the matter of love, a straight and clean desire for a clean and straight fellow creature was our Founders' ideal. They enjoined marriage between equals as the samurai's duty to the race, and they framed directions of the precisest sort to prevent that uxorious inseparableness, that connubiality which will reduce a couple of people to something jointly less than either. That Canon is too long to tell you now. A man under the Rule who loves a woman who does not follow it, must either leave the samurai to marry her, or induce her to accept what is called the Woman's Rule, which, while it excepts her from the severer qualifications and disciplines, brings her regimen of life into a working harmony with his.'

'Suppose she breaks the Rule afterwards?'

'He must leave either her or the order.'

'There is matter for a novel or so in that.'

'There has been matter for hundreds.'

'Is the Woman's Rule a sumptuary law as well as a regimen? I mean – may she dress as she pleases?'

'Not a bit of it,' said my double. 'Every woman who could command money used it, we found, to make underbred aggressions on other women. As men emerged to civilization, women seemed going back to savagery – to paint and feathers. But the samurai, both men and women, and the women under the Lesser Rule also, all have a particular dress. No difference is made between women under either the Great or the Lesser Rule. You have seen the men's dress – always like this I wear. The women may wear the same, either with the hair cut short or plaited behind them, or they may have a high-waisted dress of very fine, soft woollen material, with their hair coiled up behind.'

'I have seen it,' I said. Indeed, nearly all the women had seemed to be wearing variants of that simple formula. 'It seems to me a very beautiful dress. The other – I'm not used to. But I like it on girls and slender women.'

I had a thought, and added, 'Don't they sometimes, well – take a good deal of care, dressing their hair?'

My double laughed in my eyes. 'They do,' he said.

'And the Rule?'

'The Rule is never fussy,' said my double, still smiling.

'We don't want women to cease to be beautiful, and consciously beautiful if you like,' he added. 'The more real beauty of form and face we have, the finer our world. But costly sexualized trappings—'

'I should have thought,' I said, 'a class of women who traded on their sex would have arisen, women, I mean, who found an interest and an advantage in emphasizing their individual womanly beauty. There is no law to prevent it. Surely they would tend to counteract the severity of costume the Rule dictates.'

'There are such women. But for all that the Rule sets the key of everyday dress. If a woman is possessed by the passion for gorgeous raiment she usually satisfies it in her own private circle, or with rare occasional onslaughts upon the public eye. Her everyday mood and the disposition of most people is against being conspicuous abroad. And I should say there are little liberties under the Lesser Rule; a discreet use of fine needlework and embroidery, a wider choice of materials.'

'You have no changing fashions?'

'None. For all that, are not our dresses as beautiful as yours?'

'Our women's dresses are not beautiful at all,' I said, forced for a time towards the mysterious philosophy of dress. 'Beauty? That isn't their concern.'

'Then what are they after?'

'My dear man! What is all my world after?'

## § 6

I should come to our third talk with a great curiosity to hear of the last portion of the Rule, of the things that the samurai are obliged to do.

There would be many precise directions regarding his health, and rules that would aim at once at health and that constant exercise of will that makes life good. Save in specified exceptional circumstances, the samurai must bathe in cold water, and the men must shave every day; they have the precisest directions in such matters; the body must be in health, the skin and muscles and nerves in perfect tone, or the samurai must go to the doctors of the order, and give implicit obedience to the regimen prescribed. They must sleep alone at least four nights in five; and they must eat with and talk to anyone in their fellowship who cares for their conversation for an hour, at least, at the nearest clubhouse of the samurai once on three chosen days in every week. Moreover, they must read aloud from the Book of the Samurai for at least ten minutes every day. Every month they must buy and read faithfully through at least one book that has been published during the past five years, and the only intervention with private choice in that matter is the prescription of a certain minimum of length for the monthly book or books. But the full Rule in these minor compulsory matters is voluminous and detailed, and it abounds with alternatives. Its aim is rather to keep before the samurai by a number of sample duties as it were, the need of, and some of the chief methods towards health of body and mind, rather than to provide a comprehensive rule; and to ensure the main-tenance of a community of feeling and interests among the samurai through habit, intercourse and a living contemporary literature. These minor obligations do not earmark more than an hour in the day. Yet they serve to break down isolations of sympathy, all sorts of physical and intellectual sluggishness and the development of unsocial preoccupations of many sorts.

Women samurai who are married, my double told me, must bear children – if they are to remain married as well as in the order – before the second period for terminating a childless marriage is exhausted. I failed to ask for the precise figures from my double at the time, but I think it is beyond doubt that it is from samurai mothers of the Greater or Lesser Rule that a very large proportion of the future population of Utopia will be derived. There is one liberty accorded to women samurai which is refused to men, and that is to marry outside the Rule, and women married to men not under the Rule are also free to become samurai. Here, too, it will be manifest there is scope for novels and the drama of life. In practice, it seems that it is only men of great poietic distinction outside the Rule, or great commercial leaders, who have wives under it. The tendency of such unions is either to bring the husband under the Rule, or take the wife out of it. There can be no doubt that these marriage limitations tend to make the samurai something of an hereditary class. Their children, as a rule, become samurai. But it is not an exclusive caste; subject to the most reasonable qualifications, anyone who sees fit can enter it at any time, and so, unlike all other privileged castes the world has seen, it increases relatively to the total population, and may indeed at last assimilate almost the whole population of the earth.

## § 7

So much my double told me readily.

But now he came to the heart of all his explanations, to the will and motives at the centre that made men and women ready to undergo discipline, to renounce the richness and elaboration of the sensuous life, to master emotions and control impulses, to keep in the key of effort while they had abundance about them to rouse and satisfy all desires, and his exposition was more difficult.

He tried to make his religion clear to me.

The leading principle of the Utopian religion is the repudiation of the doctrine of original sin; the Utopians hold that man, on the whole, is good. That is their cardinal belief. Man has pride and conscience, they hold, that you may refine by training as you refine his eye and ear; he has remorse and sorrow in his being, coming on the heels of all inconsequent enjoyments. How can one think of him as bad? He is religious; religion is as natural to him as lust and anger, less intense, indeed, but coming with a wide-sweeping inevitableness as peace comes after all tumults and noises. And in Utopia they understand this, or at least the samurai do, clearly. They accept Religion as they accept Thirst, as something inseparably in the mysterious rhythms of life. And just as thirst and pride and all desires may be perverted in an age of abundant opportunities, and men may be degraded and wasted by intemperance in drinking, by display, or by ambition, so too the nobler complex of desires that constitutes religion may be turned to evil by the dull, the base and the careless. Slovenly indulgence in religious inclinations, a failure to think hard and discriminate as fairly as possible in religious matters, is just as alien to the men under the Rule as it would be to drink deeply because they were thirsty, eat until glutted, evade a bath because the day was chilly, or make love to any bright-eyed girl who chanced to look pretty in the dusk. Utopia, which is to have every type of character that one finds on earth, will have its temples and its priests just as it will have its actresses and wine; but the samurai will be forbidden the religion of dramatically lit altars, organ music and incense, as distinctly as they are forbidden the love of painted women or the consolations of brandy. And to all the things that are less than religion and that seek to comprehend it, to cosmogonies and philosophies, to creeds and formulae, to catechisms and easy explanations, the attitude of the samurai, the note of the Book of the Samurai, will be distrust. These things, the samurai will say, are part of the indulgences that should come before a man submits himself to the Rule; they are like the early gratifications of young men, experiences to establish renunciation. The samurai will have emerged above these things.

The theology of the Utopian rulers will be saturated with that same philosophy of uniqueness, that repudiation of anything beyond similarities and practical parallelisms, that saturates all their institutions. They will have analysed exhaustively those fallacies and assumptions that arise between the One and the Many, that have troubled philosophy since philosophy began. Just as they will have escaped that delusive unification of every species under its specific definition that has dominated earthly reasoning, so they will have escaped the delusive simplification of God that vitiates all terrestrial theology. They will hold God to be complex and of an endless variety of aspects, to be expressed by no universal formula nor approved in any uniform manner. Just as the language of Utopia will be a synthesis, even so will its God be. The aspect of God is different in the measure of every man's individuality; and the intimate thing of religion must, therefore, exist in human solitude, between man and God alone. Religion in its quintessence is a relation between God and man; it is perversion to make it a relation between man and man; and a man may no more reach God through a priest than love his wife through a priest. But just as a man in love may refine the interpretation of his feelings and borrow expression from the poems and music of poietic men, so an individual man may at his discretion read books of devotion and hear music that is in harmony with his inchoate feelings. Many of the samurai, therefore, will set themselves private regimens that will help their secret religious life, will pray habitually and read books of devotion, but with these things the Rule of the order will have nothing to do.

Clearly the God of the samurai is a transcendental and mystical God. So far as the samurai have a purpose in common in maintaining the State and the order and progress of the world, so far, by their discipline and denial, by their public work and effort, they worship God together. But the fount of motives lies in the individual life, it lies in silent and deliberate reflections; and at this the most striking of all the rules of the samurai aims. For seven consecutive days in the year, at least, each man or woman under the Rule must go right out of all the life of man into some wild and solitary place, must speak to no man or woman, and have no sort of intercourse with mankind. They must go bookless and weaponless, without pen or paper or money. Provisions must be taken for the period of the journey, a rug or sleeping sack – for they must sleep under the open sky – but no means of making a fire. They may study maps beforehand to guide them, showing any difficulties and dangers in the journey, but they may not carry such helps. They must not go by beaten ways or wherever there are inhabited houses, but into the bare, quiet places of the globe – the regions set apart for them.

This discipline, my double said, was invented to secure a certain stoutness of heart and body in the members of the order, which otherwise might have lain open to too many timorous, merely abstemious, men and women. Many things had been suggested, swordplay and tests that verged on torture, climbing in giddy places and the like, before this was chosen. Partly it is to ensure good training and sturdiness of body and mind, but partly, also, it is to draw their minds for a space from the insistent details of life, from the intricate arguments and the fretting effort to work, from personal quarrels and personal affections, and the things of the heated room. Out they must go, clean out of the world.

Certain great areas are set apart for these yearly pilgrimages beyond the securities of the State. There are thousands of square miles of sandy desert in Africa and Asia set apart; much of the Arctic and Antarctic circles; vast areas of mountain land and frozen marsh; secluded reserves of forest, and innumerable unfrequented lines upon the sea. Some are dangerous and laborious routes; some merely desolate; and there are even some sea journeys that one may take in the halcyon days as one drifts through a dream. Upon the seas one must go in a little undecked sailing boat, that may be rowed in a calm; all the other journeys one must do afoot, none aiding. There are, about all these desert regions and along most coasts, little offices at which the samurai says goodbye to the world of men, and at which they arrive after their minimum time of silence is overpast. For the intervening days they must be alone with Nature, necessity and their own thoughts.

'It is good?' I said.

'It is good,' my double answered. 'We civilized men go back to the stark Mother that so many of us would have forgotten were it not for this Rule. And one thinks. . . . Only two weeks ago I did my journey for the year. I went with my gear by sea to Tromsö, and then inland to a starting-place, and took my ice axe and rucksack and said goodbye to the world. I crossed over four glaciers; I climbed three high mountain passes, and slept on moss in desolate valleys. I saw no human being for seven days. Then I came down through pine woods to the head of a road that runs to the Baltic shore. Altogether it was thirteen days before I reported myself again, and had speech with fellow creatures.'

'And the women do this?'

'The women who are truly samurai – yes. Equally with the men. Unless the coming of children intervenes.'

I asked him how it had seemed to him, and what he thought about during the journey.

'There is always a sense of effort for me,' he said, 'when I leave the world at the outset of the journey. I turn back again

and again, and look at the little office as I go up my mountainside. The first day and night I'm a little disposed to shirk
the job – every year it's the same – a little disposed, for example,
to sling my pack from my back and sit down, and go through
its contents and make sure I've got all my equipment.'

'There's no chance of anyone overtaking you?'

'Two men mustn't start from the same office on the same
route within six hours of each other. If they come within sight
of each other, they must shun an encounter, and make no sign
– unless life is in danger. All that is arranged beforehand.'

'It would be, of course. Go on telling me of your journey.'

'I dread the night. I dread discomfort and bad weather. I only
begin to brace up after the second day.'

'Don't you worry about losing your way?'

'No. There are cairns and skyline signs. If it wasn't for that,
of course we should be worrying with maps the whole time.
But I'm only sure of being a man after the second night, and
sure of my power to go through.'

'And then?'

'Then one begins to get into it. The first two days one is apt
to have the events of one's journey, little incidents of travel and
thoughts of one's work and affairs, rising and fading and
coming again; but then the perspectives begin. I don't sleep
much at night on these journeys; I lie awake and stare at the
stars. About dawn, perhaps, and in the morning sunshine, I
sleep! The nights this last time were very short, never more than
twilight, and I saw the glow of the sun always, just over the
edge of the world. But I had chosen the days of the new moon,
so that I could have a glimpse of the stars. . . . Years ago, I went
from the Nile across the Libyan Desert east, and then the stars
– the stars in the later days of that journey – brought me near
weeping. . . . You begin to feel alone on the third day, when
you find yourself out on some shining snowfield, and nothing
of mankind visible in the whole world save one landmark, one
remote thin red triangle of iron perhaps, in the saddle of the
ridge against the sky. All this busy world that has done so much
and so marvellously, and is still so little – you see it little as it
is – and far off. All day long you go and the night comes, and

it might be another planet. Then, in the quiet waking hours, one thinks of one's self and the great external things, of space and eternity, and what one means by God.'

He mused.

'You think of death?'

'Not of my own. But when I go among snows and desolations – and usually I take my pilgrimage in mountains or the north – I think very much of the Night of this World – the time when our sun will be red and dull, and air and water will lie frozen together in a common snowfield where now the forests of the tropics are steaming. . . . I think very much of that, and whether it is indeed God's purpose that our kind should end, and the cities we have built, the books we have written, all that we have given substance and a form, should lie dead beneath the snows.'

'You don't believe that?'

'No. But if it is not so – I went threading my way among gorges and precipices, with my poor brain dreaming of what the alternative should be, with my imagination straining and failing. Yet in those high airs and in such solitude, a kind of exaltation comes to men. . . . I remember that one night I sat up and told the rascal stars very earnestly how they should not escape us in the end.'

He glanced at me for a moment as though he doubted I should understand.

'One becomes a personification up there,' he said.

'One becomes the ambassador of mankind to the outer world.

'There is time to think over a lot of things. One puts one's self and one's ambition in a new pair of scales. . . .

'Then there are hours when one is just exploring the wilderness like a child. Sometimes perhaps one gets a glimpse from some precipice edge of the plains far away, and houses and roadways, and remembers there is still a busy world of men. And at last one turns one's feet down some slope, some gorge that leads back. You come down, perhaps, into a pine forest, and hear that queer clatter reindeer make – and then, it may be, see a herdsman very far away, watching you. You wear your pilgrim's badge, and he makes no sign of seeing you. . . .

'You know, after these solitudes, I feel just the same queer disinclination to go back to the world of men that I feel when I have to leave it. I think of dusty roads and hot valleys, and being looked at by many people. I think of the trouble of working with colleagues and opponents. This last journey I outstayed my time, camping in the pine woods for six days. Then my thoughts came round to my proper work again. I got keen to go on with it, and so I came back into the world. You come back physically clean – as though you had had your arteries and veins washed out. And your brain has been cleaned too. . . . I shall stick to the mountains now until I am old, and then I shall sail a boat in Polynesia. That is what so many old men do. Only last year one of the great leaders of the samurai – a white-haired man, who followed the Rule in spite of his one hundred and eleven years – was found dead in his boat far away from any land, far to the south, lying like a child asleep. . . .'

'That's better than a tumbled bed,' said I, 'and some boy of a doctor jabbing you with injections, and distressful people hovering about you.'

'Yes,' said my double; 'in Utopia we who are samurai die better than that. . . . Is that how your great men die?' . . .

It came to me suddenly as very strange that even as we sat and talked, across deserted seas, on burning sands, through the still aisles of forests, and in all the high and lonely places of the world, beyond the margin where the ways and houses go, solitary men and women sailed alone or marched alone, or clambered – quiet, resolute exiles; they stood alone amidst wildernesses of ice, on the precipitous banks of roaring torrents, in monstrous caverns, or steering a tossing boat in the little circle of the horizon amidst the tumbled, incessant sea, all in their several ways communing with the emptiness, the enigmatic spaces and silences, the winds and torrents and soulless forces that lie about the lit and ordered life of men.

I saw more clearly now something I had seen dimly already in the bearing and the faces of this Utopian chivalry, a faint persistent tinge of detachment from the immediate heats and hurries, the little graces and delights, the tensions and stimulations of the daily world. It pleased me strangely to think of this steadfast yearly pilgrimage of solitude, and how near men might come then to the high distances of God.

§ 8

After that I remember we fell talking of the discipline of the Rule, of the Courts that try breaches of it, and interpret doubtful cases – for though a man may resign with due notice and be free after a certain time to rejoin again, one deliberate breach may exclude a man for ever – of the system of law that has grown up about such trials, and of the triennial council that revises and alters the Rule. From that we passed to the discussion of the general constitution of this World State. Practically all political power vests in the samurai. Not only are they the only administrators, lawyers, practising doctors and public officials of almost all kinds, but they are the only voters. Yet, by a curious exception, the supreme legislative assembly must have one-tenth, and may have one-half of its members outside the order, because, it is alleged, there is a sort of wisdom that comes of sin and laxness which is necessary to the perfect ruling of life. My double quoted me a verse from the Canon on this matter that my unfortunate verbal memory did not retain, but it was in the nature of a prayer to save the world from 'unfermented men'. It would seem that Aristotle's idea of a rotation of rulers, an idea that crops up again in Harrington's *Oceana*,[7] that first Utopia of 'the sovereign people' (a Utopia that, through Danton's[8] readings in English, played a disastrous part in the French Revolution), gets little respect in Utopia. The tendency is to give a practically permanent tenure to good men. Every ruler and official, it is true, is put on his trial every three years before a jury drawn by lot, according to the range of his activities, either from the samurai of his municipal area or from the general catalogue of the samurai, but the business of this jury is merely to decide whether to continue him in office or order a new election. In the majority of cases the verdict is continuation. Even if it is not so the official may still appear as a candidate before the second and separate jury which fills the vacant post. . . .

My double mentioned a few scattered details of the electoral methods, but as at that time I believed we were to have a number of further conversations, I did not exhaust my curiosities upon this subject. Indeed, I was more than a little preoccupied and inattentive. The religion of the samurai was after my heart, and it had taken hold of me very strongly. . . . But presently I fell questioning him upon the complications that arise in the Modern Utopia through the differences between the races of men, and found my attention returning. But the matter of that discussion I shall put apart into a separate chapter. In the end we came back to the particulars of this great Rule of Life that any man desirous of joining the samurai must follow.

I remember how, after our third bout of talking, I walked back through the streets of Utopian London to rejoin the botanist at our hotel.

My double lived in an apartment in a great building – I should judge about where, in our London, the Tate Gallery squats, and as the day was fine and I had no reason for hurry, I went not by the covered mechanical way but on foot along the broad, tree-set terraces that follow the river on either side.

It was afternoon, and the mellow Thames Valley sunlight, warm and gentle, lit a clean and gracious world. There were many people abroad, going to and fro, unhurrying but not aimless, and I watched them so attentively that were you to ask me for the most elementary details of the buildings and terraces that lay back on either bank, or of the pinnacles and towers and parapets that laced the sky, I could not tell you them. But of the people I could tell a great deal.

No Utopians wear black, and for all the frequency of the samurai uniform along the London ways the general effect is of a gaily coloured population. You never see anyone noticeably ragged or dirty; the police, who answer questions and keep order (and are quite distinct from the organization for the pursuit of criminals) see to that; and shabby people are very infrequent. People who want to save money for other purposes, or who do not want much bother with their clothing, seem to wear costumes of rough woven cloth, dyed an unobtrusive brown or green, over fine woollen underclothing, and so achieve a decent comfort in its simplest form. Others outside the Rule of the samurai range the spectrum for colour, and have every variety of texture; the colours attained by the Utopian dyers seem to me to be fuller and purer than the common range of stuffs on earth; and the subtle folding of the woollen materials witness that Utopian Bradford is no whit behind her earthly sister. White is extraordinarily frequent; white woollen tunics and robes into which are woven bands of brilliant colour, abound. Often these ape the cut and purple edge that distinguishes the samurai. In Utopian London the air is as clear and less dusty than it is among high mountains; the roads are made of unbroken surfaces, and not of friable earth; all heating is done by electricity, and no coal ever enters the town; there are no horses or dogs, and so there is not a suspicion of smoke and scarcely a particle of any sort of dirt to render white impossible.

The radiated influence of the uniform of the samurai has been to keep costume simple, and this, perhaps, emphasizes the general effect of vigorous health, of shapely bodies. Everyone is well grown and well nourished; everyone seems in good condition; everyone walks well, and has that clearness of eye that comes with cleanness of blood. In London I am apt to consider myself of a passable size and carriage; here I feel small and mean-looking. The faint suspicions of spinal curvatures, skew feet, unequal legs, and ill-grown bones that haunt one in a London crowd, the plain intimations – in yellow faces, puffy faces, spotted and irregular complexions, in nervous movements and coughs and colds – of bad habits and an incompetent or disregarded medical profession, do not appear here. I notice few old people, but there seems to be a greater proportion of men and women at or near the prime of life.

I hang upon that. I have seen one or two fat people here – they are all the more noticeable because they are rare. But wrinkled age? Have I yet in Utopia set eyes on a bald head?

The Utopians have brought a sounder physiological science than ours to bear upon regimen. People know better what to do and what to avoid, how to foresee and forestall coming trouble, and how to evade and suppress the subtle poisons that blunt the edge of sensation. They have put off the years of decay. They keep their teeth, they keep their digestions, they ward off gout and rheumatism, neuralgia and influenza and all those cognate decays that bend and wrinkle men and women in the middle years of existence. They have extended the level years far into the seventies, and age, when it comes, comes swiftly and easily. The feverish hurry of our earth, the decay that begins before growth has ceased, is replaced by a ripe prolonged maturity. This Modern Utopia is an adult world. The flushed romance, the predominant eroticisms, the adventurous uncertainty of a world in which youth prevails, gives place here to a grave deliberation, to a fuller and more powerful emotion, to a broader handling of life.

Yet youth is here.

Amidst the men whose faces have been made fine by thought and steadfast living, among the serene-eyed women, comes youth, gaily coloured, buoyantly healthy, with challenging eyes, with fresh and eager faces. . . .

For everyone in Utopia who is sane enough to benefit, study and training last until twenty; then comes the travel year; and many are still students until twenty-four or twenty-five. Most are still, in a sense, students throughout life; but it is thought that unless responsible action is begun in some form in the early twenties, will undergoes a partial atrophy. But the full swing of adult life is hardly attained until thirty is reached. Men marry before the middle thirties, and the women rather earlier, few are mothers before five and twenty. The majority of those who become samurai do so between twenty-seven and thirty-five. And between seventeen and thirty, the Utopians have their dealings with love, and the play and excitement of love is a chief interest in life. Much freedom of act is allowed them so that their wills may grow freely. For the most part they end mated, and love gives place to some special and more enduring interest, though indeed there is love between older men and fresh girls, and between youths and maturer women. It is in these most graceful and beautiful years of life that such freedoms of dress as the atmosphere of Utopia permits are to be seen, and the crude bright will and imagination of youth peeps out in ornament and colour.

Figures come into my sight and possess me for a moment and pass, and give place to others; there comes a dusky little Jewess, red-lipped and amber-clad, with a deep crimson flower – I know not whether real or sham – in the dull black of her hair. She passes me with an unconscious disdain; and then I am looking at a brightly smiling, blue-eyed girl, tall, ruddy and freckled warmly, clad like a stage Rosalind[9] and talking gaily to a fair young man, a novice under the Rule. A red-haired mother under the Lesser Rule goes by, green-gowned, with dark green straps crossing between her breasts, and her two shock-headed children, bare-legged and lightly shod, tug at her hands on either side. Then a grave man in a long fur-trimmed robe, a merchant, maybe, debates some serious matter with a white-tunicked clerk. And the clerk's face—? I turn to mark the straight, blue-black hair. The man must be Chinese. . . .

Then come two short-bearded men in careless indigo-blue raiment, both of them convulsed with laughter – men outside the Rule, who practise, perhaps, some art – and then one of the samurai, in cheerful altercation with a blue-robed girl of eight. 'But you *could* have come back yesterday, Dadda,' she persists. He is deeply sunburnt, and suddenly there passes before my mind the picture of a snowy mountain waste at nightfall and a solitary small figure under the stars. . . .

When I come back to the present thing again, my eye is caught at once by a young negro, carrying books in his hand, a prosperous-looking, self-respecting young negro in a trimly cut coat of purple-blue and silver.

I am reminded of what my double said to me of race.

# RACE IN UTOPIA

Above the sphere of the elemental cravings and necessities, the soul of man is in a perpetual vacillation between two conflicting impulses: the desire to assert his individual differences, the desire for distinction and his terror of isolation. He wants to stand out, but not too far out, and on the contrary he wants to merge himself with a group, with some larger body, but not altogether. Through all the things of life runs this tortuous compromise, men follow the fashions but resent ready-made uniforms on every plane of their being. The disposition to form aggregations and to imagine aggregations is part of the incurable nature of man; it is one of the great natural forces the statesman must utilize, and against which he must construct effectual defences. The study of the aggregations and of the ideals of aggregations about which men's sympathies will twine, and upon which they will base a large proportion of their conduct and personal policy, is the legitimate definition of sociology.

Now the sort of aggregation to which men and women will refer themselves is determined partly by the strength and idiosyncrasy of the individual imagination, and partly by the reek of ideas that chances to be in the air at the time. Men and women may vary greatly both in their innate and their acquired disposition towards this sort of larger body or that, to which their social reference can be made. The 'natural' social reference of a man is probably to some rather vaguely conceived tribe, as the 'natural' social reference of a dog is to a pack. But just as the social reference of a dog may be educated until the reference to a pack is completely replaced by a reference to an owner, so on his higher plane of educability the social reference of the civilized man undergoes the most remarkable transformations. But the power and scope of his imagination and the need he has of response sets limits to this process. A highly intellectualized mature mind may refer for its data very consistently to ideas of a higher being so remote and indefinable as God, so comprehensive as humanity, so far-reaching as the purpose in things. I write 'may', but I doubt if this exaltation of reference is ever permanently sustained. Comte, in his 'Positive Polity', exposes his soul with great freedom, and the curious may trace how, while he professes and quite honestly intends to refer himself always to his 'Greater Being' Humanity, he narrows constantly to his projected *Western Republic* of civilized men, and quite frequently to the minute indefinite body of Positivist subscribers. And the history of the Christian Church, with its development of orders and cults, sects and dissents, the history of fashionable society with its cliques and sets and every political history with its cabals and inner cabinets, witness to the struggle that goes on in the minds of men to adjust themselves to a body larger indeed than themselves, but which still does not strain and escape their imaginative grasp.

The statesman, both for himself and others, must recognize this inadequacy of grasp, and the necessity for real and imaginary aggregations to sustain men in their practical service of the order of the world. He must be a sociologist; he must study the whole science of aggregations in relation to that World State to which his reason and his maturest thought direct him. He must lend himself to the development of aggregatory ideas that favour the civilizing process, and he must do his best to promote the disintegration of the aggregations and the effacement of aggregatory ideas that keep men narrow and unreasonably prejudiced one against another.

He will, of course, know that few men are even rudely consistent in such matters, that the same man in different moods and on different occasions is capable of referring himself in perfect good faith, not only to different, but to contradictory larger beings, and that the more important thing about an aggregatory idea from the State-maker's point of view is not so much what it explicitly involves as what it implicitly repudiates. The natural man does not feel he is aggregating at all, unless he aggregates *against* something. He refers himself to the tribe; he is loyal to the tribe, and quite inseparably he fears or dislikes those others outside the tribe. The tribe is always at least defensively hostile and usually actively hostile to humanity beyond the aggregation. The Anti-idea, it would seem, is inseparable from the aggregatory idea; it is a necessity of the human mind. When we think of the class A as desirable, we think of Not-A as undesirable. The two things are as inevitably connected as the tendons of our hands, so that when we flatten down our little fingers on our palms, the fourth digit, whether we wish it or not, comes down halfway. All real working gods, one may remark, all gods that are worshipped emotionally, are tribal gods, and every attempt to universalize the idea of God trails dualism and the devil after it as a moral necessity.

When we inquire, as well as the unformed condition of terrestrial sociology permits, into the aggregatory ideas that seem to satisfy men, we find a remarkable complex, a disorderly complex, in the minds of nearly all our civilized contemporaries. For example, all sorts of aggregatory ideas come and go across the chameleon surfaces of my botanist's mind. He has a strong feeling for systematic botanists as against plant physiologists, whom he regards as lewd and evil scoundrels in this relation; but he has a strong feeling for all botanists, and indeed all biologists, as against physicists and those who profess the exact sciences, all of whom he regards as dull, mechanical, ugly-minded scoundrels in this relation; but he has a strong feeling for all who profess what is called Science as against psychologists, sociologists, philosophers and literary men, whom he regards as wild, foolish, immoral scoundrels in this relation; but he has a strong feeling for all educated men as against the working man, whom he regards as a cheating, lying, loafing, drunken, thievish, dirty scoundrel in this relation; but so soon as the working man is comprehended together with those others as Englishmen – which includes, in this case, I may remark, the

Scottish and Welsh – he holds them superior to all other sorts of European, whom he regards, etc. . . . .

Now one perceives in all these aggregatory ideas and rearrangements of the sympathies one of the chief vices of human thought, due to its obsession by classificatory suggestions.* The necessity for marking out classes has brought with it a bias for false and excessive contrast, and we never invent a term but we are at once cramming it with implications beyond its legitimate content. There is no feat of irrelevance that people will not perform quite easily in this way; there is no class, however accidental, to which they will not at once ascribe deeply distinctive qualities. The seventh sons of seventh sons have remarkable powers of insight; people with a certain sort of ear commit crimes of violence; people with red hair have souls of fire; all democratic socialists are trustworthy persons; all people born in Ireland have vivid imaginations and all Englishmen are clods; all Hindus are cowardly liars; all curly-haired people are good-natured; all hunchbacks are energetic and wicked, and all Frenchmen eat frogs. Such stupid generalizations have been believed with the utmost readiness, and acted upon by great numbers of sane, respectable people. And when the class is one's own class, when it expresses one of the aggregations to which one refers one's own activities, then the disposition to divide all qualities between this class and its converse, and to cram one's own class with every desirable distinction, becomes overwhelming.

It is part of the training of the philosopher to regard all such generalizations with suspicion; it is part of the training of the Utopist and statesman – and all good statesmen are Utopists – to mingle something very like animosity with that suspicion. For crude classifications and false generalizations are the curse of all organized human life.

* See Chapter 1, §5, and the Appendix.

## § 2

Disregarding classes, cliques, sets, castes and the like minor aggregations, concerned for the most part with details and minor aspects of life, one finds among the civilized peoples of the world certain broad types of aggregatory ideas. There are, firstly, the national ideas, ideas which in their perfection require a uniformity of physical and mental type, a common idiom, a common religion, a distinctive style of costume, decoration and thought, and a compact organization acting with complete external unity. Like the Gothic cathedral, the national idea is never found complete with all its parts; but one has in Russia, with her insistence on political and religious orthodoxy, something approaching it pretty closely, and again in the inland and typical provinces of China, where even a strange pattern of hat arouses hostility. We had it in vigorous struggle to exist in England under the earlier Georges in the minds of those who supported the Established Church. The idea of the fundamental nature of nationality is so ingrained in thought, with all the usual exaggeration of implication, that no one laughs at talk about Swedish painting or American literature. And I will confess and point out that my own detachment from these delusions is so imperfect and discontinuous that in another passage I have committed myself to a short assertion of the exceptionally noble quality of the English imagination.* I am constantly gratified by flattering untruths about English superiority which I should reject indignantly were the application bluntly personal, and I am ever ready to believe the scenery of England, the poetry of England, even the decoration and music of England, in some mystic and impregnable way the best. This habit of intensifying all class definitions, and particularly those in which one has a personal interest, is in the very constitution of man's mind. It is part of the defect of that instrument. We may watch against it and prevent it doing any great injustices or leading us into follies, but to eradicate it is an altogether different matter. There it is to be reckoned with, like the coccyx, the pineal eye and the

* Chapter 7, § 6.

vermiform appendix. And a too consistent attack on it may lead simply to its inversion, to a vindictively pro-foreigner attitude that is equally unwise.

The second sort of aggregatory ideas, running very often across the boundaries of national ideas and in conflict with them, are religious ideas. In Western Europe true national ideas only emerged to their present hectic vigour after the shock of the Reformation had liberated men from the great tradition of a Latin-speaking Christendom, a tradition the Roman Catholic Church has sustained as its modification of the old Latin-speaking Imperialism in the rule of the *pontifex maximus*.[1] There was, and there remains to this day, a profound disregard of local dialect and race in the Roman Catholic tradition, which has made that Church a persistently disintegrating influence in national life. Equally spacious and equally regardless of tongues and peoples is the great Arabic-speaking religion of Mahommet. Both Christendom and Islam are indeed on their secular sides imperfect realizations of a Utopian World State. But the secular side was the weaker side of these cults; they produced no sufficiently great statesmen to realize their spiritual forces, and it is not in Rome under pontifical rule, nor in Munster under the Anabaptists,[2] but rather in Thomas à Kempis[3] and St Augustine's *City of God*[4] that we must seek for the Utopias of Christianity.

In the last hundred years a novel development of material forces, and especially of means of communication, has done very much to break up the isolations in which nationality perfected its prejudices and so to render possible the extension and consolidation of such a worldwide culture as medieval Christendom and Islam foreshadowed. The first onset of these expansive developments has been marked in the world of mind by an expansion of political ideals – Comte's *Western Republic* (1848) was the first Utopia that involved the synthesis of numerous States – by the development of 'Imperialisms' in the place of national policies, and by the search for a basis for wider political unions in racial traditions and linguistic affinities. Anglo-Saxonism, Pan-Germanism and the like are such synthetic ideas. Until the eighties, the general tendency of progressive thought was at one with the older Christian tradition which ignored 'race', and the aim of the expansive liberalism movement, so far as it had a clear aim, was to Europeanize the world, to extend the franchise to negroes, put Polynesians into trousers and train the teeming myriads of India to appreciate the exquisite lilt of 'The Lady of the Lake'.[5] There is always some absurdity mixed with human greatness, and we must not let the fact that the middle Victorians counted Scott, the suffrage and pantaloons among the supreme blessings of life, conceal from us the very real nobility of their dream of England's mission to the world. . . .

We of this generation have seen a flood of reaction against such universalism. The great intellectual developments that centre upon the work of Darwin have exacerbated the realization that life is a conflict between superior and inferior types, it has underlined the idea that specific survival rates are of primary significance in the world's development, and a swarm of inferior intelligences has applied to human problems elaborated and exaggerated versions of these generalizations. These social and political followers of Darwin have fallen into an obvious confusion between race and nationality, and into the natural trap of patriotic conceit. The dissent of the Indian and Colonial governing class to the first crude applications of liberal propositions in India has found a voice of unparalleled penetration in Mr Kipling,[6] whose want of intellectual deliberation is only equalled by his poetic power. The search for a basis for a new political synthesis in adaptable sympathies based on linguistic affinities, was greatly influenced by Max Müller's[7] unaccountable assumption that language indicated kindred, and led straight to wildly speculative ethnology, to the discovery that there was a Keltic race, a Teutonic race, an Indo-European race and so forth. A book that has had enormous influence in this matter, because of its use in teaching, is J. R. Green's *Short History of the English People*,[8] with its grotesque insistence upon Anglo-Saxonism. And just now, the world is in a sort of delirium about race and the racial struggle. The Briton forgetting his Defoe,* the Jew forgetting the very word proselyte,

* *The True-born Englishman.*[9]

the German forgetting his anthropometric variations and the Italian forgetting everything, are obsessed by the singular purity of their blood, and the danger of contamination the mere continuance of other races involves. True to the law that all human aggregation involves the development of a spirit of opposition to whatever is external to the aggregation, extraordinary intensifications of racial definition are going on; the vileness, the inhumanity, the incompatibility of alien races is being steadily exaggerated. The natural tendency of every human being towards a stupid conceit in himself and his kind, a stupid depreciation of all unlikeness, is traded upon by this bastard science. With the weakening of national references, and with the pause before reconstruction in religious belief, these new arbitrary and unsubstantial race prejudices become daily more formidable. They are shaping policies and modifying laws, and they will certainly be responsible for a large proportion of the wars, hardships and cruelties the immediate future holds in store for our earth.

No generalizations about race are too extravagant for the inflamed credulity of the present time. No attempt is ever made to distinguish differences in inherent quality – the true racial differences – from artificial differences due to culture. No lesson seems ever to be drawn from history of the fluctuating incidence of the civilizing process first upon this race and then upon that. The politically ascendant peoples of the present phase are understood to be the superior races, including such types as the Sussex farm labourer, the Bowery[10] tough, the London hooligan and the Paris apache; the races not at present prospering politically, such as the Egyptians, the Greeks, the Spanish, the Moors, the Chinese, the Hindus, the Peruvians and all uncivilized people are represented as the inferior races, unfit to associate with the former on terms of equality, unfit to intermarry with them on any terms, unfit for any decisive voice in human affairs. In the popular imagination of Western Europe, the Chinese are becoming bright gamboge in colour, and unspeakably abominable in every respect; the people who are black – the people who have fuzzy hair and flattish noses, and no calves to speak of – are no longer held to be within the pale of humanity. These superstitions work out along the obvious lines of the popular logic. The depopulation of the Congo Free State by the Belgians, the horrible massacres of Chinese by European soldiery during the Pekin expedition, are condoned as a painful but necessary part of the civilizing process of the world. The worldwide repudiation of slavery in the nineteenth century was done against a vast sullen force of ignorant pride, which, reinvigorated by the new delusions, swings back again to power.

'Science' is supposed to lend its sanction to race mania, but it is only 'science' as it is understood by very illiterate people that does anything of the sort – 'scientists'' science, in fact. What science has to tell about 'The Races of Man' will be found compactly set forth by Dr J. Deniker,[11] in the book published under that title.* From that book one may learn the beginnings of race charity. Save for a few isolated pools of savage humanity, there is probably no pure race in the whole world. The great continental populations are all complex mixtures of numerous and fluctuating types. Even the Jews present every kind of skull that is supposed to be racially distinctive, a vast range of complexion – from blackness in Goa to extreme fairness in Holland – and a vast mental and physical diversity. Were the Jews to discontinue all intermarriage with 'other races' henceforth for ever, it would depend upon quite unknown laws of fecundity, prepotency and variability what their final type would be, or indeed whether any particular type would ever prevail over diversity. And without going beyond the natives of the British Isles, one can discover an enormous range of types, tall and short, straight-haired and curly, fair and dark, supremely intelligent and unteachably stupid, straightforward, disingenuous and what not. The natural tendency is to forget all this range directly 'race' comes under discussion, to take either an average or some quite arbitrary ideal as the type, and think only of that. The more difficult thing to do, but the thing that must be done if we are to get just results in this discussion, is to do one's best to bear the range in mind.

---

* See also an excellent paper in the *American Journal of Sociology* for March, 1904, 'The Psychology of Race Prejudice', by W. I. Thomas.

Let us admit that the average Chinaman is probably different in complexion, and indeed in all his physical and psychical proportions, from the average Englishman. Does that render their association upon terms of equality in a World State impossible? What the average Chinaman or Englishman may be, is of no importance whatever to our plan of a World State. It is not averages that exist, but individuals. The average Chinaman will never meet the average Englishman anywhere; only individual Chinamen will meet individual Englishmen. Now among Chinamen will be found a range of variety as extensive as among Englishmen, and there is no single trait presented by all Chinamen and no Englishman, or vice versa. Even the oblique eye is not universal in China, and there are probably many Chinamen who might have been 'changed at birth', taken away and educated into quite passable Englishmen. Even after we have separated out and allowed for the differences in carriage, physique, moral prepossessions and so forth, due to their entirely divergent cultures, there remains no doubt a very great difference between the average Chinaman and the average Englishman; but would that amount to a wider difference than is to be found between extreme types of Englishmen?

For my own part I do not think that it would. But it is evident that any precise answer can be made only when anthropology has adopted much more exact and exhaustive methods of inquiry, and a far more precise analysis than its present resources permit.

Be it remembered how doubtful and tainted is the bulk of our evidence in these matters. These are extraordinarily subtle inquiries, from which few men succeed in disentangling the threads of their personal associations – the curiously interwoven strands of self-love and self-interest that affect their inquiries. One might almost say that instinct fights against such investigations, as it does undoubtedly against many necessary medical researches. But while a long special training, a high tradition and the possibility of reward and distinction, enable the medical student to face many tasks that are at once undignified and physically repulsive, the people from whom we get our anthropological information are rarely men of more than average intelligence, and of no mental training at all. And the problems are far more elusive. It surely needs at least the gifts and training of a first-class novelist, combined with a sedulous patience that probably cannot be hoped for in combination with these, to gauge the all-round differences between man and man. Even where there are no barriers of language and colour, understanding may be nearly impossible. How few educated people seem to understand the servant class in England, or the working men! Except for Mr Bart Kennedy's *A Man Adrift*,[12] I know of scarcely any book that shows a really sympathetic and living understanding of the navvy, the longshore sailor man, the rough chap of our own race. Caricatures, luridly tragic or gaily comic, in which the misconceptions of the author blend with the preconceptions of the reader and achieve success, are of course common enough. And then consider the sort of people who pronounce judgements on the moral and intellectual capacity of the negro, the Malay, or the Chinaman. You have missionaries, native schoolmasters, employers of coolies, traders, simple downright men, who scarcely suspect the existence of any sources of error in their verdicts, who are incapable of understanding the difference between what is innate and what is acquired, much less of distinguishing them in their interplay. Now and then one seems to have a glimpse of something really living – in Mary Kingsley's[13] buoyant work, for instance – and even that may be no more than my illusion.

For my own part I am disposed to discount all adverse judgements and all statements of insurmountable differences between race and race. I talk upon racial qualities to all men who have had opportunities of close observation, and I find that their insistence upon these differences is usually in inverse proportion to their intelligence. It may be the chance of my encounters, but that is my clear impression. Common sailors will generalize in the profoundest way about Irishmen and Scotchmen and Yankees and Nova Scotians and 'Dutchies', until one might think one talked of different species of animal, but the educated explorer flings clear of all these delusions. To him men present themselves individualized, and if they classify it is by some skin-deep accident of tint, some trick of the tongue or habit of gesture, or such-like superficiality. And after all there exists today available one kind at least of unbiased anthropological evidence. There are photographs. Let the reader turn over the pages of some such copiously illustrated work as *The Living Races of Mankind*,*[14] and look into the eyes of one alien face after another. Are they not very like the people one knows? For the most part, one finds it hard to believe that, with a common language and common social traditions, one would not get on very well with these people. Here or there is a brutish or evil face, but you can find as brutish and evil in the Strand on any afternoon. There are differences, no doubt, but fundamental incompatibilities – *no!* And very many of them send out a ray of special resemblance and remind one more strongly of this friend or that, than they do of their own kind. One notes with surprise that one's good friend and neighbour X and an anonymous naked Gold Coast negro belong to one type, as distinguished from one's dear friend Y and a beaming individual from Somaliland, who as certainly belong to another.

In one matter the careless and prejudiced nature of accepted racial generalizations is particularly marked. A great and increasing number of people are persuaded that 'half-breeds' are peculiarly evil creatures – as hunchbacks and bastards were supposed to be in the middle ages. The full legend of the wickedness of the half-breed is best to be learnt from a drunken mean white from Virginia or the Cape. The half-breed, one hears, combines all the vices of either parent, he is wretchedly poor in health and spirit but vindictive, powerful and dangerous to an extreme degree, his morals – the mean white has high and exacting standards – are indescribable even in whispers in a saloon, and so on and so on. There is really not an atom of evidence an unprejudiced mind would accept to sustain any belief of the sort. There is nothing to show that the children of racial admixture are, as a class, inherently either better or worse in any respect than either parent. There is an equally baseless

---

* *The Living Races of Mankind*, by H. N. Hutchinson, J. W. Gregory and R. Lydekker (Hutchinson).

theory that they are better, a theory displayed to a fine degree of foolishness in the article on Shakespeare in the *Encyclopaedia Britannica*. Both theories belong to the vast edifice of sham science that smothers the realities of modern knowledge. It may be that most 'half-breeds' are failures in life, but that proves nothing. They are, in an enormous number of cases, illegitimate and outcast from the normal education of either race; they are brought up in homes that are the battlegrounds of conflicting cultures; they labour under a heavy premium of disadvantage. There is, of course, a passing suggestion of Darwin's to account for atavism that might go to support the theory of the vileness of half-breeds, if it had ever been proved. But then it never has been proved. There is no proof in the matter at all.

§ 3

Suppose now, there is such a thing as an all-round inferior race. Is that any reason why we should propose to preserve it for ever in a condition of tutelage? Whether there is a race so inferior I do not know, but certainly there is no race so superior as to be trusted with human charges. The true answer to Aristotle's plea for slavery, that there are 'natural slaves', lies in the fact that there are no 'natural' masters. Power is no more to be committed to men without discipline and restriction than alcohol. The true objection to slavery is not that it is unjust to the inferior but that it corrupts the superior. There is only one sane and logical thing to be done with a really inferior race, and that is to exterminate it.

Now there are various ways of exterminating a race, and most of them are cruel. You may end it with fire and sword after the old Hebrew fashion; you may enslave it and work it to death, as the Spaniards did the Caribs; you may set it boundaries and then poison it slowly with deleterious commodities, as the Americans do with most of their Indians; you may incite it to wear clothing to which it is not accustomed and to live under new and strange conditions that will expose it to infectious diseases to which you yourselves are immune, as the missionaries do the Polynesians; you may resort to honest simple murder, as we English did with the Tasmanians;[15] or you can maintain such conditions as conduce to 'race suicide', as the British administration does in Fiji. Suppose then for a moment, that there is an all-round inferior race; a Modern Utopia is under the hard logic of life, and it would have to exterminate such a race as quickly as it could. On the whole, the Fijian device seems the least cruel. But Utopia would do that without any clumsiness of race distinction, in exactly the same manner, and by the same machinery, as it exterminates all its own defective and inferior strains; that is to say, as we have already discussed in Chapter 5, § 1, by its marriage laws, and by the laws of the minimum wage. That extinction need never be discriminatory. If any of the race did, after all, prove to be fit to survive, they would survive – they would be picked out with a sure and automatic justice from the over-ready condemnation of all their kind.

Is there, however, an all-round inferior race in the world? Even the Australian blackfellow is, perhaps, not quite so entirely eligible for extinction as a good, wholesome, horse-racing, sheep-farming Australian white may think. These queer little races, the blackfellows, the Pygmies, the Bushmen, may have their gifts, a greater keenness, a greater fineness of this sense or that, a quaintness of the imagination or what not, that may serve as their little unique addition to the totality of our Utopian civilization. We are supposing that every individual alive on earth is alive in Utopia, and so all the surviving 'black-fellows' are there. Every one of them in Utopia has had what none has had on earth, a fair education and fair treatment, justice and opportunity. Suppose that the common idea is right about the general inferiority of these people, then it would follow that in Utopia most of them are childless and working at or about the minimum wage, and some will have passed out of all possibility of offspring under the hand of the offended law; but still – cannot we imagine some few of these little people – whom you must suppose neither naked nor clothed in the European style, but robed in the Utopian fashion – may have found some delicate art to practise, some peculiar sort of carving, for example, that justifies God in creating them? Utopia has sound sanitary laws, sound social laws, sound economic laws; what harm are these people going to do?

Some may be even prosperous and admired, may have married women of their own or some other race, and so may be transmitting that distinctive thin thread of excellence to take its due place in the great synthesis of the future.

And indeed, coming along that terrace in Utopia, I see a little figure, a little bright-eyed, bearded man, inky black, frizzy haired and clad in a white tunic and black hose, and with a mantle of lemon yellow wrapped about his shoulders. He walks, as most Utopians walk, as though he had reason to be proud of something, as though he had no reason to be afraid of anything in the world. He carries a portfolio in his hand. It is that, I suppose, as much as his hair, that recalls the 'Quartier Latin'[16] to my mind.

## § 4

I had already discussed the question of race with the botanist at Lucerne.

'But you would not like,' he cried in horror, 'your daughter to marry a Chinaman or a negro?'

'Of course,' said I, 'when you say Chinaman, you think of a creature with a pigtail, long nails and insanitary habits, and when you say negro you think of a filthy-headed black creature in an old hat. You do this because your imagination is too feeble to disentangle the inherent qualities of a thing from its habitual associations.'

'Insult isn't argument,' said the botanist.

'Neither is unsound implication. You make a question of race into a question of unequal cultures. You would not like your daughter to marry the sort of negro who steals hens, but then you would also not like your daughter to marry a pure English hunchback with a squint, or a drunken cab tout of Norman blood. As a matter of fact, very few well-bred English girls do commit that sort of indiscretion. But you don't think it necessary to generalize against men of your own race because there are drunken cab touts, and why should you generalize against negroes? Because the proportion of undesirables is higher among negroes, that does not justify a sweeping condemnation. You may have to condemn most, but why *all*? There may be – neither of us knows enough to deny – negroes who are handsome, capable, courageous.'

'Ugh!' said the botanist.

'How detestable you must find Othello!'[17]

It is my Utopia, and for a moment I could almost find it in my heart to spite the botanist by creating a modern Desdemona and her lover sooty black to the lips, there before our eyes. But I am not so sure of my case as that, and for the moment there shall come nothing more than a swart-faced, dusky Burmese woman in the dress of the Greater Rule, with her tall Englishman (as he might be on earth) at her side. That, however, is a digression from my conversation with the botanist.

'And the Chinaman?' said the botanist.

'I think we shall have all the buff and yellow peoples intermingling pretty freely.'

'Chinamen and white women, for example.'

'Yes,' I said, 'you've got to swallow that, anyhow; you *shall* swallow that.'

He finds the idea too revolting for comment.

I try and make the thing seem easier for him. 'Do try,' I said, 'to grasp a modern Utopian's conditions. The Chinaman will speak the same language as his wife – whatever her race may be – he will wear costume of the common civilized fashion, he will have much the same education as his European rival, read the same literature, bow to the same traditions. And you must remember a wife in Utopia is singularly not subject to her husband. . . .'

The botanist proclaims his invincible conclusion: 'Everyone would cut her!'

'This is Utopia,' I said, and then sought once more to tranquillize his mind. 'No doubt among the vulgar, coarse-minded people outside the Rule there may be something of the sort. Every earthly moral blockhead, a little educated perhaps, is to be found in Utopia. You will no doubt find the "cut" and the "boycott",[18] and all those nice little devices by which dull people get a keen edge on life, in their place here, and their place here is somewhere—'

I turned a thumb earthward. 'There!'

The botanist did not answer for a while. Then he said, with some temper and great emphasis: 'Well, I'm jolly glad anyhow that I'm not to be a permanent resident in this Utopia, *if our daughters are to be married to Hottentots*[19] by regulation. I'm jolly glad.'

He turned his back on me.

Now did I say anything of the sort? . . .

I had to bring him, I suppose; there's no getting away from him in this life. But as I have already observed, the happy ancients went to their Utopias without this sort of company.

## § 5

What gives the botanist so great an advantage in all his Anti-Utopian utterances is his unconsciousness of his own limitations. He thinks in little pieces that lie about loose, and nothing has any necessary link with anything else in his mind. So that I cannot retort upon him by asking him, if he objects to this synthesis of all nations, tongues and peoples in a World State, what alternative ideal he proposes.

People of this sort do not even feel the need of alternatives. Beyond the scope of a few personal projects, meeting Her again, and things like that, they do not feel that there is a future. They are unencumbered by any baggage of convictions whatever, in relation to that. That, at least, is the only way in which I can explain our friend's high intellectual mobility. Attempts to correlate statesmanship, which they regard with interest as a dramatic interplay of personalities, with any secular movement of humanity, they class with the differential calculus and Darwinism as things far too difficult to be anything but finally and subtly wrong.

So the argument must pass into a direct address to the reader.

If you are not prepared to regard a worldwide synthesis of all cultures and polities and races into one World State as the desirable end upon which all civilizing efforts converge, what do you regard as the desirable end? Synthesis, one may remark in passing, does not necessarily mean fusion, nor does it mean uniformity.

The alternatives fall roughly under three headings. The first is to assume there is a best race, to define as well as one can that best race, and to regard all other races as material for extermination. This has a fine modern biological air ('Survival of the Fittest'). If you are one of those queer German professors who write insanity about Welt-Politik,[20] you assume the best race is the 'Teutonic'; Cecil Rhodes[21] affected that triumph of creative imagination, the 'Anglo-Saxon race'; my friend, Moses Cohen,[22] thinks there is much to be said for the Jew. On its premises, this is a perfectly sound and reasonable policy, and it opens out a brilliant prospect for the scientific inventor for what one might call Welt-Apparat[23] in the future, for national harrowing and reaping machines, and race-destroying fumigations. The great plain of China ('Yellow Peril')[24] lends itself particularly to some striking wholesale undertaking; it might, for example, be flooded for a few days, and then disinfected with volcanic chlorine. Whether, when all the inferior races have been stamped out, the superior race would not proceed at once, or after a brief millennial period of social harmony, to divide itself into sub-classes, and begin the business over again at a higher level, is an interesting residual question into which we need not now penetrate.

That complete development of a scientific Welt-Politik is not, however, widely advocated at present, no doubt from a want of confidence in the public imagination. But we have a very audible and influential school, the Modern Imperialist school, which distinguishes its own race – there is a German, a British and an Anglo-Saxon section in the school, and a wider teaching which embraces the whole 'white race' in one remarkable tolerance – as the superior race, as one, indeed, superior enough to own slaves, collectively if not individually; and the exponents of this doctrine look with a resolute, truculent, but slightly indistinct eye to a future in which all the rest of the world will be in subjection to these elect. The ideals of this type are set forth pretty clearly in Mr Kidd's *Control of the Tropics*.[25] The whole world is to be administered by the 'white' Powers – Mr Kidd did not anticipate Japan – who will see to it that their subjects do not 'prevent the utilization of the immense natural resources which they have in charge'. Those other races are to be regarded as children, recalcitrant children at times, and without any of the tender emotions of paternity. It is a little doubtful whether the races lacking 'in the elementary qualities of social efficiency' are expected to acquire them under the chastening hands of those races which, through 'strength and energy of character, humanity, probity, and integrity, and a single-minded devotion to conceptions of duty', are developing 'the resources of the richest regions of the earth' over their heads, or whether this is the ultimate ideal.

Next comes the rather incoherent alternative that one associates in England with official Liberalism.

Liberalism in England is not quite the same thing as Liberalism in the rest of the world; it is woven of two strands. There is Whiggism, the powerful tradition of seventeenth-century Protestant and republican England, with its great debt to republican Rome, its strong constructive and disciplinary bias, its broad and originally very living and intelligent outlook; and interwoven with this there is the sentimental and logical Liberalism that sprang from the stresses of the eighteenth century, that finds its early scarce differentiated expression in Harrington's Oceana, and after fresh draughts of the tradition of Brutus[26] and Cato[27] and some elegant trifling with noble savages, budded in 'La Cité Morellyste', flowered in the emotional democratic naturalism of Rousseau, and bore abundant fruit in the French Revolution. These are two very distinct strands. Directly they were freed in America from the grip of conflict with British Toryism, they came apart as the Republican and Democratic parties respectively. Their continued union in Great Britain is a political accident. Because of this mixture, the whole career of English-speaking Liberalism, though it has gone to one unbroken strain of eloquence, has never produced a clear statement of policy in relation to other peoples politically less fortunate. It has developed no definite ideas at all about the future of mankind. The Whig disposition, which once had some play in India, was certainly to attempt to anglicize the 'native', to assimilate his culture, and then to assimilate his political status with that of his temporary ruler. But interwoven with this anglicizing tendency, which was also, by-the-bye, a Christianizing tendency, was a strong disposition, derived from the Rousseau strand, to leave other peoples alone, to facilitate even the separation and autonomy of detached portions of our own peoples, to disintegrate finally into perfect, because lawless, individuals. The official exposition of British 'Liberalism' today still wriggles unstably because of these conflicting constituents, but on the whole the Whig strand now seems the weaker. The contemporary Liberal politician offers cogent criticism upon the brutality and conceit of modern imperialisms, but that seems to be the limit of his service. Taking what they do not say and do not propose as an indication of Liberal intentions, it would seem that the ideal of the British Liberals and of the American Democrats is to favour the existence of just as many petty, loosely allied, or quite independent nationalities as possible, just as many languages as possible, to deprecate armies and all controls, and to trust to the innate goodness of disorder and the powers of an ardent sentimentality to keep the world clean and sweet. The Liberals will not face the plain consequence that such a state of affairs is hopelessly unstable, that it involves the maximum risk of war with the minimum of permanent benefit and public order. They will not reflect that the stars in their courses rule inexorably against it. It is a vague, impossible ideal, with a rude sort of unworldly moral beauty, like the gospel of the Doukhobors.[28] Besides that charm it has this most seductive quality to an official British Liberal, that it does not exact intellectual activity nor indeed activity of any sort whatever. It is, by virtue of that alone, a far less mischievous doctrine than the crude and violent Imperialism of the popular Press.

Neither of these two schools of policy, neither the international laissez-faire of the Liberals, nor 'hustle to the top' Imperialism, promise any reality of permanent progress for the world of men. They are the resort, the moral reference, of those who will not think frankly and exhaustively over the whole field of this question. Do that, insist upon solutions of more than accidental applicability, and you emerge with one or other of two contrasted solutions, as the consciousness of kind or the consciousness of individuality prevails in your mind. In the former case you will adopt aggressive Imperialism, but you will carry it out to its 'thorough' degree of extermination. You will seek to develop the culture and power of your kind of men and women to the utmost in order to shoulder all other kinds from the earth. If on the other hand you appreciate the unique, you will aim at such a synthesis as this Utopia displays, a synthesis far more credible and possible than any other Welt-Politik. In spite of all the pageant of modern war, synthesis is in the trend of the world. To aid and develop it, could be made the open and secure policy of any great modern empire now. Modern war, modern international hostility, is, I believe, possible only through the stupid illiteracy of the mass of men and the conceit and intellectual indolence of rulers and those who feed the public mind. Were the will of the mass of men lit and conscious, I am firmly convinced it would now burn steadily for synthesis and peace.

It would be so easy to bring about a world peace within a few decades, was there but the will for it among men! The great empires that exist need but a little speech and frankness one with another. Within, the riddles of social order are already half solved in books and thought, there are the common people and the subject peoples to be educated and drilled, to be led to a common speech and a common literature, to be assimilated and made citizens; without, there is the possibility of treaties. Why, for example, should Britain and France, or either and the United States, or Sweden and Norway, or Holland, or Denmark, or Italy, fight any more for ever? And if there is no reason, how foolish and dangerous it is still to sustain linguistic differences and custom houses, and all sorts of foolish and irritating distinctions between their various citizens! Why should not all these peoples agree to teach some common language, French for example, in their common schools, or to teach each other's languages reciprocally? Why should they not aim at a common literature, and bring their various common laws, their marriage laws and so on, into uniformity? Why should they not work for a uniform minimum of labour conditions through all their communities? Why, then, should they not – except in the interests of a few rascal plutocrats – trade freely and exchange their citizenship freely throughout their common boundaries? No doubt there are difficulties to be found, but they are quite finite difficulties. What is there to prevent a parallel movement of all the civilized Powers in the world towards a common ideal and assimilation?

Stupidity – nothing but stupidity, a stupid brute jealousy, aimless and unjustifiable.

The coarser conceptions of aggregation are at hand, the hostile, jealous patriotisms, the blare of trumpets and the pride of fools; they serve the daily need though they lead towards disaster. The real and the immediate has us in its grip, the accidental personal thing. The little effort of thought, the brief sustained effort of will, is too much for the contemporary mind. Such treaties, such sympathetic international movements, are but dream stuff yet on earth, though Utopia has realized them long since and already passed them by.

# THE BUBBLE BURSTS

§ 1

As I walk back along the river terrace to the hotel where the botanist awaits me, and observe the Utopians I encounter, I have no thought that my tenure of Utopia becomes every moment more precarious. There float in my mind vague anticipations of more talks with my double and still more, of a steady elaboration of detail, of interesting journeys of exploration. I forget that a Utopia is a thing of the imagination that becomes more fragile with every added circumstance, that, like a soap-bubble, it is most brilliantly and variously coloured at the very instant of its dissolution. This Utopia is nearly done. All the broad lines of its social organization are completed now, the discussion of all its general difficulties and problems. Utopian individuals pass me by, fine buildings tower on either hand; it does not occur to me that I may look too closely. To find the people assuming the concrete and individual is not, as I fondly imagine, the last triumph of realization, but the swimming moment of opacity before the film gives way. To come to individual emotional cases, is to return to the earth.

I find the botanist sitting at a table in the hotel courtyard.

'Well?' I say, standing before him.

'I've been in the gardens on the river terrace,' he answers, 'hoping I might see her again.'

'Nothing better to do?'

'Nothing in the world.'

'You'll have your double back from India tomorrow. Then you'll have conversation.'

'I don't want it,' he replies compactly.

I shrug my shoulders, and he adds, 'At least with him.'

I let myself down into a seat beside him.

For a time I sit restfully enjoying his companionable silence, and thinking fragmentarily of those samurai and their Rules. I entertain something of the satisfaction of a man who has finished building a bridge; I feel that I have joined together things that I had never joined before. My Utopia seems real to me, very real; I can believe in it until the metal chair-back gives to my shoulder blades, and Utopian sparrows twitter and hop before my feet. I have a pleasant moment of unhesitating self-satisfaction; I feel a shameless exultation to be there. For a moment I forget the consideration the botanist demands; the mere pleasure of completeness, of holding and controlling all the threads, possesses me.

'You *will* persist in believing,' I say with an aggressive expository note, 'that if you meet this lady she will be a person with the memories and sentiments of her double on earth. You think she will understand and pity, and perhaps love you. Nothing of the sort is the case.' I repeat with confident rudeness, 'Nothing of the sort is the case. Things are different altogether here; you can hardly tell even now how different are—'

I discover he is not listening to me.

'What is the matter?' I ask abruptly.

He makes no answer, but his expression startles me.

'What is the matter?' and then I follow his eyes.

A woman and a man are coming through the great archway – and instantly I guess what has happened. She it is arrests my attention first; long ago I knew she was a sweetly beautiful woman. She is fair, with frank blue eyes that look with a sort of tender receptivity into her companion's face. For a moment or so they remain, greyish figures in the cool shadow, against the sunlit greenery of the gardens beyond.

'It is Mary,' the botanist whispers with white lips, but he stares at the form of the man. His face whitens, it becomes so transfigured with emotion that for a moment it does not look weak. Then I see that his thin hand is clenched.

I realize how little I understand his emotions.

A sudden fear of what he will do takes hold of me. He sits

white and tense as the two come into the clearer light of the courtyard. The man, I see, is one of the samurai, a dark, strong-faced man, a man I have never seen before, and she is wearing the robe that shows her a follower of the Lesser Rule.

Some glimmering of the botanist's feelings strikes through to my slow sympathies. Of course – a strange man! I put out a restraining hand towards his arm. 'I told you,' I say, 'that very probably, most probably, she would have met some other. I tried to prepare you.'

'Nonsense,' he whispers, without looking at me. 'It isn't that. It's – that scoundrel—'

He has an impulse to rise. 'That scoundrel,' he repeats.

'He isn't a scoundrel,' I say. 'How do you know? Keep still! Why are you standing up?'

He and I stand up quickly, I as soon as he. But now the full meaning of the group has reached me. I grip his arm. 'Be sensible,' I say, speaking very quickly and with my back to the approaching couple. 'He's not a scoundrel here. This world is different from that. It's caught his pride somehow and made a man of him. Whatever troubled them there—'

He turns a face of white wrath on me, of accusation, and for the moment of unexpected force. 'This is *your* doing,' he says. 'You have done this to mock me. He – of all men!' For a moment speech fails him, then; 'You – you have done this to mock me.'

I try to explain. My tone is almost propitiatory.

'I never thought of it until now. But he's— How did I know he was the sort of man a disciplined world has a use for?'

He makes no answer, but he looks at me with eyes that are positively baleful, and in the instant I read his mute but mulish resolve that Utopia must end.

'Don't let that old quarrel poison all this,' I say almost entreatingly. 'It happened all differently here – everything is different here. Your double will be back tomorrow. Wait for him. Perhaps then you will understand—'

He shakes his head, and then bursts out with, 'What do I want with a double? Double! What do I care if things have been different here? This—'

He thrusts me weakly back with his long white hand. 'My God!' he says almost forcibly, 'what nonsense all this is! All these dreams! All Utopias! There she is—! Oh, but I have dreamt of her! And now—'

A sob catches him. I am really frightened by this time. I still try to keep between him and these Utopians, and to hide his gestures from them.

'It's different here,' I persist. 'It's different here. The emotion you feel has no place in it. It's a scar from the earth – the sore scar of your past—'

'And what are we all but scars? What is life but a scarring? It's *you* – you who don't understand! Of course we are covered with scars, we live to be scarred, we are scars! We are the scars of the past! These *dreams*, these childish dreams—!'

He does not need to finish his sentence, he waves an unteachable destructive arm.

My Utopia rocks about me.

For a moment the vision of that great courtyard hangs real. There the Utopians live real about me, going to and fro, and the great archway blazes with sunlight from the green gardens by the riverside. The man who is one of the samurai, and his lady, whom the botanist loved on earth, pass out of sight behind the marble flower-set Triton[1] that spouts coolness in the middle of the place. For a moment I see two working men in green tunics sitting on a marble seat in the shadow of the colonnade, and a sweet little silver-haired old lady, clad all in violet and carrying a book, comes towards us and lifts a curious eye at the botanist's gestures. And then—

'Scars of the past! Scars of the past! These fanciful, useless dreams!'

## § 2

There is no jerk, no sound, no hint of material shock. We are in London, and clothed in the fashion of the town. The sullen roar of London fills our ears. . . .

I see that I am standing beside an iron seat of poor design in that grey and gawky waste of asphalt – Trafalgar Square, and the botanist, with perplexity in his face, stares from me to a poor, shrivelled, dirt-lined old woman – my God! what a neglected thing she is! – who proffers a box of matches. . . .

He buys almost mechanically, and turns back to me.

'I was saying,' he says, 'the past rules us absolutely. These dreams—'

His sentence does not complete itself. He looks nervous and irritated.

'You have a trick at times,' he says instead, 'of making your suggestions so vivid—'

He takes a plunge. 'If you don't mind,' he says in a sort of quavering ultimatum, 'we won't discuss that aspect of the question – the lady, I mean – further.'

He pauses, and there still hangs a faint perplexity between us.

'But—' I begin.

For a moment we stand there, and my dream of Utopia runs off me like water from an oiled slab. Of course – we lunched at our club. We came back from Switzerland by no dream train but by the ordinary Bâle[2] express. We have been talking of that Lucerne woman he harps upon, and I have made some novel comment on his story. I have touched certain possibilities.

'You can't conceivably understand,' he says.

'The fact remains,' he goes on, taking up the thread of his argument again with an air of having defined our field, 'we *are* the scars of the past. That's a thing one can discuss – without personalities.'

'No,' I say rather stupidly, 'no.'

'You are always talking as though you could kick the past to pieces; as though one could get right out from oneself and begin afresh. It is your weakness – if you don't mind my being frank – it makes you seem harsh and dogmatic. Life has gone easily for you; you have never been badly tried. You have been lucky – you do not understand the other way about. You are – hard.'

I answer nothing.

He pants for breath. I perceive that in our discussion of his case I must have gone too far, and that he has rebelled. Clearly I must have said something wounding about that ineffectual love story of his.

'You don't allow for my position,' he says, and it occurs to me to say, 'I'm obliged to look at the thing from my own point of view. . . .'

One or other of us makes a move. What a lot of filthy, torn paper is scattered about the world! We walk slowly side by side towards the dirt-littered basin of the fountain, and stand regarding two grimy tramps who sit and argue on a further seat. One holds a horrible old boot in his hand, and gesticulates with it, while his other hand caresses his rag-wrapped foot. 'Wot does Cham'lain *si*?' his words drift to us. 'W'y, 'e says, wot's the good of 'nvesting your kepital where these 'ere Americans may dump it flat any time they like? . . .'

(Were there not two men in green sitting on a marble seat?)

## § 3

We walk on, our talk suspended, past a ruthlessly clumsy hoarding, towards where men and women and children are struggling about a string of omnibuses. A newsvendor at the corner spreads a newspaper placard upon the wood pavement, pins the corners down with stones, and we glimpse something about:–

MASSACRE IN ODESSA.[3]

DISCOVERY OF HUMAN REMAINS AT CHERTSEY.

SHOCKING LYNCHING OUTRAGE IN NEW YORK STATE.

GERMAN INTRIGUES GET A SET-BACK.

THE BIRTHDAY HONOURS. – FULL LIST.

Dear old familiar world!

An angry parent in conversation with a sympathetic friend jostles against us. 'I'll knock his blooming young 'ed orf if 'e cheeks me again. It's these 'ere brasted Board Schools—'[4]

An omnibus passes, bearing on a board beneath an incorrectly drawn Union Jack an exhortation to the true patriot to 'Buy Bumper's British-Boiled Jam'. . . .

I am stunned beyond the possibility of discussion for a space. In this very place it must have been that the high terrace ran with the gardens below it, along which I came from my double to our hotel. I am going back, but now through reality, along the path I passed so happily in my dream. And the people I saw then are the people I am looking at now – with a difference.

The botanist walks beside me, white and nervously jerky in his movements, his ultimatum delivered.

We start to cross the road. An open carriage drives by, and we see a jaded, red-haired woman, smeared with paint, dressed in furs and petulantly discontented. Her face is familiar to me, her face, with a difference.

Why do I think of her as dressed in green?

Of course! – she it was I saw leading her children by the hand!

Comes a crash to our left, and a running of people to see a cab-horse down on the slippery, slanting pavement outside St Martin's Church.[5]

We go on up the street.

A heavy-eyed young Jewess, a draggled prostitute – no crimson flower for her hair, poor girl! – regards us with a momentary speculation, and we get a whiff of foul language from two newsboys on the kerb.

'We can't go on talking,' the botanist begins, and ducks aside just in time to save his eye from the ferule of a stupidly held umbrella. He is going to treat our little tiff about that lady as closed. He has the air of picking up our conversation again at some earlier point.

He steps into the gutter, walks round outside a negro hawker, just escapes the wheel of a hansom,[6] and comes to my side again.

'We can't go on talking of your Utopia,' he says, 'in a noise and crowd like this.'

We are separated by a portly man going in the opposite direction, and join again. 'We can't go on talking of Utopia,' he repeats, 'in London. . . . Up in the mountains – and holiday-time – it was all right. We let ourselves go!'

'I've been living in Utopia,' I answer, tacitly adopting his tacit proposal to drop the lady out of the question.

'At times,' he says, with a queer laugh, 'you've almost made me live there too.'

He reflects. 'It doesn't do, you know. *No!* And I don't know whether, after all, I want—'

We are separated again by half a dozen lifted flagstones, a burning brazier and two engineers concerned with some underground business or other – in the busiest hour of the day's traffic.

'Why shouldn't it do?' I ask.

'It spoils the world of everyday to let your mind run on impossible perfections.'

'I wish,' I shout against the traffic, 'I could *smash* the world of everyday.'

My note becomes quarrelsome. 'You may accept *this* as the world of reality, *you* may consent to be one scar in an ill-dressed compound wound, but so – not I! This is a dream too – this world. *Your* dream, and you bring me back to it – out of Utopia—'

The crossing of Bow Street gives me pause again.

The face of a girl who is passing westward, a student girl rather carelessly dressed, her books in a carrying-strap, comes across my field of vision. The westward sun of London glows upon her face. She has eyes that dream, surely no sensuous nor personal dream.

After all, after all, dispersed, hidden, disorganized, undiscovered, unsuspected even by themselves, the samurai of Utopia are in this world, the motives that are developed and organized there stir dumbly here and stifle in ten thousand futile hearts. . . .

I overtake the botanist, who got ahead at the crossing by the advantage of a dustcart.

'You think this is real because you can't wake out of it,' I say. 'It's all a dream, and there are people—I'm just one of the first of a multitude – between sleeping and waking – who will presently be rubbing it out of their eyes.'

A pinched and dirty little girl, with sores upon her face, stretches out a bunch of wilting violets in a pitifully thin little fist, and interrupts my speech. 'Bunch o' vi'lets – on'y a penny.'

'No!' I say curtly, hardening my heart.

A ragged and filthy nursing mother, with her last addition to

our Imperial People on her arm, comes out of a drinkshop and
stands a little unsteadily, and wipes mouth and nose comprehensively with the back of a red chapped hand. . . .

## § 4

'Isn't *that* reality?' says the botanist, almost triumphantly, and
leaves me aghast at his triumph.

'*That!*' I say belatedly. 'It's a thing in a nightmare!'

He shakes his head and smiles – exasperatingly.

I perceive quite abruptly that the botanist and I have reached
the limits of our intercourse.

'The world dreams things like that,' I say, 'because it suffers
from an indigestion of such people as you.'

His low-toned self-complacency, like the faded banner of an
obstinate fort, still flies unconquered. And you know, he's not
even a happy man with it all!

For ten seconds or more I am furiously seeking in my mind
for a word, for a term of abuse, for one compendious verbal
missile that shall smash this man for ever. It has to express total
inadequacy of imagination and will, spiritual anaemia, dull
respectability, gross sentimentality, a cultivated pettiness of
heart. . . .

That word will not come. But no other word will do. Indeed
the word does not exist. There is nothing with sufficient vituper-
ative concentration for this moral and intellectual stupidity of
educated people. . . .

'Er —' he begins.

No! I can't endure him.

With a passionate rapidity of movement I leave his side,
dart between a carriage and a van, duck under the head of a
cab-horse, and board a 'bus going westward somewhere – but
anyhow, going in exactly the reverse direction to the botanist.
I clamber up the steps and thread my swaying way to the seat
immediately behind the driver.

'There!' I say, as I whack myself down on the seat and pant.

When I look round the botanist is out of sight.

§ 5

But I am back in the world for all that, and my Utopia is done.

It is good discipline for the Utopist to visit this world occasionally.

But from the front seat on the top of an omnibus on a sunny September afternoon, the Strand and Charing Cross corner and Whitehall and the great multitude of people, the great uproar of vehicles, streaming in all directions, is apt to look a world altogether too formidable. It has a glare, it has a tumult and vigour that shout one down. It shouts one down, if shouting is to carry it. What good was it to trot along the pavement through this noise and tumult of life, pleading Utopia to that botanist? What good would it be to recommend Utopia in this driver's preoccupied ear?

There are moments in the life of every philosopher and dreamer when he feels himself the flimsiest of absurdities, when the Thing in Being has its way with him, its triumphant way, when it asks in a roar, unanswerably, with a fine solid use of the current vernacular, 'What Good is all this – Rot about Utopias?'

One inspects the Thing in Being with something of the diffident speculation of primitive man, peering from behind a tree at an angry elephant.

(There is an omen in that image. On how many occasions must that ancestor of ours have had just the Utopist's feeling of ambitious unreality, have decided that on the whole it was wiser to go very quietly home again, and leave the big beast alone? But, in the end, men rode upon the elephant's head, and guided him this way or that. . . . The Thing in Being that roars so tremendously about Charing Cross corner seems a bigger antagonist than an elephant, but then we have better weapons than chipped flint blades. . . .)

After all, in a very little time everything that impresses me so mightily this September afternoon will have changed or passed away for ever, everything. These omnibuses, these great stalwart, crowded, many-coloured things that jostle one another and make so handsome a clatter-clamour, will all have gone;

they and their horses and drivers and organization; you will come here and you will not find them. Something else will be here, some different sort of vehicle, that is now perhaps the mere germ of an idea in some engineer student's brain. And this road and pavement will have changed, and these impressive great buildings; other buildings will be here, buildings that are as yet more impalpable than this page you read, more formless and flimsy by far than anything that is reasoned here. Little plans sketched on paper, strokes of a pen or of a brush, will be the first materializations of what will at last obliterate every detail and atom of these re-echoing actualities that overwhelm us now. And the clothing and gestures of these innumerable people, the character of their faces and bearing, these too will be recast in the spirit of what are now obscure and impalpable beginnings.

The new things will be indeed of the substance of the thing that is, but differing just in the measure of the will and imagination that go to make them. They will be strong and fair as the will is sturdy and organized and the imagination comprehensive and bold; they will be ugly and smeared with wretchedness as the will is fluctuating and the imagination timid and mean.

Indeed Will is stronger than Fact, it can mould and overcome Fact. But this world has still to discover its will, it is a world that slumbers inertly, and all this roar and pulsation of life is no more than its heavy breathing. . . . My mind runs on to the thought of an awakening.

As my omnibus goes lumbering up Cockspur Street[7] through the clatter-rattle of the cabs and carriages, there comes another fancy in my mind. . . . Could one but realize an apocalyptic image and suppose an angel, such as was given to each of the seven churches of Asia,[8] given for a space to the service of the Greater Rule! I see him as a towering figure of flame and colour standing between earth and sky, with a trumpet in his hands, over there above the Haymarket against the October glow; and when he sounds, all the samurai, all who are samurai in Utopia, will know themselves and one another. . . .

(Whup! says a motor brougham, and a policeman stays the traffic with his hand.)

All of us who partake of the samurai would know ourselves and one another!

For a moment I have a vision of this resurrection of the living, of a vague, magnificent answer, of countless myriads at attention, of all that is fine in humanity at attention, round the compass of the earth.

Then that philosophy of individual uniqueness resumes its sway over my thoughts, and my dream of a world's awakening fades.

I had forgotten. . . .

Things do not happen like that. God is not simple, God is not theatrical, the summons comes to each man in its due time for him, with an infinite subtlety of variety. . . .

If that is so, what of my Utopia?

This infinite world must needs be flattened to get it on one retina. The picture of a solid thing, although it is flattened and simplified, is not necessarily a lie. Surely, surely in the end, by degrees and steps, something of this sort, some such understanding as this Utopia must come. First here, then there, single men and then groups of men will fall into line – not indeed with my poor faulty hesitating suggestions, but with a great and comprehensive plan wrought out by many minds and in many tongues. It is just because my plan is faulty, because it mis-states so much and omits so much, that they do not now fall in. It will not be like *my* dream, the world that is coming. My dream is just my own poor dream, the thing sufficient for me. We fail in comprehension, we fail so variously and abundantly. We see as much as it is serviceable for us to see, and we see no farther. But the fresh undaunted generations come to take on our work beyond our utmost effort, beyond the range of our ideas. They will learn with certainty things that to us are guesses and riddles. . . .

There will be many Utopias. Each generation will have its new version of Utopia, a little more certain and complete and real, with its problems lying closer and closer to the problems of the Thing in Being. Until at last from dreams Utopias will have come to be working drawings, and the whole world will be shaping the final World State, the fair and great and fruitful

World State, that will only not be a Utopia because it will be this world. So surely it must be—

*The policeman drops his hand. 'Come up,' says the 'bus driver, and the horses strain; 'Clitter, clatter, cluck, clak,' the line of hurrying hansoms overtakes the omnibus going west. A dexterous lad on a bicycle with a bale of newspapers on his back dodges nimbly across the head of the column and vanishes up a side street.*

*The omnibus sways forward. Rapt and prophetic, his plump hands clasped round the handle of his umbrella, his billycock hat[9] a trifle askew, this irascible little man of the Voice, this impatient dreamer, this scolding Optimist, who has argued so rudely and dogmatically about economics and philosophy and decoration, and indeed about everything under the sun, who has been so hard on the botanist and fashionable women, and so reluctant in the matter of beer, is carried onward, dreaming dreams, dreams that with all the inevitable ironies of differences may be realities when you and I are dreams.*

*He passes, and for a little space we are left with his egoisms and idiosyncrasies more or less in suspense.*

*But why was he intruded? you ask. Why could not a modern Utopia be discussed without this impersonation – impersonally? It has confused the book, you say, made the argument hard to follow, and thrown a quality of insincerity over the whole. Are we but mocking at Utopias, you demand, using all these noble and generalized hopes as the backcloth against which two bickering personalities jar and squabble? Do I mean we are never to view the promised land again except through a foreground of fellow travellers? There is a common notion that the reading of a Utopia should end with a swelling heart and clear resolves, with lists of names, formation of committees, and even the commencement of subscriptions. But this Utopia began upon a philosophy of fragmentation, and ends, confusedly, amidst a gross tumult of immediate realities, in dust and doubt, with at the best one individual's aspiration. Utopias were once in good faith projects for a fresh creation of the world and of a most unworldly completeness; this so-called*

*Modern Utopia is a mere story of personal adventures among Utopian philosophies.*

*Indeed, that came about without the writer's intention. So it was the summoned vision came. For I see about me a great multitude of little souls and groups of souls as darkened, as derivative as my own; with the passage of years I understand more and more clearly the quality of the motives that urge me and urge them to do whatever we do. . . . Yet that is not all I see, and I am not altogether bounded by my littleness. Ever and again, contrasting with this immediate vision, come glimpses of a comprehensive scheme in which these personalities float, the scheme of a synthetic wider being, the great State, mankind, in which we all move and go like blood corpuscles, like nerve cells, it may be at times like brain cells, in the body of a man. But the two visions are not seen consistently together, at least by me; and I do not surely know that they exist consistently together. The motives needed for those wider issues come not into the interplay of my vanities and wishes. That greater scheme lies about the men and women I know, as I have tried to make the vistas and spaces, the mountains, cities, laws and order of Utopia lie about my talking couple, too great for their sustained comprehension. When one focuses upon these two, that wide landscape becomes indistinct and distant; and when one regards that, then the real persons one knows grow vague and unreal. Nevertheless, I cannot separate these two aspects of human life, each commenting on the other. In that incongruity between the whole and the individual inheres the incompatibility I could not resolve, and which, therefore, I have had to present in this conflicting form. At times that scheme does seem to me to enter certain men's lives as a passion, as a real and living motive; there are those who know it almost as if it was a thing of desire; even for me, upon occasion, the little lures of the immediate life are seen small and vain, and the soul goes out to that mighty Being, to apprehend it and serve it and possess. But this is an illumination that passes as it comes, a rare transitory lucidity, leaving the soul's desire suddenly turned to presumption and hypocrisy upon the lips. One grasps at the Universe and attains – Bathos. The hungers, the jealousies, the prejudices and habits have us again, and we are forced back to think that it is so and not otherwise that we are meant to serve the mysteries; that in these blinkers it is we are driven to an end we cannot understand. And then, for measured moments in the night-watches or as one walks alone or while one sits in thought and speech with a friend, the wider aspirations glow again with a sincere emotion, with the colours of attainable desire. . . .*

*That is my all about Utopia, and about the desire and need for Utopia, and how that planet lies to this planet that bears the daily lives of men.*

# Appendix

# SCEPTICISM OF THE
# INSTRUMENT

*A paper read before the Oxford Philosophical Society,*
*November 8th, 1903.*

It seems to me that I may most propitiously attempt to interest
you this evening by describing very briefly the particular metaphysical and philosophical system in which I do my thinking,
and more particularly by setting out for your consideration one
or two points in which I seem to myself to differ most widely
from current accepted philosophy.

You must be prepared for things that will strike you as crude,
for a certain difference of accent and dialect that you may not
like, and you must be prepared too to hear what may strike
you as the clumsy statement of my ignorant rediscovery of
things already beautifully thought out and said. But in the end
you may incline to forgive me some of this first offence. . . .
It is quite unavoidable that, in setting out these intellectual
foundations of mine, I should lapse for a moment or so towards
autobiography.

A convergence of circumstances led to my having my knowledge of concrete things quite extensively developed before I
came to philosophical examination at all. I have heard someone
say that a savage or an animal is mentally a purely objective
being, and in that respect I was like a savage or an animal
until I was well over twenty. I was extremely unaware of the
subjective or introverted element in my being. I was a Positivist
without knowing it. My early education was a feeble one; it
was one in which my private observation, inquiry and experiment were far more important factors than any instruction, or
rather perhaps the instruction I received was less even than
what I learnt for myself, and it terminated at thirteen. I had
come into pretty intimate contact with the harder realities of

life, with hunger in various forms, and many base and disagree-able necessities, before I was fifteen. About that age, following the indication of certain theological and speculative curiosities, I began to learn something of what I will call deliberately and justly, Elementary Science – stuff I got out of *Cassell's Popular Educator* and cheap textbooks – and then, through accidents and ambitions that do not matter in the least to us now, I came to three years of illuminating and good scientific work. The central fact of those three years was Huxley's[1] course in Comparative Anatomy at the school in Exhibition Road. About that as a nucleus I arranged a spacious digest of facts. At the end of that time I had acquired what I still think to be a fairly clear and complete and ordered view of the ostensibly real universe. Let me try to give you the chief things I had. I had man definitely placed in the great scheme of space and time. I knew him incurably for what he was, finite and not final, a being of compromises and adaptations. I had traced his lungs, for example, from a swimming bladder, step by step, with scalpel and probe, through a dozen types or more; I had seen the ancestral caecum shrink to that disease nest, the appendix of today, I had watched the gill slit patched slowly to the purposes of the ear and the reptile jaw suspension utilized to eke out the needs of a sense organ taken from its native and natural water. I had worked out the development of those extraordinarily unsatisfactory and untrustworthy instruments, man's teeth, from the skin scutes of the shark to their present function as a basis for gold stoppings, and followed the slow unfolding of the complex and painful process of gestation through which man comes into the world. I had followed all these things and many kindred things by dissection and in embryology – I had checked the whole theory of development again in a year's course of palaeontology, and I had taken the dimensions of the whole process, by the scale of the stars, in a course of astronomical physics. And all that amount of objective eluci-dation came before I had reached the beginnings of any philo-sophical or metaphysical inquiry, any inquiry as to why I believed, how I believed, what I believed, or what the funda-mental stuff of things was.

Now following hard upon this interlude with knowledge, came a time when I had to give myself to teaching, and it became advisable to acquire one of those Teaching Diplomas that are so widely and so foolishly despised; and that enterprise set me to a superficial but suggestive study of educational method, of educational theory, of logic, of psychology, and so at last, when the little affair with the diploma was settled, to philosophy. Now to come to logic over the bracing uplands of comparative anatomy is to come to logic with a lot of very natural preconceptions blown clean out of one's mind. It is, I submit, a way of taking logic in the flank. When you have realized to the marrow, that all the physical organs of man and all his physical structure are what they are through a series of adaptations and approximations, and that they are kept up to a level of practical efficiency only by the elimination of death, and that this is true also of his brain and of his instincts and of many of his mental predispositions, you are not going to take his thinking apparatus unquestioningly as being in any way mysteriously different and better. And I had read only a little logic before I became aware of implications that I could not agree with, and assumptions that seemed to me to be altogether at variance with the general scheme of objective fact established in my mind.

I came to an examination of logical processes and of language with the expectation that they would share the profoundly provisional character, the character of irregular limitation and adaptation that pervades the whole physical and animal being of man. And I found the thing I had expected. And as a consequence I found a sort of intellectual hardihood about the assumptions of logic, that at first confused me and then roused all the latent scepticism in my mind.

My first quarrel with the accepted logic I developed long ago in a little paper that was printed in the *Fortnightly Review*[2] in July, 1891. It was called the 'Rediscovery of the Unique', and re-reading it I perceive not only how bad and even annoying it was in manner – a thing I have long known – but also how remarkably bad it was in expression. I have good reason for doubting whether my powers of expression in these uses have very perceptibly improved, but at any rate I am doing my best now with that previous failure before me.

That unfortunate paper, among other oversights I can no longer regard as trivial, disregarded quite completely the fact that a whole literature upon the antagonism of the one and the many, of the specific ideal and the individual reality, was already in existence. It defined no relations to other thought or thinkers. I understand now, what I did not understand then, why it was totally ignored. But the idea underlying that paper I cling to today. I consider it an idea that will ultimately be regarded as one of primary importance to human thought, and I will try and present the substance of that early paper again now very briefly, as the best opening of my general case. My opening scepticism is essentially a doubt of *the objective reality of classification*. I have no hesitation in saying that is the first and primary proposition of my philosophy.

I have it in my mind that classification is a necessary condition of the working of the mental implement but that it is a departure from the objective truth of things, that classification is very serviceable for the practical purposes of life but a very doubtful preliminary to those fine penetrations the philosophical purpose, in its more arrogant moods, demands. All the peculiarities of my way of thinking derive from that.

A mind nourished upon anatomical study is of course permeated with the suggestion of the vagueness and instability of biological species. A biological species is quite obviously a great number of unique individuals which is separable from other biological species only by the fact that an enormous number of other linking individuals are inaccessible in time – are in other words dead and gone – and each new individual in that species does, in the distinction of its own individuality, break away in however infinitesimal degree from the previous average properties of the species. There is no property of any species, even the properties that constitute the specific definition, that is not a matter of more or less. If, for example, a species be distinguished by a single large red spot on the back, you will find if you go over a great number of specimens that red spot shrinking here to nothing, expanding there to a more general redness, weakening to pink, deepening to russet and brown, shading into crimson, and so on, and so on. And this is true not only of biological species. It is true of the mineral specimens constituting a mineral species; and I remember as a constant refrain in the lectures of Prof. Judd[3] upon rock classification, the words 'they pass into one another by insensible gradations'. That is true, I hold, of all things.

You will think perhaps of atoms of the elements as instances of identically similar things, but these are things not of experience but of theory, and there is not a phenomenon in chemistry that is not equally well explained on the supposition that it is merely the immense quantities of atoms necessarily taken in any experiment that mask by the operation of the law of averages the fact that each atom also has its unique quality, its special individual difference. This idea of uniqueness in all individuals is not only true of the classifications of material science; it is true, and still more evidently true, of the species of common thought, it is true of common terms. Take the word *chair*. When one says chair, one thinks vaguely of an average chair. But collect individual instances, think of armchairs and reading-chairs, and dining-room chairs and kitchen chairs, chairs that pass into benches, chairs that cross the boundary and become settees, dentists' chairs, thrones, opera stalls, seats of all sorts, those miraculous fungoid growths that cumber the floor of the Arts and Crafts Exhibition, and you will perceive what a lax bundle in fact is this simple straightforward term. In co-operation with an intelligent joiner I would undertake to defeat any definition of chair or chairishness that you gave me. Chairs just as much as individual organisms, just as much as mineral and rock specimens, are unique things – if you know them well enough you will find an individual difference even in a set of machine-made chairs – and it is only because we do not possess minds of unlimited capacity, because our brain has only a limited number of pigeonholes for our correspondence with an unlimited universe of objective uniques, that we have to delude ourselves into the belief that there is a chairishness in this species common to and distinctive of all chairs.

Let me repeat; this is of the very smallest importance in all the practical affairs of life, or indeed in relation to anything but philosophy and wide generalizations. But in philosophy it matters profoundly. If I order two new-laid eggs for breakfast, up come two unhatched but still unique avian individuals, and the chances are they serve my rude physiological purpose. I can afford to ignore the hens' eggs of the past that were not quite so nearly this sort of thing, and the hens' eggs of the future that will accumulate modification age by age; I can venture to ignore the rare chance of an abnormality in chemical composition and of any startling aberration in my physiological reaction; I can, with a confidence that is practically perfect, say with unqualified simplicity 'two eggs', but not if my concern is not my morning's breakfast but the utmost possible truth.

Now let me go on to point out whither this idea of uniqueness tends. I submit to you that syllogism is based on classification, that all hard logical reasoning tends to imply and is apt to imply a confidence in the objective reality of classification. Consequently in denying that, I deny the absolute validity of logic. Classification and number, which in truth ignore the fine differences of objective realities, have in the past of human thought been imposed upon things. Let me for clearness' sake take a liberty here – commit, as you may perhaps think, an unpardonable insolence. Hindoo thought and Greek thought alike impress me as being overmuch obsessed by an objective treatment of certain necessary preliminary conditions of human thought – number and definition and class and abstract form. But these things, number, definition, class and abstract form, I hold are merely unavoidable conditions of mental activity – regrettable conditions rather than essential facts. *The forceps of our minds are clumsy forceps, and crush the truth a little in taking hold of it.*

It was about this difficulty that the mind of Plato played a little inconclusively all his life. For the most part he tended to regard the *idea* as the something behind reality, whereas it seems to me that the idea is the more proximate and less perfect thing, the thing by which the mind, by ignoring individual differences, attempts to comprehend an otherwise unmanageable number of unique realities.

Let me give you a rough figure of what I am trying to convey in this first attack upon the philosophical validity of general terms. You have seen the results of those various methods of black-and-white reproduction that involve the use of a rectangular net. You know the sort of process picture I mean – it used to be employed very frequently in reproducing photographs. At a distance you really seem to have a faithful reproduction of the original picture, but when you peer closely you find not the unique form and masses of the original, but a multitude of little rectangles, uniform in shape and size. The more earnestly you go into the thing, the closer you look, the more the picture is lost in reticulations. I submit the world of reasoned inquiry has a very similar relation to the world I call objectively real. For the rough purposes of every day the network picture will do, but the finer your purpose the less it will serve, and for an ideally fine purpose, for absolute and general knowledge that will be as true for a man at a distance with a telescope as for a man with a microscope, it will not serve at all.

It is true you can make your net of logical interpretation finer and finer, you can fine your classification more and more – up to a certain limit. But essentially you are working in limits, and as you come closer, as you look at finer and subtler things, as you leave the practical purpose for which the method exists, the element of error increases. Every species is vague, every term goes cloudy at its edges; and so, in my way of thinking, relentless logic is only another phrase for a stupidity – for a sort of intellectual pigheadedness. If you push a philosophical or metaphysical inquiry through a series of valid syllogisms – never committing any generally recognized fallacy – you nevertheless leave a certain rubbing and marginal loss of objective truth and you get deflections that are difficult to trace, at each phase in the process. Every species waggles about in its definition, every tool is a little loose in its handle, every scale has its individual error. So long as you are reasoning for practical purposes about the finite things of experience, you can every now and then check your process, and correct your adjustments. But not when you make what are called philosophical and theological inquiries, when you turn your implement towards the final absolute truth of things. Doing that is like firing at an inaccessible, unmarkable and indestructible target at an unknown distance, with a defective rifle and variable cartridges. Even if by chance you hit, you cannot know that you hit, and so it will matter nothing at all.

This assertion of the necessary untrustworthiness of all reasoning processes arising out of the fallacy of classification in what is quite conceivably a universe of uniques, forms only one introductory aspect of my general scepticism of the Instrument of Thought.

I have now to tell you of another aspect of this scepticism of the instrument which concerns negative terms.

Classes in logic are not only represented by circles with a hard firm outline, whereas they have no such definite limits, but also there is a constant disposition to think of negative terms as if they represented positive classes. With words just as with numbers and abstract forms there are definite phases of human development. There is, you know, with regard to number, the phase when man can barely count at all, or counts in perfect good faith and sanity upon his fingers. Then there is the phase when he is struggling with the development of number, when he begins to elaborate all sorts of ideas about numbers, until at last he develops complex superstitions about perfect numbers and imperfect numbers, about threes and sevens and the like. The same is the case with abstracted forms, and even today we are scarcely more than heads out of the vast subtle muddle of thinking about spheres and ideally perfect forms and so on, that was the price of this little necessary step to clear thinking. You know better than I do how large a part numerical and geometrical magic, numerical and geometrical philosophy, has played in the history of the mind. And the whole apparatus of language and mental communication is beset with like dangers. The language of the savage is, I suppose, purely positive; the thing has a name, the name has a thing. This indeed is the tradition of language, and even today we, when we hear a name, are predisposed – and sometimes it is a very vicious disposition – to imagine forthwith something answering to the name. *We are disposed, as an incurable mental vice, to accumulate intension in terms.* If I say to you Wodget or Crump, you find yourself passing over the fact that these are nothings, these are, so to speak, mere blankety blanks, and trying to think what sort of thing a Wodget or a Crump may be. And where this disposition has come in, in its most alluring guise, is in the case of negative terms. Our instrument of knowledge persists in handling even such openly negative terms as the Absolute, the Infinite, as though they were real existences; and when the negative element is ever so little disguised, as it is in such a word as Omniscience, then the illusion of positive reality may be complete.

Please remember that I am trying to tell you my philosophy, and not arguing about yours. Let me try to express how in my mind this matter of negative terms has shaped itself. I think of something which I may perhaps best describe as being off the stage or out of court, or as the Void without Implications, or as Nothingness or as Outer Darkness. This is a sort of hypothetical Beyond to the visible world of human thought, and thither I think all negative terms reach at last, and merge and become nothing. Whatever positive class you make, whatever boundary you draw, straight away from that boundary begins the corresponding negative class and passes into the illimitable horizon of nothingness. You talk of pink things, you ignore, if you are a trained logician, the more elusive shades of pink, and draw your line. Beyond is the not pink, known and knowable, and still in the not pink region one comes to the Outer Darkness. Not blue, not happy, not iron, all the *not* classes meet in that Outer Darkness. That same Outer Darkness and nothingness is infinite space, and infinite time, and any being of infinite qualities; and all that region I rule out of court in my philosophy altogether. I will neither affirm nor deny if I can help it about any *not* things. I will not deal with not things at all, except by accident and inadvertence. If I use the word 'infinite' I use it as one often uses 'countless', 'the countless hosts of the enemy' – or 'immeasurable' – 'immeasurable cliffs' – that is to say as the limit of measurement rather than as the limit of imaginary measurability, as a convenient equivalent to as many times this cloth yard as you can, and as many again and so on and so on. Now a great number of apparently positive terms are, or have become, practically negative terms and are under the same ban with me. A considerable number of terms that have played a great part in the world of thought, seem to me to be invalidated by this same defect, to have no content or an undefined content or an unjustifiable content. For example, that word Omniscient, as implying infinite knowledge, impresses me as being a word with a delusive air of being solid and full, when it is really hollow with no content whatever. I am persuaded that knowing is the relation of a conscious being to something not itself, that the thing known is defined as a system of parts and aspects and relationships, that knowledge is comprehension, and so that only finite things can know or be known. When you talk of a being of infinite extension and infinite duration, omniscient and omnipotent and Perfect, you seem to me to be talking in negatives of nothing whatever. When you speak of the Absolute you speak to me of nothing. If however you talk of a great yet finite and thinkable being, a being not myself, extending beyond my imagination in time and space, knowing all that I can think of as known and capable of doing all that I can think of as done, you come into the sphere of my mental operations, and into the scheme of my philosophy. . . .

These then are my first two charges against our Instrument of Knowledge, firstly, that it can work only by disregarding individuality and treating uniques as identically similar objects in this respect or that, so as to group them under one term, and that once it has done so it tends automatically to intensify the significance of that term; and secondly, that it can only deal freely with negative terms by treating them as though they were positive. But I have a further objection to the Instrument of Human Thought, that is not correlated to these former objections and that is also rather more difficult to convey.

Essentially this idea is to present a sort of stratification in human ideas. I have it very much in mind that various terms in our reasoning lie, as it were, at different levels and in different planes, and that we accomplish a large amount of error and confusion by reasoning terms together that do not lie or nearly lie in the same plane.

Let me endeavour to make myself a little less obscure by a most flagrant instance from physical things. Suppose someone began to talk seriously of a man seeing an atom through a microscope, or better perhaps of cutting one in half with a knife. There are a number of non-analytical people who would be quite prepared to believe that an atom could be visible to the eye or cut in this manner. But anyone at all conversant with physical conceptions would almost as soon think of killing the square root of 2 with a rook rifle as of cutting an atom in half with a knife. Our conception of an atom is reached through a process of hypothesis and analysis, and in the world of atoms there are no knives and no men to cut. If you have thought with a strong consistent mental movement, then when you have thought of your atom under the knife blade, your knife blade has itself become a cloud of swinging grouped atoms, and your microscope lens a little universe of oscillatory and vibratory molecules. If you think of the universe, thinking at the level of atoms, there is neither knife to cut, scale to weigh nor eye to see. The universe *at that plane to which the mind of the molecular physicist descends* has none of the shapes or forms of our common life whatever. This hand with which I write is in the universe of molecular physics a cloud of warring atoms and molecules, combining and recombining, colliding, rotating, flying hither and thither in the universal atmosphere of ether.

You see, I hope, what I mean when I say that the universe of molecular physics is at a different level from the universe of common experience; – what we call stable and solid is in that world a freely moving system of interlacing centres of force, what we call colour and sound is there no more than this length of vibration or that. We have reached to a conception of that universe of molecular physics by a great enterprise of organized analysis, and our universe of daily experiences stands in relation to that elemental world as if it were a synthesis of those elemental things.

I would suggest to you that this is only a very extreme instance of the general state of affairs, that there may be finer and subtler differences of level between one term and another, and that terms may very well be thought of as lying obliquely and as being twisted through different levels.

It will perhaps give a clearer idea of what I am seeking to convey if I suggest a concrete image for the whole world of a man's thought and knowledge. Imagine a large clear jelly, in which at all angles and in all states of simplicity or contortion his ideas are imbedded. They are all valid and possible ideas as they lie, none in reality incompatible with any. If you imagine the direction of up or down in this clear jelly being as it were the direction in which one moves by analysis or by synthesis, if you go down for example from matter to atoms and centres of force and up to men and states and countries – if you will imagine the ideas lying in that manner – you will get the beginning of my intention. But our Instrument, our process of thinking, like a drawing before the discovery of perspective, appears to have difficulties with the third dimension, appears capable only of dealing with or reasoning about ideas by projecting them upon the same plane. It will be obvious that a great multitude of things may very well exist together in a solid jelly, which would be overlapping and incompatible and mutually destructive when projected together upon one plane. Through the bias in our Instrument to do this, through reasoning between terms not in the same plane, an enormous amount of confusion, perplexity and mental deadlocking occurs.

The old theological deadlock between predestination and free will serves admirably as an example of the sort of deadlock I mean. Take life at the level of common sensation and common experience and there is no more indisputable fact than man's freedom of will, unless it is his complete moral responsibility. But make only the least penetrating of analyses and you perceive a world of inevitable consequences, a rigid succession of cause and effect. Insist upon a flat agreement between the two, and there you are! The Instrument fails.

It is upon these three objections, and upon an extreme suspicion of abstract terms which arises materially out of my first and second objections, that I chiefly rest my case for a profound scepticism of the remoter possibilities of the Instrument of Thought. It is a thing no more perfect than the human eye or the human ear, though like those other instruments it may have undefined possibilities of evolution towards increased range and increased power.

So much for my main contention. But before I conclude I may – since I am here – say a little more in the autobiographical vein, and with a view to your discussion, to show how I reconcile this fundamental scepticism with the very positive beliefs about worldwide issues I possess, and the very definite distinction I make between right and wrong.

I reconcile these things by simply pointing out to you that if there is any validity in my image of that three-dimensional jelly in which our ideas are suspended, such a reconciliation as you demand in logic, such a projection of the things as being in accordance upon one plane, is totally unnecessary and impossible. They can never come together upon one plane.

This insistence upon the element of uniqueness in being, this subordination of the class to the individual difference, not only destroys the universal claim of philosophy, but the universal claim of ethical imperatives, the universal claim of any religious teaching. If you press me back upon my fundamental position I must confess I put faith and standards and rules of conduct upon exactly the same level as I put my belief of what is right in art, and what I consider right practice in art. I have arrived at a certain sort of self-knowledge and there are, I find, very distinct imperatives for me; but I am quite prepared to admit there is no proving them imperative on anyone else. One's political proceedings, one's moral acts are, I hold, just as much self-expression as one's poetry or painting or music. But since life has for its primordial elements assimilation and aggression, I try not only to obey my imperatives, but to put them persuasively and convincingly into other minds, to bring about *my* good and to resist and overcome *my* evil as though they were the universal Good and the universal Evil in which unthinking men believe. And it is obviously in no way contradictory to this philosophy, for me, if I find others responding sympathetically to any notes of mine or if I find myself responding sympathetically to notes sounding about me, to give that common resemblance between myself and others a name, to refer these others and myself in common to this thing as if it were externalized and spanned us all.

Scepticism of the Instrument is for example not incompatible with religious association and with organization upon the basis of a common faith. It is possible to regard God as a Being synthetic in relation to men and societies, just as the idea of a universe of atoms and molecules and inorganic relationships is analytical in relation to human life.

The repudiation of demonstration in any but immediate and verifiable cases that this Scepticism of the Instrument amounts to, the abandonment of any universal validity for moral and religious propositions, brings ethical, social and religious teaching into the province of poetry, and does something to correct the estrangement between knowledge and beauty that is a feature of so much mental existence at this time. All these things are self-expression. Such an opinion sets a new and greater value on that penetrating and illuminating quality of mind we call insight, insight which when it faces towards the contradictions that arise out of the imperfections of the mental instrument is called humour. In these innate, unteachable qualities I hold – in humour and the sense of beauty – lies such hope of intellectual salvation from the original sin of our intellectual instrument as we may entertain in this uncertain and fluctuating world of unique appearances. . . .

So frankly I spread my little equipment of fundamental assumptions before you, heartily glad of the opportunity you have given me of taking them out, of looking at them with the particularity the presence of hearers ensures, and of hearing the impression they make upon you. Of course such a sketch must have an inevitable crudity of effect. The time I had for it – I mean the time I was able to give in preparation – was altogether too limited for any exhaustive finish of presentation; but I think on the whole I have got the main lines of this sketch map of my mental basis true. Whether I have made myself comprehensible is a different question altogether. It is for you rather than me to say how this sketch map of mine lies with regard to your own more systematic cartography.

# Notes

## ON UTOPIAN SOURCES

Wells is defining his *modern* utopia against the tradition of the great speculative utopias from Plato (427–347 BC) to William Morris (1834–96). Wells was indebted to his predecessors, especially for his concept of a dedicated elite (neither aristocracy nor democracy) that would administer his utopia. However, his utopia is 'modern' because of its global nature, its reliance on science and technology, and scientific planning, and its sense that utopia is a process, not a specific goal. He freely admits he does not have the answer for many of the problems he identifies. Wells's utopia is also secular, not religious.

During the first chapter on 'Topographical' matters Wells notes Plato, whose *Republic* (380–70 BC) and *Laws* (350–40 BC) are possibly the first discussions of the 'ideal society' in Western literature, and Thomas More (1478–1535), *Utopia* (1516): the work that gave a name to the genre of writing about ideal societies. Such writing was boosted by the examination of ideal societies during the Enlightenment and the years leading up to the American (1776) and French (1789) Revolutions; and, during the nineteenth century, with the development of both Socialism, scientific theory and industrial technology. While such writing (for example, Cabet, as noted below) was based upon or produced as blueprints for practical experiments in social communities, other utopian fictions were either intended as satires or imaginative explorations in possibility. Under the influence of Wells himself, this latter branch extended into modern science fiction.

Also noted in this chapter are, in chronological order of publication: *City of the Sun* (1623) by the Italian monk Tommaso Campanella (1568–1639); *New Atlantis. A Work Unfinished* (1659) by the English statesman Francis Bacon (1561–1626); and *Naufrage des Isles Flottantes, ou Basiliade du célèbre Pilpai, Poëme Héroïque* (1753) by the French utopianist Morelly (dates unknown) who proposed communist ideas in *Code de la Nature* (1755). Here, Utopia was situated in an isolated island. Wells also cites *Armata: A Fragment* (1817) by Thomas Erskine (1750–1823), in which a ship finds its way to the world Armata by means of a channel from the South Polar regions of the earth; *Voyage en Icarie* (1848) by Etienne Cabet (1788–1856), a French lawyer who tried and failed to establish an American community based upon the ideas in his book; *Republic of the West. Order and Progress: A General View of Positivism, or, summary exposition of the system of life and thought* (1848) by Auguste Comte (1798–1857), the French philosopher who founded the 'positivist' school; and *Erewhon, or, Over the Range* (1872), a mock-utopia by the satirist Samuel Butler (1835–1902). Later utopias develop worlds formed by socialism, in various degrees of influence from Marxism or the rival strand of ethical, Christian socialism. These include *Looking Backward, 2000–1887* (1888), perhaps the most influential utopia of the late nineteenth century by the American novelist and writer on social issues Edward Bellamy (1850–98); *Freeland: A Social Anticipation* (1891) by Austrian economist Theodor Hertzka (1845–1924); *A Traveller from Altruria* (1894) by the American writer William Dean Howells (1837–1920) and William Morris's *News From Nowhere* (1890). *The Despised Sex: The Letters of Calirates to Dione* (1903) by W. T. Stead (1849–1912), which describes the visit to the Western world of a member of a lost race of Amazons from Central Africa, is one of a tradition of pre- or proto-feminist utopias, relatively neglected by Wells despite the chapter he devotes to the position of women in Utopia.

Wells seems particularly indebted to Bacon, who like Campanella sketched out a plan for a kind of scientific academy, and to Bellamy's state-socialist utopia which was answered almost immediately by William Morris whose utopia was coloured by both Marxist theory and medievalist longings. The 'Ishmaelite' encountered by Wells's narrator and his Botanist friend after their transition into this Utopian version of the Swiss Alps utters opinions that reflect Wells's opinion of Morris's pastoral utopia. Wells is concerned to establish that a truly modern Utopia cannot, like those of More, Campanella, Bacon, Morelly or Erskine, be situated upon an isolated island or another world. He also argues his case for a kind of elite-led socialism, neither state-socialism (as with Bellamy) or established on the basis of a collective freely arrived at Common Will, as with Morris. His Utopia owes much to the works of his predecessors, but it is firmly his own.

Specific points arising from Wells's references are noted below.

Andy Sawyer

## PREFACE

1.  *Kipps*: *Kipps: The Story of a Simple Soul* (1905) by H. G. Wells.
2.  *triclinic crystals*: Crystals in which the three axes are unequal and none of them is at right angles (90 degrees) to another, as opposed to cubes, where all three axes are equal in length and at right angles to the others.
3.  *Peacock's*: Possibly Ferdinand Mansel Peacock (1861–1908), *A Friendship After Plato* (1897) but Thomas Love Peacock (1785–1866) was also noted for his development of Plato's dialogue form in novels like *Nightmare Abbey* (1818).
4.  *Mr Mallock's*: Mallock's development of ancient dialogue to explore ideas in fictional form: see W. H. Mallock (1849–1923), *The New Republic: Culture, Faith and Philosophy in an English Country House* (1877).
5.  *Boswell's Johnson*: James Boswell (1740–95), *Life of Samuel Johnson* (1791). Boswell's life of Johnson is both a biography of the compiler of the celebrated *Dictionary of the English Language* (1755) and a vivid description of his times.
6.  *Following upon . . . writer's work*: These are not included in this volume.

# THE OWNER OF THE VOICE

1.  *whitish plump man*: As noted in the Introduction, something of a self-portrait of Wells. In *The Road to Wigan Pier* (1937) George Orwell (1903–50) described Wells's utopia as 'the paradise of little fat men'.

2.  *cinematograph*: Often spelt 'kinematograph'; the name given to a device patented in 1895 by the Lumière brothers, Auguste (1862–1954) and Louis (1864–1948) for projecting a series of photographs rapidly on to a screen to give the illusion of movement. Not only is this narrative a 'hybrid' narrative, it is trying to establish a different viewpoint through imitation of this very new narrative effect. Later 'stage directions' attempt to reflect the use of cinematic effects, or emphasize the images the writer wants to put in the reader's mind.

## CHAPTER I

# TOPOGRAPHICAL

1.  *Darwin*: Charles Darwin (1809–82), naturalist, whose theory of evolution by natural selection was one of the most powerful ideas of the nineteenth century.

2.  *Morris to his Nowhere*: William Morris (1834–96), artist, poet, socialist and author of *News from Nowhere: or, An Epoch of Rest* (1890). See Note on Utopian Sources.

3.  *the flying machine*: The first successful flight (120 feet) in a powered aeroplane had only recently (December 1903) been made by Orville Wright.

4.  *Mr Hewins*: William Albert Samuel Hewins (1865–1931), political economist, historian, politician, who was the first director of the London School of Economics, 1895–1903.

5.  *Sirius*: Also known as the 'Dog Star' in the constellation *Canis Major*: the brightest star in the night sky.

6.  *Fujiyama*: The tallest mountain in Japan. Yokohama, Japan's major port, is 70 miles to the north-east.

7.  *Matterhorn*: Swiss mountain near the border with Italy, popular with climbers. The Theodule pass links Italy and Switzerland.

8.  *Lucendro Pass*: The 'Voice' and the Botanist are hiking in the Lepontine Alps on the borders of Italy and Switzerland. Much of the subsequent action lies in the Utopian 'analogue' of this

region and the city of Lucerne in the north of Switzerland, with Wells referring to specific locations.

9.  *Lantern*: The 'cinematograph' effect described earlier by the Author, presenting the transition from Earth to Utopia as if in a flash of the 'rather defective lantern'.

10. *Orion*: One of the most prominent constellations in the night sky of the northern hemisphere. The 'Great Bear' is the constellation also known as the Plough or the Big Dipper.

11. *Scientific languages*: There was a movement to develop artificial languages in the latter half of the nineteenth century. Esperanto, the best known of these, was published in 1887 by Ludwig L. Zamenhof (1859–1917). La Langue Bleue or 'Bollak' was published 1899–1902 by Leon Bollack (1859–?). 'New Latin' may be 'Latine sine flexione' (Latin without flexions), also known as Interlingua, an attempt in 1903 by the Italian mathematician Giuseppe Peano (1858–1932) to develop a simplified Latin as a common language. Volapuk was invented around 1879 by Johan Martin Schleyer (1831–1912).

12. *Lord Lytton*: Edward George Bulwer-Lytton (1803–73), novelist; in reference to *The Coming Race* (1871).

13. *Archbishop Whateley*: Richard Whately (1787–1863), Archbishop of Dublin; see his *Logic* (1826).

14. *Significs*: See Victoria Alexandrina Maria Louisa Stuart Wortley (1837–1912), *What is Meaning? Studies in the Development of Significance* (1903).

15. *Professor Mark Baldwin*: James Mark Baldwin (1861–1934), American experimental psychologist who applied Darwinian evolutionary ideas to his theories of development.)

16. *Aristotle*: Aristotle, Athenian philosopher (384–22 BC), pupil of Plato.

17. *Sidgwick's Use of Words in Reasoning*: Alfred Sidgwick (1850–1943), *The Use of Words in Reasoning* (1901).

18. *Bosanquet's Essentials of Logic*: Bernard Bosanquet (1848–1923), *The Essentials of Logic. Being Ten Lectures on Judgment and Inference* (1895).

19. *Bradley's Principles of Logic*: F. H. Bradley (1846–1924), *The Principles of Logic* (1883).

20. *Sigwart's Logik*: Christopher Sigwart (1830–1904), *Logik* (1895).

21. *Wordsworthian*: William Wordsworth (1770–1850), poet.

22. *Nature*: British scientific journal, founded 1869 and still published, for which Wells wrote. Its first issue (4 Nov. 1869) quoted

Wordsworth's lines: 'To the solid ground/Of Nature trusts the Mind that builds for aye' from his 'A Volant Tribe of Bards on Earth are Found'.

23. *Frognal*: In Hampstead, North London.

24. *Mr Chamberlain*: Joseph Chamberlain (1836–1914), pro-imperial politician.

25. *the King*: Edward VII (1841–1910), reigned 1901–10.

26. *Sandow*: Presumably Eugene Sandow (1867–1925), a professional strongman and physical fitness promoter.

27. *Mr Arnold White*: Arnold White (1848–1925), miscellaneous writer, notably on urban degeneration.

28. *Mr Roosevelt*: Theodore Roosevelt (1858–1919), then President of the United States.

29. *Michelangelo's 'Last Judgement'*: Painting for the Sistine Chapel by the Italian artist Michelangelo Buonarroti (1475–1564).

30. *Epistemon's vision*: See François Rabelais (1494–1553), *Gargantua and Pantagruel* (1535), bk 2, ch. 30.

31. *Hampdens*: The village Hampdens: an expression for amateur politicians; after John Hampden (1594–1643), statesman, whose refusal to pay 'ship money' in 1636 deepened the crisis that led to the English Civil War. The phrase is from Thomas Gray (1716–71), 'Elegy Written in a Country Churchyard' (1751): 'Some village-Hampden, that with dauntless breast/The little Tyrant of his fields with stood' (lines 57–8).

32. *You figure him doing it*: Another interjection by the Author to emphasize the descent down the mountain to encounter an actual utopia.

## CHAPTER 2

# CONCERNING FREEDOMS

1. *Man versus the State*: Allusion to Herbert Spencer (1820–1903), the philosopher of 'Social Darwinism', *The Man versus the State* (1884).

2. *Schopenhauer*: Arthur Schopenhauer (1788–1860), German pessimist philosopher.

3. *Empedocles*: Empedocles (c. 500–c. 430 BC): Greek philosopher who professed prophetic and miraculous powers. His theory of Earth, Water, Fire and Air as the four fundamental elements was taken up by Aristotle.

4. *Heraclitus*: Heraclitus (c. 540–415 BC), Greek pessimist meta-

physician who considered change, rather than stability, to underlie existence.

5. *Ruskins*: John Ruskin (1819–1900), philo-medievalist social critic. Wells is suggesting that a future 'Ruskin's' nostalgia for the past would extend to the technology the real Ruskin would have attacked. See also Ch. 3, note 18.

6. *Mr Belloc*: Hilaire Belloc (1870–1953), poet and author.

7. *Rip-Van-Winkle*: Washington Irving (1783–1859), *Rip Van Winkle*, first published as a short story in 1819.

8. *Devil's Bridge*: Bridge over the River Reuss associated with a legend that it was built with the devil's help.

9. *Pompeii*: Roman city near Naples, destroyed AD 79 by the eruption of Vesuvius.

10. *Mr Hardy*: Thomas Hardy (1840–1928), novelist.

11. *George Gissing*: George Gissing (1857–1903), novelist.

12. *You figure . . . the Voice*: Another interjection by the Author, emphasizing the slightly pompous romanticism of the Voice.

13. *bitted*: From 'bit', the metal mouthpiece of a bridle: he is controlled by his obsession like a horse is controlled by its bit.

14. *M. Santos Dumont*: Alberto Santos-Dumont (1870–1932), Brazilian inventor who developed powered airships and in 1901 flew around the Eiffel Tower in a hydrogen airship. He later experimented with heavier-than-air powered aircraft.

15. *Mrs Henry Wood*: See *Memorials of Mrs Henry Wood* (1894), née Ellen Price (1814–87), popular novelist, best known for *East Lynne* (1861).

16. *ale that is Kops'*: A brand of non-alcoholic beer, favoured by the Temperance movement.

17. *Metchnikoff*: Elie Metchnikoff, (1845–1916), Russian embryologist, *The Nature of Man: Studies in Optimistic Philosophy* (1903).

## CHAPTER 3

# UTOPIAN ECONOMICS

1. *twaindy*: Two dozen or 24. The duodecimal (units of 12) system of currency here was also used in Wells's *When the Sleeper Wakes* (1899).

2. *Donisthorpe*: Wordsworth Donisthorpe (1847–1914), miscellaneous writer; *A System of Measures of Length, Area, Bulk, Weight, Value, Force, Etc.* (1895).

3.  *Newton*: Isaac Newton (1642–1727), natural philosopher cele-
    brated for his laws of motion, optics and gravitation. In his
    *Philosophiae Naturalis Principia Mathematica* (1687) he argued
    that the universe operated by simple mathematical laws.

4.  *undignified use*: More's Utopians used gold for chamber pots
    and chains.

5.  *Wonderland*: Lewis Carroll (1832–98), *Alice in Wonderland*
    (1865).

6.  *Principles of Sociology*: Franklin Henry Giddings, *The Principles
    of Sociology. An Analysis of the Phenomena of Association and
    of Social Organization* (1896).

7.  *Economic Studies*: (1880) by Walter Bagehot (1826–77).

8.  *Carlyle*: Thomas Carlyle (1795–1881), historian and social
    critic.

9.  *Dalton*: John Dalton (1766–1844), chemist.

10. *Davy*: Sir Humphry Davy (1778–1829), chemist.

11. *Joule*: James Prescott Joule (1818–89), physicist.

12. *Adam Smith*: Adam Smith (1723–90), political economist.

13. *Oneida Community*: Founded in 1848, a communitarian experi-
    ment led by John Humphrey Noyes (1811–86) in New York State.

14. *Statute of Mortmain*: Land granted to a church in perpetuity.

15. *Caveat vendor*: (Latin) 'seller beware', as opposed to *Caveat
    emptor* ('buyer beware').

16. *Hippodamus*: Hippodamus of Miletus (*c.* 500 BC), the most
    famous Greek town planner.

17. *agora*: (Greek) Public square or market.

18. *Road-making under Mr Ruskin's auspices*: In reference to an
    1874 experiment in which Ruskin set undergraduates to work in
    order to teach them the value of manual labour.

19. *Hawthorne*: Nathaniel Hawthorne (1804–64), *The Blithedale
    Romance* (1852) satirizes the 'Brook Farm Institute', an Ameri-
    can utopian community founded in 1841; see also *Passages from
    the French and Italian Notebooks* (1883); *Passages from the
    American Notebooks* (1883); *Passages from the English Note-
    books* (1870).

20. *linotype machine*: Typesetting machine.

21. *Sutherland*: George Sutherland (1855–1905), *Twentieth Century
    Inventions. A Forecast* (1901).

22. *Tobin shaft*: Or Tobin tube: 'A device for admitting fresh air into
    a room in an upward direction, invented by Martin Tobin of
    Leeds' (*Oxford English Dictionary*).

23. *Greek capital*: The head of a column in classical Greek style.

## CHAPTER 4

# THE VOICE OF NATURE

1. *botryoidal*: 'Minerals presenting an aggregation of large sections of small globes are called botryoidal' (*Oxford English Dictionary*).

2. *poseur*: Affecting a character or attitude.

3. *Ishmaelite*: A social outcast, from the biblical Ishmael, son of Abraham and his handmaid Hagar (Genesis 16: 11–13).

4. *Nazarite*: Following the example of the ancient Jewish sect which abstained from wine and cutting their hair.

5. *Pianotist and Pianola*: Trademarks of kinds of player piano: a piano fitted with a mechanism to enable it to play automatically, developed in the 1890s.

6. *samurai*: The first mention of the 'samurai', the order of 'voluntary noblemen', neither hereditary aristocracy nor elected democracy, which administers Utopia (see Ch. 9). Wells takes the term from the Japanese warrior class, who led the modernization of Japan during the nineteenth century, but they owe something to the 'Guardians' of Plato's *Republic*, to medieval monks or knights, and to the Civil Service that administered the British colonies. In *The Shape of Things to Come* (1933), a similar body of selfless experts/administrators is the Air and Sea Control. Wells may have taken the idea directly or indirectly from Inazo Nitobe's *Bushido: the Soul of Japan*, originally published in 1905. In Ch. 39 of *First and Last Things* (1908) he refers to contemporary interest in the Japanese philosophy of Bushido as a source for the 'organized brotherhood' of *A Modern Utopia*.

7. *Cicerone*: A guide or escort; a term originally given in the eighteenth century to those guides who showed travellers around Italian antiquarian sites, explaining their history.

8. *reductio ad absurdum*: (Latin) Reducing to an absurdity: demonstrating that the logical result of a position is something contradictory or absurd.

9. *Gladstone*: William Ewart Gladstone (1809–98), British statesman, several times Prime Minister and an eventual (unsuccessful) advocate for Irish Home Rule.

## CHAPTER 5

# FAILURE IN A MODERN UTOPIA

1.  *den of the sweater*: The 'sweat-shop', such as in the clothing industry in London's East End, where gangs of workers toiled in poor conditions for low wages.

2.  *Alsatia*: A name given in the seventeenth century to London's Whitefriars district, where debtors could claim sanctuary; thus, a refuge for undesirables or lawbreakers.

3.  *The Fertility of the Unfit*: (1903) by W. A. Chapple (1864–1936).

4.  *Petticoat Lane and Park Lane*: The first is a famous market street in London's poor East End; the second is one of the West End's wealthiest residential streets.

5.  *Malthus*: Thomas Robert Malthus (1766–1834), political economist most famous for his attempts to demonstrate that population, unchecked by war, disease or social control, increases faster than the growth in food supply.

6.  *Baron Cecil*: Robert Arthur Talbot Gascoyne-Cecil (1830– 1903), 3rd Marquess of Salisbury, statesman, Prime Minister 1886–1902.

7.  *Knights Templars*: Twelfth-century military order who protected pilgrims to the Holy Land. Wells is suggesting more historical sources for his 'Samurai'.

8.  *Cromwell's Ironsides*: Parliamentary cavalry during the English Civil War and the Commonwealth (1642–60) led by Oliver Cromwell (1599–1658) who was Lord Protector of England from 1649 until his death.

9.  *Cromwell Road*: At the Natural History Museum, established in its present location in 1880 but formerly part of the British Museum in Bloomsbury.

10.  *Northumberland Avenue*: Street in central London running from Victoria Embankment bordering the River Thames to Trafalgar Square.

11.  *Galton*: Sir Francis Galton (1822–1911), the founder of eugenics. Wells accepted the need to prevent 'undesirable traits' from being passed along the genetic line, but was uneasy about the totalitarian implications of such prevention.

12.  *Bertillon*: Alphonse Bertillon (1853–1914), French criminologist.

13.  *Deeming or Crossman*: Reference to celebrated murder cases. In 1892 Australian police investigating the murder of the wife of

Frederick Bailey Deeming (1853–92) discovered that Deeming had previously murdered another wife and family in England. In 1904 a former convict named Crossman committed suicide to escape arrest for murder and was found to have a long string of bigamous marriages, with at least two of the women missing. Newspaper accounts commented on the similarity with the Deeming case.

14. *Rousseauism*: Doctrine propounded by Jean-Jacques Rousseau (1712–78), French philosopher, but here meaning those who advocate a 'return to nature'.

CHAPTER 6

## WOMEN IN A MODERN UTOPIA

1. *Essay on the Principles of Population*: In which Malthus set forward his theory about the relationship between population and the means of subsistence (see Ch. 5, note 5).
2. 'red in tooth and claw': from *In Memoriam* (1850), section 56, line 15. By Alfred, Lord Tennyson (1809–92).
3. *Mankind in the Making*: (1903) by H. G. Wells.
4. *Socrates*: Socrates (*c.* 470–399 BC), Athenian philosopher under whom Plato studied.
5. *Man and Woman*: Henry Havelock Ellis (1859–1939), *Man and Woman. A Study of Human Secondary Sexual Characters* (1894).
6. *Social Origins* and *Primal Law*: Andrew Lang (1844–1912), *Social Origins* (1903) and J. J. Atkinson (?–1899), *Primal Law* (1903).
7. *Jowett*: Benjamin Jowett (1817–93), philosopher.
8. *History of American Socialisms*: (1870) by John Humphrey Noyes.
9. *History of Socialism in the United States*: (1903) by Morris Hillquit.
10. *The Thelema of Rabelais*: The communistic Abbey of Theleme, in *Gargantua* (1535) by François Rabelais (see Ch. 1, note 30).

CHAPTER 7

## A FEW UTOPIAN IMPRESSIONS

1.  *Pilatus*: Swiss mountain near Lucerne, so called because of the 'cap' (Latin *pileus*) of white cloud that covers it.
2.  *Frankenstein*: Victor Frankenstein, the creator of the 'monster' in Mary Shelley (1797–1851), *Frankenstein* (1818).
3.  *Channel tunnel*: Various plans for bridges or tunnels across the English Channel were devised during the nineteenth century, but none came to fruition until 1994.
4.  *L'Art Nouveau*: (French) Literally 'New Art', a style of art flourishing in the 1890s and early 1900s, characterized by decorative effects drawn from organic forms, especially leaves and vegetation.
5.  *Leonardo*: Leonardo da Vinci (1452–1519), Florentine painter and sculptor.
6.  *Dürer*: Albrecht Dürer (1471–1528), German painter.

CHAPTER 8

## MY UTOPIAN SELF

1.  *Gradgrind*: The harsh schoolmaster in Charles Dickens (1812–70), *Hard Times* (1854).
2.  *Begbie away!*: Possibly a reference to Sir Matthew Baillie Begbie (1819–94), Canadian judge, a colourful character who was the first judge of the new colony of British Columbia from 1858 during the turbulent gold rush years. Known as an energetic counsel and a 'hanging judge', he also took the side of the native and Chinese immigrant peoples in many disputes.
3.  *Queen Anne villa*: Victorian 'villa' or middle-class detached house in the architectural style of the reign (1702–14) of Queen Anne (1665–1714). This is the style recommended by the architect when Kipps decides to build a house in Bk 3, Ch. 1 of *Kipps*.

CHAPTER 9

## THE SAMURAI

1.  *Bight of Benin*: Part of the Gulf of Guinea on the West African coast, extending about 400 miles along the coasts of Ghana, Togo, Benin and Nigeria; named after the former Kingdom of Benin.

2.  *Mahomet*: Muhammad (AD 570–632), founder of Islam.

3.  *Whistler*: James Abbott McNeill Whistler (1834–1903), American artist who settled in England.

4.  *Dan and Beersheba*: The most northern and southerly cities of the biblical Israel.

5.  *House of Salomon*: The scientific academy in Bacon's *New Atlantis*.

6.  *Henley*: William Ernest Henley (1849–1903), poet. The lines beginning '*Out of the night that covers me*' are the first four lines of Henley's 'Invictus' (1875). It was a popular Victorian poem, especially for its last lines: 'I am the master of my fate:/ I am the captain of my soul'.

7.  *Oceana*: James Harrington (1611–77), *The Common-Wealth of Oceana* (1656).

8.  *Danton's*: Georges Jacques Danton (1759–94), French revolutionary leader.

9.  *stage Rosalind*: The heroine of Shakespeare's *As You Like It* (1599).

## CHAPTER 10

# RACE IN UTOPIA

1.  *pontifex maximus*: (Latin) Chief priest; pope.

2.  *Anabaptists*: Radical Protestants who seized control of Munster in 1534.

3.  *Thomas à Kempis*: (1380–1471), German theologian.

4.  *City of God*: (AD 413–25) by Augustine of Hippo (AD 354–430).

5.  *'The Lady of the Lake'*: (1810) by Sir Walter Scott (1771–1832).

6.  *Mr Kipling*: Rudyard Kipling (1865–1936), novelist and poet.

7.  *Müller's*: Friedrich Max Müller (1823–1900), orientalist.

8.  *Short History of the English People*: (1874) by John Richard Green.

9.  *The True-born Englishman*: *The True-born Englishman: A Satire* (1701) by Daniel Defoe (1660–1731), author of *Robinson Crusoe* (1719).

10. *Bowery*: Slum area of New York City.

11. *Deniker*: *The Races of Men* (1900) by Joseph Deniker (1852–1918).

12. *A Man Adrift*: *A Man Adrift. Being Leaves from a Nomad's Portfolio* (1899) by Bart Kennedy (1861–1930).

13.  *Mary Kingsley*: Mary Harriet Kingsley (1862–1900), traveller and writer.

14.  *The Living Races of Mankind*: (1900) by Henry Neville Hutchinson (1856–1927).

15.  *As we English did with the Tasmanians*: The native inhabitants of Tasmania were exterminated by the British settlers of Australia between 1803 and 1876. Wells refers to this in the first chapter of *The War of the Worlds* (1898).

16.  *Quartier Latin*: The 'Latin Quarter' or 'Left Bank' of Paris, known as a centre for intellectual and artistic activities.

17.  *Othello*: Play (1604) by William Shakespeare (1564–1616), in which the black ('Moorish') hero marries the white Desdemona who is falsely accused of infidelity.

18.  *the 'cut' and the 'boycott'*: To 'cut' is to ignore someone publicly and openly; a 'boycott' is a more organized refusal to deal with someone, as by not trading with them.

19.  *Hottentots*: One of the indigenous peoples of South Africa.

20.  *Welt-Politik*: (German) International politics.

21.  *Rhodes*: Cecil John Rhodes (1853–1902), imperialist after whom the states of Northern and Southern Rhodesia (now Zambia and Zimbabwe) were named.

22.  *Moses Cohen*: A Jewish viewpoint is given through the use of a common, even stereotypical, name.

23.  *Welt-Apparat*: (German) In this sense, a worldwide political 'machine' or World-State.

24.  *Yellow Peril*: The fear of the Chinese and Japanese nations, documented in much fiction of the time. See the novel *The Yellow Danger* (1889) by M. P. Shiel (1865–1947).

25.  *Control of the Tropics*: *The Control of the Tropics* (1898) by Benjamin Kidd (1858–1916).

26.  *Brutus*: Marcus Junius Brutus (*c*. 85–42 BC), a conspirator against Caesar.

27.  *Cato*: Marcus Porcius Cato (234–149 BC), known as Cato the Censor.

28.  *Doukhobors*: Gospel of the Doukhobors: a late eighteenth-century Russian peasant heretic sect who believed in the goodness and creativity of God, and the doctrine of loving one's neighbour.

CHAPTER 11

# THE BUBBLE BURSTS

1.  *Triton*: Greek sea-god, often represented as part fish.
2.  *Bâle*: Now spelt Basle: Swiss town bordering France and Germany.
3.  *Odessa*: Ukrainian city on the Black Sea, the location of several attacks on the country's Jewish population.
4.  *Board Schools*: Compulsory municipal schools, largely for the working-class population.
5.  *St Martin's Church*: St Martin-in-the-Fields, on the east side of Trafalgar Square.
6.  *hansom*: Light horse-drawn cab used for public transport.
7.  *Cockspur Street*: Leading from Trafalgar Square westward to Pall Mall and the Haymarket.
8.  *seven churches of Asia*: The Book of Revelation in the Bible was addressed to the 'seven churches which are in Asia' (Revelation 1:4).
9.  *billycock hat*: Felt hat with a broad rim.

APPENDIX

# SCEPTICISM OF THE INSTRUMENT

1.  *Huxley*: Thomas Henry Huxley (1825–95), naturalist, under whom Wells studied 1884–5 at the Normal School of Science.
2.  *Fortnightly Review*: Influential periodical published 1865–1934 and afterwards as *Fortnight* until 1954.
3.  *Prof. Judd*: John Wesley Judd (1840–1916), geologist under whom Wells studied during his last disastrous year (1886–7) at the Normal School of Science.

G. C. and A. S.